5H

D0014200

"WARNING: UNIDENTIFIED OBJECT APPROACHING!"

The alarm sounded throughout the *Shenandoah*, computer and human voices calling out in an uncanny duet.

"Recommendation, Commander?" the human voice continued alone.

"Battle Stations."

The alarm gong echoed through the ACC. The main hatch slid shut. The armored hatch followed. All compartments were completely sealed by the time the all-hands signal blared.

"All hands, all hands. Battle Alert! Battle Alert! All hands man your battle stations." And then came the words veterans and trainees alike dreaded to hear: "This is not a drill. Repeat, this is not a drill!"

⊘ SIGNET

(0451)

DISTANT REALMS

☐ **THE COPPER CROWN: The First Novel of *The Keltiad* by Patricia Kennealy.** When their powers of magic waned on ancient Earth, the Kelts and their allies fled the planet for the freedom of distant star realms. But the stars were home to two enemy star fleets mobilized for final, devastating war . . . "A gorgeous yarn!"—Anne McCaffrey.

(143949—$3.50)

☐ **THE THRONE OF SCONE: The Second Novel of *The Keltiad* by Patricia Kennealy.** Aeron, Queen of the Kelts, has fled to the stars on a desperate mission to find the fabled Thirteen Treasures of King Arthur, hidden for hundreds of years. But while she pursues her destiny, all the forces of Keltia are mobilizing for war. "Brilliant!"—Anne McCaffrey.

(148215—$3.50)

☐ **BAD VOLTAGE by Jonathon Littell.** For half-breed Lynx and his gang, the Livewires, existence on the streets of post-nuke Paris is the condition of the moment. But when the Downsiders and Uptowners clash in cybernetic battle, Lynx struggles to free himself of the world that is slowly claiming his soul.

(160142—$3.95)

☐ **FANG, THE GNOME by Michael Greatrex Coney.** Here is an enthralling excursion into an age when mythical creatures roamed the lands, men fought for ideals of chivalry, and the majestic dream of Arthur and his Knights of the Round Table first cast its spell on humans and gnomes. "Rich, striking and original!"—*Kirkus Reviews.*

(158474—$3.95)

☐ **NOT FOR GLORY by Joel Rosenberg.** What begins as one final mission—not for glory but for the very life of the people of Metzada—is transformed into a series of campaigns that will take General Shimon Bar-El from world to world and into intrigue, danger, and treacherous diplomatic games that may save Metzada and its mercenaries—or be its ultimate ruin . . . "A swift-paced, brutal, excellent, political novel about the soldier of the future."—David Drake, author of *Hammer Slammers.*

(158458—$3.95)

Prices slightly higher in Canada

Buy them at your local bookstore or use this convenient coupon for ordering.

NEW AMERICAN LIBRARY
P.O. Box 999, Bergenfield, New Jersey 07621

Please send me the books I have checked above. I am enclosing $_____
(please add $1.00 to this order to cover postage and handling). Send check or money order—no cash or C.O.D.'s. Prices and numbers are subject to change without notice.

Name_____

Address_____

City _____ State _____ Zip Code _____

Allow 4-6 weeks for delivery.
This offer, prices and numbers are subject to change without notice.

STARCRUISER SHENANDOAH

Squadron Alert
by
Roland J. Green

A SIGNET BOOK

NEW AMERICAN LIBRARY

A DIVISION OF PENGUIN BOOKS USA INC.

To Eleanor Wood, who found a homeport
for *Shenandoah* by having more faith
in me than I had in myself

And to John Silbersack,
who provided that homeport

NAL BOOKS ARE AVAILABLE AT QUANTITY DISCOUNTS
WHEN USED TO PROMOTE PRODUCTS OR SERVICES.
FOR INFORMATION PLEASE WRITE TO PREMIUM MARKETING DIVISION.
NEW AMERICAN LIBRARY. 1633 BROADWAY.
NEW YORK. NEW YORK 10019.

Copyright © 1989 by Roland J. Green

All rights reserved

Map illustration by Pat Tobin

SIGNET TRADEMARK REG. U.S. PAT. OFF. AND FOREIGN COUNTRIES
REGISTERED TRADEMARK—MARCA REGISTRADA
HECHO EN DRESDEN. TN

SIGNET, SIGNET CLASSIC, MENTOR, ONYX, PLUME, MERIDIAN
and NAL BOOKS are published by New American Library, a division of
Penguin Books USA Inc., 1633 Broadway, New York, New York 10019

First Printing, September, 1989

1   2   3   4   5   6   7   8   9

PRINTED IN THE UNITED STATES OF AMERICA

Principal Characters

Commander Pavel BOGDANOV, U.F.N.: Executive officer, *Shenandoah*

Colonel Indira CHATTERJE: Chief medical officer, Victoria Command

First Lieutenant Lucco DiVRIES, U.F.N.: On leave from U.F.S. *Valhalla*

Brigadier Dominic FEGELI: CO, Alliance forces on Victoria ("the Bonsai Force")

Second Lieutenant Louis FERRARO, U.F.N.R.: Engineering officer and tender pilot, supply ship *Leon Brautigan*

Commander Shintaro FUJITA: Chief engineer, *Shenandoah*

Governor Martin HOLLINGS: Governor of the Freeworld States Alliance Territory of Seven Rivers, on Victoria

Major General Mikhail KORNILOV: Commanding general, Victoria Command

Rear Admiral Sho KUWAHARA: Commander, Victoria Squadron, and senior naval officer, Victoria Command

Brigadier General Marcus LANGSTON: Commanding general, Victoria Brigade, Victoria Command

Captain Paul LERAY, F.S.N.: C.O., heavy cruiser *Audacious,* and senior naval officer of the "Bonsai Force"

Captain Rose LIDDELL, U.F.N.: C.O., battlecruiser *Shenandoah*

Principal Characters

Second Lieutenant Charles LONGMAN, U.F.N.: Launcher Division, *Shenandoah*

Admiral Marya LOPATINA, F.S.N.: Commanding Alliance reinforcements to Victoria

First Lieutenant Brian MAHONEY, U.F.N.: Training Department, *Shenandoah*

Commander Joanna MARDER, F.S.N.: Executive officer, *Audacious*

Master Chief Petty Officer Chelsea NETSCH, U.F.N.: Senior petty officer, Training Department, *Shenandoah*

Major Liw NIEG: Intelligence, Victoria Command

Colonel Sun Ji PAK: C.O., 96th Independent Regiment, the principal Alliance ground unit on Victoria

First Lieutenant Karl POCHER, U.F.N.R.: C.O., *Leon Brautigan*

First Lieutenant Mahmoud SA'ID, U.F.N.R.: Executive officer and navigator, *Leon Brautigan*

Admiral John SCHATZ, U.F.N.: Commander, Eleventh Fleet, Federation Navy

First Lieutenant (acting Captain) Candice SHORES: C.O., Scout Company, Victoria Brigade

Second Lieutenant Brigitte TACHIN, U.F.N.: Weapons Department, *Shenandoah*

Commander Ahmed TOURKMANI, U.F.N.: *Shenandoah* project officer, Riftwell Dockyard

Rear Admiral Mordecai UZEL, F.S.N.: Chief of staff to Admiral Lopatina

First Lieutenant Elayne ZHENG, U.F.N.: *Shenandoah,* on detached duty with 879th Attacker Squadron

Glossary

AG: Attacker Group

ETA: Estimated Time of Arrival

EWO: Electronic Warfare Officer

FADS: Future Admiral Delusion Syndrome

F.S.N.: Freeworld States' Navy

IFF: Identification, Friend or Foe

kheblass: Merishi obscenity, literally meaning "too clumsy to climb"

JOW: Junior Officer of the Watch

kropis: The most important domestic animal of the Merishi; bulls in the mating season are a byword for bad temper

LI: Light Infantry

OTC: Officers' Training Course

skeerish: Merishi bird, notorious for its piercing, raucous cry

SOPS: Senior Officer Present in Space

U.F.N.: United Federation Navy

TO: Table of Organization

TOAD: Temporary Out-of-Area Duty

TOQ: Transient Officers' Quarters

TUCE: Taken Up from Civilian Economy

XO: Executive Officer

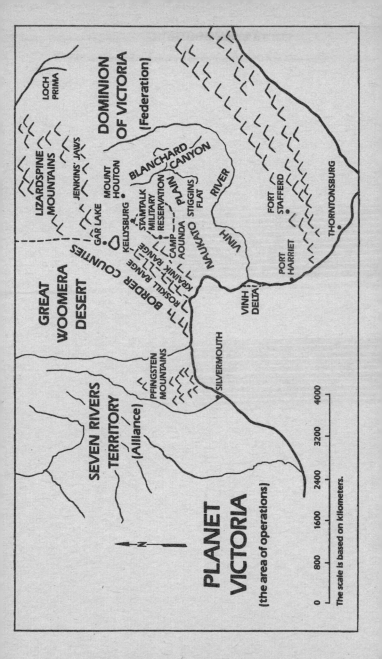

Prologue

Admiral John Schatz read his Command Secret order for the fifth time. It told him nothing he hadn't learned on the third reading.

The Eleventh Military Zone of the United Federation of Starworlds was ordered to establish a permanent naval squadron in the Victoria planetary system, as well as an orbital base for the squadron and ground facilities for an expanded garrison. As commander of the Eleventh Fleet, Schatz was expected to provide the squadron.

He dropped the order into his desk drawer and asked his computer to do three things: invite his opposite number, General Berkson, commander of the Eleventh Army, to dinner the next day; request the immediate presence of his chief of staff, Commodore Sho Kuwahara; and display a map of the planet Victoria.

The map appeared in seconds. Schatz had just started picking out the cities from the gray-blue ocean and gray sandy continents when the immaculately uniformed commodore entered. By standing orders, he didn't knock.

"What do you know about the planet Victoria?" Schatz said, without taking his eyes from the map.

"Our share of the dual-sovereignty problem," Kuwahara replied. "The Federation settlement's a daughter colony of Southern Cross. Technically it's a dominion of the Britannic Union, but we've always conceded their dominions Federation status along with the parent worlds. Is this being changed?"

The admiral shook his head. Kuwahara looked relieved. "Good. We need the Union navy."

He looked at the ceiling and continued his recitation. "Seven River is a territory of the Freeworld States Alliance. If it's like most such, the Pentarchy pulls the strings fairly directly."

"They do."

"Total population of Victoria is about three million, in a sixty-forty ratio in favor of the Federation. The gravity is lower than Standard, the atmosphere thinner, the mean temperature lower, and the average humidity lower. The people are concentrated at lower altitudes, near water supplies, in the temperate zones or tropics."

"The Alliance has an independent regiment and a heavy cruiser assigned to Seven Rivers. We have a nominal brigade, with one regular battalion, one reserve, and two territorials, which is what they call their militia. A transport division, with either two or three ships. Major General Kornilov's our CO. Not brilliant, but reliable for the long run."

"Would you say that Victoria's a potential headache?"

"Any dual-sovereignty planet's more trouble than one with a single government. Victoria, I would say, is mostly potential."

"Ten minutes ago, I'd have agreed with you. Now we both have to change our minds."

Schatz pulled out the order and passed it across the desk. Kuwahara's thin face twitched expressively as he read it.

"It mentions no change in the nonprovocation policy, I see," the commodore said as he handed the order back.

"No. Expanding base facilities is allowed under existing agreements."

"Suppose the Alliance disagrees?" Kuwahara asked.

The nonprovocation policy between the Federation and the Alliance called for minimal garrisons on dual-sovereignty planets, those shared between the two human superpowers. The intention was to discourage local hotheads from provoking trouble in the hope of being quickly rescued.

Like most senior Federation officers, Schatz thought the policy demanded miracles from the diplomats and soldiers left on the spot. Also like most, he regarded performing those miracles a part of his job. The policy and the miracles together had saved the Federation and the Alliance a good many crises and at least two wars over the past century.

On Victoria, the miracle might have to be larger than usual, because of the convoluted command structure. General Kornilov was nominally subordinate to the commander of the Eleventh Army. In fact, he had to reckon with the governor-general of the dominion of Victoria, who had his orders (not always the same ones, either) from Southern Cross and the Britannic Union. He also had to listen to the Military Council of Victoria, which included the minister of war as *ex officio* chairman and equal numbers of senators, members of Parliament, and retired territorial officers.

Kornilov's virtues as a combat leader were yet to be proved. He certainly had the knack of fitting into three chains of command at once. Schatz wasn't sure that might not be more valuable in any crisis on Victoria.

"The Alliance hitting the panic button is outside what we'll be expected to handle ourselves," Schatz said. "I still want to review all of our organic intelligence sources, just in case. Charlemagne is a long and insecure link away."

The eight hundred light-years to the Federation capital cut both ways. Eleventh Fleet might not learn what it needed to know until it was too late. Charlemagne might not find out what Eleventh Fleet had done until it was too late to stop it.

Schatz sat down and cleared the screen. "Now, what do we have available for a squadron?"

"We've light craft to burn—"

"*Will* you stop using that phrase."

Kuwahara smiled. Their genial argument was two years old. "We have enough unassigned light vessels to form several squadrons. I imagine that Admiral Baumann would be happier with at least one capital ship."

"The Empress would bust us to steward second class in the Hospitality Squadron if we didn't send one. So what do we have?"

"With your permission, Admiral?"

Schatz nodded and unlocked his terminal. Kuwahara quickly conjured up a roster of Eleventh Fleet's capital ships.

"The only one that doesn't have a firm assignment is *Valhalla*, and she's in Dockyard for her three-year overhaul."

"I don't think we want a carrier. Too formidable for

Victoria and too likely to be needed elsewhere. What about *Shenandoah*? How close is she to recommissioning? If I remember the specs on her class, she was designed to carry an attacker squadron. Have they left that alone?"

The fleet table vanished, replaced by the vital statistics and history of U.F.S. *Shenandoah*.

"Dockyard's left well enough alone," Schatz said with satisfaction. "Now, how fast can we have her off Victoria?"

Kuwahara frowned. "I'd estimate she could be on her way in thirty Standard days, if we let her shake down on the way to Victoria."

"That would look too much like panic. Not what we want, with a new ship and crew."

"Exactly what I thought, Admiral. If anything went wrong, we'd be worse off than before. Not to mention that quite a few people will already be nervous, with the history of the name."

Schatz contemplated the historical data. He decided that he was one of the people it made nervous.

The first *Shenandoah* recorded in the file was a First American Civil War Confederate commerce raider that stayed at sea long after the war was over, technically a pirate. The second was a dirigible of the United States Navy, lost in a storm. The third was a 21st-century American aircraft carrier, lost in one of that century's nasty little wars—Schatz couldn't remember which one.

The lugubrious tale went on into space. One *Shenandoah* had been lost during the Starworld Revolution in 2104, another in the Merishi War's one-fleet action forty years later. A century and a half of peace, then the century of the Hive Wars and three successive *Shenandoah*s lost, two in action, one missing.

The postwar recovery ended in the Alliance Secession, and the Federal authorities revived the name for a battlecruiser. She'd just been tested when that dubious half-crisis, half-war ended, and she went into the Riftwell Fleet Reserve Depot with almost indecent haste.

She'd been pulled out and overhauled twice, for two crises with the Baernoi. Both times, the confrontation with the porcine nonhumans stopped at bad language and ship movements. Both times, *Shenandoah* went back into reserve right after her shakedown cruise.

These overhauls made it inevitable that when Eleventh Fleet was authorized a new capital ship, they were ordered to recommission *Shenandoah*. She was more than a century old but, as far as commissioned service was concerned, pratically brand new.

"It could be worse," Schatz admitted. "None of the losses were dishonorable. We can look on it as trying to break the jinx."

"We could also change the name."

"Not without passing it all the way up to the Empress, and you know what she'd say to that. Meanwhile, we have to start pushing *Shen* out of Dockyard tonight. I won't be a party to changing a ship's name on the eve of her commissioning ceremony."

"I think I could handle that," Kuwahara said. "If you could authorize me to drop rank—"

"I'm sure you could if I did," Schatz said. He grinned, then pulled another order out of his desk and handed it over.

"Congratulations, Rear Admiral Kuwahara."

The chief of staff's face remained creditably expressionless as he read the order. Then he grinned back and gripped Schatz's hand.

"I can't imagine what tales you told the Promotion Board, but thank you for telling them. *Shenandoah* may not be so grateful, though. Who else did you have in mind as her captain?"

"Rose Liddell."

"She doesn't have the real killer instinct, from what I've heard."

"Sho, you and I were part of that lucky minority to have ship duty the one time the Baernoi woke up with such hangovers that they *had* to try their tusks on somebody.

"Rose is one of the majority. Her 'killer instinct' is no worse than an unknown quantity. She does have a strong record in practical leadership, administration, and diplomacy. That makes her closer to what *Shen* and Victoria will need than anybody else available."

"She's also very well read," Kuwahara admitted. He hesitated. "Will she command the squadron?"

Kuwahara's ambition was, if not naked, wearing no more than shorts. Schatz smiled. If he hadn't approved of

Kuwahara's hopes to be commander-in-chief some day, he wouldn't have nudged the Promotion Board over the man's second star. However, it wouldn't hurt Kuwahara to sweat just a little bit. . . .

"No need to afflict a ship just getting on her feet with an admiral. We'll give Rosie some attacker type for exec and she can be SOPS for a bit. Meanwhile, you can stay on as my chief as long as you want, now that you've got all the rank you need. I don't think Chilly Willi is going to yank me in the middle of this Victoria business.

"Or you can start briefing your replacement and packing your gear for ship duty. The Victoria squadron is yours, if you want it.

"Now, while you're imitating the donkey with the two bales of hay, I suggest a drink."

Schatz's desk drawer disgorged a bottle of Briggs Commercial Bourbon and two glasses, which quickly overflowed with the ruddy brown Monticellan whiskey. Schatz raised his.

"To *Shenandoah*. God bless her and all who sail in her!"

Outside the Officers' Club window, a dustdevil was gathering strength for its march on Fort Stafford. Major General Kornilov contemplated the pale gray swirls for a moment, then turned his attention back to the screen in front of him.

White circles flashed into sight, glowing and overlapping. They covered sixty percent of the area occupied by First Battalion of the Victoria Brigade. In places, the density of the fragmentation bomblets raining down guaranteed casualties to even troops under cover.

At least they all were under cover, as much as the terrain allowed them in ten minutes. First Battalion was doing very nicely in the simulations. Were they ready for a live-ammunition field exercise?

Try one company first, and see what happens. Less to lose if something goes wrong, and less warning to the Pentarchs that the Victoria Brigade is gearing up for combat. Now, which company?

Approaching footsteps sounded on the carpet behind the high-backed chair. Kornilov swiveled to face the sound.

"Hello, Mark."

Brigadier General Marcus Langston, CO of the Victoria

Brigade, saluted. "Evening, Mikhail. I suppose you could tell me something about the rumor?"

"What rumor is that?"

Langston recited the substance of the orders Kornilov had received that morning. The senior general only realized how forbidding he looked when he saw Langston reflexively dropping into a karate stance.

"Sorry, Mark. I was just thinking that it's a pity Philip Stoneman didn't investigate the propagation speed of rumors when he was discovering subspace. I think he might have found something that travels faster than light without leaving normal space."

"Likely enough. Is there anything my informants left out?"

"Not worth noting."

Kornilov tapped a bar order into the arm of his chair and leaned back. It automatically adjusted to the shifting of his hundred kilos. Victoria's lighter gravity reduced them to ninety-two but didn't shrink his bulk.

He wished he could adjust as easily to the problems of hosting a Navy squadron and maybe a larger garrison. At least they wouldn't be his problems anymore if the garrison grew too large; they'd send somebody senior to take over. The Britannic Union might also recruit some high-ranking help for their governor-general, if the dominion's government wasn't too afraid of having the Union's hand strengthened. Then just maybe the Federation would give Kornilov a third star. . . .

No. Victoria had long been a dead end—if not your last post before retirement, then a sign that you'd better start thinking about retirement instead of promotion. Mark Langston was an exception, and Kornilov didn't care. Others like Colonel Liu, the chief of staff, had turned themselves into a problem by caring too much.

"Where do we expand the ground bases?" Langston asked.

"Right here, to begin with. After that, we build in the Startalk Training Area. It already has enough water. Or do you expect us to have the resources to put in a complete infrastructure from the ground up?"

"I'm a brigade commander, not a magician," Langston said. "R & R will be a problem, unless we get a full brigade. They can provide their own."

"What's the problem? Mount Houton and Kellysburg are both less than a hundred kloms. Either one will do."

"Neither will do, unless you want incidents. When was the last time we had any cooperation from either mayor?"

"That could change, with the next election."

"Which isn't until next year. That squadron's going to be overhead inside of two months."

Knowing Admiral Schatz's reputation, Kornilov thought that estimate conservative. "I suppose we could limit the expansion to Fort Stafford."

"Yeah, but the nearest area for large-unit training is three hundred kloms away. Startalk's right in the middle of the Naukatos Plain. Nothing but spikeweed until you get close to the towns."

"All right, Mark. This is no election, but I'd like you to cast a vote anyway."

Langston ran both hands through his wiry, gray-shot curls. "I vote for Startalk. Keeping up combat efficiency takes priority over kissing civilians."

"Let's drink to combat efficiency; may we have it when we need it," Kornilov said. "Now, where in the devil's name is that—"

The waitress appeared, carrying a tray with two glasses flanking a frosted bottle of Rurik Dynamo vodka. Kornilov turned his glower into a smile.

"Just leave the bottle, and thanks."

The woman fled in obvious relief. She was new, which meant unused to senior officers. Maybe she also felt guilty about doing her Federal Service in such a soft billet as an officers' club.

Nothing to be done about that, either, as long as the Victoria Brigade had to accommodate its full quota of Federal Service people with only one active battalion. At least this crisis might give all the FS people something more demanding—

Langston finished pouring out two glasses and raised his.

"To combat efficiency?"

Kornilov nodded and drank. He hoped he was wrong, that Victoria Command had more officers than Mark and a few company commanders who would recognize combat efficiency when it bit them in the balls.

If he wasn't . . .

He decided that one way of setting a good example would

be no more drinking. Starting tomorrow, of course. Duty called, but not so loudly that it wouldn't be a crime to waste this bottle. . . .

"So, when can I have my ship?" Captain Rose Liddell asked.

Rear Admiral Durgin, the Riftwell Dockyard superintendent, frowned. "Thirty-two days. Possibly four or five less, if Ahmed here cancels his Koran reading group."

"I begin to regret the day I organized it," Commander Tourkmani said. "But so few of even the believers seem to know what God sent to the Prophet. So much superstition has crept in." He shook his head.

"God sent the Koran to the Prophet, that His Word might be known," Liddell said. She smiled. "To lesser men, God sent heads and hearts and hands to hold tools, that other work may be accomplished. I will not speak for God, but I will pray that He knows of both your good heart and your sense of duty."

"I do not recognize the poet," Tourkmani added. "I know I should, but to my shame—"

"No shame," Liddell said. "I made that up myself."

"Then God bless your gift of poetry," the commander said.

"Let's hope God will bless our efforts to push our elderly virgin out of this Dockyard," the superintendent interrupted. He'd obviously been up since well before Captain Liddell was even contemplating her morning tea.

"Indeed, or Admiral Schatz will send something other than a blessing," Tourkmani said. "Now, I can indeed suspend the Koran reading and perhaps gain a whole hour. I can gain days, if some of the transferred people can be assigned—"

The superintendent was starting to nod when Liddell used a deliberately coarse interjection. This won her the undivided attention of both Dockyard officers.

"A polite translation: I'll fight that all the way up to Schatz. Those orphans have mostly signed up for TOAD assignments to get ship duty. I won't have them kidnaped for your bloody workshops!"

"Captain, with all due respect, I was not contemplating asking any of them to withdraw from ship duty," Tourkmani said. "I was only hoping to find some volunteers among those not assigned to *Shenandoah*, to work on her while waiting for their own ships."

Liddell recognized the tone of a man who'd wanted the whole herd but was pretending to be satisfied with a cow and a calf. *Well, the man's more on your side than not. Let's keep him that way.*

"I don't have any problem with that. I'll even drop a word in my own exec's ear, as soon as I know who he is. There may be slack times even for *Shenandoah*'s people."

"Then what are we talking about, as far as when we'll have the ship ready?" Admiral Durgin's tone indicated he didn't like having junior officers making deals as if he was blind, deaf, or civilian.

"Twenty-eight days, if we're lucky," Tourkmani said. "We have Schatz on our side, which may be all the luck we need. If not, perhaps I should reconvene the reading group for prayer."

"I'll join you," Liddell said.

Twenty-eight days. Less than a single Dominion month, before I become one of the elect: captain of a capital ship in the Federation Navy. Twenty-seven years of training, studying, and even a little dreaming, and now the moment is here.

A silent prayer at least seemed appropriate.

Lord, give me a good crew and the skill to be the captain they need.

One

The warm fulfillment faded swiftly. Brigitte Tachin suddenly found herself crying.

The young surgeon lieutenant she knew only as Rafael leaned over her.

"Brigitte, did I hurt you?"

"Oh no. I'm no virgin."

"That's obvious."

The tone was flattering. Two vagrant tears ambled down her cheeks. She wiped her eyes with the sheet, and no more came. She rolled over, facing Rafael.

"I could say the same about you."

He hugged her, exactly what she wanted. *I was luckier than I deserved, setting out to pick up someone for company tonight.*

She didn't believe in omens. Still, it was a good start to her Temporary Out-of-Area Duty with Eleventh Fleet. Charlemagne and home were still far away, but TOAD duty no longer felt quite so much like exile.

She turned down the fruit juice Rafael offered and snuggled under the blankets, close but not quite touching. He sipped from the frosted tumbler and traced both of her heavy brown eyebrows with one finger.

"You know, you didn't even say if you're a first or a second lieutenant. If you're a first lieutenant, I've been bedding a superior officer."

"*Quelle horreur!*" Tachin exclaimed. "No danger of that. Signing up for TOAD will bring me into the zone for promotion next year. Otherwise, I'd still need two years or a medal for that next stripe."

"Are you on a ship or at a base?"

Rafael's hopeful tone was more flattery. She didn't want to remind him how many bases Eleventh Fleet had to cover its assigned sixty-odd planets.

"Shenandoah."

"Oh ho. You're going to be sweating. It's all over the base that she's being rushed out as flagship of a new squadron."

"Do they say where?"

"No. But you'll have a good captain. Rose Liddell was Deputy Chief of Staff for Personnel for two years. They said she was good to work for. Maybe she'll even fight off the Hermit."

"The who?"

"Bogdanov, your exec. Hardshell Russian Baptist from Rurik. If he could run a starship single-handed, he'd do it."

Liddell and Bogdanov sounded like the classic nice-captain/hard-exec combination. In theory this made for a well-run ship. She was about to learn how it worked in practice.

"I'm in Weapons," Tachin said. "Know anything about our Weapons Officer?"

"Not even the name, I'm sorry. I'm afraid that if you're an Alliance spy, you've wasted the evening."

"I could spend quite a few this way without feeling I'd wasted any of them."

He hugged her again, in a way that flashed DESIRE in big, glowing holographic letters. She was tired and only half aroused, but she resolved to make a valiant effort. Rafael deserved it, if only for saving her from what she might otherwise have found in bed.

Her effort seemed valiant enough. Rafael fell asleep right afterward, and Tachin discovered that he snored. Since she wasn't going to spend the night, this didn't matter.

She slipped out of bed and let her gaze linger on Rafael for a moment before pulling the blankets up to his chin. He was really good looking in a rather colorless blond way and very fit in spite of his indoor job.

She wondered what her perverse insistence on handsome partners meant. One result was certainly long bouts of celibacy. She was too short and thin flanked for many tastes.

A look in the mirror on the bathroom door suggested that the flanks could use some work. She'd come straight out from Charlemagne, eight hundred light-years and fifty ship days on a transport with a limited menu and less room to exercise. At least that was one virtue of *Shenandoah*: a battlecruiser could accommodate everything short of a swimming pool.

Dressed and booted, Tachin slung her coat over one arm and rumpled Rafael's hair with the other hand. Then she retraced her steps—hall, elevator, downstairs hall, the reception desk (could a reception robot be programmed to leer?), and finally the thermolock to the outside.

The wind reminded her to pull on her coat. As she stepped within reach of the taxi stand's sensors, it lit up.

"'Name and destination, please?" came the mechanical inquiry.

"Second Lieutenant Brigitte Tachin, Transient Officers' Quarters."

A brief hum, then an unapologetic, "Ten minutes, ma'am."

The wind seemed to grow colder. Tachin stepped away from the taxi stand and looked away from the streetlights until the stars began to appear.

Clouds had covered half the sky since she and Rafael came in. Only one of the local constellations she recognized was still in sight. It was the one called (in polite company) the Jewels.

Downhill, lights danced as a shuttle lifted from the field. Tachin followed it with her eyes until it vanished in the clouds. She searched the sky for Dockyard, then remembered that the asteroid would have been below the horizon even without the clouds.

She turned her back on the wind, which didn't help much. The thought struck her to run back to Rafael's room and admit she was too homesick to spend the night alone. He deserved that much honesty.

Honesty, mon cul! *Self-pity, and asking him to tolerate it. I'm not the first star sailor to be a long way from home.*

Not for the first time, Tachin wondered if she'd been wise, staying so close to home on her first assignments. An enlisted term aboard the Charlemagne-Alcuin Base shuttle, then the officers' course, then the Alcuin Arsenal: none of them more than five light-seconds from the vineyards of the Gretton Valley.

With hindsight, that hadn't been wise at all. But all she'd known then was how reluctant she was to leave the big, warm, rambling house among the terraces.

At least I did it, so when Grandfather decided he would keep the vineyards in the family cost what may, I was already in the Navy. When I knew what my sisters would have to give up, if I left the Navy or even didn't do well . . .

As she turned to face the wind, lights glowed down the road. A taxi purred up to the stand. The door opened, and the ID slot lit up to receive her card. She pushed it in and waited until vulgar noises turned into words.

"Second Lieutenant Brigitte Tachin. Transient Officers' Quarters. Please climb in, ma'am."

As the door closed behind her, a last look at the sky told her the clouds were swallowing the Jewels.

Captain Liddell reached the shuttle terminal full of good will and her staff's going-away brunch. The good will faded when she learned that *Shenandoah* didn't have a dedicated shuttle.

"Count the people going up to my ship," she instructed the operations chief.

"Your ship?"

Liddell opened her overcoat. The dress uniform with four stripes and twice that many ribbons had its usual effect. The chief didn't notice the spot where a bit of egg had parted company with the fork on its way to Liddell's mouth.

"I'm Captain Rose Liddell, CO of *Shenandoah*. Now, you may be new here. But if you don't count the people for *Shenandoah* before I'm back from the head, you'll be reducing your chances of growing old."

"Aye-aye, ma'am."

The count turned up fifty-eight people on their way to *Shen* this morning. That was more than enough to justify a dedicated shuttle under *Shenandoah*'s Priority Two.

Liddell reminded herself to say a special prayer of thanks for Admiral Schatz's invoking that priority. How many favors he'd used up in the process and what he'd expect from her in return, she neither knew nor cared. This morning, her people could ride straight up to their ship and get to work. Otherwise they'd be twiddling their thumbs in the Dockyard's waiting room while Admiral Durgin's transport staff tried to conjure ferries out of the rock.

By the time the shuttle's departure time showed on the display, the waiting room was half filled, many of the people wearing *Shenandoah* patches. Rather than loom over them with her rank or hide in the operations office, Liddell ducked out to the observation deck. The wind had dropped; she could just endure the cold if she kept moving.

The deck ran completely around the circular terminal. Three directions gave Liddell a view of nothing but barracks, landing pads, and workshops that could have been dropped on any one of twenty planets without causing a raised eyebrow.

The fourth direction showed her the boneyard, with the stripped hulks of retired hangar queens lying half buried in the snowdrifts. Beyond them rose the hills of Riftwell, gray-green masses striped with snow and fringed with trees. Except for the trees—local Gate of Paradise and imported pines, instead of tailored oak—it might have been Heller Field on Dominion the day she boarded her first ship.

A shuttle decelerated through the sound barrier with a crack and a rumble, then swooped toward the terminal. As the landing probe engaged it, Liddell realized she was no longer alone.

A female second lieutenant, about her own height and coloring, was standing by the railing. The sight of the shuttle seemed to have hypnotized her.

"Are you for *Shenandoah*, too?" Liddell asked. The lieutenant started, and her salute was pure reflex. Liddell was wearing her favorite overcoat, a Ranger thermal with no rank insignia.

"Yes, ma'am. Second Lieutenant Brigitte Tachin, Weapons Department."

"Do you have any attacker time?"

"No. But I did a year at the Alcuin Arsenal. I'm from Charlemagne: the Gretton Valley wine country."

"I thought I recognized the accent. You're one of the TOADS, aren't you?"

"Yes, ma'am. My first starship time was the transport out here."

"You'll survive. I did my enlisted service as half the

25

Supply Department of a courier-ship tender out of Dominion. Then my first assignment out of OTC was *Skanderbeg*, under Simon Burroughs. That was before he got famous, of course."

No need to mention how much time I spent keeping clear of the other half of that Supply Department. He didn't make a boor of himself, though. Just a bore.

"Are we going to have an attacker squadron aboard *Shenandoah*, ma'am?"

"If Admiral Schatz can scrape one up we will. I'm not making bets either way. You do the same, and save your money for extra cabin stores. Schatz has almost cured our Support Command of trying to save money on the food for remote-duty ships, but they keep having relapses."

Tachin was looking a bit confused, as if asking, *Who's this with access to all the high-level gossip?*

"Excuse me, Lieutenant. I'm Captain Rose Liddell. In about—" she looked at the tower clock "—two hours, I'm going to be your commanding officer."

"Yes, ma'am."

Tachin's voice was suddenly as frigid as the wind. "With your permission, ma'am?" She looked toward the door.

"Of course." They exchanged salutes. Liddell let Tachin gain enough of a lead that the lieutenant wouldn't have to run to stay ahead, then followed.

So much for all those Outstanding *ratings in Leadership. I saw what I once was: half woman, half girl, joining her first starship and fighting off fear and homesickness. I forgot that I was as nervous as a stray kitten and as ready to scratch even a helping hand.*

"Now hear this, now hear this," the loudspeaker boomed. "All personnel embarking for *Shenandoah*, please report to Gate A. Repeat, all personnel for *Shenandoah* report to Gate A immediately. That is all."

Sixty kilometers above Dockyard, *Shenandoah* hung shimmering against the stars.

Brigitte Tachin tried to see if the load the tug was pulling away from the ship was really a folded meteor shield. Everyone else aboard the shuttle seemed to be equally curious. She backed away from the port, looking for one that wasn't barricaded with feet, elbows, and rumps.

She'd just spotted a completely untenanted one when the cabin's forward screen finally came on. A slow drift back toward seats began, as the screen requested that "ALL HANDS STRAP IN FOR DOCKING MANUEVERS."

Since Tachin knew she had a good ten minutes before the shuttle captain lost patience with diehards, she headed for the port anyway. She wanted to go on seeing her home for the next two or three years with her own eyes.

As she reached the port, she discovered that Captain Liddell had had the same idea. Tachin saluted, backed away, and started to apologize. She stopped when she saw that the captain probably didn't even know she had company. A teaching sister praying in the chapel couldn't have been less conscious of the outside world.

Well, not quite. The sister probably wouldn't have prayed with a portable computer unfolded across one arm. She also wouldn't have been muttering things that invoked God but were a long way from being prayers.

Curious beyond discretion, Tachin stayed in sight of both the port and the computer's display and began comparing them. Like most capital ships, *Shenandoah* was a series of spheres linked by a heavy framework inside a mirror-finished outer hull. Like a battleship, she had four spheres—Bow (weapons and command), First Midships (quarters), Second Midships (stores and life support), and Stern (major systems, including power pile, drive, shield, and gravity generators).

Unlike a battleship, she could embark an attacker squadron. If she'd been a carrier, her bow would have been a gigantic hangar, able to house, maintain, and launch thirty to fifty of the forty-meter craft without anyone working up a sweat. Aboard a battlecruiser like *Shenandoah*, a single squadron of a dozen attackers had to perch like migrating whitemasks on the girders linking the Bow and First Midships.

This fact seemed to be connected with Captain Liddell's language. *Shenandoah*'s main strength and protection lay in the four spheres themselves, with hulls sixty centimeters thick and internal bulkheading and bracing in proportion. The outer hull provided a mirror surface to reflect lasers and an extra barrier against kinetic-energy slugs, shaped charges, and particle beams.

With the outer hull in place, *Shenandoah* should have had

27

the appearance of a slightly flattened cylinder with pointed ends, four hundred meters long, a hundred and twenty meters in diameter, and almost completely featureless except for serial numbers, signal lights, and deployed antennae. Now she showed one crucial difference.

Where a launcher hatch should have sealed the hull, a long rectangular hole gaped black against the mirror finish. A second look showed Tachin tiny lights gleaming red and yellow in the blackness. She knew that with that hatch open and the meteor shield gone, far too much delicate equipment was naked to space.

Tachin felt a junior officer's relief that she wasn't the woman standing beside her, now folding up the computer and tapping the stained carpet with one small foot. If anything had gone wrong, it might not be Brigitte Tachin's problem.

If it was aboard *Shenandoah*, it had to be Captain Liddell's.

"Oh, Lieutenant Tachin," Liddell said. "Glad to see you. Unless this problem involves the Weapons Department, I'm going to borrow you for a few hours."

"Yes, ma'am."

"Don't you want to know why?"

"I . . . well, I assumed—"

"Don't assume anything about four-stripers, including that all our orders are legitimate. We only think we're gods. However, in this case I think the order's in the clear." She was unfolding the computer again as she spoke.

"I want to try holding on to that tug with our meteor shield, without shouting over the radio. I want you to ferry down to the superintendent's office with the request. Do you know your way around the Dockyard?"

"I studied the plans on the way out from Charlemagne. I've never actually been there."

"I've only been there twice myself. You'll do. The point is, until we know what's wrong, the quieter the better. Embarrassing Durgin's no way to keep him cooperative."

Tachin mentally noted this lesson in leadership. She also wondered whether Liddell was more concerned about Admiral Durgin's embarrassment than she was about *Shenandoah*'s. On a more practical point, she spoke aloud.

"What if the shield's on its way to some other ship, ma'am?"

"Then I'll request that the order be countermanded. The other ship probably doesn't have an attacker-sized hole in her outer hull. *Shenandoah* does."

"Yes, ma'am."

The text of a politely sulphurous memorandum scrolled across the computer's screen, then crept out of the print slot. Liddell folded the memorandum, squeezed hard to seal it, stamped it with her ID, and handed it to Tachin.

"Good luck, Lieutenant."

Two

Warrant Officer Hobson had been on duty in *Shenandoah*'s Personnel Office for nine days. Several times he'd wished his desk had its own private shield generator. He didn't need one against the young lieutenant leaning on the desk now, but he devoutly wished the man would take himself elsewhere.

Lieutenant Longman had orders from the executive officer to do exactly that. Reminding him how seriously to take the Hermit's orders might solve the problem peacefully.

"I appreciate your wanting to know the roster for the Launcher Division," Hobson said. The most contemplative of Buddhist priests could hardly have matched his tone of infinite patience with human folly.

"But I can't. Really, I can't. It isn't complete yet. Besides, launcher problems could affect how many people you're assigned."

"I know that, Mr. Hobson," Longman said. He managed to avoid sounding petulant by not playing with the earring in his left ear. It was within the bounds of regulation jewelry. So was the length of his beard. Both made Hobson wonder what Longman wore on a dirtside leave.

"I don't need a complete count. Just an approximate one. I've done some preliminary calculations. The more I know in advance about my personnel resources, the better I can program solutions."

You've guessed the Hermit's standards well enough. Two points to you, then subtract one for saying "your" personnel resources.

30

In Hobson's thirty years in the Navy, he'd learned early and practiced carefully the rule that favors had to be earned. Right now, Second Lieutenant Charles Varin Longman was a good many points short of earning the favor he wanted.

"Lieutenant, the best thing you can do for yourself is head down to the airlock and suit up. When Bogdanov asks for you, he likes you to at least try to meet yourself coming back. It'll help that you took time to work out some solutions in advance, but it won't help enough if you don't move out."

"Chief, I can order the roster."

Hobson turned on all his dignity. "Sir, with all due respect, you can't. Not unless you are formally installed as Acting Launcher-Division Officer. That requires laying this whole matter before the captain. Meanwhile, Commander Bogdanov is going to be waiting. Instead of you, he'll get a report that you're arguing with me over regulations."

After which report, he's likely to slaughter us both impartially, but I'm betting you don't know that yet.

At least Longman's glare was adult. "I'd hoped for more cooperation, Mr. Hobson. I also hope something will happen to make me forget this."

You and me both, sir.

"Eh?"

I'm slipping. I must have subvocalized.

"Just that I'm sorry I can't help you as much as I'd like to, sir. But I'm sure you'll find a way through."

Balked, Longman was suddenly so eager to leave that he nearly collided with a lanky first lieutenant entering the Personnel Office. The new arrival waited until Longman was well on his way before looking at the yeoman clerk. Hobson looked at her, then back at the lieutenant, then gave a double thumbs-up.

She's clear.

"Lieutenant Mahoney, welcome aboard!" They slapped palms, and Brian Mahoney grinned.

"Chief, aren't you getting a little old to fight young bulls like Longman?"

"If they want a piece of my pasture, they don't get it free. Although maybe I should watch myself. I nearly told that young *skeerish* what he could do with himself."

"I'd have been a witness that he was threatening you witn an illegal order."

"Yeah, and we'd have all been run off the ship. It might not have ended there, either. Longman's family grows admirals like some people grow pimples. I think he's related to two active and three retired flag officers. You want that much rank on your case?"

"I wouldn't do it for everybody, Chief."

"No, thank God. Otherwise you ought to put in for a Section Five discharge. But what's with you being aboard *Shen*? Last I heard, you were on *Valhalla*."

"I was. Didn't you also hear we had a toxic-cargo leak after that Jump-triggered fire?"

"Something like that. No casualties, though."

"Correction: one casualty, and you're looking at him. Nothing heroic about it, either. I was the one person in the exposed area with a malfunctioning breathing mask. The dose put me in hospital. I'm still on a medical waiver for ship duty. That's why I'm plans officer for the Training Department. I'll probably wear a second hat as Orientation Division Officer, too, if Captain Liddell organizes one."

"Oh, she will. I talked with Shumrick at his retirement party. He was Chief of the Ship when she commanded *Zulu*. The Orientation Division was one lieutenant and one petty officer. Anything they didn't do or have done, she did herself and made sure they knew it. Just them and nobody else."

"Nice to know some people don't change. Particularly the ones I still owe. Maybe I'll be able to figure out how to pay them back."

"You don't need to lose any sleep over that, Lieutenant. Not with me, anyway."

Is this his idea of a feeler for negotiations? Brian Mahoney is the damndest combination of blarney and sneakiness I've never been able to outwit!

"Actually, there is something I could do. It might cost me a little sleep, but not much. If you haven't made up the officers bunk roster yet, put Longman with me."

Hobson realized that he'd just been outnegotiated again. Brian Mahoney was the ideal man to keep someone like

Longman from making trouble. If he did that, Hobson's own job would be a bloody sight easier. Now, what to do for Mahoney?

One easy question, Ken. Just send him enough people for the Orientation Division. No, one thing more: give him the address of the Three Palms, if he doesn't have it already. Good drinking spots aren't all that common on Riftwell.

Hobson's fingers had worked along with his mind. The officers' bunkroom assignments scrolled past, until they reached "D-4." Hobson tapped in "Longman, Charles V., Second Lieutenant."

"That makes you as senior, Longman, Elayne Zheng, and one vacancy. Zheng's another transfer from *Valhalla*, I think. I hope she can cope with a FADS case like Longman."

"She is. She's also going to be wilder than a rutting *kropis* if we don't embark an attacker squadron. Radar watch on our shuttles isn't enough to keep an AG type tame."

"It all counts on the bonus," Hobson said. "Anything else?"

"Not that I can think of. I'd better get down to the Training Office and start the inventory of materials. The new inventory, that is. We keep getting new shipments every other day, and Bell's decided I'm inventory officer."

"Open space and a good ship, sir." This time Hobson saluted Mahoney.

As the lieutenant vanished, the yeoman looked up from her terminal. "FADS, Chief?"

"Future Admiral Delusion Syndrome. Lieutenant Longman thinks he's going to be an admiral. It's conceivable that he's wrong. Understand?"

"Yes. I think so."

"You think? You actually can perform such a rare and difficult feat? Then could I make a suggestion? Apply this mystical power of thought to figuring out how we can bunk four hundred and sixty-eight enlisted in space intended for four hundred and twenty."

"Aren't we supposed to get people pods if we're embarking that many passengers?"

"These," Hobson said heavily, "are not passengers. They're ship's complement. Passengers, if any, will be extra. So will any high-priority cargo. We may get people pods then. We also may not. Don't bet anything you can't afford to lose on our getting them."

"All right, Chief."

The yeoman swiveled her chair back to the screen, pulled on her helmet and microphone for the verbal-command link to the computer, and went to work. Hobson considered pulling out his desk bottle of Killarney Mist, then remembered that Captain Liddell's leadership style was very much like his. *Everybody toes the line until they've earned the right to relax.*

Shenandoah was going to be a very regulation ship until Liddell decided all the bad actors had been smoked out. Regulations were unkind to drinking on duty, and Rose Liddell had made enough allowances for Kenneth Hobson to last both of them a lifetime.

In fact, he was still in the Navy because she'd stood up as a witness for him the second time he failed a blood-alcohol test for being drunk on duty. He'd lost three years' seniority and paid a stiff fine, but he'd stayed sane and reasonably sober ever since.

Hobson saw that the yeoman was lost in her work. He punched up the roster of petty officers with Instructor ratings and started checking for those without fixed assignments already. As he did, he mentally fitted an ancient tune with new words.

"Roll on, *Killarney, Takeda, Renown.*
This shiny new lady is getting me down."

The three spacesuited officers made a human trefoil as they floated in the space between *Shenandoah*'s Bow and First Midships spheres. With helmets touching, they could talk without using their radios. The launcher problem wasn't a crisis yet, but it wasn't something they wanted turned into messhall gossip either.

Commander Fujita tapped Longman's computer with a gloved hand. "I assume you didn't do your calculations just for their entertainment value."

"No, sir."

"Would you be prepared to recommend closing the hatch?" Commander Bogdanov asked.

Having devoutly wished for the undivided attention of the

chief engineer and the executive officer, Longman began to repent. Trying to demonstrate initiative, he'd only succeeded in having a major decision thrust on him.

And it's not just my mechanical knowledge they're testing. It's my loyalty—Shenandoah *against my own arse. Will I shy away from a decision to protect that arse, or risk it to save their precious ship from having a great big gaping hole in her side while they're trying to fix things?*

Longman looked about the bay, running down a mental checklist. Stress meter in place, tested (old, but it worked), and feeding to his computer. Manual override activated. Nothing and nobody dangling or loose.

"Yes."

In a vacuum, with none of them touching any part of the ship, they heard and felt nothing. They only saw the fifty-meter rectangle of stars overhead slowly narrow, then vanish. Longman's breath went out in a *wssssh* of relief.

The bay lights brightened, and he repeated his scan of the bay. "Sir," he began. "One of the hatch joint covers was a little slow to close. If the hinges—"

"Later, Lieutenant," Fujita said. "Right now you've proved that your calculations are as sound as mine in one area. Did you take them any further?"

"If I'm being asked to offer a working hypothesis—"

"You are." *The commanders might have been a duet.*

"I'd say the stress fracture began with that meteor impact the year after the Erasmus Crisis. It remained at a subdetection level until the tugs moved *Shenandoah* to the Dockyard. What brought it up to the danger level was probably a combination of additional stresses. Also, the stress scans have been cut back in the interests of saving time."

Longman was glad Fujita's face was unreadable behind his tinted face-plate. It was no secret that Fujita had turned down an offer from the Dockyard to make extra scans with their own people.

Rumor said that this wasn't trying to show off what he could do with his own people. Captain Liddell had ordered it because the Dockyard offered to do the work with TOADS volunteers already assigned to *Shenandoah*—making the ship a gift out of her own resources, so to speak.

Loyalty is vital. And everyone has a different definition of it. With five admirals in the family, why the devil couldn't one of them add that little detail before sending me off to Officer's Training Course!

Forget rumors. The fact was that a key beam in the Launcher Two structure would never hold up under regular use of the launcher. Even without an embarked attacker squadron, *Shenandoah* could hardly afford to have one of her shuttle/attacker launchers out of action in a potential combat zone. The big missile-carrying buses used the heavy launchers, too.

"I had only approximate data on the exact site and extent of the fracture until now," Longman continued. "But I worked out various techniques for the repairs, depending on these factors. I also made two assumptions. One was that we wouldn't have time to remove the whole beam and replace it. The other was that we would be using only ship's personnel and equipment."

Time to blow the whistle on Chief Hobson? I really could have offered rosters for each approach if he'd helped. No, Bogdanov wants the display or me fixing the beam with my teeth in about two minutes.

Longman had spent his own money on the best multi-environment microcomputer. The benign vacuum inside *Shenandoah*'s outer hull was nothing to electronics intended to survive six atmospheres of methane at a hundred below. The combinations and permutations of what could be done to put Launcher Two back in service marched past with the disciplined precision of light infantry on parade.

"I see you managed another limitation," Fujita said when the screen was clear. "You'll be limiting EVA in this space rather substantially. The supporting framework is going to be spiderwebbed halfway across it."

"Sir, I'm sorry if I didn't—"

"No apologies necessary," the engineer said. "You had your priorities in order. Leaping around during EVA saves time, but it isn't as critical as a functioning launcher. We'll both want personal copies of all your material. Then we'll run it through the main computer and lay it before the captain. I would like you—"

"Now hear this, now hear this," came a woman's voice, in a creditable imitation of an all-hands announcement. "Will the picnic in Bay One please report to the Bow dock for the captain's arrival?''

By the time the announcement was done, Longman had recognized the voice of the Weapons Officer, Commander Zubova. The two senior officers were already on their way toward the airlock, soaring on a precise path through the projecting structures inside the bay.

Longman added curses on zero-g athletes to those on uncooperative warrant officers. He carefully locked his computer to his belt, then followed his superiors at a more sedate velocity.

Three

"Return File T657-KY to Memory," Brian Mahoney ordered the computer.

"Returning . . . returned," the reply came. Telltale lights flashed on the console, confirming the words.

"Acknowledging return. Switch to Record/Transmit."

"Return acknowledged. Switching to Record/Transmit."

Mahoney stared at the warm yellow bulkheads. They no longer seemed to clash with the blue-green hatch. Either he was getting used to the Training Department office or he was too busy to worry about esthetics.

More likely the second. Mahoney closed his eyes and slowed his breathing. It didn't help. He couldn't find words that would make his third memorandum about more simulator capsules any different from the first two. Or at least different enough to attract more attention from Lieutenant Commander Bell.

A tap on the back of Mahoney's chair made him turn. Chief Petty Officer Netsch was looking down at him with her usual maternal smile. Mahoney pulled off his helmet and unclipped his mask.

"Yes, Chief?"

"If you're trying to get those extra sim rigs—"

"Were you listening in?"

"No, just making an educated guess."

Mahoney refused to make an issue of it. He felt so tired so often these days that he knew his temper was unpredictable. He wondered if fighting for that medical waiver had been a mistake.

"Well, if you're in the guessing business, can you guess why I'm sticking to my guns?"

"No guess needed. If we get the usual percentage of new people and have a busy cruise, hands-on training won't be enough. We'll need at least six more simulators to take up the slack. Problem is, where do we put them?"

"I don't know. But damn it, there's got to be some space on a ship this size!"

"If we have passengers, freight, and an embarked squadron, we won't have room to set up another water cooler!

"Are we going to be carrying freight and passengers during the whole cruise? Or will we unload at Victoria?"

"Probably the second. You've got an idea, Lieutenant?"

"Call it another educated guess. The only part of the cruise where we'll be packed to the overhead is the transit to Victoria. We can juggle the training schedules for that long. If we load the extra simulators in with the freight, we can set them up once we've unloaded. We'll be out there as a cruising warship a lot longer than we'll be transiting as a glorified passenger-cargo liner."

Netsch grinned. "I like. We'd still better have places picked for setting up the extra six. Otherwise—"

"Now hear this. Now hear this. Captain coming on board. Repeat, captain coming on board."

The intercom screen above the hatch showed the inboard side of the Bow dock, sideboys, and department heads already in formation. Netsch muttered something about "checking on how Hoffman's doing with those graphics tests." Mahoney waved good-bye as the petty officer vanished into the bowels of the Training Section.

Netsch's real vocation was for teaching; she was one of the rare petty officers who avoided ceremonial like Heller's Rot. It made for compatibility with Mahoney, who was usually happy that first lieutenants were too low on the chain of military evolution to be needed at fancy-dress brawls.

Of course, he might be luckier in the Navy than he'd been in the seminary or in marriage. Two of the people who helped so far were aboard *Shen*, Hobson and now Rose Liddell. Hobson had as good as spoonfed him through some rough spots in recruit training. Liddell had taken a green second lieutenant, too old and too uncertain of himself for his job, and turned that job into a continuous test of skills she knew he had. By the time he'd passed all those tests, the doubts were gone and the age no longer mattered.

The hatch in Bay Four irised; Rose Liddell drifted through. Bosun's pipes wheetled and everyone with a hand to spare saluted. Liddell returned the salutes and gripped a handhold in the overhead. Mahoney heard the familiar combination of warmth and crispness in her voice as she thanked everyone for the welcome aboard and suggested that they get back to work.

The screen remained live, showing the rest of the shuttleload streaming through the hatch. Mahoney went back to work on the memorandum, sparing only an occasional glance at the screen. Not much chance of recognizing anybody in that mob scene, and the memo was finally shouting "Write me! Write me!" now that he knew what he wanted to say.

One memo suggested another, that one a third, and by then he saw Hobson had delivered the roster of Instructor-qualified petty officers. He called that up and started annotating it, making two alternative lists, one for twelve simulators they had and one for the eighteen to twenty they really needed.

He'd just finished the second list when the hatch opened and Elayne Zheng floated in. She'd let her hair grow since they'd said good-bye in *Valhalla*'s sick bay, but otherwise she hadn't changed. Her dark elf's face showed all five ethnic groups in her ancestry if you looked at it long enough but never the same one two minutes running.

Mahoney unbelted and pushed himself up from his chair. A foot hooked under its arm held him in place as Zheng approached close enough to let him kiss her lightly on the forehead.

Then she grabbed him by both shoulders and kissed him properly. "Hey, Brian. Good to see you. Lungs all flushed out?"

"I'm on waiver for shipboard duty. That's why they stuck me here in Training. I'm not supposed to do EVA."

"I'm sure *Shen* will survive without you pulling on a suit. I suppose you pulled me into your bunkroom?"

"Do Merishi climb? You, me, and a FADS case named Charlie Longman. I thought we'd be a match for him."

"Who's the fourth?"

"Any other old *Valhalla* types floating around?"

Zheng turned upside down relative to Mahoney and anchored herself with two fingers hooked under the base of his desk display.

"Nobody that I know. Stokowski retired. Rieke transferred to Eighth Fleet, DeVries is on TDY at Chandler Base, and Kharku is staying with *Val*. It is not true, incidentally, that Captain Prange threatened mutiny if Kharku was transferred."

"What about Candy Shores?"

"Candy?" Zheng grinned. "If—"

"Now hear this! Now hear this! All hands to damage-control stations. All hands to damage-control stations. This is a drill. Hull breach in Second Midships Frame 87. Repeat, this is a drill. Breach in Midships Frame 87. This is a drill."

Zheng jackknifed to pull her breathing mask out of her belt pouch. Mahoney did the same to retrieve his from the fastener strip under his desk. When they were both masked and the hatch had shut, he told Zheng to monitor the hatch telltales. Then he plugged his mask into the intercom and cleared his throat.

"All Training Office compartments, this is Lieutenant Mahoney. Damage and casualty report!"

"Sills, Compartment One. All clear."

"Yakov, Compartment Two. All clear."

"Baltsa, Compartment Three. We only caught half the alarm. This is a drill?"

"Affirmative."

"No damage or casualites."

Mahoney ran through the eight compartments of the Training Office in half that many minutes. Compartment Eight was the largest, housing nine simulators. Netsch answered, sounding peeved.

"Eight here. No damage. One casualty."

"Who?"

"Hoffman. She didn't take her mask into the simulator with her. Those things aren't airtight and she couldn't get out in time. I've ruled her as needing a brain regen." More calmly, Netsch added, "Hoffman knows everything about graphics but not a whole lot about ships."

"You know what to do about people like that, Chief. I won't jiggle your elbow."

"Okay, Lieutenant."

Mahoney turned to see Zheng handing him one of the

emergency oxygen bottles. The breathing mask held a five-minute supply. That plus the support of standard shipboard coveralls for human skin was usually enough to let people evacuate the area of a major hull breach. Beyond that, the collapsible helmet, gloves, and hour's supply of oxygen packaged in the emergency bottles came into play.

Mahoney checked the pressure gauge of the bottle to make sure no one had been using it to cure hangovers, then started to undo the outer seal. As he did, both screen and telephone intercoms blared.

"Now hear this. Now hear this. Secure from drill. Repeat, secure from drill. That is all."

Mahoney resealed the bottle, pulled off his mask, and rubbed his face where the edges of the mask had scraped the skin. Zheng hung up the bottle and pulled off her own mask.

"Liddell's not wasting much time, is she?"

"In her situation, would you?"

"Probably not. Anyway, what were you going to say about Candy Shores?"

"Rumor says we're on our way to Victoria. If that's true, Candy's going to be standing on a mountaintop waving hello to us. They popped her aboard *Beng Dzhou* as soon as the Dockyard took over security, her and about thirty others from the LI detachment."

"Good luck to her. Victoria's no garden spot, but Candy always did prefer field duty. If they put her in Scout Company, she'll be up to her neck in honey."

The ocher and rust hills bordering the Naukatos Plain rolled away to the west. Jutting up among them was the rocky outcropping Scout Company had christened the Thumb. From the edge of Costello's Flats to the Thumb was two kilometers. With their battledress adjusted to desert camouflage, the troopers were lost to the naked eye at a tenth of that distance.

First Lieutenant Candice Nikolaevna Shores, 108 Light Infantry Brigade, formerly attached to U.F.S. *Valhalla*, contemplated the scene with satisfaction. Being shipped in on virtually no notice to take over as company exec was bad enough. She was an outsider replacing a popular officer who'd been posted to Third Battalion as Assistant Operations Officer. The battalion needed Lieutenant Coombes more than Scout Company did, but the troopers might not buy the big picture.

They were doing their job, though. This field exercise against simulated snipers threatening the new base perimeter was going like a drill. So had everything else she'd seen them do in the last thirty-two days. Captain Abelsohn was behind her all the way, too. If things just went on this way for another thirty-two days. . . .

Shores pushed her mask up onto her helmet and scanned the horizon. She knew the mask was needed for prolonged exposure to the deep desert. Low humidity would get you in the short run and mites could get you in the long. She also knew the mask wasn't supposed to cut your peripheral vision. She wondered who the mask designer had bought to have that notion written into the training manual.

The Scouts' close air support was in position. One lifter was high, the other two so low that even from this little ridge Shores could see only the puffs of dust when they used their fans to hold position.

Everything nominal there. One lifter high to scan, draw, decoy, and jam enemy responses, and return fire if it lasted long enough. Two lifters low, with a mix of weapons to tackle anything short of a spaceship. Their gunners could pick the right combination in the time it took to feed target information into the computers and pop up into firing position.

The rest of the company's lifters were back in a secure LZ, with a platoon guarding them. Unless they'd been "borrowed" for the field logistics exercise General Langston was supposed to be running, over beyond the Roskill Range. Langston had a long-standing habit of springing that kind of surprise. It didn't win him any popularity contests with the people who wanted to retire on Victoria without actually handing in their—

"Son of a bitch!"

Shores and her escort, Lance Corporal Sklarinsky, stared at the swelling yellow-black cloud beside the Thumb. A moment later the cloud swallowed the Thumb, and the roar of the explosion reached them.

Shores flipped her pickups clear of her ears. For a Light Infantryman, standard infantry gear always felt like a committee's compromise. Without her armor she felt half naked; without its sensors she felt half blind and half deaf.

Well, most infantrymen through the ages have survived with even less, when they survived at all.

The smoke cloud wouldn't tell her anything more. Shores scanned the landscape. At first even the nearest platoon seemed to have vanished. Her stomach turned to stone. Then she realized that they must have gone to ground. Fifty meters away, she picked out two troopers shifting position, low-crawling a meter at a time.

Shores realized that she hadn't heard Captain Abelsohn on the company command circuit. She jerked her mask back on.

"All Bedrock units! This is Huntress. Status report!"

"Huntress, this is Hammer's CP. Hammer's down. Head injury from a flying rock. Unconscious. One KIA, five other WIA. No missing."

"Hammer" was Captain Abelsohn's call sign for this exercise. He'd been with 2nd Platoon, closest to the Thumb. 1st Platoon was back with the transport, clear of immediate danger, but the rest . . .

Shores felt the stone in her belly turn to something heavier, like power-pile shielding. She was now in command of Scout Company, facing a guerrilla threat that was no longer simulated.

"2nd Platoon, ground and freeze! 3rd Platoon, manuever to provide covering fire for 2nd. 4th and 5th, take position for all-around defense. 3rd, when you're in position, detach one squad to help 2nd Platoon evacuate the wounded. Then cover their withdrawal into the 4th-5th perimeter."

"Huntress, this is Frontier," began the senior platoon commander, from 5th Platoon. "We don't know what the threat is—"

"No, and until we do we don't get any closer to it. Or would you rather ditch our wounded?"

That was a low blow, but Shores had neither time nor patience for argument. If she ended up looking unaggressive, she'd be out of Scout Company in hours. Meanwhile, she wasn't going to have neglected wounded on her conscience.

Sometimes the best thing to do for the wounded was to leave them and push the enemy back. Her tactics courses had been full of examples of firefights lost because a unit was paralyzed by concern for its casualties.

Shores didn't think this was one of those times. The "enemy" had set off one big bang, probably by remote control. They probably weren't anywhere they could be reached, no matter how "aggressively" she pushed Scout Company forward on a cold or even nonexistent trail.

Scout Company might not like their acting CO's orders, but they obeyed. Shores watched the two platoons form the defensive perimeter in what looked like slow motion through her binoculars. She knew they were actually moving as fast as possible without making naked targets of themselves.

In eight minutes the perimeter was formed, 3rd Platoon in position, and the wounded on their way out of the explosion area. The acting CO of 2nd Platoon (the CO was one of the casualties) reported that he was forming a rear guard of two squads and asked if Huntress had any further orders.

"No. Just one comment. Well done, everybody. Now I think we'd better tell the upper echelons."

Radio communication on Victoria was only just reliable enough for tactical purposes. Shores knew she had a choice between a multiple relay through ground stations, which meant delay, and a one-stage relay through Milsat 8, which meant sending a high volume of security-critical material that the Alliance could record in haste and unscramble at leisure.

Before Shores could decide, she saw that the high lifter had been joined by the low flight and two complete strangers. She wasn't entirely surprised to see the Scout Company lifters break out of formation and head for the wounded, while the other two skimmed toward her. After that, she wasn't surprised at all to see one lifter land and General Langston climb out.

Like most Federation field-grades, Langston went fully armed. He carried a standard pulse rifle with grenade launcher and a custom-made bandolier with grenades and magazines alternating. He trailed the rifle and signaled with his free hand to the airborne lifter to circle.

"All right, Lieutenant Shores. I've been lucky enough to hear most of what happened. I still want to hear it in your own words." The intensity in Langston's brown eyes and level voice made Shores feel stripped of uniform as well as armor. She almost forgot field regulations and saluted.

"Captain Abelsohn had deployed the company with four platoons in line and one for lifter security. . . ."

The general listened silently. Shores was sweating in spite of the chill wind. She began a mental countdown to the moment of her relief from Scout Company.

Then Langston smiled. "You said it for me, Lieutenant. Well done, everybody. That includes you. Going baldheaded for the enemy makes sense only if there's an enemy to go baldheaded for."

"You don't think there was anybody in reach? That was my guess, but I wouldn't call it more than that."

"Sometimes it takes more courage to admit you're guessing than to take the point in enemy territory. I'm glad you've got both kinds. But, answering your question: that was my guess, too.

"We still want more than guesses about something that slammed eight of our people. The medevac lifters are coming back with a chemical analysis kit. Maybe we can get an idea of what kind of HE made that bang.

"I've put a request in for a complete record of all RIs in the area. If that was a radio-command detonation, somebody may have heard the signal."

"They'd have to have observation for a command detonation," Shores put in.

"If you don't mind a lousy picture, you can use a spy-eye the size of a golf ball. Or a hundred of them. Personally, I suspect the explosion was triggered on the spot. That means either an Alliance arms cache or a dump of mining explosives."

"Mining explosives? They wouldn't be rigged to blow at an intruder alarm, would they? That's illegal!"

"A lot of what the miners did fifty years ago was illegal. They thought the planet would develop enough to make the profits worth the risk. If somebody's supply dump included data on what he'd found, he might very well make sure nobody else could learn anything from it. Or the explosives might have become unstable with age.

"We'll have to check Economic Development records," Langston went on. "Meanwhile, an accident with a cache of mining explosives makes a good cover story. We can't deny it completely, but we can avoid everyone accusing the Alliance."

That took a load off Shores's mind. She didn't think war was immoral, or she'd never have put on a uniform. She did think fighting the wrong people by mistake was a crime.

But what about Langston's superiors? Langston, everybody said, was on his way to three stars. The rest of the senior officers on Victoria had no hope of promotion unless they had to fight a war.

Not much a first lieutenant can do about it if they do get galloping promotionitis, either.

Langston slung his pulser. "I thought of pulling Coombes back from Third Battalion to take over the Scouts. But you seem to be on top of things. Want me to confirm you as CO?"

Lord, give me the wisdom to know what I ought to want, even if you won't give it to me.

Shores didn't know if it was an answered prayer or another lucky guess. Somehow she knew that giving up Scout Company would be failing to pursue a fleeing enemy.

"They're good people. I couldn't ask for better. I'll take it."

"Fine. I'm going to organize C Company for a low-altitude search. Then I'll be back, unless I need to go in and extract that chem kit personally."

"Good hunting, sir. And . . . thank you."

Langston probably didn't hear. He was already climbing into the lifter, and its fans were turning. Shores wound up saluting the lifter's belly armor, then she turned back to her company.

Suddenly Victoria didn't look so bad. There might be captain's bars hidden somewhere in its deserts.

And if you're thinking like that, Candy, what are you doing throwing stones at other people's promotionitis?

Four

As Bogdanov and Fujita left Captain Liddell's office, the lights in the passageway dimmed. A voice announcement raised faint echoes from the shadows.

"Now hear this. Now hear this. Day-night illumination cycle commences at 2000. Repeat, day-night illumination cycle commences at 2000. That is all."

Fujita anchored himself with one hand and opened his computer with the other. Bogdanov hooked his toes onto a holdstrip on the bulkhead. Both scanned the passageway for anything that had suddenly become hard to see in the artificial twilight.

Spacemen had long known the wisdom of maintaining the human diurnal cycle aboard ship. Navy regulations were strict about obstacles and emergency facilities being visible under both full and emergency illumination, visible and infrared.

Somewhere in the middle, people sometimes forgot about the need to find things "at night." Fujita knew why: people assumed that "night" would become either full or emergency lighting before anything had to be done. He thought that assumption was tempting Fate, Murphy, and everything else that killed people and wrecked ships.

No nighttime perils lurked in the passageway, except for a gap in the overhead paneling that Fujita knew was an access panel removed for maintenance on a dust scrubber. The two officers detached themselves and drifted down the passageway to the elevator.

As the elevator door closed behind them, Bogdanov whispered, "How much do you think Captain Liddell was hiding about our mission?"

"Nothing she was sure about. Certainly. Maybe a few guesses or rumors. She hates rumors—they lead to unnecessary speculation."

Fujita was whispering, too, but he hoped the slight edge in his voice was sending Bogdanov the right message. That tactless question was no way to begin a cruise under Captain Lidddell.

Bogdanov shrugged. "So I have heard. Certainly it can do no harm, if we are ready not only to cruise but to fight. That means we must adopt a solution for Launcher Two that allows high-intensity operations."

Fujita considered. All the evidence pointed to *Shen* getting a squadron. Nothing was missing except written orders and the actual hardware.

"I agree, but I don't think there'll be any problems, not with Longman on the job. Did you know that every solution he presented was optimized for minimal shift in the ship's center of mass? They all work out safe to eight decimal places."

"Longman thinks a long way ahead when he deals with machinery."

"But not so far ahead with people?"

That had to be brought into the open, even if Bogdanov did owe at least one promotion to Longman's Aunt Diana.

"No. I know that for me to call someone tactless is the pot calling the kettle black. But God and duty require the truth."

"Agreed. What do you require?"

"I require nothing. But if you have three Engineering people you can spare for the Launcher Two team, preferably structural-mainenance experts . . ."

"I'll see what I can do. But if I send three, that gives Engineering a six-to-five majority on the team. By regulations, that means the team head has to be from Engineering. Captain Liddell won't care about regulations as long as the job's done. Do you want to gamble on Longman doing it?"

"If your people will turn a deaf ear to Longman's tantrums—" Bogdanov began. Then he shrugged. "I am asking much, that you assign one of your officers to damp-ing Longman when he needs it. But that is also a job that must be done."

"I'll try Lieutenant Uhlig," Fujita said. "If all else fails, he can stuff Longman into a handy locker any time the boy's mouth runs away with him."

The hiss of the elevator faded and the door opened. Fujita blinked. The passageway outside the Officers' Mess was fully illuminated. Then he saw the two technicians performing arcane rituals over the entrails of the beverage dispenser at the entrance.

"What's wrong?" Bogdanov asked.

Both technicians downed tools and saluted. That wasn't required for working parties, but Bogdanov's reputation carried more weight than regulations.

"Tannic-acid erosion in the tea tank," the senior technician said. "No, sir, I'm not joking. Somebody was careless about the bond they used the last time they fixed the valves. We'd have been up to our belly buttons in Asok Black by tomorrow."

"Clearly a major crisis," Bogdanov said. Fujita looked at him. Had the Executive officer suddenly sprouted a sense of humor? Or was he speaking seriously, fueled by his well-known passion for tea? A rigid teetotaler and fitness fanatic, Bogdanov allowed himself one known vice: ten cups of tea a day. It was a standing joke in the fleet that his insides were so thoroughly tanned he might live halfway into his second century.

Inside, meals were still cafeteria-style, but the full menu was not only displayed but available. Fujita pulled out his own set of chopsticks, picked a bulb of hot tea, then surveyed the vegetarian dishes.

As the dispenser spit out a pack of rice-and-onion loaf, Fujita looked at his watch. He could allow himself a whole half hour for dinner and still be back at the Engineering Master board in time to launch the next watch properly.

Elayne Zheng peeled off her underwear and floated nude above the table in the middle of Bunkroom D-4. Except for the pattern of scratches on the bulkheads and floor, nothing distinguished the bunkroom from a dozen other junior officers' accomodations Brian Mahoney had seen.

A central cabin with a table in the middle that doubled as

a desk, and a locker in each corner. Two curtained sleeping alcoves, each with an upper and lower bunk and more storage. A head just the right size to guarantee banging elbows or shins at least once a day. Everything theoretically supposed to work under both zero-g and artificial gravity.

In Mahoney's opinion, nothing in the room worked as well in zero-g as Elayne Zheng's body. It had the grace of a well-designed and versatile tool. He respected it without sharing the opinion of those who found it desirable as well.

Mahoney himself still wore his underwear and slippers. There was still a bit of the seminarian in him and a lot of the native of Killarney's damp, cool North Continent.

Zheng opened the curtain on her bunk and stowed a viewer in the net over the foot. Then she sprang lightly into the air again and turned a slow somersault before catching herself with one hand on each of Mahoney's shoulders.

Mahoney grinned. "Either you're planning to seduce me or we're embarking an attacker squadron. Unless you've developed some new passions lately?"

"I won't spoil a good friendship. They're a lot harder to come by than good affairs. It's a squadron. They've got people on Launcher Two round the clock. What else could they be planning?'

"Troop shuttles, drones, spare buses."

"We're a battlecruiser, not a *kheblass* transport! Weapons has enough launchers for its missiles. The only drone aboard is you, and I don't want to see you launched. You have your redeeming qualities, even if it takes the main computer to find them."

The door signal chimed.

"Hello?"

"Lieutenant Tachin. I'm assigned to this bunkroom."

Zheng pushed off from Mahoney and hit the door opener with her feet. A small dark woman with European features and huge eyes with even darker circles under them floated in.

"Is my baggage here?" She looked around the cabin, noting the two lockers already claimed by Mahoney and Zheng and the third labeled "Longman." "The captain drafted me for a mission to the Dockyard. I just got back."

"What did you have?" Zheng asked.

"Just the basic shipboard kit. I'm one of the TOADS, out from First Fleet."

"Long way from home," Mahoney said.

"You win the prize for the hundredth person to say that," Tachin replied. "That's one reason why I didn't bring any cabin stores. I didn't know a good place to pick them up."

"When we get leave, I'll give you the two-stellar tour," Zheng said. "Meanwhile, you were probably lucky. There's been a problem with pilfered baggage aboard the shuttles. Now, I was just going to take a bath, but you look like you need one worse than I do."

"I showered this morning, but I have been running all day, it's true. If somebody can loan me a robe? . . ."

Mahoney tossed a pair of his pajamas at Tachin. They would fit her like combat boots on a cat, but if she preferred to keep something on, that was her decision. The most unbreakable rule of shipboard etiquette was "What makes you comfortable is allowed, as long as it doesn't make anyone else uncomfortable."

Tachin pulled the curtains behind her. Zheng floated close to Mahoney and whispered in his ear, "I think she'd better bunk in my upper. Any objections?"

"I was hoping you'd offer. I've never known a FADS case like Longman who didn't think they had a chance with anybody that interested them."

The informal rule for mixed bunkrooms was that you could chose the sex of whoever shared an alcove with you. Some people chose the sex that interested them, some the one that didn't.

People who chose a bunkmate of the interesting sex and found that interest not returned were a problem. Then there was that dismal minority who had neither preferences nor manners. The Navy sometimes resorted to transferring them to the Army.

The door chimes sounded again.

"Hello?" Mahoney said.

"Lieutenant Longman. Who's senior?"

"Me," Mahoney said. Zheng had been in uniform for eighteen years but an officer for only four against his six.

"Who's 'me'?"

"First Lieutenant Brian Mahoney. Now come on in." He let his tone make it an order.

The door slid open, and Charles Longman floated in. He reminded Mahoney of himself twenty years before, with legs and arms so long he couldn't always keep track of them. Longman's blond hair was matted where it didn't stick out in spikes, and he brought a distinctive and unwelcome smell. Zheng floated near the overhead, ignoring Longman's careful survey of her body.

"Is that your baggage on the rack outside?" Mahoney asked.

"No. It's for a Lieutenant Tachin."

"That's our fourth bunkmate," Mahoney said.

Longman floated over to his own locker, ignoring the hint. Whoever had dropped off Tachin's baggage should have signaled, but that was no excuse for Longman not lending a hand to a bunkmate who didn't have one to spare.

The curtains of the port alcove parted and Tachin floated out, shrugging into the borrowed pajama tops. "Hello," Longman said. "You're Brigitte Tachin?"

"So the priest who baptized me said," Tachin replied. The pajama bottoms parted company with the tops and tried to part company with her. Mahoney launched himself out into the passageway.

He returned with Tachin's baggage. A small package was strapped to the topmost bag. Mahoney recognized Rose Liddell's handwriting on the package label.

Longman looked disappointed when he found that Tachin had not only sorted out her clothing but vanished into the bathroom. He stretched out in midair and rubbed his eyes.

"How long are you going to be, Brigitte? You've been running errands for the captain. I spent most of the afternoon in a suit, working on Launcher Two."

"Most of those errands had to do with your launcher, Lieutenant," Tachin's voice replied. "I won't be long. I'll be even quicker if somebody could pull my toilet kit out of the green bag."

Longman jumped at Tachin's baggage so fast that he collided with Zheng on the same mission. This left Mahoney to extract the toilet kit and thrust it through the waterlock in the bathroom door.

"Thanks," Tachin said.

Longman rubbed his head. "I suppose you wouldn't consider bathing together, Brigitte?"

"I consider many things without doing them," was the

reply. A moment later the sounds of a sponge bath gave way to the sound of the air blower. Then the bathroom door opened. A clothed and clean Brigitte Tachin and a few drops of water floated out.

Longman had gone off to sulk in his upper bunk. Both he and Tachin missed the look passing between Zheng and Mahoney.

His eyes said, *I don't care how hard Longman's working. He's bad news.*

Zheng's reply was, *Let's plan a natural division of labor. Longman fixes the launcher. Tachin fixes him if he gets out of line. I fix you if you come running to her rescue when she doesn't need it.*

All this made excellent sense, except that he shouldn't have needed Elayne to remind him about not rescuing Tachin.

Since his alcove was occupied by a Longman radiating bad temper, Mahoney sat down at the central table, pulled the terminal toward him, and opened the keyboard. It would take longer to key in the last few memos than using voice, but right now he wanted complete silence.

Five

"Now hear this. Now hear this. Artificial gravity will be activated in two minutes. Repeat, this is the two-minute warning for artificial gravity. Secure all unsecured articles immediately! That is all."

Captain Liddell took her eyes off the screen picture of Commander Tourkmani and studied her office. Not that she expected to find anything ready to fall, but a final check never did any harm.

Her bulb of tea looked too close to the edge of her desk. She moved it to the center holdpad, then ordered the computer, "Open all doors to the passageway."

On the screen, Tourkmani assumed a wounded look.

"You doubt the quality of our work on your gravity generators?

"I like to hear anything going wrong nearby without somebody having to remember to tell the Old Lady."

"Of course."

The one-minute warning came. Liddell sat down in her chair. On the screen, Tourkmani's Siamese cat Kadin climbed on to his lap, then put her paws on his shoulder and began nuzzling his ear.

"Now hear this. Now hear this. Artificial gravity being activated. Ten, nine, eight, seven, six, five, four, three, two, one—activation!"

An invisible hand gently pushed Captain Liddell into her chair. It pushed harder and harder, until she felt as if her chest would cave in. Had the generators gone out of control? The display on her desk told her no, the field had only reached .87 Standard.

It happens every time. I really have to spend less time on the yoga and more on the centrifuge when we're in zero-g.

From the reception room came a faint thump. From outside in the passageway came assorted distant thumps and crashes. Raised human voices followed them. It sounded more like seniors listing the vices of juniors than like personnel casualties. As the display showed one full Standard gravity, Liddell began breathing again.

She didn't breathe easily until all departments had sent in negative reports on damage and casualties, or none worse than spills and bruises. When she turned back to the screen, Tourkmani was still there, hands clasped across his generous stomach. Kadin had now maneuvered herself into a position across the back of his neck and was industriously washing a forepaw.

"Thank you for waiting," she said. "I hope I wasn't keeping you from anything important."

"God does not count against a man's years the time spent comforting children and animals," Tourkmani said. He scratched Kadin behind the ears. Liddell saw that the cat was pregnant.

"There's also the Dockyard superintendent, who's closer than God and less charitable."

"True. As I was saying, I want a list of the Dockyard people you absolutely *must* have for your shakedown cruise. Please don't put anyone on it unless their absence would endanger your ship."

"Is Captain Prange on your . . . back again?"

"Indeed, and more so than usual."

"He's that kind."

"I know. I also think he now expects that if he gives offense, the offended party will be ordered to ignore it."

Meaning that Prange thinks there's something blowing up that will make Schatz jump through hoops, if it will help speed up Valhalla's *overhaul.*

It would be nice when Prange got his star and got out of a ship's command circuits. But then he might be in a whole squadron's. . . .

Leave it be, Rosie. Prange isn't your fight. This time.

"Let's stay out of Prange's path, if he's mobilizing. Will twenty-four hours be soon enough for the list? There's no way I can produce it without a department heads' meeting."

"Soon enough, Captain. I thank you."

They shook hands at each other and the screen blanked. Liddell reached for her bulb of tea, discovered that it was both cold and leaking, and decided to take advantage of gravity. She could drink her next tea out of a real cup.

[Commissioning minus fourteen days]

Elayne Zheng glared at the packing container as if it had just propositioned her on duty.

"That's not our sensor sim rig, Brian. They come in a 325. That's a 638. With the opticals, our rig won't even fit in a 638!"

Mahoney protested. "Lanie, I go by what the label says. I don't have time to scan everything that comes past me. We'd have lighters clustered five deep and the superintendent turning into a dragon."

"My ulcer bleeds for you," Zheng said, but she grinned. Now that most of the major repairs were done, supplies were coming aboard in a steady stream. Some days the stream reached flood level. This had been one of those days.

"Well, order up some tools and let's see who forgot what."

Two officers and three technicians with tools and strong backs made quick work of the mystery container. In the middle of the disassembled panels sat a simulator for the master engineering panel of a *Muscaro*-class light cruiser.

"Did somebody swap containers on the lighters? Or is this squadron cargo?"

Mahoney addressed his questions to the overhead, but they weren't rhetorical. Having more equipment or stores than you needed meant that somebody else probably had less. Besides, Bogdanov fumed as much about overages as about shortages, a rare case of rigidly obeying orders producing justice.

"Better get on the horn to the dispatcher at the depot," Zheng said. "Of course, there's probably a three-hour backlog of complaints. Who's that saint you Romans pray to when things are completely hopeless?"

"Saint Jude."

"Try him. I can't think of anything else to straighten this out. No, wait a minute. When's the next ferry to the Dockyard?"

"Forty-five minutes, unless they've cut back."

"They're more likely to add. Can you keep our air flowing while I drop over to the depot? I think a toe to someone's pants might do more than a call in less time."

[Commissioning minus twelve days]

" 'Chute deployment!" Brigitte Tachin called.

"Affirmative," the reply came from the other console.

"Nav and target data filed!"

"Affirmative."

"Panel release!"

"Affirmative."

"Missile ejection!" Tachin held her breath.

"Affirmative!"

First sign of pleasure from that old croutonard!

"Engine ignition." This time she managed to speak in a normal voice instead of a near shriek.

"Affirmative."

"Aerodynamic stabilization."

"Affirmative."

Tachin sighed softly, counted to twenty, then said, "Manual simulation test on Re-entry Pod JT98802+ completed. Secure the consoles and let's take a break. We can do the realtime test later."

"Yes, ma'am."

Warrant Officer Nishimura stood up, stretching like a gigantic cat. Tachin sat quietly at her console while Nishimura ordered everything shut down. As they left the bay, Tachin looked back over her shoulder at the gray pod, five times her height.

In theory, it had plunged into the atmosphere of a planet (*don't call it Victoria*) with its cargo of six cruise missiles. Programmed, ejected, and now flying free, the six missiles were closing their targets at two kilometers a second. When they arrived—Tachin didn't know whether the warheads were conventional or special.

No, that wasn't quite true. She'd been conscientious during her year at the Alcuin Arsenal, memorizing vital statistics with a voracious appetite. A Mark Seventy-seven Model Four weighing in at 1.62 tons was carrying a K193 warhead, tactical fusion adjustable from three to forty kilotons.

Six miniature suns would blaze to life. Their life would bring death, swiftly to those lucky enough, in six target areas.

Tachin still needed the break, but she'd lost her appetite.

[Commissioning minus nine days]
Lieutenant Uhlig nodded. Charles Longman swallowed.

"Maximum cycle rate!"

Every moving part in Launcher Two seemed to blur. Longman knew this was an illusion, even when they were pushing the machinery to the limit. Maybe it was the sweat of fear that two weeks' work was about to fail its last test.

The beam under his feet began to vibrate faintly as the cycle rate increased. That didn't concern him; it wasn't part of his project. Just the same, he'd scanned it for stress fractures and come up negative.

In fact, all the beam scans in the structure surrounding his repairs had come up negative. Lieutenant Uhlig had been a lot easier to deal with after that. Longman couldn't tell if it was the negative results or just Longman's having made the scans at all.

That's about the thousandth time you wished people's motives were as easy to figure out as stress loads.

Not that people were impossible. Longman now understood his bunkmates clearly.

Zheng doesn't like FADS cases. Mahoney doesn't like anyone Tachin doesn't like. And Tachin doesn't like anyone who's warm for her.

An alarm screamed.

"Meter Six shows a 256 percent jump in the stress load!" someone shouted. He was adding quite unnecessarily to Longman's own stress load, since his own helmet display was showing him the same thing.

Bile rose in Longman's throat. He swallowed hard, got himself under control, then looked at the display again.

"Cut Meter Six off the circuit," he ordered.

Longman watched the signal blink out. The other meters continued to show no signs of dangerous stress loads. If there'd been anything going wrong in the area of Six, it ought to have shown up on at least some of the others.

"Khoraji, take one of the spares and replace Six."

Launchers had too bloody many moving parts—one reason they were both a challenge and a nightmare. None of those parts were moving anywhere near Khoraji's route to Meter Six.

Khoraji worked so fast that Longman hadn't even finished mentally undressing Brigitte Tachin when the replacement meter came on line. He felt like cheering as its readings fell into the same nominal pattern as the others'.

"I thought it might be meter trouble," Longman said. "Some of those meters showed signs of being field rebuilds."

"Good thinking," Lieutenant Uhlig said. His tone held respect. Longman only hoped he'd pass that respect along when he reported the tests to Commander Fujita.

With all the meters correctly measuring the stress loads on *Shenandoah*'s structure, Longman's repairs passed their last test by a generous margin. He was at the end of what, please God, would be his last fifteen-hour day. Otherwise he'd have felt like dancing.

At last Uhlig nodded, Longman slapped the manual power switch, and Launcher Two subsided into inert metal and ceramics. Uhlig lifted the filter from his helmet faceplate, showing a broad grin. He leaned over until his helmet touched Longman's.

"Charlie. Go to the wardroom and order us a round of drinks. I'll clean up here and fiddle the paperwork. I may even put you in for a commendation, if you have the sense not to ask for it."

"Can do."

[Commissioning minus five days]

The detailed print report on the Thumb incident was on Admiral Schatz's desk when he returned to it after his late-morning swim. He read the report over a lunch of eel salad and rolls, then called Kuwahara.

The chief of staff read the report with the expression of a man eating half-spoiled food. When he reached the account of the cover story, his patience ended.

"A cache of mining explosives? What happens to that if it gets out that the explosives were Baernoi military demolitions?"

"It won't. Security is Mikhail Kornilov's middle name."

"Can he control everyone who might talk where unfriendly ears could hear?"

"As well as anyone can. Were you thinking of any particular kind of unfriendly?"

"Kellysburg and Mount Houton ears. Both towns seem to be opposed to the new base. How can we be sure this isn't anti-Federation activity?"

"I'd bet it is," Schatz said blandly. "I'd also bet there's something like it on at least half the planets in the Federation. If we tried to stamp it out, we'd have the Alliance Secession all over again, only bigger.

"We also have the Baernoi perched in the wings. Anybody who gets really desperate knows they have someplace to go."

Kuwahara suggested a number of places where all sorts of secessionists could go and what they could do when they got there. Then he bowed. Schatz braced himself, knowing this promised either sarcasm or something embarrassing.

"I think we should address seriously Captain Prange's requests for more workers on *Valhalla*."

"What requests?"

"To the superintendent, and through Commander Tourkmani, to Captain Liddell."

Schatz briefly echoed Kuwahara's remarks of a few minutes before. He stopped before he ran out of breath and glared at Kuwahara.

"Why didn't you tell me this before?"

"Sir, I wanted to make sure that Captain Prange hadn't breached HQ security to gain access to intelligence on the Victoria situation. Good guessing is one thing. Unauthorized taps are another."

"What did you learn?

"No proof of any security breaches. Captain Prange appears to have relied on his network of personal contacts."

Schatz nodded. Prange was independently wealthy, a bachelor, and famous for his parties. Rumor said that he stopped just short of blackmail to get information from his guests.

Kuwahara went on. "Also, *Shenandoah*'s being rushed

into commission has been no real secret for weeks. That alone could have been enough data for an officer of Captain Prange's caliber."

"Right. He didn't get that Federation Star from a catalog. So Prange is clear?"

"Provisionally."

"Fine. We'll let him turn slowly in the wind until we know more. If he's guilty, we can run him up to the masthead. If he's innocent, we can cut him down. Meanwhile, there's *Shenandoah* to commission, in—how long?"

"Five days. I just received the preliminary plan for the commissioning ceremony." Kuwahara handed over four sheets.

Schatz began to smile as he read the plan. It had Rose Liddell's stamp all over it.

"Trust Rosie to do things in style," he said, as he pulled out a stylus and scribbled, "Approved with enclosed amendments. J. Schatz, COMFLT." on the last sheet. "She wants to build *esprit de corps* by doing things on the grand scale." The admiral's smile widened. "They're going to be even grander than she expects."

"Indeed?"

"I'm going to be the transferring officer. I'm going to receive *Shen* from Durgin and pass her on to Rosie. You're going to be there, and everybody from both Fleet and Army Headquarters we can load into a shuttle. On *Shenandoah*'s commissioning day, nothing short of a full-scale Baernoi invasion is going to take the lights off her."

Kuwahara was beginning to smile too. "Are we sending a message to Captain Prange?"

"Is the Pope faithful to his wife?"

"What about the little matter of workers for *Valhalla*?"

"Beg, borrow, or steal a shuttle. Head up to Dockyard and arrange a conference with Rosie and the superintendent. Prange, too, if necessary, but play that one by ear. If Rosie and the super are already on the same wavelength, no need to give Prange any rope he doesn't need.

"Once you've got the transfer roster arranged, you can start shipping people over to *Valhalla*. But not one more than Rosie and the super want to go. I mean it, Sho. If Prange comes over uninvited to try grabbing more, kick his *cojones* up around his ears."

Kuwahara bowed. "A sound solution, in theory. In practice, I must remind you that Captain Prange is ten years younger than I am and also a third dan."

He straightened. "Captain Prange would be a better captain now if he spent less time thinking about what a fine admiral he will be some day."

Six

Captain Abelsohn saw Lieutenant Shores to the door of his hospital room over her protests. In bed, the captain looked more bored and uncomfortable than sick. When he tried to walk, the concussion's marks showed.

"Oh, I'm supposed to have my sense of balance back in another week or two," Abelsohn said. "The doctors may even be right. Even then, it'll be light duty for a while. Don't think you're just keeping my chair warm. As far as I'm concerned, Scout Company's yours."

"Thanks, Captain. If I'm up to the job, it's mostly because you made it easy. They're trained like a *yana* pack."

They shook hands. As she went out, Shores thanked God for the wisdom of modern armies in abandoning the ancient folly of "up or out." Abelsohn could and probably would spend the rest of his career doing what he did best: commanding rifle companies and teaching others to do the same. He'd never be forced to choose between turning into an inferior field-grade or an outright civilian.

The first person Shores met after she passed the duty nurse was General Kornilov. He returned her salute, then signaled her to fall in beside him.

"I pulled a triceps at the weights this morning," the general said. "So I had Dr. Chatterje inject it with Staminol. She says no more weights for a while."

"Watch out!" Shores called. The warning came too late. Kornilov collided head-on with the first of a line of gurneys rolling down the corridor, under the surveillance of an orderly walking beside the sixth. The orderly's mouth opened to swear, then his eyes widened as he recognized the general. Improbably, his hand darted inside the neck of his smock.

"Down!" Shores screamed. She flung herself at Kornilov as the orderly drew a miniature pistol. Hitting the general was like hitting a brick wall. By luck she caught him in midstride. They both crashed to the floor.

Fffup! The first shot flew overhead and struck the wall with the vicious crack of an explosive round.

"Security!" the duty nurse shouted from behind them. Alarms howled. The orderly waved the pistol uncertainly, then whirled as footsteps sounded behind him. He turned and fired, missing Dr. Chatterje but hitting the wall beside her. Fragments clawed one side of her face into a bloody mask.

Shores was drawing her own pistol when Security arrived, faster than she'd expected. She remembered that the psychiatric ward was nearby.

"Take him alive!" Kornilov thundered.

The order came a trigger-pull too late. Shores had a glimpse of the would-be assassin's face—eyes staring, pupils contracted, skin sweat-slimed and gray. Then a burst from the guard's carbine flung the man out of her view. It also spread most of his chest over the wall behind him.

"Durak!" was all that Kornilov could find the breath to say.

Shores now had her pistol drawn and was trying to point it in all directions at once. She gave up only when three more guards appeared, as well as so many staff that she couldn't have fired safely.

"Lieutenant Shores," Kornilov said.

"Sir?"

"If you are considering an intimate relationship with me, I have a suggestion. Do not initiate it by inserting your elbow into my groin."

"Sorry, sir."

Kornilov rose, brushed himself off, flexed his hurt arm, then went over to kneel beside Dr. Chatterje. The look on his broad face was fear and love fighting to get through the professional mask. Only when the colonel had been loaded on a gurney and sent off to Emergency did he turn back to Shores.

"Lieutenant, I would like to assign you as my bodyguard for an hour or so. Until General Langston can send a detail, at least."

"Thank you, sir, but if we're going on alert—"

"What makes you think we're going on alert?"

"But—"

"Correct that statement. You weren't thinking. There could be many reasons for someone to shoot at me. Only a few of them would justify an alert. In fact, one reason for this attempt on my life could be forcing an unnecessary alert. Somebody could be trying to wage psychological warfare against us."

Shores looked at the floor and walls, shining clean two minutes ago and now slaughterhouse red. As far as she was concerned, whoever was trying to wage psychological warfare was succeeding.

Captain Liddell initialed the printed report on the repairs to Launcher Two and slipped it into her desk drawer. As she closed the door, the chime on the teapot tinkled.

"Kado's 'Rainbow Suite'?" Fujita asked.

Liddell nodded as she poured three cups full of steaming Surajian Clove Blend. "A friend gave it to me when I made commander. It replaced one that played only 'The Old Forty-five.' "

Fujita shuddered politely and bowed, sitting down as he sipped his tea. Bogdanov gulped his tea, meanwhile staring into space in a manner that would have been too rude to overlook in anyone except the Hermit. Liddell knew he must be mentally rehearsing responses to everything that could possibly go wrong with the morrow's commissioning ceremony.

The Hermit had even less charm than the stories said. He also had an even wider range of skills. No one had done more, or even as much, to let *Shenandoah* meet her nearly impossible commissioning date.

And speaking of the charmless but talented—

"I noticed you didn't put Lieutenant Longman in for a commendation."

The two commanders looked at each other. Bogdanov nodded at Fujita. The chief engineer shrugged.

"I'm going to wait until he does something just as good without Uhlig at his back. Gordy Uhlig spent too much time smoothing down fur Longman had ruffled. When parts didn't arrive on time, Longman took it as a personal insult. Then he took it out on everybody within range."

"What about a 'well done' for both of them?"

"Fine," Fujita said. Bogdanov nodded and poured himself another cup of tea.

"That goes for both of you, too," Liddell added. "I am really beginning to look forward to this commission." She turned off the teapot. "There will be a department-heads meeting tomorrow night, after we've said good-bye to the admiral. Time to be announced, depending on how long the admiral's briefing takes."

The two commanders rose and saluted. Liddell watched them go, then left her office door open for a moment longer. The sounds of a living starship drifted in—muted voices, footsteps, the purr of a well-tuned ventilation system, occasional faint bursts of mechanical vibration carried through the thousands of tons of metal and ceramic to the deck under Liddell's feet.

Shenandoah's already a ship. Commissioning her tomorrow just makes it official. Now all she needs is a crew, instead of five hundred people who happen to occupy her quarters.

The office door slid shut behind Captain Liddell. The door to her cabin followed. She dialed a warm shower and heard the water start running. Her secretary had the dress uniform laid out, with a note that the sword scabbard was being polished.

By the time she'd stripped to a shower cap, Liddell was feeling so content with the universe that she started singing "'MacPherson's Lament.'"

A good deal had changed in the Officers' Club since the afternoon when Kornilov and Langston had discussed the latest rumors.

Armored shutters now covered the window. Even if they'd been open, Kornilov would have seen mostly darkness, perhaps a faint afterglow from Little Sister, possibly a glimmer of moonlight on the canal.

A second chair with terminal and displays had been pulled into position beside Kornilov. General Langston occupied it. Tables of Organization and vehicle inventories occupied both screens.

Instead of a Federal Service waitress, Candice Shores was serving the drinks—*Captain* Shores, as of about two hours ago.

"Abelsohn's not going to be back on duty before this either blows over or blows up," Langston had said when he presented her with the new insignia. "You're doing the job, so why not give you the rank?"

Langston finished a revised TO for Scout Company and printed it, then handed it to Shores. "Anything here you can't handle, Captain?"

Heavy dark eyebrows rose after a quick look. "That gives us three times the normal organic firepower. Do we get the organic supply and maintenance people to go with it?"

"No. Our theory is that if you need major resupply or maintenance, it will be a full-blown incident. We'll be coming to your rescue, with all hands on deck. Meanwhile, you'll have enough firepower to keep from being easy victims.

"We have to use Scout Company as point for the brigade," Langston added. "Until all four battalions are field-ready, anyway. We won't send you into anything without the firepower to shoot your way out again."

"We've had enough of dead intelligence sources for one crisis," Kornilov added. He poured himself another glass of apple juice.

They'd had to endure the frustration of the assassin's death. The guard's quick shooting had at least proved harmless; an autopsy proved the gunman had lethal doses of three different drugs in his body at the time he was shot.

The assassin was the only fatality. Dr. Chatterje would require a facial reconstruct and a new eye. (Kornilov remembered the pain in the one not covered with bandages until the anesthetic took hold.) The only other casualty was an orthopedic nurse who'd run out to see what was going on. He was now a patient in his own ward, his left knee wrecked by a ricocheting slug from the guard's carbine.

Shores' eyebrows came down. "Will we be pulling any of the routine security?"

"Not if I can help it," Kornilov said. "Of course, the governor-general or the Military Council can make that difficult. I'll give the scouts the highest priority for vehicles and the lowest for security duty."

"Thank you," Shores said. It struck Kornilov that she was doing a better job of arguing with vastly superior officers than he'd ever done when he was a newly promoted captain.

Langston turned off his screen. "Mikhail, if there's anything that can't wait until tomorrow—"

"Everything else can wait until I've seen the politicians," Kornilov said. He pushed his screen back, emptied his glass, and stood up.

"Captain, do you want an escort back to your quarters? General Langston has six on the bodyguard detail, in case we're traveling separately. Since we aren't, we have people to spare."

"Thank you, sir, but I don't think I'm on anybody's target list. Yet. With your permission?" She saluted.

"Good night, Captain."

Kornilov peered around the high back of his chair at Shores until she passed the sentry at the door. There was one officer of the Victoria garrison whose promotion opportunities were secure.

Correction. They were, if somewhere along the way she didn't find herself called on to do the soldier's ultimate duty.

Sharon was standing knee-deep in the long grass on the bluffs above Granville Beach. Brian Mahoney faced his wife, sand trickling over the tops of his low walking shoes.

He knew it was a dream. When they'd come to the bluffs in reality, Sharon had stripped and dared him to make love to her hidden only by the grass. He'd done it, aroused and resentful at the same time.

Now she wore all her clothes and something more: the grim face of the last days before she told him she wouldn't renew their contract. She ran her thumbs along the line of her jaw and spoke words the sea wind couldn't drown out. His memory's ears were perfect.

"You're an orphan. You've been an orphan ever since you left the seminary. Seven years is enough for anyone to grow up and stop needing a parent. You haven't done it. I won't wait another fourteen years or any part of them, hoping you'll change.

"You don't have it in you to change. God pity any woman who thinks otherwise."

He'd groaned then, burying his head in his hands. Probably this confirmed Sharon's opinion of him, but he hadn't cared.

Now he groaned again. No, he heard groaning, not his. It was higher pitched, broken, and sounded like sickness or pain rather than despair.

Mahoney awoke just enough to remember not to sit up in his bunk. He put his feet on the bristly rug and his head between his knees until he knew he could stand. The groaning went on, from a point somewhere above his left ear.

"Charlie?" The location suggested Longman as the source of the groans.

"O God."

The voice confirmed Mahoney's hypothesis but provided no other data.

"What's wrong?"

"I'm . . . I've got . . . it's like six bad hangovers—all together."

"Let me get you some—"

"God, no." Longman gagged. "If I swallow my own . . . spit I'll puke all over you."

"Can you get to the bathroom if I help you?"

"I'd better try, hadn't I? Today's commissioning day."

"Christ and all His Saints! I forgot!"

Longman had enough energy to laugh. He rolled over the edge of the bunk, dropping seventy-five kilos of dead weight into Mahoney's arms. They landed with Mahoney sprawled half out of the alcove and Longman on top of him. For a moment Mahoney wasn't sure whose stomach was going to rebel first, Longman's or his.

From his prone position, Mahoney saw Brigitte Tachin vanishing into the bathroom, bare to the waist. Several weeks' proximity to that young lady hadn't explained why she seemed to think she was unattractive. Quite the reverse, in Mahoney's opinion. No one thing about her stood out, but together her features made a harmonious whole. Brigitte soothed the eye rather than aroused it.

At this point Longman leaped to his feet, with a speed and agility that would have done credit to a martial-arts adept. A second leap took him to the bathroom door. He tore it open and plunged inside. A moment later came the sound of a stomach violently emptying itself.

Mahoney pulled on a bathrobe and pulled his toilet kit out of the net. He prayed to anyone he thought would listen that Longman didn't make too much of a mess of the bathroom. Rumor had it that Schatz would be making a spot inspection after presiding over the commissioning. Fate infallibly sent inspecting admirals to the cabins of people who'd partied too long and too late the night before.

But he couldn't recall Longman showing any signs of partying last night. He'd been red-eyed and shaky on his feet when he came in, but for him that was usual. The way he drove himself didn't excuse his manners, but they did help explain them.

The continuous vomiting gave way to occasional spasms, the sound of running water, and Brigitte Tachin murmuring soothingly. *Better her than me*, thought Mahoney. *I'd tell him to stick his head out the window.*

Elayne Zheng was already gone, having left the common room ready for inspection and a message on the screen: GOING DOWN EARLY, TO LISTEN FOR CLUES ABOUT THAT GOD-ROTTED SQUADRON!

That wasn't just curiosity anymore. They all had a stake in knowing if *Shenandoah* was going to embark a dozen attackers. If so, when and where? Mahoney had visions of getting the word and the squadron at the last moment, after they'd returned from their ten-day shakedown cruise. They'd have everything neatly arranged for the voyage out to Victoria, then have to rearrange it all! Hundreds of tons of supplies would wind up perched in the frames like tree tigers, the quarters bill would have to be changed, and maybe hotbunking adopted . . .

Change *visions* to *nightmares*.

"Now hear this. Now hear this. Special cleaning details, man your stations. Special cleaning details, man your stations. The smoking lamp is out in all spaces. The smoking lamp is out in all spaces. All hands are required to be at their commissioning stations by 0930. All hands are required—"

"Oh, piss off," Mahoney said, cutting the intercom.

The bathroom door opened. Longman tottered out, his face dripping and freshly scrubbed. He leaned with what

Mahoney thought was unnecessary force on Brigitte Tachin's bare shoulder. She wore the same as when she went in to the bathroom, plus a sour look.

"This . . . *fils de cochon* has been taking Vessegol 14 since the launcher work began."

That particular stimulant was a prescription-only drug, for good and sufficient reasons. "What doctor? Never mind, I can guess," Mahoney said. "How much?"

"Fifty mg a day."

"Really?"

"Well, sometimes I took one in the morning and a second midafternoon."

"Sometimes?"

"Two days out of three, I guess. I can't remember."

"You'd better remember by the time the surgeon has you down on her table. Otherwise—"

"No, please. If—I can't go to the surgeon with something like this. It's not an allergic reaction. Really it isn't. I'll be fine now that my stomach's empty."

Tachin laid a hand on his forehead. "It's true, he has no fever."

Longman's grin was a ghost of its usual self. "If you want to give me one, just keep your hand there."

Any sort of Vessegol overdose was serious, but was this one dangerous? Longman's system had probably adjusted to a fairly high level of the stuff. He was also right about what the surgeon's report would do to his first Evaluation and Rating Report aboard *Shen*. The admirals of the Longman clan would not be amused.

But if Mahoney and Tachin didn't haul Longman before the surgeon and something did go wrong, they would have it on their consciences. They would also have comments in their own E & Rs that would not be pleasant to see carved on their tombstones.

"Seriously," Longman said. "I'll take the responsibility if I've guessed wrong. If you can brew up some tea, I should be able to simulate fitness for duty. At least until the admiral leaves."

Tachin frowned. "I have only coffee. And those Killarney brews of yours, Brian—we want to soothe Charles's stomach, not tan it."

"All right. I'll break into Elayne's supply."

Zheng's array of teas produced something called Glowmint, which Longman said would probably do the trick. Mahoney handed two packets over to Tachin and began putting Zheng's cabin stores back the way she'd left them.

She'd forgive him stealing any amount of tea for medicinal purposes or entertaining congenial company. If he left her locker a mess, though, his *cojones* would be on their way to her family's trophy room.

Seven

The Dockyard superintendent opened the leatherbound Transfer Certificate and handed it to Admiral Schatz. The wardroom lights made the ruddy leather glow.

Schatz lifted the certificate and read it in a slightly raspy voice.

> I declare that on Standard date 19/4/547 I transfer U.F.S. *Shenandoah* to the Operating Fleet. All work preparatory to commissioning has been completed. The ship is hereby certified as in all respects ready for space.
>
> Leopold K. Durgin
> Rear Admiral, U.F.N.
> Superintendent
> Riftwell Naval Dockyard

Schatz closed the certificate and tucked it under one long arm. To Brian Mahoney, watching on the screen in the Training Department office, the admiral had more than his usual lean and hungry look. He looked like a man who'd had bad news, a short night, or both.

"What's gotten into Schatz?" he whispered to Elayne Zheng.

"My money's on constipation."

Like most Navy ships, *Shenandoah* had no compartment big enough to hold her whole crew. Commissioning ceremonies had to be on the screen, with everybody at their duty stations in full-dress uniform, as proper as if they were drawn up on a parade ground.

The full-dress uniforms and the duty stations were easy to enforce. No one could enforce propriety on Elayne Zheng, unless they caught her in a rare good mood.

"By the authority vested in me as commander of Eleventh Fleet, United Federation Navy, I accept U.F.S. *Shenandoah* from the Riftwell Naval Dockyard.

"By the same authority, I now transfer her to her commanding officer, Captain Rose Liddell." Schatz turned with nearly his usual grace and handed Liddell the certificate.

"Captain Liddell, place this ship in commission."

"Aye-aye, sir!"

Liddell saluted precisely, in spite of the sheer delight all over her face. She nodded at the Hermit, who stepped forward and saluted even more precisely.

"Commander Bogdanov. Set the first watch!"

"Aye-aye, ma'am."

He turned to the screen and barked, "All hands, set the first watch!"

No one on the screen moved, except the first lieutenant, the officer of the watch. The screen's view shifted, enlarging Captain Liddell until her round tanned face filled it.

"Admiral Schatz, Admiral Durgin, distinguished guests, I thank you. This is our *Shenandoah*'s second chance to add honor to the name. We shall do our best.

"Crew of *Shenandoah*. We've already come to know each other these past few weeks. We're setting off on a difficult job for any ship, let alone a new one. Thanks to the past few weeks, we're setting off with no illusions about its difficulty or about each other.

"This is as it should be. Ignorance has killed more people than the Hive Wars. *Shenandoah* won't add to that toll if we can help it.

"Normally I would not grant any special privileges at this point. The people of a newly commissioned ship have to earn them.

"But you've been earning them these past weeks, with your sweat and your fatigue and your late nights and early mornings. You haven't done more than I expected of you, but you've done more than I would have dared ask.

"So you've earned the privilege of not listening to long

speeches from your captain. Shipmates, I'm proud to be your captain and *Shenandoah*'s.

"Thank you."

Aboard Schatz's tender alongside, the Eleventh Fleet band struck up the Federation anthem. Captain Liddell disappeared from the screen. A full exterior view of *Shenandoah* took her place. As the band soared into the refrain, all the ship's external lights came on.

Mahoney swallowed. Irreverence was now light-years from his mind. Even Zheng looked subdued.

Brian Mahoney, this cruise will make or break you as a naval officer. If it breaks you, it will damned near break you for good and all.

Neither Schatz nor Liddell were abstainers. They still preferred yoga to alcohol for the initial stage of relaxing after a long tense day.

They took their final savasanas on the padded floor of Schatz's cabin aboard the tender. The entertainment system played Fedoseev's "Refugee Cantata." Most of the time Liddell found it incredibly lugubrious. Now it matched her mood, since she'd learned of the attempt on Kornilov's life.

At last Schatz stood. "End play," he said. The music faded. "Bar open," he added. The serving robot trundled out across the floor.

"Bourbon," Schatz said. "Lots of rocks, lots of water."

"Beervine vodka," Liddell said. "Two fingers. Straight up, on the rocks."

The robot trundled off. "You feeling abandoned tonight, Captain?" Schatz inquired.

"Mildly," she replied. She drew a pillow toward her and hugged it as Schatz vanished into the bathroom. He wore a sleeveless vest and loose trousers. He could have worn a good deal less without overexposure; he looked a good twenty years younger than his actual sixty-five Standard.

Both Schatz and Liddell intended to keep their relationship purely professional, but each found the other attractive and both knew it. It helped them over minor differences, such as Liddell's conviction that bourbon was an evil spirit.

Schatz seemed to leave his day-long grimness in the bathroom. He was smiling as he accepted his drink from the robot and sat down in the easy pose.

"Rose, some good news and some bad news. Which do you want first?"

Liddell looked at the ice cubes in her vodka. They were uncommunicative. "The bad news."

"Okay. The postshakedown leave period will have to be canceled. We don't know that *Shen*'s muscle is going to be needed, but we're not betting either way. Giving your people a week off doesn't look feasible."

Throwing glasses at admirals seldom accomplished anything. Just to be on the safe side, Liddell set her drink down.

"What about a duty-free day?"

"No problem. I'll even post it in the bulletin and lay on shuttles for families. They may have to step lively to avoid being trampled by the work gangs heading for *Valhalla*. Can you spare people for guides?"

That would mean asking people to work on a duty-free day, helping shipmates get together with their families. It would have to be a volunteer affair; how many volunteered would say a lot about morale aboard *Shenandoah*.

Liddell nodded.

"Fine. Now for the good news. You're getting an attacker squadron."

"Crammed in at the last minute? Sir, if that's your idea of good news—"

"Down spines, Rose."

"Aye-aye, sir."

"They'll be joining you off Victoria. You'll have plenty of time to unload all your extras and orient yourself to the system. *Ira Hayes* is just out of Hogan's World Dockyard. They fitted her with external cradles for attackers and shuttles. A squadron from the Fleet Reserve will ride out on her.

"Once out there, *Hayes* will join your squadron. The attackers will operate in rotation from *Shenandoah*, the Victoria Dockyard, and the Army fields. They're going to have to handle both strategic and tactical support, so they may need some help from your training people."

"They're going to have their hands full with our own crew."

"It all counts toward the bonus, Rose." Schatz held up his glass as a signal to the robot.

By the time he was halfway through his third bourbon, the admiral was growing mellow. He leaned back, tucked a pillow under his head, then rested his feet on another.

"Have you ever been on Shenandoah, Rose?"

"A daughter colony of Monticello, isn't it?"

"Yes. I spent two months Standard there, when I was a commander. I was on my way to Fed HQ, and the best connections were from Shenandoah to Monticello, then on to Charlemagne.

"I'd just checked into the TOQ when the Baernoi started making HQ itchy. A freeze order came down: all transfers suspended. Except that they didn't have a ship for me at Shenandoah. They made me disaster-relief and billeting officer. Took about three hours of work a day. Haven't had such a good vacation since.

"Lovely world. The name's old Amerind, means 'Daughter of the Stars.' There's a river by that name back in the old United States of America. Sam Briggs's family either had land in the valley or fought in the Civil War battles—"

"Which civil war?"

"The First American. Anyway, his kids had a lot to do with settling the planet, right after the marshal was killed. When they said he'd always wanted to see a planet named Shenandoah, well . . ."

Schatz emptied his glass. "Lovely world, like I said. Lots of wilderness left, and only a couple of really big cities. The Hivers took out a third, but didn't do much damage otherwise."

"Let's hope our *Shenandoah*'s that lucky. Luckier than some of her predecessors, anyway."

"They all went out fighting, Rosie." Schatz looked at the robot, then shook his head. "No, that wouldn't help a lot. I'm getting too old to want to see anybody go out, fighting or not."

He stood up, almost managing not to sway. "Rose, I'm nearly drunk and losing my professional attitude toward you. How about we say good night?"

Schatz might have been kissing his daughter when he kissed Liddell on the forehead. By the time she left the cabin, he was in a lotus position.

How can a captain arrange to get her fleet commander his share of the fun as well as the headaches?

By doing her own job.

The screen took up half of one bulkhead of Captain Paul Leray's day cabin aboard the Freeworld States Alliance heavy cruiser *Audacious*. The weather front marching across the Great Woomera Desert took up half the screen. In places along the three-thousand-kilometer front, the gray clouds shaded into brown as local winds raised dust storms.

Paul Leray wondered how many people were down there under the clouds, listening to the moan of the wind and the hiss of dust and sand. If they were lucky, they wouldn't hear the sound of sand-eaten walls cracking, letting in the angry weather.

Leray shifted the screen view, to the starscape above Victoria's north polar cap. It was beginning its spring thaw, but Leray hardly cared. His eyes were on the stars. The son and grandson of Free Engineers, he'd been born in space. Ships were the true lifebearers, the seeds for humanity. Planetary colonies were only the plants that ripened and scattered the seeds.

So why had he joined the Alliance Navy, dedicated to squabbling over those wretched dirtballs with the Federation, the Baernoi, and anybody else handy? He'd asked himself the question often enough to have given up hoping for an answer, but it wouldn't let him alone.

At least he could do something about the planetscape on the screen. He blanked the screen as a knock sounded.

"Colonel Pak's here, Captain," came the voice of his executive officer, Commander Joanna Marder. Leray was pouring out glasses of Hochwelt brandy as Marder escorted the commander of the 96th Independent Regiment into the cabin.

"Welcome aboard, Colonel." Leray pushed two glasses across the desk. Pak frowned at his without taking it.

"It's true, then? The Federation is sending a squadron with a capital ship as flag?" the colonel said. His tone seemed to accuse Leray of having personally contrived this development for his embarrassment.

"They haven't officially announced where *Shenandoah* is going," Marder pointed out.

"No, they wouldn't," Pak said sourly. "They wouldn't

want to warn us that the nonprovocation policy has been breached."

"What makes you think that?" Leray asked. Pak was a highly efficient pessimist but not usually one to make such gigantic leaps to conclusions.

"A capital ship, confronting the Bonsai Force. Isn't that enough provocation?" Pak asked.

"We aren't helpless, even facing a capital ship," Marder said sharply. "It only takes one good hit."

Pak's long-suffering look hardened. So did his voice. "Spare me the tired wisdom I have been hearing from our governor. We of the Bonsai Force will do every part of our duty, including obeying him."

That, Leray reflected, might be harder than fighting *Shenandoah* ship-to-ship. A well-handled heavy cruiser could take on a capital ship, even without attacker support. If Governor Hollings started tying his hands with orders either obscure or deliberately intended to provoke Leray into a court-martial blunder . . .

No, Hollings wasn't that big a fool. He still had too few wits and too many political connections among the Pentarchy, the five founding planets of the Alliance. They'd kept him on Victoria for twenty-two years after the end of a long and moderately distinguished military career. It was said that the Alliance forces on Victoria were kept weak to avoid a military commander senior enough to argue with Hollings.

Well, they might be small but they were efficient. "The Bonsai Force" was the name given them by Admiral Mido after an inspection twenty years before: "You are small but perfect in every detail." The federals made a joke of it. They didn't know the Allied sailors and soldiers wore it with pride.

At least Pak's surliness now had both explanation and excuse. After an audience with Hollings, most people needed a few hours alone before they were fit for human society again. Pak must have been practically dragged out the governor's door and onto the shuttle.

"Come on, Colonel," Leray said. "Drink up and leave the nonprovocation policy to the people paid to worry about it. I don't think it's gone out the hatch, for three reasons.

"One, Victoria's in a unique position. Even if they don't want to fight or expand in this area right away, the Feds know they'll have to one day. That means laying in the infrastructure now. An orbital base and one capital ship is only a little more than what they have now.

"Second, if they're building any kind of an orbital base, they could plead security. If *Shenandoah* comes out, she'll probably be called an 'escort for the base-construction force.' "

Marder nodded. The muscles of her long neck twitched as she swallowed more brandy. "I'd bet a year's salary there are outlaw colonies no more than twenty light-years from here. They'd mortgage their souls for a transport load of space-construction machinery, or even just the transport herself."

She poured herself more brandy, ignoring Leray's usual look of polite reproach, then went on. "We actually have more interplanetary spacelift in-system than the Feds. Think we should offer them a couple of ships as a 'conciliatory gesture'?"

Leray looked at Pak. "Why not?" the colonel said. "At least Hollings will have to explain why he won't allow it, if all three of us ask."

"Then we will," Leray said. "I suspect he'll agree, too. The Feds wouldn't be doing this if they thought the Baernoi were going to stick a finger into the pie. Now, whether or not they're right, I don't know. I'm not in Intelligence. I prefer to display it. But the Tuskers can't be increasing the pressure, at least.

"So that makes *Shenandoah* and whoever she brings with her unwelcome but not disastrous. It's like mites up the sinuses or a pulled Achilles tendon. We won't enjoy it, but we won't die of it."

Eight

Tension tied small knots of exquisite pain across Rose Liddell's forehead and up and down her cheeks.

"Drive full reverse," came Bogdanov's crisp voice over the intercom from the bridge.

"Drive, full reverse," Fujita replied from the engine room.

Liddell hand-activated the visual mode on the intercom, then split the screen. Now she could see as well as hear the two officers at their stations.

Fujita wore a broad smile. Most engineers were at heart children turned loose on the biggest construction sets in the universe. Some tried to hide this, but Fujita wasn't one of them.

Bogdanov surprised Liddell. His uniform actually looked as if he'd worn it for part of a Standard day. More remarkable still, he was smiling. It wasn't the predator's smile he wore when on the trail of substandard performance, either. It was a smile of genuine, if modest, pleasure.

Beyond Bogdanov, the rest of the bridge crew was silhouetted against the visual displays. The Dockyard showed up on all those displays, still closing but more slowly with each second. *Shenandoah*'s drive field was braking her from thirty kilometers a second to a dead stop with plenty of margin for error.

Not that accidents hadn't happened at this stage of coming into port. Liddell remembered as a girl watching the mediacasts of the Alexander Station accident, when a power surge sent the transport *Kuba Hill* crashing into the station's orbital warehouse.

Even then, most of the four hundred people aboard the transport might have survived if the warehouse hadn't just taken aboard a load of chemicals. When the last fragment was accounted for, everybody aboard the transport and the warehouse and a good many aboard the station itself were gone—726 people.

The thought didn't help Liddell's tension aches. Nothing would have helped now, except being able to show that the Old Lady was nervous about letting the second team maneuver *Shen* around Riftwell Dockyard.

That meant no help at all. She couldn't undermine the second team's confidence, not without weakening *Shenandoah*. Everyone qualified to handle the ship, even under high-ranking and highly critical eyes, was an invaluable resource.

Not to mention that Bogdanov seemed to enjoy shiphandling. Liddell wondered if the man was as rigidly austere as he seemed or as content to be his superiors' disciplinarian and executioner.

Bogdanov was counting down the last few hundred meters of the ship's progress.

"On station in six seconds . . . five . . . four . . . three . . . two . . . one . . . at rest!"

In the screens, Riftwell Dockyard no longer moved. On the bridge and in the Combat Center, no one moved either. Nothing moved, except the tug creeping toward *Shen* with puffs from its jets.

"Docking crew, prepare to engage tug," Bogdanov said. Another screen lit up, showing the view from the hatch where the docking crew waited. Once the tug was locked in place, *Shen* could keep her station around the Dockyard even with every power system cold-ironed.

Only the drive and shield would be, this time. If *Shen* were still here at the end of four Standard days, Admiral Schatz's opinion of the delay would be detectable, if not audible, from orbit.

Liddell killed the visual on the intercom and leaned back in the padded captain's chair. Two meters below her, the CCD officer detected the movement,

"Permission to secure?"

"Granted."

Lights came up, harness popped, and thirty-odd sets of

feet thumped carpeted decks. In two minutes the only people still seated in the Combat Center were the four helmeted figures at the four master panels.

Liddell sat up, set her terminal for "Compose," and ordered a cup of hot chocolate. Below, the CC crew members were silhouetted against the display-loaded bulkheads as they moved back and forth, unlimbering cramped muscles.

Two decks high and twenty meters across, the main Combat Center was the heart of *Shenandoah* as a war machine. It was the captain's battle station and the admiral's, if one were aboard. All data on threats and targets came in here, and all orders for combat maneuvers or weapons use went out.

The displays began fading, as one by one they went to standby mode. In another two minutes, everything was down except the four master stations, legally required to remain active as long as *Shenandoah* was in commission.

Even the minimum of displays would have looked garish in a party mall. A CC with everything online continually skated along the edge of sensory overload. Ergonomic design fought a rear-guard action against it, not always successfully.

Even without sensory overload, the cumulative effect of CC watches had been a problem as long as there'd been interstellar navies. Genetic engineering of a warrior class was the path tried by the Hivers; that precluded it for the human race. Direct human-computer linkages had proved a dead end. Over more than the short run, they destroyed too many human minds and raised the anxiety level in the survivors to dangerous heights.

The work along the road to this dead end hadn't been entirely wasted. The neurosurgeons had learned most of what they could do to repair major brain and nerve damage that way. They still couldn't keep sensory overload and "CC burnout" from flying formation with some of the brightest and toughest minds in any navy.

The bridge screens now showed the tug ready to dock. The dockmaster gave a dramatic version of the "Cut" signal, which let Liddell recognize him—Lieutenant Longman, that overdriven scion of a few too many generations of Navy.

The tug settled into place, so gently that the impact didn't register in the CC. Rocket nozzles swiveled, so that their blast would clear *Shen's* external arrays and the tug's own bloated collection of extra fuel tanks. Then Longman gave the thumbs-up and Bogdanov repeated the gesture.

"Well done, Pavel," Liddell said. Bogdanov was saluting as she switched the visual link from "Bridge" to "All stations."

"All hands, this is the captain speaking. Our shakedown cruise is finished. We're in position off Riftwell Dockyard.

"I'm sure there were times when you felt that both our ship and ourselves would really be shaken into our component molecules. This didn't happen. Instead, we learned that most of us knew our jobs and most of the rest were ready to learn. We did not, thank God, have very many passengers who could neither do nor learn.

"You've known for some time that normal postshakedown leave won't be possible. However, I've received confirmation that each watch will have twelve hours of Dockyard liberty. Special shuttles will be laid on, to bring up authorized family or affiliates. So will dirtside communications links, for arranging such visits. The first liberty period will begin at 0800 tomorrow."

From the shouts and smiles in the CC, Liddell guessed the whole ship must be echoing. *I've thrown you a crumb and you think it's the whole bloody cake! Are you loyal or just easy to please?*

Or maybe professional enough to know why it's necessary?

A lovely thought, that last one. It was every officer's dream to command such a crew.

Please, make it so. Nothing else could so thoroughly break the curse of the ship's name.

Liddell got her voice under control and continued. "All crew not on liberty will have extra duty, loading ship's stores, transit supplies and personnel, and anything else we're stuck with hauling to Victoria. We are expected to be ready to leave within thirty hours after the conclusion of the last liberty period."

This time Liddell saw smiles but heard no cheers. That matched her own feelings. Even interstellar space was a limited-threat environment, its dangers comparatively predictable.

It took the unpredictability of sapient beings to create

high-threat environments. On Victoria those sapient beings were hard at work.

Shrieks exploded behind Brigitte Tachin, reaching a pitch that sounded so mechanical she spun around. Instead of an emergency, she saw half a dozen dark-haired children under ten Standard years embracing two male petty officers from *Shenandoah*. A gray-bearded man and two women about the same age as the petty officers looked on benignly.

Tachin was suddenly sorry she'd looked back. There were any number of explanations for the particular mix of sexes, generations, and professions in that family group, but a family group it was, eight hundred light-years closer than hers.

She walked away briskly, as the shrieks subsided into animated questions from the older children and cheerful noises from the younger ones. The questions were in Arabic, which suggested one of the more conservative family styles; Arab-descended people seldom went in for megafamilies or group marriages.

Tachin increased her pace as she realized she couldn't even speculate about somebody else's family without its leading to dark thoughts about her own. She began to think that coming on liberty had been a mistake.

She'd sent a message to Rafael and he might still come up, but he wasn't family or affiliate. Even if he didn't have duty, he couldn't get a place on the special shuttles.

And if he did come around the next corner right now, all they'd have time for was another one-night (or half-day) encounter. This might—no, do the man justice, *would*—temporarily relieve the consequences of celibacy but not a cursed thing besides that!

Tachin was so absorbed in her homesickness that the two people who did come around the corner at that moment ran straight into her. She threw out both hands to catch herself, clutched someone's hair with one, and didn't pull the hair painfully only because two large hands gripped her other arm.

"Rafael?"

"I was christened Brian," Lieutenant Mahoney said. "Are you all right, Brigitte?"

"I think so." She flexed both arms. "Sorry about grabbing your hair, Elayne."

"That's all right. It's almost too long for shipboard anyway." Zheng fingercombed the damage out of her sleek black coiffure and shook Tachin's hand. "What brings you here, Brigitte?"

"Being dropped by my date, I think," she said. "Either that, or he had duty too late to get a message to the ship. He's a doctor at the base hospital."

"Affiliated?"

"Now, how would I have had time to do that? No, just a bed friend."

"Well, would you like to come along with us for lunch?" Mahoney asked. "We decided to make liberty after Charlie said he was going to. He doesn't have anything in mind except company in bed, so I thought we'd better fly distant escort. God willing, we can pick up the pieces and maybe even him before Security notices anything."

"If we can find the little bastard," Zheng muttered. "Is it just my imagination, or have they expanded the Recreation Deck since the last time I made liberty here?"

"When was that?"

"Our last liberty from *Valhalla*? You remember the twins who tried to be all things to all people and sometimes succeeded?"

"I've been trying to forget that lapse of taste."

"Whose taste? You've known me long enough to know I don't have any."

"If you shock Brigitte, Elayne, I may become dangerous. Oops! Sorry about that, Brigitte. I didn't mean to sound protective."

Tachin realized that neither Mahoney nor Zheng was entirely sober. In spite of this, lunch with them seemed like a good idea.

"Thanks for the invitation, and don't worry about protecting me. That's what a family's for, and you people are the closest thing to a family I have here."

She'd intended that to be just politeness, but when she finished speaking she realized she'd told the truth.

Admiral Kuwahara knew the legend of the Riftwell Base Flag Club. In eighty Standard years, it had used only three hundred stellars in appropriated funds. Everything else was donated money, labor, and supplies.

Looking around the walls paneled with wood that had never grown within light-years of Riftwell, Kuwahara allowed himself a touch of skepticism. Either there's been several flag officers as rich as Marshal Sforza, or else some of those donations were in the great tradition of "You've just donated a week's salary to the Flag Club Fund, haven't you, Commodore?"

Having been a lowly commodore until the previous month, Kuwahara could see the scene as vividly as if he'd been there.

He picked up the jug of elevonce and made a gesture at the empty glasses on the low table in front of him. Rear Admiral Naomi Xera shook her elegant silver-blued head.

"Thanks for the offer, Sho, but I made the mistake of letting a few friends know I was being reassigned. They all want to show me the sights of Riftwell."

"That shouldn't take more than ten minutes—"

"Don't they issue tact with the second star?"

"I asked Service Command, but they're out."

Kuwahara poured half a glass and sipped judiciously. "Do they have a shuttle billet for you up to Dockyard, or may I offer you a ride? I'm going up to watch *Shenandoah* and her squadron sail."

"Goodwill gesture?"

"You might say that."

"Come on, Sho. You know it's all over Riftwell, that you get the Victoria squadron as soon as it needs a flag."

"And as soon as my successor as chief of staff—" he raised his glass to Xera "—is ready to assume the duties of her office."

"Pull me a handy reference file on Victoria and I can start at the end of next week."

"Why Victoria in particular?"

"It's the one thing you've shown me since I arrived that might need some major decisions before I've settled in. I don't want to whine at Schatz or let the Army think they can help me."

"Coletta's threatening to be helpful again?"

"Again? Does he make a habit of it?"

"When he thinks Berkson won't notice it."

Kuwahara sighed and decided he needed the second half of his glass. When it was empty, he shrugged.

"We can't all be like Frieda Hentsch. The gods made her a lady, whatever her commission said. I wish we had her and Berkson over at Army, not Coletta."

"Hentsch won't be wasted at I Corps," Xera said. "Not if Victoria needs troops. Mind if I smoke?"

At Kuwahara's nod, she pulled a nelsyn cigar from her tunic and pulled the lighter strand. When it was drawing comfortably, she leaned back with a discontented expression at war with her body's ease.

"I sometimes wonder who the Army would rather fight, us or the Baernoi. Eleventh Army, anyway."

"Whichever would give them the high hand in the Zone," Kuwahara said sourly. He decided that he only wanted, as opposed to *needed*, another drink. "We really don't need to worry too much. Coletta's only one man, and cosmography's against him."

Some of the Federation's fourteen War Zones had a small number of heavily populated planets. There the Army was senior. Others had many planets with small populations and long light-years between them. In these, the Navy held the high hand.

Zone Eleven was the second kind, with the Baernoi on one side and the Alliance on two others thrown in for good measure. It was a physical impossibility for the three corps of Eleventh Army to be more than an appendage to the Eleventh Fleet, but that didn't keep Eleventh Army from periodically developing delusions of grandeur.

This irritated Kuwahara without particularly surprising him. Interservice rivalry, he suspected, began the day one Neanderthal tribe's stone throwers claimed that those who fought with axes were getting more than their share of the good stones.

"Here's to cosmography, then," Xera said, saluting the sky beyond the mural of the Battle of Isis with her cigar. "Coletta did warn me about Kornilov, the Victoria CG. Does he want Kornilov's job, or what?"

"Kornilov's an odd bird, I must admit. Not the usual retired-on-duty type they send to Victoria. He simply wants troops to lead and plenty of bedroom time off duty, and he doesn't care about anything else."

"Including who knows it?"

"Exactly. The Army's Promotion Boards are funny about people who want three stars. If they don't see somebody at least trying to look like Karpova or Edubo, they start making out retirement papers."

"Where does the Army find its Promotion Boards?"

"In supply pods left over from the Hive Wars, I think. But that's only a hypothesis. Would you care to offer an alternative over dinner?"

"Toss for the charge?"

Kuwahara pulled out his ID. "Badge or stats?"

"Stats."

The rectangle of encoded plastic landed with the Navy's rayed starship face-up. "Any objections to winter rolls and some Cedar Terrace '69?" Xera asked.

"None."

The wine mixed well with their previous drinks and their present moods. Both had little influence and less money to launch them on their naval careers. Both had known the pleasures of commanding a ship and had wondered if it would be all downhill from there. Kuwahara was discovering that it was not; he hoped Naomi would have the chance to make the same discovery.

The wine went even better with the winter rolls. Between mouthfuls of shellfish, pork, and vegetables, they brought each other up to date on friends promoted, retired, or on the endless cruise.

They exchanged an oily kiss over the last glass and crumb. "Damnit, Sho," Xera said. "I'm twice as glad about taking COS if it frees you up for Victoria."

"You mean you want all the help you can get if Coletta's the new dirtside CG there."

"Was I that obvious?"

"No more so than our overgrown Machiavelli on a bad day."

"Your next order of winter rolls will have laxative in them."

"There won't be a next order, if you don't want to delay the Victoria file. If you can order desert while I order a secure link, you can have it by the time we leave."

"Can do."

Kuwahara stood up and brushed crumbs off his blues.

The terminals at the tables were only medium security. The Command Secret terminals were in the meeting rooms, in the rear of the lounge.

"Naomi. I'm not going to lose sleep about Coletta. If Victoria stays only a little warm, Berkson will leave Kornilov in place. If it gets hot, I'd bet on Frieda Hentsch going out.

"If it gets very hot, I suspect the Supreme Command will put a theater commander in the pipeline to Zone Eleven. The TC will probably have a court favorite to plug in, not Coletta."

"Bet on that?"

"A graduation present for Yaso against a new ski set."

"I'll tell the boy to decide what he wants."

"Optimist!"

"It's a hard job, but somebody has to do it."

The Navy's first chief engineer, Admiral Heineman, had argued for bases like Riftwell Dockyard centuries before the first human starship entered Riftwell's system.

"Rock is cheaper to carve than steel is to forge. It isn't as tough as steel, but there's a lot more of it lying around in most systems. "Find me an asteroid."

That was the first job in setting up a Navy base in any new system. Riftwell Dockyard had been hauled into place more than two hundred Standard years before *Shenandoah* started loading for Victoria. Hardly a year had gone by since then without more usable space being nibbled out of the forty cubic kilometers of rock.

The three *Shenandoah* officers found themselves diving down dark and shiny passages: dark, because the lighting wasn't fully wired up; and shiny, because the rock sealer hadn't been scuffed and scarred by generations of feet, hands, heads, or elbows.

A massive armored lock finally let them into a place calling itself the Casbah. It held smoke, shadows, what seemed like a hectare of tables, and three doors periodically disgorging or swallowing serving robots.

"Looks like we've gone too far down," Mahoney said. "Nobody from *Shen* here."

"All the more reason for Charlie's being here," Zheng said. "No shipmates to watch."

"Come, come, Elayne," Tachin said. "Why should he have anything to hide?"

"FADS cases always hide it, whether it needs hiding or not."

"I defer to your superior knowledge," Tachin said.

Zheng mimed pulling her foot out of her mouth while Mahoney scanned the tables more carefully. Most of the shoulder patches on the well-worn coveralls were Dockyard or shuttle crews.

No *Valhalla* patches, fortunately. The carrier's crew had a reputation for regarding brawls as a way of improving muscle tone and digestion. Prange had a reputation for not discouraging them hard enough.

No empty tables, either. Mahoney was backing out of the path of a serving robot when someone shouted from the back of the room.

"Hola! Lieutenant Tachin! May I offer hospitality?"

Mahoney recognized Commander Ahmed Tourkmani, the man who really made Dockyard work.

"Shall we?" Tachin asked. "We worked together a bit while I was running errands for the Old Lady, some more during weapons training."

"Lead on."

A tall gray-haired man moved over one chair to make room for the *Shenandoah* trio. "My cousin Feroze Chakour," Tourkmani said. Chakour salaamed with old-fashioned formality.

Tachin returned the gesture. "Were those your sons and grandchildren I saw in the reception area?"

"Indeed. Also Yusef's wife and Ismail's widow. The Baernoi sent Ismail to Paradise two years ago, may God afflict them! But the women do well for the children, and Yakoub may yet marry."

Chakour smiled at Tachin. "Perhaps you would care to meet Yakoub? Women have called him handsome, and I know he is honorable."

"I thank you," Tachin said. "But I must give myself to the Navy for a few more years. It is a matter of family honor."

"Then let no more be said of it, unless you are offended?"

"Not at all."

"I will be offended if my guests perish of thirst and

hunger," Tourkmani said. "Even our kinship will not spare you my wrath, Feroze. Now, who wants what?"

They punched in orders: a huge pot of stew, flatbread, candied fiftyfruit, and a selection of drinks. Tourkmani and Chakour were conservative enough to stay with wine, and they split a bottle with Tachin. This left Mahoney and Zheng with the whiskey.

Mahoney thought of leaving some of the whiskey for Longman, then realized he neither knew nor cared if Charlie was going to show up. For all Mahoney cared, Longman could be trying to bounce a fertile pit snapper.

"To *Shenandoah*," Tourkmani said. "May she fly far and free, and bring home those she bears forth."

"Except for those who have joined the kinship of the honored dead," Tachin added.

Mahoney clinked glasses with Tachin and felt the whiskey's glow expand through him as it flowed down. Now he actively disliked the idea of Longman showing up. It would spoil his mood of believing that *Shenandoah* was the place where Brian Francis Mahoney would finally do something worthwhile.

Nine

Bogdanov turned in his seat and nodded as precisely as he saluted.

"All stations report ready to get underway, Captain."

"Thank you."

Rose Liddell took a deep breath. "Engine Control, all ahead slow."

"Aye-aye, ma'am," came Fujita's voice on the intercom.

Shenandoah's colossal power plant could be controlled from the bridge, without the intervention of a single engineer. Liddell and Fujita would use that capability when necessary. Leaving the dockyard, it was worse than unnecessary, it was dangerous. It cut a human backup out of the system at a particularly accident-prone point.

The engine-panel displays had lit up while Liddell was contemplating the philosophy of control systems. She glanced at them, then called up an exterior view on her console screen.

Just fast enough to notice, Riftwell Dockyard was drifting astern and to port.

Liddell caught her breath as the view of the space around the dockyard expanded. No sign of *Valhalla*, and a starship a third again larger than *Shen* would be impossible to miss. She must still be docked.

Liddell was aware of mixed feelings about this. Prange was considerably her senior and not an easy man to serve under. But "bare is brotherless back," even when the only available brother might be Captain Prange.

94

The Dockyard drifted entirely off the screen. A course check showed no significant deviations.

"Tug to *Shenandoah*," Tourkmani's voice came. "Permission to cast off?"

"Permission granted. Thank you."

"God be with you."

The battlecruiser's mass absorbed the modest jolt of the tug's undocking. The tug silently crossed the screen, jets playing with the deftness only to be expected of Tourkmani, who'd begun his career as a tug pilot.

Ten kilometers from *Shenandoah*, Tourkmani salvoed flares. Crimson, gold, emerald, they blazed across the starscape. Screens darkened to protect human vision, then returned to normal as the flares died.

Liddell's screen now showed the view aft. Dockyard floated there, centered but shrinking. *Ira Hayes* drifted on to the screen, two attackers already riding her external cradles, a third parked close by.

Bogdanov was subvocalizing a Russian Baptist prayer. Liddell thought a better launching for this cruise would be a chorus of "We're off to See the Wizard." Gandalf, Merlin —no, somebody named Oz; anyway, the wizard had a few surprises for his visitors.

"*Cooney* reports authorization from Dockyard Control to get underway."

Another human link in a control system. With an enemy in detection range, Dockyard Control would have been ordering everything in orbit to run or land at their discretion. With nothing to do but set up a squadron in proper cruising formation, both the dockyard and *Shenandoah* had to give permission for each junior ship to move.

Still all nominal on the displays. Liddell nodded.

"*Shenandoah* to *Cooney*. Permission to get underway."

The screen went holographic, one slowly moving spark near the edge and a second starting to move out from the center. Liddell saw that Bogdanov had already logged *Shenandoah*'s own getting underway and took another deep breath.

"0716. Victoria squadron underway for destination, Rose Liddell SOPS." She nodded at the talker.

The whistle shrilled. "All hands, all hands. Set cruising stations. Set cruising stations. That is all."

As the announcement ended, so did Captain Liddell's euphoria. Her stomach gave a rumble that she was sure must have been heard in the Combat Center. Breakfast this morning had seemed to be one of those things that could be put off—and put off, and put off. Now she was ferociously hungry.

She rang for her messenger.

"Yes, ma'am?"

"Breakfast, on the double. One of the special omelets, tea, and I think I'll splurge with an angelnut roll. Toasted, no butter."

"Aye-aye, ma'am."

As the messenger called in the order, light cruiser *Welitsch* came on with her request for permission to get underway.

[Departure plus twenty-six hours]

The conference room was too small even for three people. But, then, Brian Mahoney thought the carrier berths of Dockyard would have been too small to hold him and the first lieutenant right now.

"We need to set up the simulators *now*, Brian! We'll be too busy for heavy training once we're in the Victoria system."

"Ma'am, the problem's the same no matter how much work we have to do off Victoria. Where the devil are we going to put the bouncing things?"

"You're being stubborn, Mahoney." So much for the gesture of calling him "Brian." The first lieutenant crossed her elegant legs—Mahoney wouldn't deny her good looks and a good combat record—and frowned. "One might almost say insubordinate."

"Ma'am, it's your privilege to call my opinion anything you please. It's my privilege not to change it—without a direct order," he added, more dutifully than he felt. He'd seen Commander Charbon's eyebrows curl toward each other, the preliminary stages of a royal or at least princely reaming out.

"The direct order would have to come from Captain Liddell," Theodora Bell said. This truism didn't stop the first lieutenant's eyebrows; it merely swung her head toward the Training officer.

Somewhat to Mahoney's surprise, Charbon didn't say a

word. She merely fixed Lieutenant Commander Bell with those wide dark eyes until Bell started to stammer an excuse.

Mahoney felt an impulse to see Commander Charbon not only out of the conference room but out of the ship altogether. Preferably without a suit.

Charbon had at least one of a good leader's virtues. She knew who was loyal to their subordinates and who would throw them to the first lieutenant for an improved efficiency report. Bell was loyal to people like Mahoney, so she would have to be attacked directly.

"Let's try the executive officer first," Charbon purred. "I'm sure he gives the correct priority to training."

Mahoney risked an exchange of sympathetic looks with Bell while Charbon punched up Bogdanov's cabin.

"Good morning," Bogdanov said through the steam from his cup of tea. "Is it urgent, or can it wait until tomorrow's Officers' Call?"

"I'd rather not wait that long, if it's all the same to you," Charbon said. "It concerns the efficiency of the ship and the cooperation of the Training Department with our goals for it."

After that greeting Mahoney knew he and Bell were dead. The only question was what method of execution would be used. *Oh well, I suppose I can always try the priesthood again. Someplace far enough from Killarney that they're too short of bodies to ask about vocations.*

Clearly Charbon thought Mahoney's refusal to grab the first compartments that came to hand for getting up the extra six simulators showed a lack of concern for his duty. Bell was compounding the offense, and Charbon wanted Bogdanov to perform major surgery on both offenders.

Mahoney composed his rebuttal to Charbon, for all the good it would do, and turned to the screen. Nothing showed but Bogdanov's chiseled face and muscle-corded neck, as animated as a Delanite carving. Except that every so often the blue eyes wandered off screen, and once the high forehead wrinkled.

"I appreciate your calling me, Commander," Bogdanov said. "This will spare us having to settle it at Officers' Call."

"Oh, I quite agree. I don't want to embarrass the Training Department."

You hypocritical—!

"Neither do I, Commander," Bogdanov said. "On the other hand, I give a higher priority to reducing the amount of hotbunking. The only available compartment big enough for all six simulators is already embarked for overflow quarters. The bunks start going in tomorrow."

Charbon's startled gape plainly said, "Nobody told me." Bogdanov frowned, and Mahoney realized that when it came to executioner's faces, Charbon wasn't in the same class with the Hermit.

Mahoney used the silence to break in. "Commander, I hope we can find a compromise. I've noted down a few compartments that could hold three simulators apiece. We don't need all of them."

Bell swallowed. "Actually, we're a bit shorthanded for manning two new training centers. The equipment's not worth installing if you don't have the people to operate it."

"So three simulators with full crews would be nearly as good as six without them?" Bogdanov inquired.

"I'd guess about 80–85 percent," Mahoney put in.

"Lieutenant, refine that guess and have it to me by 1100."

"Aye-aye, sir." Mahoney substituted a salute for cheering and dancing.

"Commander Charbon, I'd like to see you in my quarters. If the Training Department is shorthanded, we can explore a few transfers. Also, we can pull files on some of our passengers and ask for volunteers."

"That smells a little like Captain Prange," Charbon said.

Bogdanov's frown was now that of the executioner filling the injector. "I am not proposing to introduce *Valhalla* standards aboard *Shenandoah*, Commander. Merely to make the best use of temporarily available resources. When can I expect to see you?"

Charbon's departure was too fast for dignity. Bell and Mahoney let her get out of sight, then left themselves. The last thing they wanted was to be around when the first lieutenant returned from her meeting with Bogdanov.

As they waited for the elevator, Mahoney realized that he could finally breathe again. "Whew! I've heard of the Hermit showing you the plate you'll be handed your head on the next time you do it on your shoes. I've never seen it."

"Neither have I," Bell said. "And I never expected to see

it used against somebody like Charbon. I thought the Hermit and Number One were the same breed."

"*Were* may be the word," Mahoney said. "I suspect Captain Liddell's got something to do with it. What, I don't know."

"But you could find out?"

Mahoney considered. He thought of Brigitte Tachin, working under a Weapons Officer who was a former squadronmate of the Hermit. He thought of Elayne Zheng, heiress to all the gossip of the attacker community, of which the Hermit had once been a distinguished member.

He even thought of Charles Longman, whose five flag-rank relatives might have sometimes been indiscreet in his presence.

"Yes, ma'am."

"Then do it. But after you get that estimate to the exec."

"Aye-aye, ma'am."

[Departure plus fifty-one hours]

"Launcher Two, you are clear for launching."

"Shuttle One, we are clear to be launched."

Disembodied voices in Charles Longman's headset and displays on the control panel two meters ahead said the same thing. He gripped the arms of his seat, imagining the pistons of Launcher Two drawing back and the charge building up to drive them forward, flinging the shuttle out into space, stressing the whole Launcher structure. . . .

The stars were all around them so suddenly that Longman's breath *whssshed* out of him; all around them except for one screen, which showed *Shen*'s hull receding steadily.

When the battlecruiser hung against the stars, the pilot's hands hovered over the controls. The computer didn't need any help. When it knew the shuttle was a safe two thousand meters from *Shenandoah*, it cut in the drive.

As the shuttle's velocity dropped by a few hundred meters per second, *Shenandoah* swept forward off the screen and vanished. Now there was nothing but stars, some larger than others, the largest of all showing only in the rear screen.

Engineer support ship *Stepan Pucinski* rode there, a hundred and fifty kilometers behind, her staff probably already checking their supply of homebrew in case there was time for a party after the conference. Even without the party, the prospect of the conference would have delighted Longman.

If only he hadn't had to pack himself into this shuttle to get there! No choice, once the request for him to join the party came down from the Engineer Squadron CO. Besides, he'd be damned if he wanted to look afraid to trust his own repairs!

Shen was now only his brightest star ahead, as *Pucinski* was the brightest aft. The pilot unstrapped, leaving the copilot to monitor the computer's execution of the flight plan. The delicate balancing of jets, drive, the gravity and solar wind of Rashid's Star, and the distribution of the shuttle's payload could be done much better by a functioning computer.

Longman's instincts forced him to listen for any signs that the computer wasn't functioning. Computers weren't his specialty, but they were machines. He understood any machine better than most people, liked any machine better than the stars.

The first were too unpredictable, the second too big. But how the devil to explain that to the five admirals born or married into the Longman family? Particularly to explain to Aunt Diana, with her three stars, her recruiting-poster looks, and self-confidence that made not only starships but stars docile?

If there was any way, I wouldn't be here. Since I am here, the only thing to do is the best I can.

Fifty times the same question, and always the same answer. *I suppose I'm making the best of a bad job. I've given up hope of doing much to build the family reputation. I'll just have to grit my teeth and try not to mar it.*

From the seat beside him, Elayne Zheng whispered, "Nervous, Charlie?"

He got out words instead of a coughing fit. "I'm not a bloody attacker jockey, claustrophobic except when I'm aboard one of those overpowered cans!"

"It takes all kinds."

She sounded less hostile than usual. To keep the conversation going, Longman asked, "Any idea why you're on the way to the conference?"

"Probably the same reason you are. The most available expert on attacker support, the most available expert on launchers. They're going to want input when they try to equip Victoria Dockyard out of that pile of parts aboard *Stepan*."

"If it wasn't for the honor of the occasion, I'd rather be in bed."

"Anyone's in particular?"

Longman managed to raise eyebrows while flushing.

"Sorry, not really my business unless I decide it's going to be mine."

"Am I supposed to bet on that?"

"Nothing you can't afford to lose."

"You have a real knack for flattery."

"I try."

"Very greatly." *My God, she's actually taking the trouble to joke with me!*

Does she know about me and agoraphobia? Or is she just trying to be friendly all at once?

Damn people! Machines don't have motives!

Mahoney caught the corner of the table with his hip as he sat down. Brigitte Tachin's cup of hot coffee slopped over onto her toast.

"Merde," she said dispassionately.

"Sorry. I started off by dropping the chalice at mass when I was an altarboy. Father Broxson said God would have something to say about that. Maybe he was right. I've been bumping and crashing my way through life ever since."

"Everywhere?"

"I don't seem to have any trouble in free fall."

Some women had also said he was comfortable company in bed, but they might have been flattering him. Certainly he hadn't had a regular partner for so long that he might be out of practice.

"Jake Polmar actually turned out to be more useful than Commander Zubova," Tachin began. Mahoney looked a question. "Weapons Maintenance Division," she added. "He's not one of the attacker jockeys, but he was Weapons Officer on *Muscaro* when Bogdanov was Captain of *Picon*."

Fweeeeettttt!

"All hands, all hands! This is an Alert Two. Repeat, this is an Alert Two. All hands report to your stations. All hands report to your stations. That is all."

Alert Two meant half the weapons and damage-control stations manned. Neither Tachin nor Mahoney had anything to do under this alert except stay out of the way of people who did. They managed this by staying seated and suspending a conversation that would have been drowned out anyway by falling trays and cutlery and scurrying feet.

When the half-empty wardroom was quiet, Mahoney looked at the green ceiling and the pale blue rug, already showing smudges. "Why is it that every new sound absorber seems to work everywhere except in wardrooms?"

"Increasing the stress tolerance of the officers, no doubt," Tachin said. "But I was saying about the Hermit . . ."

"I'm all ears."

"No, only about half."

Tachin dialed a refill for her coffee and munched the soggy toast. "Bogdanov had a reputation as a crack shiphandler. When the division commander wanted some really fancy maneuvering done, he called on *Picon*. I believe the Hermit even wrote the standard manual on light-cruiser maneuvering in atmosphere at low altitude." The last bite of toast vanished. "I'm not sure what that means, and I didn't want to seem to pry. Do people get frustrated if they're not allowed a daily dose of shiphandling?"

"Are novas bright? It's like Charlie Longman waking up a eunuch. Particularly if they were attacker jockeys, which is the purest form of shiphandling around."

"But don't light cruisers give the same chance?"

"They do. But they're so close to attackers that running a light cruiser doesn't prove you can handle something bigger. At least not to people who think attacker jockeys have all their brains in their fingers and arses.

"Bogdanov should have stayed in small ships. But he was just as good an administrator and disciplinarian as he was a shiphandler. I suppose it was being first lieutenant of *Eleanor of Aquitaine* that made his reputation there."

"I've heard of that," Tachin said. "I suppose after he cleaned up that mess, they always put him to work whipping the serfs and never let him handle a ship. *Le pauvre petit!* Like *le fou Charles*, if he was made a harem guard without being made a eunuch. Always looking, never touching."

The coffee refill arrived as the talker's pipe squealed again.

"All hands, all hands. Secure from Alert Two. Repeat, secure from Alert Two. The alert was called because of an unidentified single-ship contact on a parallel course. The contact turned out to be an emergency courier ship taking station. That is all."

Mahoney slipped up to the serving line just ahead of the returning breakfasters and came back with tea and a basket of rolls. He munched one with the nutty flavor of Novy Baikal rye and watched the coffee stain on Brigitte Tachin's upper lip. The lip was like the rest of her: by itself nothing to sing about, but very pleasant to look at where it was.

Tachin raised her eyes from her cup. Mahoney flushed, convinced she was reading on his face thoughts as unflattering as Longman's. He rushed into the rest of his explanation to cover his embarrassment.

"Anyway, I begin to understand why the Hermit's putting the whip away. The Old Lady won't let him use it, but she won't let him just sit and stew either. That's why she was letting him maneuver *Shen* so often on the shakedown. She figures either he knows enough or can learn it with practice."

"That's a risk if the captain isn't an expert shiphandler herself. Or will the Hermit take lessons from somebody else?"

"If the Old Lady orders him, he will. He probably will anyway, just to get a chance at conning a capital ship. Maybe Liddell can help him there, maybe she can't. But she'll see that he gets help, somehow."

"Then it seems not to matter if the captain is not an expert shiphandler. If she handles her people instead—Brian, why are you looking at me that way?"

"Just imagining how you would look—"

"Naked? Pardon, that was nasty. Also, you know."

"Yes, and I'm the better for knowing. I was really imagining four stripes on your shoulders."

"Me, a captain? *Imbecile*!" She aimed a punch at him. Playful as it was, it knocked the roll out of his hand. "Oh, I'm sorry."

"I should stop munching anyway. Speaking seriously, from my exalted status of eight years in the Navy, you ought to try for all the rank they'll give you. There are never enough leaders who know that the Navy's people, not machines."

"And the more there are, the easier the life of one of God's natural lieutenants becomes. True?"

"My altruism does have its limits."

"So does my appetite." Tachin pushed away her cup and plate. "I have two hours before my watch and nothing crying to be done. Would you like to join me in the gymnasium?"

"You want to punch me without rolls getting in the way, right?"

"Why not?"

Ten

The command lifter's laser blazed a dead line across the dusty street. The dust dissipated some of the beam, but a solid IR pulse remained on Candice Shores's screen.

"Pulse and dye rounds, simulated launch!" she snapped. The ammo counter beeped fifteen times. Now the ten meters beyond the deadline was sown with mines, ready to emit paralyzing ultrasonics, gruesome smells, indelible dyes, and nauseating gases at anyone who crossed the deadline.

Shores looked at the grid on the screen, showing where real mines would have fallen. "Good." She punched up a display of the active radius of the mines. They overlapped nicely, from storefront on one side to fence on the other. "Even better."

The lifter banked away and the display changed. "Huntress to Blossom Four, you're a little exposed from twenty meters, and there's two buildings that high in range."

Obeying standing orders, the sniper didn't acknowledge. He just shifted, until his telltale disappeared.

Now for a final test . . .

"Huntress to Walker Six. Unidentified ground vehicle approaching deadline along Goucher Street, twelve kph, erratic course."

"Acknowledge, Huntress. We're on it."

That cheerful message was almost literally true. The Walker Six lifter squatted at the intersection of Goucher Street and Menzies Boulevard, then soared away to the left.

"Report by data link, Walker Six."

What the lifter had done came up on Shores's screen.

Four simulated foam bombs covered the whole intersection. Ten seconds after release, the foam would be turning gluey, immobilizing people on foot, slowing moving parts in the vehicle, and covering the windshield. Thirty seconds and it would solidify, rooting pedestrians to the ground and slashing the vehicle's tires or jamming its fans.

"Good work, Walker Six."

"Thanks, Captain. Ah, we got a visual on a lifter approaching on the deck, bearing 260."

Shores had a nasty feeling about that lifter. "Climb to 400 meters," she told her pilot. The command lifter rose until the abandoned mining town Victoria Command was using for urban-security exercises lay spread out below. A colored dot was closing on the town from the southwest.

Like the foam, Shores's nasty feeling solidified as she zoomed in on the dot. It was the personal lifter of the chief of staff, Colonel Liu, with its orange stripes, white belly, and nonregulation lights.

"Huntress to all hands," Shores said. "The chief of staff is paying a visit. Walker Two, intercept and escort to ground. Other units complete the exercise. Debriefing will be at the CP as planned, time to be announced."

A lieutenant disguised as a captain might not get away with telling a notoriously touchy colonel to wait until she finished an exercise. But at least she would be getting the right message across to her own troopers.

"Battle Stations, Battle Stations, Battle Stations!"

The words blasted Paul Leray's feet off his desk. The siren wailed as he sprinted out of his cabin, his shoulder brushing the opening door.

"Battle Stations!"

The words came again as Joanna Marder burst out of her cabin, trying to drop a towel, pull on coveralls, and run, all at the same time. She succeeded remarkably well, although maybe it wasn't so remarkable, considering how fast she could get out of her coveralls on appropriate occasions.

Leray and Marder slapped shoulders as they hit the main fore-and-aft passageway and headed for their respective stations in the two Battle Command rooms. Marder had a shorter trip and was already signing on as Leray strapped himself in.

"All right," he said to the BCR duty officer. "What's wrong?"

"Unidentified ship on an intercept course, current bearing 234-79-154, current closing velocity 4.2 kps."

"Signature?"

"Nothing that matches what we'd expect out here, Captain. I didn't want to try an active scan without your orders."

"Not every friendly ship stays where we expect it, Lieutenant. As for his response to an active scan, we are a heavy cruiser. We are supposed to be able to handle anything likely to show up."

At least long enough to get off a warning. Avoiding an active scan made more sense now than it would once *Audacious* had an Alliance capital ship backing her up. If the stranger were something—better not call her *Shenandoah* —substantially superior to the cruiser, the Alliance had nothing in the Victoria system to replace her.

"All right. You need to learn when to think conservatively and when not. Otherwise, I've seen worse. In fact, I've even done it. I'll tell you about that later. Right now, I want an all-mode scan."

"Aye-aye, sir."

Radar, IR, every form of radiation detector, and visual scans went to work, building a picture of the unidentified ship in the computer. Seconds after the radar hit, the stranger began to slow.

"He's got a radar detector," the BCR officer muttered.

"So does every mining cooperative," Leray said. Not that Victoria had any asteroid miners, with its modest population and abundant surface metals. So what the devil was—?

Leray's mental alarm rang. "Signature 465, display!"

His screen split, showing the signature of the approaching ship and the signature of the Federation's observatory supply ship. They were identical.

The tension in the BCR evaporated, leaving behind the smell of sweat and a collection of red faces. Leray grinned.

"Now we know who's out there. The next question is Why?" He called the auxiliary BCR.

"Jo, call up our friends in *Leon Brautigan* and ask why they're out here when the observatory's halfway to the other side of the system."

"With pleasure, Captain."

* * *

Candice Shores faced the assembled platoon commanders and platoon sergeants of Scout Company. She was uneasily aware of Colonel Liu sitting just behind her to the left. She was more pleasantly aware of the company's first sergeant, Raoul Zimmer, standing just behind her to the right.

"I'm not giving you a 'well done' this time," she began. "I save those for something better."

The faces gave her no clues. What the Hades, when in doubt follow Sam Briggs: Every so often, somebody dies from too many facts. A lot more often, they die from too few.

"Not too much better, though. Mostly what we need is speeding things up. Coordination is good. One more security simulation, and we'll be ready for a live-fire exercise.

"Two specific areas we need to work on. One is ammunition expenditure. With our loads, we ought to be able to hold a deadline with twelve mines, an intersection with three foam bombs. We may end up with more, but let's not bet on it.

"If we have to use lethal force because we've shot ourselves dry on the nonlethals, the bystanders' relatives will be coming after us.

"The other problem is the snipers. Nothing that more practice in urban areas shouldn't cure, but we do need that. Most people won't try to jump a deadline or wrestle a troop line. More will try to pick off an exposed sniper, figuring the rest of us won't notice. They'll be wrong, of course, but the sniper will still be dead.

"Our job isn't to let local hotheads count coup on Starworld regulars. It's to remind them as gently as possible why that's a bad idea and has been for a long time."

This time Shores got polite smiles. "Any questions?"

"Yeah," said the CO of 3rd Platoon. "Why are we putting in time on security exercises?"

Now the only presence that counted was Zimmer's. Colonel Liu might have been on Deccan, for all Shores cared about him.

"We're Scouts. You all know the Scout tradition."

"If it's legal, we'll do it faster and better. If it's illegal, we'll fight it longer and harder." Several voices quoted Charissa Briggs in chorus.

"Right. The other reason is that the way we move around, we might be the first on the scene for any security problem. Nobody wants to have to use lethal force because a unit on hand isn't trained for anything else."

From behind her came a muttered, "Zing, Captain." She didn't know if the chief of staff heard, and she didn't care. The smiles facing her were now all real, but Zimmer's words counted for more than all the smiles combined.

Aboard F.S.S. *Leon Brautigan*, the Alliance ship's call was no surprise. The converted survey ship's two-man crew had been alert ever since the first radar probe.

Lieutenant Karl Pocher wondered if the Alliance officer of the watch had let himself in for a reaming. He'd faced a dilemma as old as radar. Your radar could warn your enemy of your presence at twice the range it could tell you very much about him. Which was more dangerous—mutual ignorance, or knowledge gained at the price of exposing yourself?

Brautigan slowed. As she did, the distress-call alarm battered eardrums. In the other control chair, Lieutenant Mahmoud Sa'id thrust a slim finger into his ear and worked it around.

"They really didn't have to shout."

"Maybe they're really in trouble?"

"*Audacious* doesn't get into trouble. The Djinn could rebuild her in space if he had to."

"You spaceborn are all alike. I suppose it's the variable gravity. Gives your brain cells funny shapes."

Sa'id made a gesture of flicking away filth. The distress-call alarm faded, to be replaced by the normal ship-to-ship signal. "So they want to talk," Sa'id muttered. "Any bets that it'll be Commander Marder?"

"Stop trying to redistribute the wealth and answer the nice lady, Mahmoud."

"Aye-aye, Captain."

Audacious was at the extreme outer limit of screen-signal range, or what should have been the range for most ships the size of *Brautigan*. But the survey ship had only lost her Stoneman drive, not her Jump-capable computers. That let her perform observation missions herself, as well as supplying manned and tending unmanned observatories. It also came in handy for enhancing weak visual signals.

Pocher studied the face wobbling and wavering in the middle of the screen. Too long and too large featured for beauty, it was too striking to be called plain. The long neck half exposed by the open Alliance uniform shirt was the best feature.

"Hello, Commander. Do you need help, or were you worried about us?"

"You were a mystery, then you were out of place. We don't claim the system, but guess who gets the blame if we don't investigate and somebody does get hurt?"

"Nobody's hurt," Pocher said. "We've just done all the survey and astronomical work anybody could think up. So the Navy's borrowed us for a week or two."

Marder put on a look of horror. "They called you up?"

"Can you imagine the Navy taking over our pay? We're just as reserve as ever."

"Much more congenial, I'm sure."

Commander Marder now seemed to be sharing the screen with three or four other faces. Pocher thought of interference, then remembered the cramped auxiliary stations aboard Alliance ships. They had to pack fighting power equal to Federation or Baernoi opponents into a third less space. Matching sizes as well would have given the shipyards of the Pentarchy a virtual monopoly of the Navy, and the rest of the Alliance had enough influence to at least prevent that.

"Speaking of congenial, Commander, do you people have an updated junk count of this area? We can provide one, if you want."

Pocher knew Marder hesitated before answering and thought one of the faces behind her frowned. Alliance Intelligence or just a hyperdriven patriot? Certainly Marder's answer was no surprise.

"We've been making one as we go, but thanks. Can we offer any cabin stores?"

Pocher shook his head as if this meant no more than the offer of an unwanted drink. "We're pretty well off, for a small crew."

"I suppose not everything intended for the observatory mess was unloaded?"

Pocher feigned indignation. "Everything listed for the

observatory mess was unloaded. Of course, we didn't triplecheck the accuracy of the listing. . . ."

"Remind me never to let you be supply officer aboard any ship of mine," Marder said.

Sa'id glared, but Pocher's palms-down gesture stopped anything more. Sa'id's indignation was understandable: his province of Riftwell had largely been settled by the descendants of refugees from planets that had gone over to the Alliance. An Alliance officer joking about Federation officers turning their colors was no joke to him.

Give him another year, and he'll think the same way about the Bonsai Squadron as us old Victorians. Meanwhile, I can live with a little too much patriotism better than I can live without him.

"So we can report you're on Federation survey business and need no assistance?"

"Firm and logged. I suppose we can report you're on Alliance Navy business and don't need any, either?"

"Any day *Audacious* needs help from a retired survey ship, I turn in my uniform."

"But then what will you wear, Commander?"

"Come to Eden and find out, if you can save the fare on what the observatory pays you. Godspeed and good sailing, Kurt."

"Safe voyaging, Commander."

A lifeboat's radar could have detected the sudden acceleration as *Audacious* fed power to her drive fields. From velocity matching *Brautigan*'s, *Audacious* picked up two hundred kilometers a second in less than a minute. She raced off, radar and thermal signatures fading almost at the same time.

Pocher wiped his forehead, then opened his tunic and wiped his neck and throat.

"Here." Sa'id handed him a hot cloth from the dispenser beside his couch. "Shall I dial a drink?"

"Temptation, get thee behind me—but not until tomorrow morning at the earliest." Pocher finished mopping. "Call up the record of their sensors, my friend. Let's see what they could have learned."

The playback was encouraging. "It looks like there's no way they could have learned the tender's gone. What do you think?"

"I'm not quite that optimistic. Say, 93 percent probability we're clear."

"I can live with that. Better than I can with not knowing what Louis found. Ask him for a maximum-security transmission—code, scramble, squirt, tight-beam, the works."

"On the way, Kurt."

The conference room in Paul Leray's cabin would have made a good closet for one of the Pentarchy's lesser aristocrats. Even with only Leray and Marder at the table, it was a good thing that they were friendly.

Actually, aristocrats didn't let clothes accumulate long enough to need big closets. After they'd worn something a dozen times or so, it went on its way: casuals to the recycler, permanent formals to the poor—like a son's spaceborn roommate, on leave from the Academy and invited oh so graciously to call their home his own . . .

Loyalty and fact told Leray that the Alliance was needed, if only to keep the Federation honest. But who was to keep the Alliance's rulers honest? And how, when humans couldn't afford to let the Baernoi gain any advantage while they settled their own affairs?

He punched up the sensor readings from the approach to *Brautigan* and moved to where Marder could put an arm around him if she wanted to. She did. She also rummaged in her shoulder bag and pulled out a flask.

"Brandy, Paul?"

"No."

"I told you not to keep at me."

"I didn't say a thing."

"You managed to put a whole lecture into the word *no*. Have you ever thought of going to work for Intelligence as a code expert?"

Her arm tightened as he stiffened. "Jo, your sense of humor is going, along with everything else."

"Not everything, surely, or do you have any complaints in that area?"

"We can find out—later."

His own arm tightened. *Jo may pull through after all. If I can just keep the drinking off the next assessment.*

The amber brandy settled quietly in two glasses as they

studied the sensor records. Finally Leray blanked the screen and looked at Marder.

"They're flying light."

"Almost certainly. Very light. They're not carrying any of the robot observatories or a lab pod, that's certain."

"I think they're even lighter than that."

"No tender?"

"What else would account for those figures? That tender weighs twelve tons. Everything else they could unload doesn't add up to more than ten."

"Maybe they came out with no tender."

"Into the asteroid belt? I can't think of anything worth the risks that wouldn't need the tender."

"A survey for a base asteroid?"

"At least. Remember, two of the Fed's other in-system ships haven't been sighted for a week. Three ships roaming around loose, one of them survey equipped. That adds up to more than just looking for the right-sized rock. I think they want to find out if we have any people out in the asteroids and make them nervous if we do."

"That's for Intelligence?"

"Why not?" He laid his cheek against hers. "It isn't too often that we can look good to Intelligence without giving them something they'll abuse. If they're playing games in the asteroids, maybe they'll be careful and not get their people killed. If they aren't, maybe they'll think twice before starting."

"You think of everything, Paul."

"Sarcasm is not your best garb, Jo. I just thought of something more. Recommend that we make another offer of in-system ships. If the Federation's doing something legitimate, maybe we can work together. Learn more about them, of course, but also build good will."

"And if they're doing something else?"

"We can use the ships to watch them. The old safety-in-space argument we just used on *Brautigan*."

"Mmmm," Marder said. She poured another glassful, from a flask that sounded half empty already. She wiped an amber trickle from her lower lip with the back of one long-fingered hand and raised the glass.

"To honest starmen. May we embarrass all the people who want to use our ships like chess pieces, until they let us go about our business." She kissed him, a kiss that still tasted more of Jo than brandy. "Paul, don't let me drink alone."

On the main screen on *Brautigan*'s bridge, the asteroid grew. Its ragged southern hemisphere crept off the screen entirely, then the camera zoomed in on a crack just north of what could loosely be called the equator.

"This asteroid has the average high metallic content of asteroids of Type URT in the Victoria system," Louis Ferraro's recorded voice said. "Therefore the initial metallic signature in the area of this crack was not conclusive evidence of artificial presence."

"God spare us," Sa'id muttered. "I have known five people who used that term, and I liked none of them."

"Well, Louis is not exactly in love with either of us," Pocher said. "This mission was about as much fun for him as the Hivers were for Eden. But he's doing his job."

"And explaining it at great length, but—oh, very well. I will be quiet."

"I am so grateful."

The camera now crawled into the crack, the view half obscured by puffs of gas from the maneuvering jets. Then, suddenly, the crack wasn't a crack anymore.

"God spare us," Sa'id repeated, in quite a different tone. "That is a Baernoi depot."

Ferraro's voice continued with monotonous detail, giving dimensions to the centimeter, percentages of worked and natural surfaces to the fourth decimal place, and a great deal more data already recorded in *Brautigan*'s computers.

"The depot had been stripped of all consumables and movable equipment," Ferraro concluded. "However, the remaining tie-downs and racks were of mixed Merishi and Baernoi manufacture. The Merishi material was predominantly human-export models. I have tried to obtain samples of all remaining equipment for metallurgical analysis, but the number-three waldo appears to be malfunctioning.

"I will try to repair it or, alternatively, use the number-two. If I cannot do either, I will EVA to obtain the necessary samples. Before I attempt to obtain samples, I will put a copy of this intelligence into a courier pod and discharge it.

"Request acknowledgment and instructions. Ferraro out."

This time Sa'id invoked God blasphemously and loudly. "The fool!" he concluded.

"No, just wrong," Pocher said. EVA by a man in a solo ship was strictly forbidden, except in an emergency. Ferraro probably thought this was an emergency. If *Audacious* started breathing down their necks, maybe it would be. Right now, though . . .

"*Brautigan* to Ferraro," Pocher began recording. "Acknowledging your transmission. Well done, but negative on the EVA. Repeat, negative on the EVA. Wait for further contact before 1240. Repeat, we will make further contact before 1240. Pocher out.

"Send that five minutes ago, then start powering up for a speed run."

"Black down?"

"You got it. I don't want the toilet flushing after we hit the power. *Audacious* may not be in a mood to chase us."

"And if she is?" Sa'id asked.

"We'll have to decide if it's time to show the ECM and decoys."

"It might not be a bad idea, anyway, to show people that this 'survey ship' can take care of herself."

"If there's a crisis, we'll have plenty of chances. We don't want to cause the crisis by showing off. That can look like an attack if our friend Leray has a heavy trigger finger."

"Supposing he does not, and we arrive safely?"

"We make the rendezvous in the radar shadow of the asteroid. Then we see if it's worth taking time for the samples, while everything heads for Victoria on tight-beam."

"You forgot listening to Louis take five minutes to get around to thanking us."

"I'll bet more like two minutes. He did a damned good job, and I'm going to tell him so. That should sweeten him up."

Sa'id muttered again, probably unprintably. "Jealous, Mahmoud?" Pocher asked.

"Of Ferraro? You insult me."

"Good. Louis is so damned efficient he'd be boring inside of a month. You, on the other hand . . ."

"My appreciation of your praise knows no bounds."

"Express it by setting up the power plant and blacking us

down," Pocher said as he fed the message to Ferraro into the communications module.

His years of active duty had given him much useful experience, but this was his first time for ordering someone under his command into danger. Given a choice, he'd be perfectly willing for it to be his last.

Eleven

The general alarm hooted as Candice Shores finished soaping herself. By sheer reflex she stabbed for the shower button. The overhead fixture produced only a series of rude noises. She'd forgotten that the new Camp Aounda's showers still lacked running water.

She poured the bucket over herself, grabbed a towel, and darted out of the stall. Lieutenant Halso in the next stall did the same. They collided and went down, dumping Halso's bucket of water on the floor and Shores's clothes into the puddle.

Shores looked profanely at Halso. Halso had the decency to blush.

Shores's towel was dry and her jacket not completely soaked. She improvised underwear from the towel and pulled on the jacket. Halso offered a pair of pants. The two officers didn't match in any dimension, but the pants at least stayed on, which gave Shores a little more dignity.

As she opened the bathhouse door, the alarm rose to an ear-torturing warble, then died. A human voice replaced it.

"All personnel to security action stations. All personnel to security action stations. We have a civilian demonstration in progress, bearing 130 from HQ, 200 meters outside the Camp perimeter."

"What are they demonstrating?" someone muttered, as Shores sprinted past. "If it's refrigerators, I'll buy one. Haven't had a cold beer since we moved out from Fort Stafford."

Shores began to wish she'd put on her boots, soaked or

not. They'd protect her feet from gravel cuts that might easily become mite infested. Mite foot was not her preferred method of losing Scout Company.

Two hours before, the main screen in *Shenandoah*'s Auxiliary Combat Center had shown the kaleidoscopic starscape of a Jump. Stars danced and swirled across the screen, their fire trails dazzling even with filters turned up, the colors bearing no relation to the normal colors of stars.

Experts had argued for centuries whether the color shift lay in the Jump or in the minds of the observers. Even comprehensive brain scans of crews aboard Jumping ships hadn't settled the question.

Commander Bogdanov reflected that it was easier for him not to worry about the matter. Both the stars and the human brain were the work of God, and people were in God's care as much during a Jump as at any other time.

Of course, they should also be under the care of a good navigator, like Lieutenant Commander Welch. Not like the navigator of the transport taking Bogdanov out to his first command, who took eight hours to find that they were where they were supposed to be.

That might not have been so unpleasant, if he hadn't been one of the people who found *Lackey* after she stayed in Jump so long her Stoneman Drive burned out. At least half the crew must have taken immediately lethal doses of radiation. Many of the rest hadn't objected to ending their own lives. Those whose beliefs or duty to investigate what had gone wrong kept them alive until the radiation exposure killed them slowly were not a pleasant sight.

Shenandoah wasn't going to suffer even minor inconvenience. Welch had their position fixed in the Victoria system within half an hour after testing the computer. An hour after the Jump, Victoria was centered in all screens.

Then the stars vanished, and Captain Liddell appeared, announcing a squadron alert.

"Just for practice, people. But if anybody is watching, we want to show them we're ready. So let's get it right the first time."

Bogdanov shifted uncomfortably. Centuries of ergonomics still hadn't produced command chairs equally comfortable for all the size of human beings aboard *Shenandoah*.

Bogdanov, nearly the tallest, usually felt cramped. Ten meters away, Petty Officer Wangla seemed to be swallowed in a chair of the same size.

"Screen 3, formation display," Bogdanov said. The screen on his console lost its starscape, turned into a holographic display, and showed the squadron in formation.

Shenandoah led. To either side and slightly behind were two shuttles, simulating the light or scout cruisers that would normally hold the position. The two transports followed in *Shenandoah*'s wake, with light cruiser *Cooney* bringing up the rear.

"Maximum scale on display," Bogdanov added. The gold flecks that were ships shrank to pinpoints and a new one appeared well out ahead of the flagship. Light cruiser *Welitsch* rode sensor point a thousand kilometers ahead, free to scan, report, and evade or attack once she'd reported.

"Display intervals."

Figures danced slowly across the screen. Bogdanov nodded approvingly. Eighty-six kilometers was the shortest interval between any two ships. That was the two transports, least likely to need to use their sensors or their modest weapons suite. In fact, Bogdanov remembered that *Pucinski* had so much equipment riding her outer hull in pods that she couldn't use any of her weapons.

Bogdanov watched the figures superimposed on the lights for a couple of minutes, then ordered the starscape back. He signaled for a cup of tea, content with the squadron's performance. Any clown could start at the right interval. The good shiphandler would maintain it as long as ordered.

The expert shiphandler would maintain it as long as necessary, adjusting it without orders. The expert's ship would ride through a battle able to fire, maneuver, and evade anything from hostile missile strikes to stray fragments of friendly ships that hadn't been so well handled.

Bogdanov was sipping his tea when the contact warning sounded. He preserved both his reputation and his tea by setting it down before calling: "Contact display."

"Repeating from main sensors," came the computer's polite contralto. Something like a distant candlefly appeared at the very edge of the screen—the very edge of the squadron's linked sensors, too—holding position. Bogdanov had the captain on the intercom by the time the computer had finished the standard analysis and interrogation of the contact. The verdict came up on the screen as Liddell's voice sounded in his ears.

"UNIDENTIFIED." The human and computer contraltos were a duet.

"Recommendation, Commander?" the human voice continued.

"Battle Stations."

The alarm sounded before Bogdanov could catch his breath. Liddell's hand must have been hovering millimeters above the switch plate—one of the few entirely manual switches aboard the ship. Computers could evaluate whether an alarm should be sounded; the actual order to sound it had to come from a human throat or hand.

The alarm gong echoed through the ACC. The main hatch slid shut. The armored hatch followed. The compartment was completely sealed by the time the all-hands signal blared.

"All hands, all hands. Battle Alert! Battle Alert! All hands, man your battle stations. This is not a drill. Repeat, this is not a drill!"

Candice Shores studied the demonstrators as she lay in the ditch beside Major Kufir, the exec of First Battalion. The improvised CP was closer to the demonstration than they'd expected, but neither wanted to move. They had good communication and good observation of the enemy. They also had no intention of letting the enemy see them withdraw.

In fact, Shores was having second thoughts about calling the demonstrators "the enemy" at all. They were no more than thirty men and women, in all the sizes and colors of Victoria Dominion's population, wearing scruffy earth-toned clothes and desert boots.

At least they looked scruffy from fifty meters. Shores reminded herself that clothing for Victoria's sand and mite-laden bush made you look like a shacker from some kinder planet.

"How did they get into the base area?" Shores asked.

"They came in the civilian bus," Kufir replied. "It seems that an extra crew was expected, to open another drilling site. The driver gave the authorized call sign and landed in the correct place."

Kufir pointed to a lifter bus squatting a hundred meters beyond the demonstrators. "When they came out, they were carrying shoulder bags and tool kits, just as expected. They marched up to the sensor limit, pulled their signs and banners out of the bags, and formed up as you see them."

Shores raised her glasses. The signs and banners looked new and neatly lettered. She read "NO BASE FOR REPRESSION," "REGULARS GO HOME," "STARTALK—SACRED LANDS." As she tried to make out a fourth slogan, its banner popped loose from one pole and streamed out like a flag. Kufir snorted with laughter as the demonstrators wrestled it under control.

A section from HQ Platoon scrambled down into the ditch beside the two officers. Shores noted that they wore full combat gear, with grenades as well as magazines in their bandoliers.

Kufir sat up and brushed the grit from his trousers. "Captain, I appreciate your help with the personal reconnaissance. My plan is to move one platoon of D Company to the bus and investigate the driver. He's either guilty of abetting trespass or the demonstrators are guilty of kidnaping as well as trespassing.

"A Company will move to place the civilian work crew under surveillance."

"They haven't done anything," Shores pointed out.

"Not yet," Kufir said. His tone implied that they might start sacrificing babies to the Great Sandscrabbler if they weren't watched every minute.

"Companies B, C, and E will hold the base perimeter. Your Scouts will be our reserve. I want one platoon ready to move out when D Company goes for the bus. It's a good thing you were doing security exercises just a few days ago."

It was, but for reasons Shores wasn't going to mention to Kufir. With the First Battalion CO still in Kellysburg, Kufir was senior officer at Camp Aounda—and he was notoriously hard-nosed in dealing with uncooperative civilians.

Scout Company's recent security exercises would certainly save trouble. They might save lives.

Lance Corporal Sklarinsky tramped up. He was carrying miscellaneous clothes and complete combat gear over one shoulder, a multisensor pack under the other arm. "Here, Captain."

He handed the clothes and gear to Shores, then dropped the sensor pack at Kufir's feet.

"Thanks, Sklarinsky."

"Thank the Top and Lieutenant Halso. Zimmer thought somebody ought to run the sensor pack out here. Halso showed up with the rest of the stuff when I was about ten meters out the door. Top called me back."

"Those sensors had a higher priority," Kufir said.

Sklarinsky's mutter wasn't audible, and Kufir would probably have been deaf to it anyway. Mere battalion execs didn't question the decisions of Raoul Zimmer, who had enlisted from Pied Noir before either Shores or Kufir was born.

Have to do something nice for the Top. He's thought of both my arse and my dignity, and how hard it is to preserve the second when the first is waving in the breeze.

"Two Mark 91-Ds, Mark 48 warheads," Brigitte Tachin said.

"Two Mark 91-Ds, Mark 48 warheads," Warrant Officer Nishimura muttered.

Nishimura should be repeating loud and clear, but with the sequence continuing, Tachin would leave him to Commander Zubova.

"Check readiness, Bus 29," Tachin ordered.

"Checking readiness on Bus 29," Nishimura replied, loud, clear, and correctly.

"Bus 29 ready for loading," Tachin, Nishimura, the computer's voice, and the displays all said at once.

"Load selected and ready for Bus 29, Commander," Tachin said, turning slightly toward Zubova.

"Full attention on the board, Lieutenant," Zubova said. "That's about ten megatons worth of warheads you've got lined up. You don't want an electron to wiggle without you noticing it."

Ten megatons, which may actually be killing people inside of an hour. Somehow it's different when you have that knowledge for the first time.

"Yes, ma'am. Permission to initiate loading sequence for Bus 29."

"Permission granted."

"Initiate loading sequence," Tachin said. Her fingers and Nishimura's hovered over switch plates, but the computer needed no help. READY lights changed from red to green as if a magic wand had passed over the board and the mechanical telltales flipped up.

"Bus 29 loaded. Beginning third circuit check."

No matter how many megatons we load into that bus, if we can't arm them, all we have is a very expensive kinetic-energy round.

The expense of building one of *Shenandoah*'s thirty warhead buses was not going to be wasted. All arming circuits showed green and up.

"Weapons Control to Launcher Control. Permission to load Bus 29."

"Permission granted."

It was Charles Longman. He sounded as nervous about doing it for real as she did—or was it just fear of his precious machinery letting him down?

Tachin remembered admonitions from her ethics teacher, Mother Yvonne: "Everybody deserves a little charity, until we know whether they deserve much or whether only God could show it."

"Initiating launcher loading of Bus 29," Tachin said.

"What launcher?" Zubova snapped.

"Launcher Two," Longman came back.

"Acknowledged. Bus 29 loading aboard Launcher Two—three, two, one, mark!"

Lights and telltales marked Bus 29's orderly progress out of the magazine, through the armored double airlock, and into the launcher. When the displays signaled that the Bus was in the hands of Launcher Control, Tachin felt like slumping in her seat.

"Careful about relaxing, ma'am," Nishimura said. "That model of chair, you can trigger the pod release if you lean the wrong way."

The control chairs at Weapons Primary had self-enclosing emergency pods with short-duration life-support systems. For public consumption, they were supposed to keep people who had to stay at their posts alive long enough for rescue.

Weapons, Combat Center, and Engineering people knew otherwise. The pods let them fly and fight their ship until she was vaporized or came apart around them. They might have to do it with the bodies of their shipmates floating centimeters from their pods, but they knew that too well to talk about it.

"Very careful," Zubova added. "Remember, Launcher Control's going to be doing a final systems check before pushing our bus out the door. When they relay it to you, you want to spot any anomalies about one picosecond after they show."

"Yes, ma'am." Tachin blinked her eyes, hoping they were stinging from sweat.

"Easy, Lieutenant. If you ever want a few minutes of low comedy, let me show you a film of one of my early simulator sessions. I made about as many mistakes as one human being can with only one mouth, two eyes, and two hands."

The confidential tone eased the tightness across Tachin's shoulders. "Do you think we're going to have to shoot?"

"I'm only a Weapons Officer, not a clairvoyant. So are you. Remember the difference."

As reproaches went, it was one Tachin could live with. She didn't miss a bit of data as Longman's final check of Bus 29 came across her board.

Captain Shores was lying down again, contemplating the demonstrators. She was also enjoying the greater dignity of full clothing and gear and the greater comfort of the roof of Building 12. Its fiber panels hadn't been sand scoured long enough to pit or roughen, and the air-filter housing provided concealment and a windbreak. It was a bit crowded with Shores, Sklarinsky, and two snipers from D Company, but compared to being half dressed in a ditch it was a luxury billet.

Shores finished her study of the demonstration, handed her glasses to Sklarinsky, and crawled across the roof to the rear of Building 12. It was shaped like a U, with the top toward HQ in the center of the base. Inside the U, 3rd Platoon of Scout Company was drawn up, under the eye of Sergeant Major Zimmer.

"Any change?" Zimmer called.

"Somebody sang a couple of songs. Couldn't make out the words. Otherwise nothing. They haven't even moved."

"How's the D platoon?"

That was the leader of 3rd Platoon, a young and conscientious master sergeant.

"All formed up on the perimeter road," Shores replied. "A lifter just unloaded a pallet of ammo boxes. Probably foam and gas grenades."

"Let's hope that's all we need," the sergeant muttered.

"Kufir knows doctrine," Shores added. *He may even follow it.* "I wish I thought those demonstrators knew what they were doing. Maybe we should run them through our next security exercise, so they can do a more convincing job next time."

That got a short laugh from everybody except the sergeant who still seemed to be looking for loose connections on grenade launchers or camouflage-disrupting makeup. Shores was just about to call the sergeant over when Sklarinsky shouted.

"Captain, the Ds are moving!"

Through her glasses, Shores saw the D Company platoon moving out toward the demonstrators. They had their pulsers at high port, their helmets buttoned up, and bandoliers loaded with grenades draped over their vests.

The demonstrators stood their ground. Switching frequencies, Shores heard them start chanting.

"We hold this sacred ground, not the regulars. We hold this sacred ground, not the regulars. We—"

"Attention, attention!" boomed the amplified voice of the platoon leader. "You are trespassing on a military reservation. You are also interfering with humanitarian assistance to the crew of your lifter."

"He doesn't need any assistance," several people shouted. A woman added, "He is one with us."

That made the pilot an accessory rather than a victim. Bad luck for him, good luck for the others. Kidnaping and holding hostages were far more serious offenses than trespassing.

"We can't take your word for that," the platoon leader shouted. "Clear the way to the lifter, please." Shores saw a hand signal send a team out on either side, to unsling and raise pulsers.

She also saw a squat shape rise over the crest of the ridge beyond the demonstrators. It grew into a lifter, slowed, stopped twenty meters up, and began to descend on the far side of the landing area.

Kufir's voice slammed into Shores's ears like a handball. "Reserve platoon, move out on the double! The bastards are bringing up reinforcements!"

Shores was already swinging over the edge of the roof. She landed spring-legged as Kufir's voice faded.

For once she agreed with the major. When facing an equal or superior force, even stupid people were usually cautious. Outnumbering the other side, even intelligent people could expect to get away with something stupid. When something stupid could get people killed . . .

Shores bounced to her feet, caught a bandolier as Zimmer tossed it, and sprinted for the command lifter.

Mahoney sat crosslegged on the deck of the Training Office. He'd given up hoping to be comfortable, not in full damage-control gear. Now he was trying to keep his legs functional. He was surprised at how many lumps the rug had developed since it was laid, lumps that threatened to cut off the circulation, pinch the nerves, and dislocate the joints in his legs.

Another shift of position landed him on the biggest lump of all. Mahoney sighed and leaned back against the bulkhead. The intercom squawked, then the squawks turned into words.

"All hands, all hands. We are launching busses. All damage-control parties test your gear. Repeat, all damage-control parties who have not tested your personal equipment, do so immediately."

Mahoney met Netsch's eyes. They implied a smile on the rest of her face, hidden by the mask. "If we *did* want to test our equipment, there's hardly room," she said. "Muscle cramps don't make me enthusiastic."

"Me neither. Okay, people, button up, check, and report."

The eight people of the Training Division's damage-control party pulled their helmets down and their gloves on. One by one they tested their com gear, both plug-in and radio, then turned on the air supply.

Yakov's helmet promptly started bulging and he began waving his arms frantically. Netsch grabbed one arm, reached in past it, popped the seals on the helmet, and adjusted the valve on the air supply. It went right on hissing.

"Defective feed valve, damnit!" Netsch snapped. "I'll write it up. Yakov, if this gets real, duck into Compartment 523."

"Okay, Chief."

They settled down to wait for further developments, whether they came as announcements or not. Mahoney knew that Captain Liddell took keeping her crew informed as a sacred trust. But she was now commanding a capital ship and a squadron, and she might be a little too busy to play bulletin service.

The first thing Damage Control Party 43 might know about a real situation could be a shock wave tearing through the structure of First Midships. Mahoney could imagine the nearest simulator ripping loose from its base, flying across the compartment, crushing Netsch into red paste, breaking Mahoney's arm . . .

He reminded himself that there was a fine line between using imagination to increase your alertness and abusing it until you wore yourself out. Adrenalin depletion would do no good. Checking the anchoring of the simulator rigs might help.

"Everybody except Yakov reports equipment nominal," Netsch said.

"Good. I'll report in, while the rest of you check the anchoring of the simulator rigs."

"Aye-aye, sir," Netsch said, before anyone could protest. "Damage-Control Stations are not a break from duty, people. Anyone who thinks otherwise had better pray I don't find out who they are."

The other six were down on their hands and knees by the time Mahoney had jacked into the intercom to report Party 43's condition.

As Shores reached the command lifter, the pilot threw the door open. She ducked inside, then popped her head inside the top turret. The sensors, sights, and 22-mm gun breech left just enough room for her helmeted head.

She held on as the lifter rose. It drifted out of the courtyard in a nose-high attitude, then climbed to avoid blasting the platoon with dust and gravel.

The platoon was already double-timing it toward the road as the lifter reached two hundred meters. They ran in a double column, pulsers at high port, sergeant in the lead, Zimmer bringing up the rear. Shores began a communications check with the other four platoons of Scout Company. The check with the engaged platoon could wait; they had their hands and circuits full for now.

By the time Shores knew she had good communication

with all five platoons, she also knew that Kufir had good communication with *her*. Not surprising, over this short distance. Even Victoria's weather needed more than a kilometer to work in. But having Kufir off the circuit might be handy, if the situation didn't require muscle so much as a tolerance for boredom and badly done protest songs.

"Hey, isn't that Khasim the Cook in the other lifter?" the pilot asked.

Shores shifted the sights. "Yeah. And that's his wife climbing out of it. What's going on?" Company commanders weren't senior enough to have to pretend infallibility.

"Maybe he bought a new lifter with all the money he's been making off the civvies?" the copilot asked.

"New? That thing's a piece of junk even for this Mithras-denying desert!" the pilot replied.

Khasim the Cook was the son of a Victorian mother and a Riftwell father, two meters and 125 kilos of amiability except when someone tried to sell him inferior ingredients. He made a respectable living flying meals and other portable amenities out to mining camps, isolated settlements, construction crews, and anybody else cut off by Victoria's deserts from the local simulation of civilization.

That didn't explain what he was doing here now, still less why he'd been allowed to fly in and land after the alert.

Khasim's wife, Fatima, was almost as familiar a sight as Khasim himself. A good meter eighty and spectacularly proportioned, she was now loping across the space between the two lifters. Under her arm she carried what Shores devoutly hoped was not a shotgun. Some of the demonstrators turned around to watch her progress, but none of them moved.

She reached the lifter-bus, stuck her head in the open door, and seemed to be talking with somebody there. Some of the demonstrators who'd turned around finally moved. They ran to the lifter and reached for Fatima.

The shotgun swung around, somebody struck it up, and it went off. Instantly the D Company platoon stopped and deployed, their leader falling back to stand in the middle of the line. Shores's mouth went dry.

Then Khasim himself burst out of his lifter. In one hand he carried a meter-long ladle, in the other a metal-bladed stirrer as tall as he was. He charged the demonstrators, brandishing both weapons until they blurred.

The next two minutes proved that numerical superiority wasn't always necessary for overawing rioters. Khasim and his kitchen arsenal did the job as thoroughly as the whole First Battalion could have done. The ladle and the paddle cracked heads, stung knuckles, elbows, and shoulders, made men double up and roll on the ground clutching at their groins. Before the two minutes were up, the whole thirty-odd demonstrators were in headlong flight, straight toward the deployed D Company platoon.

"D Company platoon," Shores called. "Open your ranks and let those poor clowns through. 3rd Platoon, clear the road and let them by if they keep running. Close in when they stop."

Both platoon leaders treated Shores as the SOP; neither wasted time consulting with Kufir. The deployed platoon swung open like the two halves of a door, and the demonstrators stampeded through the gap.

By the time they reached the Scout Company platoon, it was lined up on either side of the road like a guard of honor. The demonstrators were beginning to trail stragglers, and as they passed the platoon, two of these stumbled and fell.

Without orders, Zimmer waved two troopers forward to help the fallen. From their lack of resistance, Shores suspected that they'd changed their minds about regulars. Baernoi strike commandos would have looked better than Khasim!

"Let's wrap this up," Shores said. "Hover fifty meters above the demonstrators and turn on the loudspeakers." She switched circuits. "So far so good, people. End this without anymore bloodshed, and it'll be even better. Top, would you mind having a little talk with our friend Khasim?"

"On the way, Captain."

Twelve

"All buses launched," Charles Longman repeated. "All launches nominal. Beginning electronic checks." He nodded to Master Chief Electrician Flora Menambres. She could train anything with a chip in it to sing the Baernoi Hymn of War.

The electronic checks of the launcher system would take at least two minutes. Longman wouldn't have minded if they took two hours. Long enough, anyway, for him to wash the sweat off with a shower, preferably with a friend, and take a cup or stick of something. Longman didn't much care what it was, how strong, or whether it was legal. He wanted to spend an hour or two in puddle mode.

No chance of that, in the middle of a live Alert One. As a substitute, he conjured up a picture of the buses he'd just finished launching.

Twelve had gone out, each with its own particular combination of long-range seekers, short-range defenders, decoys, jammers, and God and Weapons only knew what else. All twelve now formed a cluster around *Shen*, holding formation on her but ready to receive commands for independent action.

Three-quarters of the battlecruiser's weapons load was still aboard, ready to be fed into the launchers. If the enemy didn't force *Shenandoah* to raise her shields, the individually programmed and guided weapons would be substantially more accurate than the ones aboard the buses.

But if the shields went up, then any missile aboard *Shenandoah* had to stay aboard until the shields went down again. The shields' property of repelling anything with mass worked both ways. A shield would even contain a fusion explosion until it destroyed the ship's shield generator.

The buses also had dead-man switches that turned them into vengeful demons if *Shenandoah*'s enemies were too strong for her. Their drives were designed for high speed and short life; if their last command was to chase an enemy ship, that ship was going to be well and truly chased.

Longman shivered. He'd tried to calm himself by reviewing the role of his launchers in *Shenandoah*'s tactics. He'd only managed to bring himself back to the edge of his nerves by thinking about the buses' deadly loads.

He still couldn't put off taking the Weapons test much longer without Aunt Diana taking notice. But if he took it and failed, everybody up in the family tree would throw sticks and nuts at him.

Oh, it's going to be fun either way!

"Electronics check completed," Menambres said. "Launcher Three had a power surge launching Bus 22. The circuit breakers show some deterioration."

"Log them and bring up the board for the mechanical checks," Longman said.

"Aye-aye, sir."

Longman took a deep breath. The job wasn't what his nerves needed, but it was better than nothing.

Mikhail Kornilov held out his glass as Indira Chatterje raised the jug of fruit juice.

They clinked glasses. "To your recovery, and may you have no patients when you are ready to deal with them again," Kornilov said.

"You're an optimist, Mikhail," the doctor said. "I thought that was a bad thing for a general to be." But her smile lit up the whole visible side of her face.

"Surely you've had surgical cases where you expected no problems but prepared for them anyway?"

"Every one, since I was a resident."

"Then you understand at least one principle of combat command," Kornilov said. "Let's hope Markee Hinman understands it as well."

In two days Chatterje was leaving medical matters in Victoria Command to her deputy and going back on the operating table, for a synopt implant and a regen on her major scars. When she got out of bed after that, Kornilov hoped she'd take off the mask, at least when they were alone. His assurances that he'd seen far worse sights than the damaged half of her face had collided with her pride.

The chime on the desk terminal sounded, soft but insistent. Then a sitar began to play, just as insistent and much louder. To Kornilov it sounded like a giant earnester singing badly off-key. Perhaps that was why Indira had programmed the terminal with that signal; it was almost impossible to ignore.

Chatterje slapped the remote switch. The screen swiveled and displayed the codes for a Commanders' Confidential Bulletin.

"If you want me to leave—" she began.

"Colonels and above are cleared for CCBs, regardless of branch of service," Kornilov reminded her. "All it will mean is you getting the bulletin before the chief of staff."

"I can contain my grief over that," Chatterje said, pulling her legs up onto the sofa and resting her chin on them.

"Maximum print size," Kornilov said. He felt just a little too comfortable to move right now, even if a CCB at this time of the morning probably meant trouble.

The CCB rolled across the screen. *Shenandoah* was in-system, as of five hours ago, but giving no ETA. A demonstration outside Camp Aounda had been broken up without the use of lethal force or military casualties and almost without casualties to the demonstrators.

"Son of a bitch," Kornilov muttered. He hardly expected Captain Liddell to broadcast information that would let the Alliance calculate her squadron's course to Victoria. It would still be nice to have another senior officer to share the burden of being ordered around by the civilians.

So far, most of Victoria Command's preparations had been with Kornilov's authority. The only exception had been preparing the reserve and militia battalions of the Victoria Brigade for the field. That had needed the approval of the Dominion's president, prime minister, governor-general, and Military Council. To do them justice, they had all come through in two days, with only a *pro forma* admonition about "preserving harmonious civil-military relations."

Now that those relations showed signs of becoming discordant, civilians in the chain of command all the way up to the Federation Senate would go on the alert.

Civilian approval was needed to ensure adequate resources for the soldiers. Nor did the Federation appoint to high office the kind of fool who regarded ignorance of military matters as a form of civic virtue.

What still threatened was a longer and more divided chain of command than usual. It could be worse, but it was one reason why Kornilov had given up drinking for the duration. His stomach could endure either vodka or being second-guessed by civilian superiors, but not both.

Kornilov spoke his own code and the chief of staff's. By the time the screen showed a paper-piled desk, the general was seated at the terminal.

Ludmilla Vesey, the deputy chief of staff, peered over the top of the desk. Then she jumped to her feet and saluted.

"I'm sorry, sir. I was getting in my exercises while General Liu's on his way to Camp Aounda."

"No problem, Milla. When did he leave?"

Vesey looked frantically around for her watch before discovering it on her wrist. "0837. He's riding a courier, and I sent an armed shuttle as escort. I've warmed up another to carry the recorder team Weapons Group is sending over. They should be on the way by 1030."

From behind him, Kornilov heard a strangled giggle. Milla Vesey was functioning as usual: twice as fast and probably twice as efficiently as her superior, assuming that lesser minds would be able to fill in the details of what she'd done without help.

If she could stop that—and also stop looking as if her uniforms were both cut and put on in the dark—she might hope for more than a graveyard promotion to colonel.

"Sorry, sir," Vesey said, reading Kornilov's face. "We got word on the riot at 0750. The chief was all ready to lift out by 0800, but I had his pilot stall until I could warm up the escort. By the time he left, the demonstration was over.

"He still didn't have a recorder team, so I asked Intelligence for one. They didn't have any to spare, and neither did Public Information."

Kornilov made a mental note to find out why. If either office was going to behave like a commissar, he wanted plenty of warning. Also the names of possible replacements for both chiefs and a few of their subordinates.

"I knew Weapons Groups had stood down, and their damage-evaluation teams have the right training and equipment. So I called them up, and Nickie Kampfer is sending a team and an AOP. He wanted to send it straight out, but I talked him into waiting for armed transport. They should still be on the way in about ten minutes."

From Fort Stafford to Camp Aounda was about ninety minutes for a shuttle running at its maximum low-altitude speed. "Did the people at the camp make any records?"

"I haven't been able to reach anyone who knows. I told them to at least make audios of all the interrogations and action reports. I thought you'd approve."

Kornilov wanted to crawl down the circuit and kiss Ludmilla Vesey's feet.

"Well done, Colonel Vesey. *Damned* well done. Have Liu report to me as soon as he touches down. The battalion CO, too."

"Right away, sir."

Kornilov blanked the screen and leaned back in the chair. Programmed for Chatterje's fifty kilos, it nearly dumped his hundred-plus on the rug. This time Chatterje didn't strangle her giggle.

"Mikhail, try not to break an arm until I have binocular vision again."

The chimes sounded again. This time Kornilov had the message on screen before the sitar started whining. It was a request to call the chairman of the Military Council.

"The civilians are mobilizing already, I see," he muttered in Russic, then ordered increased circuit security and the chairman's number.

"All lines to this number are currently in use," came a dulcet voice with more than a trace of broad vowels in its Anglic. "Please state your priority, then be ready to record your message."

Kornilov said something he hoped would not be recorded. Chatterje laughed out loud.

"How long is it going to take to identify this bloody bogey?" Captain Liddell muttered.

Not programmed to recognize rhetorical questions, the

computer replied, "Indeterminate time, given the present data."

"Update and display," Liddell said. "Command circuit and display for the exec and navigator, too."

Thirty seconds later the data was on screen and the other two officers were on line. "Smell anything about this profile, Dave?" she asked.

Navigator Welch was *Shen*'s ship-recognition expert. Given two minutes with a bogey's signature, he could make an 80-percent reliable guess about its identity. With visual data, he might need another two minutes with the *Jane*'s file, but then his reliability rose to 90 percent.

Today wasn't Dave Welch's chance to shine. He spent four minutes and a good deal of cranky swearing on the signature before coming up with the same answer as the computer.

Bogdanov said something impolite in Russic. "Thanks, Dave," Liddell put in. "I suspect one of three things: a communications casualty, an outlaw colony ship, or a bandit. No bets on what kind of bandit. We want a better ID on this character."

"Recommend we send *Cooney* for a closer look," Welch said. "Next to us, she's got the best combination of legs and sensors. If we set up a real-time link to her readings, maybe I can make a better-educated guess sooner."

"Reasonable. Pavel?"

"If that ship is fast enough, she could stay below the ID threshold for anybody but us. And we're the best equipped to meet an attack."

"Also reasonable."

Here's where the burden of command reaches about five Gs. Doctrine says the flagship doesn't go barging into unknown-threat situations. The facts say we'd do the best job. Common sense says—what?

Come on, Rosie! Or didn't you want to be a capital-ship skipper as badly as you thought?

"*Cooney* and one of the shuttles. The shuttle won't have the legs to keep up with the cruiser, but she won't need them. Her job is to watch and report. Pavel, punch up the orders and flash them for me. Also punch up a request for a scout cruiser in the first reinforcements for the squadron."

"Not just a scout?"

"No, we'll need something that can—"

"Data update on unidentified ship," the computer said. "Ship now opening range, accelerating rapidly."

"Continuous update on course and acceleration," Liddell said. "Visual mode."

Her screen showed rapidly changing figures. Both Bogdanov and Welch swallowed expletives. Some of the sensor crews weren't as controlled.

"Look at that bastard go!"

"That's a warship!"

"Maybe a merchant ship with a light—"

"Bounce the theories! Nobody can afford to load that big a drive into anything that has to make a profit. Not us, not the Alliance, not the Baernoi, not the Creator."

Liddell let the chatter go on until she judged everyone had relieved the tension, then said, "Quiet in the Combat Center, please."

In the hush, she watched the figures march on. The unidentified ship finally dropped below sensor threshold, moving as fast as *Shenandoah*'s maximum in-system speed and heading straight for the plane of the Victoria system's elliptic.

Liddell's last impulse to open up *Shen*'s drive and run down the bogey vanished. A chase now meant a trivial chance of overtaking the bogey and a nontrivial chance of running into something too big for *Shenandoah*'s unshielded hull to handle.

Starships always cruised, Jumped, and if possible fought well above the plane of the elliptic, where the density of what Philip Stoneman had called "the Creator's leftovers" was higher. The speed of the bogey's departure suggested that she was more than an unidentified warship.

Her captain had to be either desperate, bold, or very knowledgeable about the Victoria system. None of these were characteristics Rose Liddell wanted to see in a possible enemy.

Liddell blanked her screen, took off her helmet, and closed her eyes. As the CC and its perennial sensory overload receded, her thoughts expanded to fill the vacancy. With this expansion came intuition, telling her what to do next.

The original plan had been for the squadron to split. *Pucinski*, the troop transport *Marat*, and one light cruiser were supposed to head for the asteroid belt, pick an asteroid suitable for the Victoria Dockyard, and start converting it. *Shenandoah* and the rest of the squadron were to head straight for Victoria.

Now an unidentified, possibly hostile warship could be roaming the asteroid belt. She might outgun a Federation light cruiser, she could certainly outrun one, and that light cruiser would be the engineers' only protection.

So why not move the whole squadron into the asteroids, and come out only when Victoria Dockyard was ready to move? That could be just a few days, if the engineers were willing to install the drive and navaids first, then go on with the other work once they were underway.

No "ifs" about it. Carving out the dockyard on the move would be a technical challenge, and engineers were addicted to technical challenges.

The authorities on Victoria might not be so happy. Even General Kornilov might prefer the squadron in a ball-of-yarn formation around Victoria.

Liddell couldn't help that. A working dockyard was more important than soothing nerves, even the nerves of prospective superior officers. But she was glad she hadn't sent in a squadron ETA. Now the first Victoria would learn of the change of plans was when *Cooney* brought the news.

Liddell stood up and stretched, ignoring the pain of muscles uncramping too suddenly. Sitting down, she pulled her helmet back on.

"Pavel, signal *Cooney* to rendezvous for visual data transmission and a possible shuttle docking. Everybody else maintain course and speed. As soon as *Cooney* acknowledges, give me an all-hands circuit. There's been a slight change of plans."

"Aye-aye, ma'am."

Thirteen

"Sandstorm coming up, Captain," the lifter's pilot said. "Better let me take over."

Candice Shores muttered a reluctant assent and slid out of the seat. The copilot couldn't hide relief as his regular partner replaced a groundpounder working on her qualifying hours.

"Don't worry, Captain," the pilot added. "We'll angle across the front of this mother and be in clear air inside of an hour. If you're qualified for night flying—"

"I am," Shores said, with more emphasis than tact. She began to wish there were another week or two in the month, for everybody who'd handled the demonstration to calm down and stop snapping at each other. The higher-ups weren't looking for scapegoats—yet—but the amount of interest they were showing in the whole affair was enough to jangle anyone's nerves.

The two days since the demonstration had been too few to unjangle Shores's. Unfortunately, the month had only two more days to run, and she had to get in three more cockpit hours or miss her month's quota toward her pilot's rating.

"Well, you can bring us down at the depot and take us all the way back. You won't need more than a few extra minutes for the month. I can jiggle the log for that much."

"Thanks. Really, I appreciate that," Shores added, realizing that she'd sounded almost petulant.

"No sweat. Hey, what's that off around 290?"

Shores was the first to identify the big command lifter

climbing steadily up from the desert. Its camouflage blended equally well with the hills, the desert, and the rising sandstorm.

The command lifter matched course and speed with Shores's with the ease of expert piloting and extra power. A blinker light flashed from the cockpit.

"Air dock right in front of a sandstorm?" the copilot growled when the message was done. "Who do they think they are?"

"Somebody with enough rank to use an M-476B," Shores said. "Probably too much rank to argue with.

"No need for you to stay docked if they want me over there a while. They can drop me off at the depot when they're through."

"Unless that storm swings wide enough to hit the depot," the pilot put in. "If the pilot's got enough hours to be in a 476, he ought to have enough sense not to try punching through a sandstorm."

"He ought to," the copilot agreed darkly, but he was already maneuvering the lifter to a stable course and altitude. The command lifter's pilot did the rest. In five minutes the docking latches *thunked* into place. The two lifters were now a single flying machine, stable and strong enough to cover any distance under normal flying conditions.

Shores popped the hatch, and the desert wind filled the cockpit. They were too high for mites, so she left her mask off and took a deep breath. Too dry, not too cold, and, above all, fresh. All she missed was the smell of the sea.

She walked out on the lifter's skirt. The fans slowed until she could see the individual blades. A thousand meters below, an ocher patch of mineral salts crept into the center of her field of vision and stayed there.

As she crossed to the skirt of the command lifter, the hatch behind slammed shut and the one ahead opened. She scrambled through it, nearly falling into the red-lit passenger compartment.

"Good evening, ma'am. General Langston will see you now."

A muscular arm lifted her to her feet. She faced Command Master Sergeant Koritz, Langston's combined steward, valet, and bodyguard.

"Thank you, Sergeant. How's the family?"

"I'm trying to talk Serena out of enlistment on a waiver."

"She could always ship out."

Koritz's face hardened. Shores realized she'd hinted that Serena Koritz might want to run away from a combat theater.

"Sorry, Sergeant. I should know you and yours better than that."

"No offense taken, ma'am."

Shores hoped so. There were a number of mysteries about Jacob Koritz, including his reasons for being steward to three successive brigade commanders, but no mystery about what insulting him could do to a junior officer's career.

"Jake," came Langston's voice. "You've got a perfectly good haunch of first lieutenant hanging in the freezer. Lay off Captain Shores."

"Yes, sir. Has the captain dined?"

"Never mind if you have or not, Captain. I haven't, and I'm not going to eat alone. Two warmups, Jake."

"Yes, sir."

Shores slipped aft into the private office. General Langston was sprawled in a red-padded chair, a cup of tea clamped to a console within easy reach. Without rising, he motioned Shores to a folding seat.

They were halfway through fresh cups of tea before Langston started talking. Or, rather, started interrogating Shores. The questions came fast. Fortunately there were few she couldn't answer with at least an "I don't know but I'll find out."

Gradually the questions focused on Major Kufir. Shores thought she was keeping the edge out of her voice fairly well, until Langston suddenly banged his cup down and fixed her with his famous Laser Stare. She'd heard so many tales of it that she'd begun to doubt its existence. She doubted no more.

"Are you hiding something, Captain?"

"No, sir."

"No personal connection with Major Kufir?"

"No, sir."

"I doubt that, Captain."

"If . . ." Shores began, rejected several openly insubordinate replies, and plunged ahead as best she could.

"If Major Kufir is being investigated in connection with the demonstration—"

"That, Captain, is an obvious conclusion. It is also an incorrect one."

"Then could I ask for a little background, sir? Major Kufir is a very aggressive officer, but a highly competent one. Doing anything to him would affect the whole First Battalion. Since Scout Company is currently operating with the battalion—"

"All right. I suppose you're entitled to that much background. But what you're about to hear was a classification about three degrees above Command Secret."

Langston's tone was distinctly warmer. Shores ventured a modest joke.

"Something like 'Commit suicide after hearing'?"

"About that."

Langston poured more tea. "Next incarnation, I'm going to come back on some planet where they grow coffee.

"*Shen* and her squadron are in-system," he began. "*Brautigan* found Baernoi tracks while looking for a dock-yard asteroid. Kornilov's ordered the squadron to cover *Brautigan*. He's also onboard *Cooney*, on his way out to *Shen* for a little planning session.

"I imagine he thinks security for *Brautigan* and a fast, secure planning session are more important than standing on rank. Meanwhile, he's left me running the Army side of Victoria Command, complete with glitches.

"One glitch is finding a safe place to put the chief of staff. He'll need some sort of a paper command, plus a deputy who's expendable as far as other units are concerned."

"You were thinking of Major Kufir?" Shores phrased it as a question, even though she had no doubts.

"Among others. I didn't want to decide until I'd heard you. You're the only officer connected with the demonstration I hadn't talked to. It sounds like you don't consider Major Kufir expendable at this point."

"No, sir, I don't, and it's not just concern for my own company's relations with First Battalion."

"Good, because you won't be operating with First Battalion for the next few weeks. We're shifting Scout Company over to Second Battalion, which is coming up on field-ready. You'll start by playing their opponent in the field-readiness exercises."

Hmm. Colonel Lovis of Second Battalion is somebody

you're grooming for when you take over from Kornilov in Victoria Command. So I have to make him sweat, but lose in the end.

Like the Laser Stare, the small-group politics of provincial garrison's was the subject of a host of rumors. Unlike the Laser Stare, Shores had never doubted the politics. *Valhalla* was a good school for that.

All right, General Langston. I'll go along with that, but only for a price. Such as a few more Command Secrets . . .

"Who's going to be the new chief of staff? Colonel Vesey?"

Langston's cup clattered to the table. Fortunately it was empty. His dark face darkened further.

The general's head jerked. "I suppose you're asking only because you're concerned with the Scouts' relations with HQ?"

"Yes—no, sir." Langston's face remained hard. "At least not entirely. I've never had any problems with General Liu. But I suspect I'd have fewer with Colonel Vesey."

"You and a lot of other people, starting with Kornilov. Although I doubt that I'm telling you anything you don't know."

"Let's say, sir, that both officers have distinctive reputations."

"I prefer you when you're not trying to be tactful," Langston said.

He smiled. "Seriously, Captain, one of the ideas I had was making you deputy in the new command, with the acting rank of major. That new command may not stay entirely paper, and you could handle anything up to half a battalion."

Shores found herself in the rare condition of being not only speechless but blushing. Langston's smile widened.

"I didn't come all the way out here for a highly irregular interrogation just because you were the last witness. You were also the best officer involved in the demonstration. Too good, I decided, to be assigned as damper field for our friend Liu."

Shores managed to get out a coherent, "Thank you, sir."

Three knocks sounded on the door. Sergeant Koritz's voice followed.

"General, the pilot says we can't stay docked more'n another five minutes and still outrun the storm. I figured

Captain Shores would want to take something back to her crew, so I put in another couple warmups."

"How long?"

"Two—no, one minute."

"Thanks, Sergeant," Shores said. She stood up. "With your permission, sir?"

"Good-bye, Captain, and good luck."

Koritz was stuffing the three meals into an insulated shoulder bag when Shores passed forward. After looking around to be sure everyone's eyes were elsewhere, he reached under a panel and pulled out a silvery bottle.

"Another kind of warmup, Captain. God keep you."

A bottle of Koritz's private stock was harder to come by than promotion to field-grade. Shores couldn't find words; all she could do was grin. Koritz grinned and punched the hatch.

Outside, the wind was stronger and throwing fluky gusts from all directions. Shores needed her goggles against the sand, and even then grains crept under the cheek pads.

Braced in the hatch of her own lifter, she watched Langston's command machine undock and slide away into the twilight. Beyond it the stormwall was closer, higher, and darker, except toward the fringes. There the sunset turned the lighter plumes to crimson and virulent pink.

Deep in the sandwall, faint yellow flashes danced furtively. Static electricity, the scientists said. The spirits who rode the storms, the Old Worshipers said.

From a messhall window, it was easy to believe the scientists. When you were riding the same sky as the storm, the Old Worshipers made more sense. Those sandstorms were the real rulers of Victoria's deserts.

Shores scrambled into the lifter and reached for a water bottle as the hatch shut out the storm.

On Rose Liddell's screen, the Alliance scout cruiser shrank rapidly to a pinpoint indistinguishable from the stars. In two more minutes she'd vanished from sight entirely.

Not from *Shenandoah*'s sensors, or the awareness of the electronic warfare boards. They rode herd on the Alliance ship as long as they could, another eight minutes.

"Contact lost," the first lieutenant finally reported.

"Call in the shuttles," Liddell said. With lighter hulls and no shields, they couldn't hold squadron speed above Matter Density 4.0. The Matter Density was already at 2.8 and rising steadily, as the squadron raced toward the plane of the elliptic.

Liddell didn't wait for the acknowledgment before switching her screen to holo mode and starting to evaluate formations for the squadron's approach to the asteroids.

Victoria Command's approval of her initiative in changing course was flattering and useful. Kornilov's coming out for a planning session was even more so—not to mention a hint that nothing was expected to go seriously wrong dirtside in the next ten days.

Neither solved her own problem of sneaking up on *Brautigan* without laying a trail a trainee sensor operator aboard a mining barge could pick up.

Brautigan had been under electronic silence since she reported her find to Victoria. Her full message had still given *Shenandoah*'s computers enough data to work out the supply ship's approximate position. Liddell knew where to go and how soon to turn on her IFF.

How to hide it that she knew where to go? She considered, displayed, and discarded a dozen formations. Which one offered the best combination of protection, ambiguity, and sensor coverage against both bogeys and stray rocks?

They needed the ambiguity. At least one unknown ship in this system had legs and sensors equal to anything in the squadron. Given a clue where *Brautigan* might be, the unknown ship might make an end run around the squadron, then make mischief for *Brautigan*.

Liddell played with her screen until she'd worked out a satisfactory compromise. *Shen* would ride tilted crosswise to her course to give all sensors and launchers a clear field. The two transports tucked in close behind *Welitsch*, positioned to cover *Shen*'s few blind spots. Shuttles docked and their hardworked would be free to catch up on their sleep.

"Shuttles docked," the first lieutenant reported.

"Acknow . . . ledge," Liddell said. It came out that way because she'd looked at the time. Thirty-eight minutes on the displays, to reach a decision that she should have been able to make in five and in combat would have to make in two.

The shuttle crews weren't the only people aboard *Shenan-*

doah who needed to catch up on their sleep. Liddell calculated ETA in IFF range of *Brautigan* for the planned course and speed.

Eleven hours. Barring emergencies, the Old Lady was going to spend at least eight of those hours sipping sherry (if not the good stuff she was saving for Kornilov and *Brautigan*'s people), taking a shower, and sleeping.

Above all, sleeping. Her mind was slowing down just when she needed it working faster than ever. How lack of sleep had overtaken her this way was a mystery. It had never happened before.

But then, she'd never taken a capital ship and a squadron into a possible war zone before.

"Wake up, friends. We have company."

Louis Ferraro's voice finally eroded a path into Karl Pocher's consciousness. He sat up, nearly banged his head on the locker overhead in spite of the restraints, and unsnapped.

By the time he'd floated over to the screen, Ferraro had assumed his listeners were awake and begun to report on the contact. Pocher had to tell him three times to go back and start at the beginning. The third time, he had to shout. Ferraro looked aggrieved.

Pocher was now awake enough to remember his manners. "Sorry, Louis. Mahmoud and I went down pretty hard when we did go down." Ferraro's eyebrows rose. "No, we didn't do any of the things you're thinking about, either. That's what makes it so annoying."

Ferraro's eyebrows were under control, but the rest of his face was eloquent. The sexual activities of his superiors were beneath his notice, it seemed to say, particularly when duty called.

Which it was doing, even if it was calling in Louis Ferraro's voice. Pocher prodded Sa'id awake, and they sat down to listen to Ferraro's report.

The receiver on the cable linking the tender and *Brautigan* had picked up *Shenandoah*'s IFF. Range was approximately 12,000 kilometers; no speed or accurate bearing and therefore no ETA.

"If the squadron is only twelve K out, the ETA will be any minute," Sa'id pointed out.

"I know," Ferraro said smugly. "I went and groomed before I called you. I can handle screen—"

"Louis, this is not an emergency. If you take *Shenandoah*'s call, I will personally break a random selection of three fingers."

"Yes, sir."

Pocher didn't know who broke the circuit first. He turned from the blank screen to Sa'id.

"Which of us looks worse without a bath?"

Sa'id grimaced. "I do, but it is my fate, not my fault."

"You mean your face," Pocher said, putting a hand on his friend's shoulder and gently pushing him aft. "Go and wash."

The shower burbled and hissed into life. Pocher called up an external scan on the screen. Ten kilometers away, the tender glimmered faintly, snugged down to the surface of the asteroid. The view also showed a jagged spur of the smaller rock *Brautigan* had grappled and maneuvered into position. Shielded by rock from any observer not between them and linked by a secure glass-fiber cable, the two ships had done a pretty good imitation of uninhabited space for the past two days.

A faint reflection from the screen told Pocher his hair desperately needed combing. He'd just finished that when Ferraro came back on the screen.

"Oh, I almost forgot, sir. We were cut off before I could mention the Dockyard Suitability Evaluation I did for the asteroid."

"*Which* asteroid?" Pocher wasn't about to be bought off by tact from Ferraro, even if it was a pleasant surprise.

"This one," Ferraro said, pointing at the deck. "I only have 94 percent of the data for a nominal evaluation, but within those parameters—"

"Yes?"

"This asteroid has an 86 percent suitability."

Pocher was impressed in spite of himself. A DSE was normally two people's work for a whole day. The tender's smaller computer must have slowed Ferraro down even more. If he'd done it right, he'd damned near given the Navy its dockyard all hot and ready to serve when the squadron made rendezvous.

Which would make everybody in the squadron very happy with *Leon Brautigan* and her crew.

"Damned good work, Louis. Shoot the study over here and I'll run a check on it with our computer—"

"Sir, I already did that. The only other check required is one on *Shenandoah*'s main. Unless they wish to complete the data?"

"That's up to them," Pocher began.

The call chime broke in and Mahmoud popped out of the shower, clothed except for his feet but with his hair still tangled. He lunged for Pocher's comb, collided with his friend, and knocked the comb into a parabola that took it into the passageway.

The last thing Pocher saw before he answered the incoming call was Ferraro heroically trying not to laugh.

In twenty-seven years in the Navy, Captain Liddell had never figured out what to call her first meal after waking up. She seldom ate it at anything like conventional breakfast hours, by ship time. She also seldom missed having tea and toast and fruit as part of it, no matter what else she might have, and she never had anything chemical even if a wardroom party were erupting down the passageway.

She treated the meal as breakfast in another way. She was off-circuit for everything short of an Alert One emergency. If the backlog of print work was thicker than her little finger, she'd make the concession of looking over some of it with the second cup of tea. Otherwise she kept half an hour out of each twenty-four to call her soul her own.

So *Brautigan*'s report reached Liddell when she signaled that she was back on-circuit. She was studying the summary of the Dockyard Suitability Evaluation when the surgeon came on.

"Captain, we've got emergency surgery."

"Life threatening?"

"No. But it's a weird case. Would you believe appendicitis?"

"Frankie, have you been drinking this early?"

"It's 1830, and I've asked myself the same question. But I've scoped and scanned our boy. It's appendicitis. He had major regen after some lava burns. Rescue work on Teuffelsheim, five years ago."

"But if he'd sprouted a new appendix, it should have been picked up."

"Should have been but wasn't. I'm sure you've seen it

147

before. Everybody thinks the person before them was so reliable they would have found anything wrong, so some essential checks don't get made."

In the Personnel Division, Liddell had sometimes been up to her third rib in similar situations. She gave Doctor Mori a disgusted look.

"What's his name?"

"Want to name a shuttle?"

"Come on, Frankie. I know you better than that. I just want to visit the man when you're through sealing him up."

Electrician Second Class Morton Gellis would be operated on that night and receiving visitors within twenty-four hours. Liddell promised to be one, then left Mori to scrub while she recorded a message for the exec.

"Pavel, send two shuttles to rendezvous with *Leon Brautigan*. Use the two freshest crews. Put an armored LI squad aboard one and a full antiship load in the other's racks. Everybody will be under the orders of *Brautigan*'s CO, Lieutenant Pocher, until we arrive.

"Also, arrange time on our main for the final check on a DSE. They say the asteroid the Baernoi were using looks just right. That doesn't break my heart.

"I'll be on-circuit but doing my yoga for the next twenty minutes."

She thought of calling Captain Steckler aboard *Pucinski*, but that would be an unnecessary and unsecured communication. In another two hours it would be out of the power of the Alliance, the Baernoi, or anyone else to find a cheap way of interfering with the rendezvous. If Wolfgang hadn't intercepted the message already, he'd just have to cool his hairy heels.

Liddell dropped her robe and began a sun salutation. She needed the relaxation that comes with well-exercised muscles. Battle plans weren't supposed to survive contact with the enemy, but this one hadn't even lasted that long!

"The LI people are in position," the shuttle copilot said. "Loaded for Baernoi and anything else we're likely to find out here. Of course it's the unlikely things that kill you."

This was too old a truth about war and space to require comment, except possibly about second lieutenants who thought it was a profound insight. Pocher found that he'd exhausted his day's supply of rudeness on Louis Ferraro.

"Strap in, people," the pilot said. She slapped controls in the apparently random pattern of the expert. "We're about to rendezvous with *Shen*."

Drive and internal gravity died in the same moment. Pocher learned that his straps weren't quite as snug as he'd thought. He was tightening them when the cockpit armor irised and *Shenandoah* leaped at him.

From five hundred meters away, she seemed to fill half the sky. Pocher automatically scanned her mirrored finish for signs of sloppy polishing or minor damage.

Ice crystals from the shuttle's jets swirled past the window as the pilot pushed her ship closer. The ice vanished as docking cables *chunked* into place at bow and stern. *Shenandoah* grew steadily and not too rapidly larger, the sign of good people on the docking crew as well as in the shuttle.

"My God, I didn't realize just how *big* she was," Ferraro said.

"Eh?" Pocher replied. He'd just finished deciding that *Shenandoah* looked like a tight ship, as well as behaved like one.

"I said, I didn't realize—"

"Yeah, I heard you. Really I did. Haven't you ever seen anything this size?"

"Skipper, I've never served in anything larger than a converted light cruiser. I've never seen anything larger than a Province-class heavy."

An ungallant pleasure at finding a chink in Ferraro's armor of competence warred with skepticism. "Didn't you ever get to Riftwell?"

"They gave me a waiver for all the basic courses because of my merchant service. It was all on-board training, mostly in the Pied Noir system's two supply ships."

Neither of which, probably, was a quarter the size of the battlecruiser. Even a Province-class heavy was half the length and a third the diameter.

"Better start getting used to it. No point in gawking like a tourist if you're going to be slumming with the big-ship Navy. They take off their pants one leg at a time, just like us."

"I hope so, Skipper." Ferraro sounded neither amused nor reassured.

The steady inward motion continued. The forward edge of the dock crept upward, until bulkheads dripping equipment cut off the stars.

The hatch slid closed. Two bangs signaled a solidly completed docking to Pocher's ear. A long pattering as the passenger collar latched itself into place around the hatch ended in the whine of the hatch opening.

Pocher swallowed to clear his ears, but the pressure in shuttle and ship were identical. He scooped his shoulder bag out from under his seat and stood up as the smell of *Shenandoah* washed over him.

A big ship, a clean ship, a new ship, her life-support tuned, her machinery in top form, her crew willing to sweat to keep things that way and then take the time to wash off the sweat afterward. Not the old hacks that served Victoria, with machinery too often repaired and recyclers too feeble to let the machinists wash.

Not *Brautigan*, as much as Pocher loved her or at least respected her long and faithful service. Not anything but what *Shenandoah* really was, the big-ship Navy that Pocher thought he'd forgotten but now knew he hadn't forgotten or even stopped missing.

Fourteen

Captain Liddell had retracted the bulkhead between her office and her conference room. This was hardly necessary for nine people, but it made Kornilov more comfortable. He hadn't realized how accustomed he was to the vast open spaces of Victoria until he boarded *Cooney* and had to spend two days in a cabin about the size of his Fort Stafford bathroom.

The retracted bulkhead left a room four meters by eight, respectable even for *Shenandoah*. Displays filled one end, while a robot bar-buffet crouched protectively in front of Captain Liddell's desk at the other end. The walls held original art, mostly landscapes, except for one portrait of an elderly man with a long bald skull and a gray spade beard.

As senior officer present, Kornilov had the head of the table. As host, Liddell had the foot. On either flank sat the other four captains of the squadron, Captain Steckler of the 82nd Engineering Squadron, Commander Bogdanov, and Kornilov's chief of intelligence.

In Kornilov's experience, nine people could prove too many for a meeting expected to yield major decisions. Fortunately this meeting had no such purpose, as he'd quickly learned. His pleasure at this surprise outweighed his annoyance at Liddell's having her agenda so firmly fixed in advance. It was, after all, a concession for him to be coming out to *Shenandoah* instead of calling Liddell in to Victoria.

The concession now seemed wise. Standing on rank might be useful with a junior who would take a kilometer if given a centimeter, like Captain Prange. Liddell could be wooed into reason and moderation, and she probably wouldn't even think of intriguing with your chief of staff. . . .

The thought of intrigues led to Kornilov mentally undressing Captain Liddell. If the body matched the sleek dark hair and the small-featured face, it would be worth seeing. Anyone whose uniform hid their figure so well was probably spare of flesh, but her movements spoke of grace and hinted at fitness.

Certainly she would have the same dignity, clothed or otherwise. That was a quality far rarer than good bodies, even among military professionals. Kornilov knew he lacked it, thanks to what forty years of good living had done to a body already designed for weightlifting or wrestling.

Kornilov put Captain Liddell's clothes back on and his mind back to duty.

A hand wearing a desert glove rose above a boulder fifty meters toward the lip of the canyon. Candice Shores lay still and so flat that her breath kicked up puffs of dust. The hand wigwagged a signal: "UNIDENTIFIED CIVILIANS APPROACHING ON FOOT IN THE CANYON."

Sklarinsky muttered something, but no louder than the faint whine of the desert wind. Shores rolled over on her back and contemplated faint wisps of cloud that seemed to scar rather than decorate the hard blue sky overhead.

Civilians in the area were a complication she hadn't expected. Assuming, that is, they were really civilians. Lieutenant Colonel Lovis of Second Battalion had an unorthodox streak in him. Infiltrating the area Scout Company had "secured" with people disguised as civilians was the kind of thing to expect from him.

With one hand Shores signaled Sklarinsky to grab the com operator's camera and follow her. With the other she signaled one of the two squads of the ambush team to do the same.

Seven Scouts low-crawling downhill made less noise than a kitten playing. The civilians in the canyon were tramping along, fat, dumb, and happy, when Shores focused her binoculars on them.

Four of the civilians towed a lifter with handlines, two others lay prone beside the shrouded cargo. It looked like a pile of crates, about three meters by two, and half a meter high.

The civilians looked like the genuine article, and desert-bred to boot. Their coveralls were faded and their boots scuffed pale; the men all wore beards much too long for regulars. One of the women had an abo-style hairdo peering from under her headdress.

Two hundred meters past the watchers, the civilians stopped where the canyon forked. The two riders dismounted, two more took their place, and the whole party moved off down the left-hand fork of the canyon.

Shores watched them at top magnification until the rock formation known as the Devil's Privy hid them. Then she hand-signaled a return to their previous position, for everyone except the two sentries.

On the way, she tried to think what to do next. This wasn't part of the military reservation; the civilians had every right to be where they were. But what were they doing?

And how to find out? Each fork of the canyon forked again within a few kilometers, to form a still-unsurveyed maze covering more than two thousand square kilometers and full of places where a whole battalion could lose itself or be ambushed.

By the time Shores had returned to her post, she knew what to do next: go on with the exercise and meanwhile find out if anyone had seen these civilians before. Even learning that nobody would tell her anything would be better than a wild-grumbler chase into the canyon.

Sklarinsky checked the film counter and handed the camera back. Shores rolled on her back again, eased a rock out from under her left shoulder, and breathed slowly. She wished she could unseal her mask and dry off her face, but being this low to the ground guaranteed mites as soon as the sun dropped a bit.

Far off, a heat-cracked rock split, and the echoes rolled down the canyon.

"Thank you, General Kornilov," Liddell said. "Does anyone have any questions?"

"Yes," the Intelligence colonel said. "I haven't heard any mention of our surveying a second Dockyard asteroid."

"With that unknown ship in-system, I'm reluctant to send the survey party out in anything less than a light cruiser,"

Liddell said. "We have more urgent uses for *Welitsch* and *Cooney*."

Both cruiser captains looked relieved. Kornilov had them mentally labeled as hot for the fray and reluctant to be anywhere else.

Not to mention that light cruisers were, if Kornilov's experience was typical, not particularly suitable for embarking survey parties. Just two passengers aboard *Cooney* had evicted the executive officer from his cabin and forced hotbunking all the way down to the Supply warrant officer.

"We also have a significant amount of data already gathered by Victoria Command's previous flights," Liddell went on. "I would like to analyze that thoroughly before assuming we need to go rock-hunting again."

Kornilov nodded. "I concur."

That would keep the civilians off Liddell's back, unless and until they started ignoring Kornilov. The general hoped that day would be a long time coming.

He also hoped that Captain Steckler and his engineers were as good as they thought they were. A hastily surveyed asteroid might not fall apart the minute its passage crew fired up the drive. Carving big chunks of rock out of it was another matter. Even the best engineers were hardly up to gluing an asteroid back together.

"Any problems with shore leave, when authorized?" *Cooney*'s captain asked.

"None that we anticipate now," Kornilov said. "I can give more accurate data when I know your leave schedule."

"We'll tell you as soon as we know ourselves," Liddell said. Her eyebrows told Kornilov that he'd kept doubt off his face but not out of his voice. "Thank you, everyone. General Kornilov, might I have the pleasure of your company for a drink?"

The reflective inside of the camocover stretched among boulders trapped even the minute heat from the field cooker. That warmed Scout Company's HQ people and reduced HQ's infrared signature. There was no perfect concealment from modern sensors, but you could throw a lot of ambiguity into the signature you did have. The more ambiguity, the more chance the other guy would say "Oh, Cold Iron take it!" and leave you alone until you were somewhere else, such as landing in his backyard.

Sergeant Zimmer was looking at the cup of stew in his hand without really seeing it. He inhaled the steam, then looked at Captain Shores.

"What you saw down there in the canyon does smell like something I've heard. Nothing hard, maybe C-Three or thereabouts. But quite a lot of it."

C-Three meant both the data and the sources were open to question. But—

"To hell with the quality. What does the quantity tell you?"

"Still nothing hard. But from what I hear from friends, it looks like the locals are moving back and forth in time with our maneuvers. Real tight match in time, too. Either they're watching us more'n we suspect, or some of our people aren't keeping their lips zipped."

Shores made a mental note to find out which and see what could be done about it. "Any incidents?"

Zimmer shook his head. "Mostly they've stayed out of eyeball range, and outside the reservation there's been a live-and-let-live policy."

"Any pattern to the movements?"

"Between Mount Houton and the wild country west of the Vinh River. I don't know which way is going and which way is coming, and neither does anybody else. It was real good we got a hard visual on them today, film and all."

Shores recognized one of Zimmer's camouflaged compliments. "Maybe we can do something about the live-and-let-live policy after today."

"Maybe, if it wasn't for that damned demonstration. Last thing Kornilov wants is to give the locals a good excuse for another one. Bouncing a bunch of people for being where it's all right for them to be would be a real good one."

"You've got a point."

They both did. Live-and-let-live was fine if you knew the other guy wasn't a threat. If you didn't . . .

If you didn't, the first thing was to find out. Memory of basic-tactics courses led to memories of other things, followed by a flash of intuition. If Scout Company could hide its outposts from a Second Battalion that was looking for them, what about hiding them from locals who weren't?

Outposts that would be equipped to record the height, weight, sex, load, weapons, bedroom habits, and DNA of everyone found where they shouldn't be.

That assumed Intelligence cooperation from Victoria Command and the company's staying power. She couldn't do more than guess about the first, but she had a reliable judge of the second right beside her.

"Top, if we didn't have anything else to do, could the company stay in the bush another three, four days beyond the end of the exercise?"

Zimmer frowned, then nodded slowly. "It would help if they had a day's field stand-down, or some extra leave afterward."

"How about both, if we can swing it?"

Zimmer grinned. "For that, they'd take out the Bonsai Force's HQ!"

"Another sherry before dinner?" Liddell asked.

"Thank you, no. I have broken my abstinence as much as I have, because the alternative would be insulting your sherry."

"As you wish."

Liddell hadn't really wanted another drink and suspected that half her bar could go down Kornilov's gullet before he started showing it. She waited until the general's eyes wandered back to the portrait of her father, then stoppered the decanter.

"General, if I might take this chance to be rather blunt: are there security problems for shore leave you didn't mention?"

Kornilov leaned back and steepled his fingers on his stomach. "That's one of the things we're investigating, without knowing what we will find or when we will find it. But you want more details than that, of course." Liddell nodded politely as Kornilov straightened up.

"The Victoria Brigade is an odd hybrid. Weapons, HQ, and one rifle battalion are regulars. Another battalion is reserves, mostly ex-regulars now Victorian residents or citizens. The regulars are field-ready, the reserve battalion nearly so.

"The question mark is the two territorial battalions—our local militia. Normally militia aren't brigaded with regulars or reserves. Victoria is an exception. Its population is small, and this looked like a good way of implementing the nonprovocation policy."

"The territorial battalions have regular or reserve cadres, but even many of these are Victorians, and everybody else is local. Some of the locals come from areas with strong antigovernment sentiments."

"Not pro-Alliance?"

"Not even necessarily anti-Federation. Merely against the current state of affairs, with no very clear idea of what they're for."

Liddell pretended to smell a questionable odor.

Kornilov shrugged. "We have lived with this situation for twenty years. I would expect us to go on living with it, but for two circumstances."

"The demonstration is one. What's the other?"

"The demonstration is one, and not just because it took place. It took place on the day the news of your arrival in-system reached Victoria. I hope this is a coincidence."

"I also hope it is just a coincidence that about half the demonstrators have business or family ties to members of the territorials."

"There's bound to be some coincidence. Militia units on planets like Victoria are as much social clubs for leading citizens as they are military units. Or is Victoria an exception?"

"No. We have, of course, ordered the territorial battalions into Federation service. They are working hard, but their absentee rate for drills has been high. Also, they report abnormally severe shortages of equipment."

"Not weapons and ammunition?"

"No."

"Desert conditions—"

"The territorial battalions train in the desert at most once year."

"It still sounds more like crime than rebellion. We could go over recent reports of outlaw colonies—"

The call to dinner interrupted her. Before she could rise, Kornilov hurried on. "Most Victorians own at least one weapon and a modest supply of ammunition. Also, they may have other sources. What is missing is shelters, medical supplies, communications equipment. What they would need for armed resistance but could not so easily improvise."

Liddell rose and took Kornilov's offered arm. "I suppose it doesn't really matter if our people stumble on rebels or thieves. Both will kill to cover their tracks."

"Exactly," Kornilov said. They stepped aside in unison as the bulkhead slid back again.

One last robot was scuttling away from the table, now set with Liddell's family tableware and a set of crystal wine glasses. The buffet had practically disappeared under a load of covered dishes and freshly opened bottles. The captain's steward made a delicate adjustment to a salad bowl, turned, and saluted.

"At your service, ma'am, General Kornilov."

"Thank you, Jensen."

The exercises were over and a field stand-down for the whole Second Battalion and attached units was about to begin. From the look on the Battalion CO's face, Candice Shores wondered what else was about to start.

"Captain Shores, CO of Scout Company. Major Nieg, from Command Intelligence."

Major Nieg smiled. His face looked about twenty-two, except for eyes that looked about fifty. He was short and so wiry he made Candice Shores feel plump. She wondered if he was an ex-Ranger. The Federation's tame ninjas often wound up in Intelligence after giving up field assignments—or between them.

"Colonel Lovis tells me you gave his battalion a serious workout," Nieg said.

"They made us sweat, too," Shores said. In a real war, the Scouts could have chopped up two, maybe three companies, but why not be polite? Lovis was really doing a sound job of turning his overweight and undertrained reservists back into field-ready troopers.

"Good," Nieg said. "Because this exercise is about to be prolonged by about four days. At least that's the cover story. But from now on, it's for—yes, Captain?"

Shores wanted to answer, but the grin on her face was too wide.

"If you're wondering about your proposal, yes, it's been approved. The Scouts and Second Battalion will carry it out. That's why we're sending out two convoys, not one."

Nieg opened his traveling case and they crouched around

it to see its miniature display. The amount of data marching across the screen left Shores moderately impressed. Apparently most of the rumors Zimmer heard had been recorded in Intelligence files, as precisely as the data allowed.

Shores didn't mention Zimmer; Intelligence types were more often than not paranoid about anything they considered poaching on their territory. She only said that she wasn't surprised at the pattern.

"How so?" Nieg asked.

"If somebody was preparing for trouble—to make it or meet it—in the Kellysburg-Mount Houton area, this offers good cover—"

"Cover?" interrupted Nieg.

"Didn't you say we were in a hurry, Major?" Lovis asked. "Then how about letting Captain Shores have her say?"

Nieg jerked his head. "Caves," Shores said. "Some with water. Most with no mites. It's hard to shadow somebody in that area, and easy to ambush them if they try. That's why we didn't go after the party we saw. I sent a squad down to the canyon branch, and they found four perfect ambush sites before they'd lost the trail."

"I read your report, Captain," Nieg said. "Now, since we are in a hurry, I want plans for a network of outposts in the area before we leave this room."

Nieg made some adjustments to the controls of the display. "That puts it in open mode. Now you can use it without wiping the memory or setting off the demo charge."

"The—how big?" Shores asked.

"Enough to blow a standard lifter out of the sky, or kill us all," Nieg said mildly. "I didn't have the case wrapped with heavy-alloy wire for extra fragmentation."

"I'm grateful," Shores said, hoping the sarcasm wasn't too blatant. She loathed boobytraps, even "friendly" ones.

"Don't worry, Captain," Nieg said. "Boobytraps trap only boobies, and you aren't one. Now, why don't you go first, since this was your idea originally?"

"What forces do we have available?"

"The whole Scout Company in outposts, randomly moved about within the parameters we agree on. One company of Second Battalion in rotation, assigned to the outposts, with all their movements randomized. We'll even drop them a minimum of five kilometers from each outpost."

"Just so they have their IFF and passwords ready," Shores said. "If my people go out there with live ammo, it's going to be unhealthy to look unfriendly."

"No problem, Captain," Lovis said.

Shores bent down and went to work. The ideal was to cover the whole area with a grid of randomly moving, sensor-loaded, heavily armed Federation patrols and outposts. Eventually such a grid would gather enough intelligence about the locals' movements to permit shadowing, searching, arresting, ambushing, or whatever combination the threat justified.

Shores rather hoped that the locals' antics weren't a threat. She also knew that her job was to assume the worst and use her quarter-million stellars' worth of training and experience to guard against it.

She was sweating by the time she stood up. "That's my best judgment, based on what you've given me. Sure we can't pass it through a bigger machine?"

"Sure we can't publish it on the bulletin service?" Nieg replied. Lovis frowned at the mockery in the major's voice; the major raised pencil-thin eyebrows.

"We've been through that before," Nieg added. "My orders give me very little discretion."

"I don't suppose you'd trust my people even if you had it," Lovis growled.

"Probably not," Nieg said. "But I trusted Captain Shores, and she came through magnificently."

"I'd feel better if you put that in writing," Lovis said.

Shores slumped into the nearest chair, the strength draining out of her. She wanted to be proud of what she'd done—a staff-trained major's job at least—but they were taking away the pleasure with their squabbling. Not to mention making it pretty obvious that one of Nieg's jobs was to check Second Battalion's loyalty. Shores didn't know what was worse: the thought of disloyalty or the paranoia of Intelligence.

Fifteen

The forward bulkhead of the shuttle's passenger cabin was the same color as the Victoria desert. Elayne Zheng could judge that precisely; the screen displayed an arc of gray desert with stars above it. *Marat* had faded into the fringes of the atmosphere until she was no longer even the brightest star.

The last of the sky vanished, and a range of pale rust mountain slid past, a hundred kilometers below. The screen split, the upper part showing the view and the lower showing the shuttle's position on a map.

The shuttle was sliding in over the coast about a thousand kilometers south of the Vinh Delta. Another two thousand, and they'd be landing at Fort Stafford. From there lifters would take the people assigned to Camp Aounda to their posts. From her experience with Army transport people, Zheng expected it would take longer to get from Fort Stafford to Camp Aounda than it had taken to reach Victoria from the asteroids.

"Your attention, please. We are now subject to atmospheric disturbances. Please return to your seats, check your harnesses, and secure any loose objects."

Zheng hadn't unbuckled; ten years riding attackers set certain habits firmly. She stuffed her empty tea bag into the waste slot and twisted her head from side to side to ease a stiff neck.

This gave her for the first time a good view of the officer seated across the aisle.

"Lucco DiVries?"

"Elayne! Welcome to Victoria." They reached across the aisle to shake hands and slap shoulders.

"I thought you were still back on Riftwell."

The other lieutenant shook her head. "I put in for long leave to visit my brother Mark. He's got a little organics still outside Mount Houton. Between what he sells the farmers and what he puts on his own fields, they make out pretty well. He's always telling me he could make out better if I'd loan him enough to move coastward, so I thought I'd check him out."

"I'm coming down on duty."

"AAP for that new base?"

"Haven't you heard of security?"

"Isn't that one of the lesser gods of the Ptercha'a?"

"*All* the Catmen's gods are lesser."

"What, a pantheon that inspires—"

"Lucco, the Ptercha'a pantheon didn't keep a bunch of them from going rogue on Agamemnon. My uncle was killed trying to round them up. So I don't buy most of the stories about the noble Catmen. I think we spend a lot too much time picking up after them, and after their Merishi masters."

"Sorry."

"Let's call it an accident and talk about something else. Know any good watering spots around Fort Stafford?"

"Never been to Fort Stafford except in transit. But I know a couple of good places in Mount Houton."

"What do they serve, synthos glazed with sand?"

"You'd be surprised."

"I'm sure I would be."

"Pleasantly surprised."

"Want to bet?"

"You're on. Price of the first dinner?"

"Fair enough."

Zheng suspected it would be a while before they were able to settle that bet. The Advanced Air Party would be lucky to get six hours' sleep out of the twenty-two in a Victorian day until *Ira Hayes* brought her squadron in. Then the ground detachments would take over, and when she'd caught up on her sleep she'd be ready to go into town.

Nice to have someone to look up when I do. Nicer still that he's unattached. I don't know what I want to happen, but I do know I was contemplating tripping Charlie Longman a few days ago. . . .

"Your attention, please. Upon landing at Fort Stafford, all personnel will be confined to the base. All personnel proceeding onward will draw their personal weapons from their baggage."

Zheng looked at the speaker as if it had said she was an inferior bed partner. Then she looked at Lucco DiVries, in time to see him hastily erasing a frown.

"Any ideas?"

"Your guess is as good as mine. It could be anything from a barroom brawl with civilians to the Baernoi attacking."

Zheng remembered the hastily suppressed frown. But pressing DiVries would be futile."

"And me without an attacker to ride!" she muttered. "Oh well, they only said you would see many worlds if you joined the Navy. They didn't say which ones, or when."

On the screen, the land below turned dark as they crossed into night. Far to the north of their course, a faint glow crept across the desert. The map told Zheng she was seeing the settlements trailing out into the desert south of Mount Houton.

Four mornings in a row Charles Longman had performed a little ritual when he reached his office. Never mind that the office was a table-terminal clamped to a section of tunnel wall ten meters short of where the insulation, sealing, and pressure all ended at a glazerock wall. It was an office, and it deserved a routine.

First he would heat a cup of coffee (in a sealed jug, to get it hot enough with only half pressure in the crew spaces). Then he would pull his files, for any work that should have been done the night before and would have to be done before lunch. Finally he would tap into the camera network and contemplate *Shenandoah* riding majestically ten kilometers out. This last was, strictly speaking, against regulations, but Longman was sure that if anyone were going to make a fuss about it the camera network would have been much more secure. He could have broken what security they had when he was eleven!

This morning the coffee was hot and sweet, the file almost empty of urgent work, and one of his reports had come back studded with praise. Longman was ready to sing when he punched through to the camera network.

The song was stillborn as one view after another failed to turn up *Shen*. Nine, ten, eleven, twelve cameras—no more, and that meant no *Shenandoah*.

"What the devil?"

"You rang?" Nickie Gallifet said from the next desk. Farther up the tunnel heads turned.

"May Death Commandos piss in your beer," Longman growled. "Where's *Shen*?"

"Didn't you hear?" Nickie asked. "She's on her way to Victoria. Some sort of trouble, so they asked for a flag-showing trip. Ball-of-yarn pass in low orbit, weapons demonstration, the whole nine meters."

"I thought it was some more Baernoi stuff they found out on the Pimple," said somebody farther down the tunnel. Several other tenants promptly hushed him with explicit descriptions of what happened to waggletongues under Captain Steckler.

Longman craned his neck, trying to see who'd spoken, with an eye to pumping him that evening. Everyone seemed determined to crawl into their terminals. He turned back to his own, muttering, "Nobody tells me anything."

After five minutes he began to feel slightly less undressed. If the work continued at the same pace for another two days, he'd be able to trade this terminal for a portable or even a welder. Getting into a suit and working up a decent sweat could make him forget a lot of things, including being out here on a barely armed asteroid with the Baernoi maybe coming and *Shenandoah* certainly going.

Electrician Second Class Morton Gellis was a wiry man of indeterminate ancestry. Everything about him was under-sized except his ears and, Brian Mahoney quickly discovered, his ego.

The Sick Bay lounge was six meters by eight, and it held half a dozen people besides Gellis, Mahoney, and Brigitte Tachin. Gellis somehow managed to reduce all the rest to an audience for his patter.

"Oh, I don't understand why they're sending me over to Training for light duty," he said cheerfully. "This was even easier than the first time I had my appendix out. But I suppose orders are orders. Will I have time for my courses? I wanted to sit for the First Class exam this cruise."

"You'll have a lot more time for your courses if you don't waste time finding excuses for not doing your work," Mahoney said.

"And the courses won't make a bit of difference to your rating if I keep hearing your questioning orders," Brigitte Tachin added. "Or Lieutenant Mahoney, or Warrant Officer Nakamura."

For the first time Gellis looked slightly subdued. "You won't tell Su—Nakamura?"

"The less I hear from you, the less he'll hear about you. Fair enough?"

Gellis nodded. He actually seemed at a loss for words.

"I'd add Chief Netsch to the list of people I don't want to hear from about you," Mahoney said. "Otherwise, I expect we'll see eye to eye. Training Department's likely to be busy, now that we've dumped our passengers, so you'll have plenty of chances to shine. I'll even promise not to try kidnaping you when it comes time for your evaluation."

Gellis smiled cautiously.

"*Wheeetttt!* Now hear this. Now hear this. The captain will address all hands."

The screen flickered, and Rose Liddell looked out of it. "In about one hour, we will be maneuvering for a ball-of-yarn pass over Victoria in low orbit. We will be passing over both Federation and Alliance territory. This operation has been requested by Victoria Command and accepted by the Alliance governor."

She grinned. "So in theory, it's something we can do in our sleep. In practice, *Shenandoah* doesn't do anything that way. In thirty minutes, this ship will go to Alert Two. When we maneuver, we will go to Alert One and stay there until the pass is completed.

"I don't expect any trouble. But we'll be ready for it. The people down there know all about our weapons and sensors. They might not know how ready we are to use them. It will save a lot of grief if there aren't any mistakes about that.

"I expect everyone to do as well as I know you can. Thank you, and good luck."

The screen switched back to the intercom-duty petty officer's bearded face, which rattled off a stream of routine announcements. Gellis was looking aggrieved by the time the screen blanked entirely.

"Not a word on who we have to worry about," he said.

"Oh?" Mahoney said. "Is it anybody unusual? A Hiver revival, or maybe the K'thressh have developed spaceflight?"

"Well, I've heard rumors—"

"The kind of rumors worth talking about?" Mahoney asked.

"Put that way, not really, sir," Gellis said. *Glory be, the man can tell sarcasm when he hears it! Maybe he won't drive me to drink after all.*

Tachin stood up. "Brian, if you'll excuse me, I'd better report to Weapons. It sounds as if the captain's going to launch armed buses. I want to see if Twelve and Nineteen are still down, and who's going to be on the launchers."

For a moment they stood close. She pressed Mahoney's hand—those supple fingers were amazingly long for such a small woman—then scurried out the door.

"Cut there, and there," the sergeant said. "Clear the area, everybody except the cutter gang."

He didn't look at Candice Shores, but she knew she was included in the request and would have been if she'd worn three stars. She backed off twenty meters from the sealed cave entrance, then ten more. The cutter was supposed to work only on the sealing compound holding the rocks in place, but cutters weren't infallible and rocks were seldom homogenous. Not to mention boobytraps . . .

The cutter whined into action. Shores looked at her watch. Outpost Green Four reported the sealed cave just before *Shenandoah* started her low pass. It took Shores and the combat engineer and security teams twenty minutes to lift in. Five more minutes, and *Shen* would be visible overhead. Not for long, in the ribbon of sky visible at the top of the canyon, but long enough to boost the troops' morale.

Devil take the troops' morale, mine *needs boosting!*

It wasn't much consolation that her plan for collecting intelligence on civilian movements seemed to be working. As fast as it achieved one goal, someone asked Scout Company to pursue another. The orders usually came from Brigade or Second Battalion, but Shores thought she saw Major Nieg's hand in and on them.

What does it take to keep that bastard happy? If it's some-thing impossible, who can I trust to stop him?

The vibration reaching her soles through the rock faded. The cutter team hoisted their equipment and stepped back. The bomb-disposal people rolled their drone forward and switched it on. A sharp squeal in her earplugs made Shores cringe, as the fuse-jammer field came on. On eight indepen-dently articulated donut wheels, the drone rolled forward into the cave.

"Hey! Look there!" someone shouted, before a sergeant shouted her down. Shores looked up. High and bright and utterly remote, *Shenandoah* was riding overhead.

With her glasses set at maximum magnification, Shores could make out *Shen*'s silhouette. Around and above her rode shuttles, a light cruiser, and what could only be weap-ons buses.

Shores started counting the buses, but just then the engi-neer's leader shouted.

"We're through into one damned big cave, Captain!"

He held out a display pad. "Goes straight in about twenty meters, too straight to be natural. Then it makes a real sharp turn, runs another ten meters that looks more natural, and expands. Fifty meters by twenty, at least. We're trying to check for shape and contents, but that'll be easier if we turn off the jammer."

"Leave it on. Get a couple of volunteers with recorders and lights and I'll get a couple for a security team. Then we can go in and make an eyeball check."

"Yes, ma'am."

Shores didn't know if she'd crossed the line between courageous leadership and foolishly sticking her neck out. She was sure that she'd finally come up with something big, and she wanted to see it for herself before serving it up on a platter for Major Nieg.

"Steady as she goes," Commander Bogdanov said. His voice, just above a whisper, didn't match the uncontrollable grin on his face.

Captain Liddell took off her helmet and rubbed both ears until the circulation started in them again. Did the helmet need adjustment, or was her head swelling because so far everything with *Shenandoah* was working out well?

Hard to tell. This low pass is a fool's errand, or it would be if the man who sent us on it was a fool. Since he isn't . . .

Bogdanov returned to monitoring the displays that traced *Shenandoah's* delicate balancing act—her drive field against Victoria's gravity. She was too low to keep full orbital velocity for more than an hour or two without using her drive.

But this low, too much drive could make her hard to control. The hundred and fifty kilometers between her and the desert was a small margin of safety for major control problems.

Liddell thanked the Creator for Pavel Bogdanov's ship-handling skill. Clearly that was his major religion, after the Baptist Communion. Being a martinet was a secondary faith, which he clung to only when not allowed to practice either of the first two.

On the screen, the green area around Mount Houton and along its reservoir was creeping off the lower edge. It represented two centuries of sweat and sore muscles and mite inflammations, but the whole area could have been dropped into the space between Fort Stafford and the sea.

Minutes took *Shenandoah* across the High Waste and for the tenth time into Alliance territory. Liddell counted the spots of green that marked more sweat and soreness and children coughing from mite-lung.

We could solve half the planet's problems by pulling everybody out of the desert, both Federation and Alliance. Buying them out plus extra desalinization and organics plants for the coastal areas would be cheaper than keeping this squadron overhead for a couple of years.

Liddell punched up the radar-mapping display. Good radar maps of Victoria existed, but *Shenandoah*, like any capital ship, was equipped to make her own. Liddell had ordered the radar watch to do it; the homemade maps would serve as a check against the official ones, if nothing else.

Bogdanov listened to something, then signaled Liddell to put her helmet back on. The sharp pulsing of a long-range spaceborne radar scan jumped out of the earplugs. She didn't even need to call up the signature on her screen.

"Well, well. *Audacious* has us on her radar. Too bad there's nothing we can do to make their day more interesting."

"Brigade reported a patrol checking out another arms cache, about twenty minutes ago," Bogdanov said. "Suppose we show what we can do to support ground units if they're in a fixed position by our next pass?"

Liddell considered. It meant more low-altitude maneuvering but no useful intelligence for *Audacious*. It would also let *Shenandoah* combine this flag-showing pass with a live-firing exercise that was badly overdue.

"Pavel. Find the firing range closest to the coordinates for the patrol and ask for permission to use it."

"Aye-aye, Captain."

Two of the buses riding twenty kilometers higher had live missiles with HE or flash warheads aboard. She'd let Weapons Department take things from there. She needed to know even more than *Audacious*, just how alert Weapons' sharpshooters might be.

Sixteen

Candice Shores wondered what leading the way into nonexistent danger did for a leader's reputation.

An hour in the cave had turned up no danger except falling over your own feet if you stepped beyond the circle of light without pulling down your night goggles. As far as hostile activity, living or robotic, was concerned, the cave was as quiet as a House of Meditation.

"Turn off the damper?" the engineer sergeant asked for the third time,

Shores wanted to say yes. Her voice was beginning to rasp, from having to shout instead of using the jammed radios. Her ears were beginning to ache from the echoes of those shouts, trapped under two hundred meters of rock.

Her guts told her to ignore throat and ears.

"Leave it on," she said.

The sergeant seemed about to argue, when they all heard a shout mixing fear, surprise, and anger. It came again, turning into a stream of curses and obscenities. Several people were shouting at once. Some were soldiers, at least one a local civilian.

Shores cupped her hands and shouted, "Full power on all lights! Patrol, report!"

On infrared and on visible light, the darkness retreated. High up on the west wall of the cave, a cluster of struggling forms appeared on a ledge.

Her two-trooper security squad had loaded, unlocked, and aimed without orders. Beyond that they didn't know what to do, and neither did Shores.

Luck and fast action on the ledge saved her reputation. Two rounds went *spunnnggg* on the rock floor, to either side of the drone. A Scout Company corporal gripped the sniper's carbine, smashing it and the man's hands against the wall. A Second Battalion private knocked the man's legs out from under him. The rest of the mixed squad covered a man and a woman emerging from a crack in the rock. All were dressed like locals.

"Good work," Shores called. "Now bring 'em down."

"No!" the man in the crack screamed. He flung himself between two Second Battalion privates. One staggered and would have gone off the ledge if her comrade hadn't gripped her arm. This left the man a clear path, to plunge over the edge and fall ten meters to the floor.

The corporal on the ledge drew his stun injector. The woman struggled and screamed and needed three people to hold her until the stun took hold. The fight seemed to be out of the sniper; he slumped boneless in the corporal's arms almost at once.

"Pop your belt ropes and rig harnesses," the corporal ordered. Both Scout and Second Battalion people unsealed their belts and unwound the microfilament lines inside. In another minute, both prisoners were on their way down to the floor.

Shores and the engineer sergeant were the first to grab the prisoners' feet and drag them not too gently away from the wall. The squad on the ledge started down. Shores turned, to move the rest of the engineers and security team until they could keep an eyeball watch on the whole cave every minute until reinforcements came in. Reinforcements on the order of another squad of engineers, a Scout Company platoon, and Second Battalion's assigned company could—

"God!"

The engineer sergeant shrieked as the "stunned" man stabbed him in the belly. He doubled up, bringing his carbine within reach of the man. The man snatched it and fired expertly one handed.

Everyone went flat before they realized he wasn't shooting at live targets. His slugs chopped into the drone, chewing out bits of the shell and the curcuitry.

Return fire made a bloody ruin of one leg. "Head shot!" Shores screamed. The man had to have a final card, one to be played once the damper no longer jammed signals to radio-controlled detonators.

The "stunned" woman rolled violently to the right, under the man's feet. He flung his arms wide and toppled, landing on top of the sergeant. The sergeant locked both his arms around the man's free hand. The man howled, writhed, brought the carbine around, and fired a burst into the woman's head with the muzzle almost touching her forehead.

By then Shores was close enough to snatch the carbine out of the man's hands, reverse it, and knock him out with the butt. Then she gripped it until she stopped wanting to pound the man's head into the same bloody mess as the woman's.

She whirled at footsteps behind her, nearly shooting two medics.

"Sorry. You've come to the right place."

"The lieutenant started us in as soon as we heard the shooting," the senior medic said. She looked at the bodies and crossed herself.

"Tie the local up before you work on him," Shores said. "He's got some sort of stun immunity."

"Tie him—" began the other medic.

"If you don't," Shores said heavily, "you'll be held responsible for his not reaching HQ alive." The medic gulped, and his partner put a hand on his shoulder and pushed him to his knees.

They'd just gone to work when a lieutenant from Second Battalion and another squad hurried in. The officer took one look, posted his men, then waited for orders.

Shores straightened up, feeling as if the whole roof of the cave had just landed on her shoulders. She popped the magazine from the carbine. As she set it down, the long rumble of a distant explosion floated down the tunnel. Shores jerked.

"What the devil?"

The answer came on the radio. "*Shenandoah*'s laying down a pattern on the Dobulev Range. Warheads, lasers, the whole load. Hey, we're reading you loud and clear. What happened to the damper?"

"It got shot up," Shores said. Sweat flooded her eyes, stinging and half-blinding her. She wiped it away with the back of her hand, took a deep breath, and gagged as the smells of violent death flooded in.

Now, to brief the lieutenant, say something nice to the corporal on the ledge because this wasn't his fault, and find a nice quiet corner to be sick in.

"Captain, we're picking up hot traffic from the Blanchard Canyon area. It's going on to the Brigade net."

"What happened?" Liddell asked, not moving or even raising her voice. Time to come to full alert later, if it turned out to be something that needed adrenalin expended to solve it.

"We're just getting fragments, scrambled and coded," the communications watch officer said. "But I'd be surprised if it wasn't something with shooting and casualties. They wouldn't be shouting like this, at least not First or Second Battalions."

Casualties didn't necessarily mean shooting. Flash floods were a hazard of Victoria. So were demon-lizard frenzies, falls, and lifter accidents.

Still, Blanchard Canyon was in the middle of the area Brigade was searching for rebels—or, at least, for people who were behaving suspiciously in order to find out what they were. Liddell decided that the officer wasn't pushing the panic button.

"Continuous monitoring, unscrambling, and decoding," she ordered.

"Aye-aye, ma'am. Put it through to you?"

"No. Not unless somebody starts talking about antiship weapons. Then you scream."

"Loud and clear, ma'am."

Liddell spoke quietly to Bogdanov. "Pavel. Raise the squadron's orbit by twenty kilometers."

"Thirty would be better, if we're planning on launching a bus."

Liddell conjured up figures on her screen. "So it would. And I'm going to launch two more buses. One with a full range of decoys, the other with a load of Mark 71s."

This deep in the atmosphere, a bus launched higher up could maintain its speed with auxiliary rockets. One launched now would use up too much power and time taking station. Liddell wanted both buses ready for action the moment they were launched.

"What kind of warheads on the Mark 71s?"

Liddell felt in her breast pocket for the red key card. "Nuclear. And alert the other key officers."

"Aye-aye, Captain."

Twilight on Victoria was a dirty, unappetizing part of the day, with the sunset colors going or gone and the stars not yet blazing. Candice Shores had been too busy to look at the sunset, and she'd be back indoors before the stars came out.

In fact, she was going indoors right now. She stepped up to the hospital shelter, and the medic on duty nodded instead of saluting. They were not only in the field, they were damned close to being in combat.

"You got Sergeant Kiggle in here?"

She probably owed her life to the engineer sergeant—him and the—call her a rebel. Kiggle was not only a regular, he was also alive to be thanked.

"The medevac took him out half an hour ago," the medic said. "He was stable enough to travel. Surgeon says he's got a better'n even chance of making it."

"Damn. Not about his making it, about his being gone."

"Win some, lose some," the medic said. "I got your Corporal Esteva lying down, if that's any help."

"Esteva? I didn't know he was hurt." The man who'd done good work on the ledge had looked ready for another six rounds with the rebels when Shores talked to him five minutes after the shooting.

"I was supposed to check him in overnight. Orders from a visiting major."

Shores remembered the third lifter that had flown in with the medevac and its escort. Distance and twilight hid the insignia, but if it had been from Brigade HQ . . .

"Small wiry major, Asian look to him?" The medic was silent. "Ordered you not to talk about him, too?" More silence gave Shores her answer. She pushed past the medic, through the double door, and past the life-support module to the second cot. Esteva was sitting on it, shirtless and doing breathing exercises as he watched something in a viewer propped against his pillow.

"How are you doing, Corporal?"

"I'd like to get back to my squad. Any chance of that?"

"How long are you supposed to be under observation?"

"Until morning. Surgeon's orders."

"When did those orders come through?"

"Well, ma'am—"

"Was it after Major Nieg visited?"

"I didn't know—" Esteva began, stopped, then grinned. "Yeah. I didn't know that was his name, but I made him as Intelligence right away. He pumped me about the other people up on the ledge, mostly the Second Battalion types. Wanted to know if they'd been slow in moving or anything like that."

"If they'd been . . ." Shores was too angry to complete the sentence.

Esteva saved her from standing with her mouth gaping. "I told him the truth—that I'd been too damned busy to see what anybody else was doing 'less they were doin' it to me."

"Oh lord," Shores breathed. "That'll just make him suspect you."

"Maybe not," Esteva said. "I offered to take a truth-scan, but he didn't ask."

That didn't make a lot of sense, if Nieg were the kind of man anybody that high up in Intelligence practically had to be. Shores disagreed with the popular image of Alliance Intelligence as the great bogey, but only because she thought Federation Intelligence ought to share the dishonor.

"Well, if you've skated through this far, I won't try to spring you. Nieg probably doesn't want you talking to everybody and his uncle. Can I get you anything?"

"Just tell the squad what you told me. The reservists, too, if you can catch up with them."

"Will do. I'll see if I can't put through a commendation for you, too. Don't expect too much, though. They don't hand out much for BBA-classified stuff like this."

"Thanks anyway, ma'am."

Shores went out, determined to keep her promises to Esteva but more concerned with catching up with Major Nieg. This whole business was probably classified Blabbers Boiled Alive, the legendary highest secrecy classification. That meant *she* would be answering the major's questions if she didn't at least ask him a few before talking to anyone else.

My Scouts and me, we can fight anybody on Victoria. Maybe we can even take on Intelligence.

*   *   *

"Concluding eleventh orbit," the Helm officer of the watch intoned solemnly. She sounded like a brand-new priest afraid the devil would snatch her away if she let any pleasure creep into her voice.

"Position check," Liddell rasped. She rubbed her eyes and drank half a glass of water as the data came up.

"All right, people," she said. Everyone on the bridge looked at her expectantly.

Are my eyes as red as theirs? We all look like we've been on a very wearing but not terribly fun shore leave.

"We've passed in visual range of every settlement on Victoria, except the mines on Loch Prima. We'll maneuver to pass over them on the way to high orbit. We have carried out our orders from Victoria Command."

Liddell listened to the echo effect as her orders passed to the squadron, drank more water, and watched the screen. They were on the day side of Victoria, with a thin silver river scrawling a path across the uninhabited badlands below.

The river seemed to jerk, then leaped southward, off the bottom of the screen. The displays sang a silent duet with the engines, as *Shenandoah* broke out of orbit and climbed toward the stars.

Liddell picked up her glass and emptied half of it before she realized the water was making her throat burn and her teeth ache. Thoughts of contamination and having to go hat in hand to Kornilov raced by, followed by recognition.

"Commander Bogdanov, I thought you were an abstainer."

"I am. But I know where to obtain medical supplies for emergency use."

"Is this an emergency?"

"Captain, if I handed you a mirror I might be accused of attempted murder."

She must be tired enough to hallucinate if she thought the Hermit was joking. She levered herself out of the command chair and managed to stand with a little help from the chair and more from Bogdanov's muscles.

"Thank you, Pavel." She walked to the elevator. "Set a high orbit that lets everybody catch up on their sleep. Wake me about 1300, and schedule a department heads' meeting for 1430."

"Agenda?"

"Shore leave, any problems this low pass turned up, anything we learn about the trouble in Blanchard Canyon. Fill in the rest yourself."

"We have visual confirmation of *Shenandoah*'s orbit," the intercom said. The speaker in Captain Leray's cabin had deteriorated in the past few days. Today it was distorting past recognition most voices, except Jo Marder's.

"Thank you," Leray said.

"A geostationary orbit, over Fort Stafford. Sounds like they're going to take it easy."

Leray didn't need an intercom to hear Jo Marder. She was sitting in the corner chair, barefoot, a glass cradled in her lap.

"What else would you do in their position?" Leray asked.

"Aside from bombarding Fort Stafford, if I thought it would get whoever ordered that pass—"

"Jo—"

"Are you getting more afraid of Intelligence, or losing your sense of humor?"

"Rebellion isn't funny, and the Federation worries just as much about it as we do."

"They're a damned sight more tactful!"

"They can afford to be."

"Now it's the party line." Marder shook her head. "Don't you trust your jammers?"

"What I don't trust is your tongue when you've had a few too many."

"My tongue's pretty damned good, even when it tastes of brandy." She stuck it out at him, then rose and hugged him so smoothly he wondered if she really were as drunk as she sounded. "Feel it," she added, poking her tongue into his ear.

He gently pushed her away, without breaking the embrace. He didn't want to do it. He also really didn't trust those jammers anymore, and the cleaner his slate the easier his coming visit to Silvermouth.

However, another round and dinner wouldn't do any harm. He dialed for both, then let his own chair recline.

"Jo, unless whatever happened in Blanchard Canyon blows up a storm, we have it easy for five or six days. That's the earliest ETA we have on any Federation reinforcements. If those are minor, we may have it easy until the Dockyard asteroid is in Victoria orbit.

"So I think we can both afford to be out of the ship for a while. Long enough for a courier visit to Silvermouth, at least."

"Fine. I'll have all-modes copies of our data on *Shenandoah*'s pass ready. Anything else that needs a courier?"

Leray shook his head. A record of eighteen hours of *Shenandoah*'s signals, sensor emissions, and maneuvers was something he really didn't mind giving Intelligence. Analyzed with more resources than *Audacious* could muster, it might even reveal something useful to the Bonsai Squadron.

This wouldn't keep him from passing on the usual extra copies. One at least would go to Colonel Pak. Another would go to a grounded spaceborn businessman in the capital. He had no known ties to any government or military but considerable resources for getting information to the Naval Staff without Intelligence or the Federation hearing about it.

Marder stood up, wiggling her toes in Leray's rug. She stood straight, with only flushed cheeks to show that she'd left sobriety some distance behind.

"I'll put the EI team onto it tonight. We should be able to leave tomorrow, if they don't fumble."

"Scan it yourself before you freeze it," Leray added.

"Why?"

"The EI people know sensors and signals. They don't know ships and squadrons and tactics, at least not as well as you do."

Besides, the more you work the less you drink.

For a moment Marder seemed to have read his thoughts, as her long face twisted. Then she saluted precisely and went out.

Seventeen

The elevator down into the atrium squealed gruesomely. Brian Mahoney winced. Elayne Zheng clapped her hands over her ears, knocking over Lucco DiVries's drink with one elbow. DiVries rolled his eyes to heaven as he tried to mop off his trousers and ordered another round.

Brian Mahoney was thinking that the charms of shore leave on Victoria were mightily overrated. Or was it the charms of Kellysburg, a city with few military visitors before the establishment of Camp Aounda?

With another screech, the elevator climbed out of the atrium, carrying one of the two serving robots. From the shape of their stained and dented cases, Mahoney judged the robots were military surplus—Second Hive War surplus. From the amount of noise it made, the elevator might go all the way back to the Colonial period, but Victoria hadn't been discovered until nearly a century after that.

Hennessey's Bar and Grill was certainly left over from the Hive Wars. The atrium had originally been an underground warehouse for emergency supplies. Victoria was never attacked, so the buildings on the surface were cleared away by wrecking crews instead of Hiver bombs. A hole ten meters deep and twenty wide offered plenty of room for three levels of tables, linked by two elevators and winding stairs.

As the second robot delivered the table's round of drinks, Mahoney looked over the railing. The bottom of the atrium held three small tables, a couple of bonsai-style local trees, and a pond of brass-tinted green water. Once a year

Hennessey opened the dome and let the rain fill the pond. Otherwise it used waste water from the East Bank recycler, deodorized but otherwise left pretty much raw. Enough moisture to fight off the mites was all the pond was expected to provide.

"How are you getting on with Mort Gellis?" Zheng asked, sipping gin and brokenheart juice.

"You know him?"

"Enough to recognize the type. Technically brilliant but no leadership aptitude. Sort of an enlisted version of our Charlie."

"He doesn't seem that driven."

"Who's driving him? Not five admirals, that's for sure. Maybe La Tachin and the Sumo will be unhappy if Gellis doesn't make First, but—and speak of the devil!"

Mahoney craned his neck to follow Zheng's finger. Brigitte Tachin was settling into a chair at a table on the second level of the atrium. She wore a tailored black suit; Mahoney remembered her talking about "black's slimming effect."

Not that she really needed it. Mahoney was determined to one day find a way of convincing Brigitte that she was quite attractive outside as well as inside. So far, all he had was the determination; the way kept eluding him.

Meanwhile, Tachin's outside had glances homing on her from several other tables. A tall man in bush clothes was the first to do more than glance. He said something to his three companions, then stood up.

Under the table, Mahoney felt Zheng's hand on his knee. "Insatiable?" he began.

"Quiet. That man's making his move too soon. Some of his friends don't like him making it at all."

"Who's been trying to protect Brigitte from my protection?"

"That man's lady friend doesn't want to protect La Tachin."

By now DiVries was looking at the unfolding action. From his frown he seemed to agree with Zheng's analysis.

Mahoney decided to let those two handle it, since they were so damned sure they knew what it was. He doubted that Brigitte would let anyone come between her and exploring her chances with a man that good looking.

Although now that he looked more closely, one of the local men did seem to be trying to hold the lady by the wrist. The third man (black haired, clean-shaven, a little pudgy) was standing up and stepping out from behind the table.

The tall man stopped by Tachin's table. She nodded, and he sat down. The other woman jumped up with a sound that might have been intended for a scream.

Already alert, DiVries and Zheng moved faster than Mahoney. DiVries punched the combination for alerting the manager. Zheng vaulted over the railing and started scrambling down. Mahoney wondered what she would use when she reached Brigitte, other than her sharp tongue, then remembered that Elayne almost always carried a folding-blade knife.

The angry woman didn't seem to know who she wanted to deal with first—Tachin, her own friend, or the man trying to restrain her. Her indecision gave the pudgy man time to punch the second man in the stomach. He folded up, gagging and letting the woman go. She practically flew to Tachin's table, knocking her friend against the wall.

Before he could move again, the woman snatched Tachin's chair out from under her. At the same time Elayne Zheng swung down to join the party, the manager's daughter popped out of the office with a riot gun, and the elevator fell all the way from the top of the atrium with one of the robots aboard.

The crash as the elevator hit bottom froze everyone, including Mahoney, at the head of the stairs. He watched the robot roll out, smoking like a hot coal, clatter across the gravel, and topple into the pond. A memorable stench rose when water and circuitry met. He nearly fell on the steps but arrived in time to find Brigitte on her feet and the other two women facing each other in unarmed—combat stance.

The tall man grabbed his friend by the shoulder. She jerked as if he'd been dwarfer fungus. "I don't care how many bouncer friends she has," the woman snarled. "No damned Feddie—"

"We're not contracted, and I'm over the age of consent," the man snapped. "So is the officer."

"Officer? When she can't go out without—" the woman began.

At that point Brigitte Tachin kicked the woman smartly in the knee. As she staggered, her friend caught her and pulled her back, wrapping his arms around her torso gently but so thoroughly that he actually lifted her feet clear of the rug. She kicked his shins hard enough to make him yelp and called him all the names she'd doubtless been ready to use on Tachin and Zheng.

Mahoney found himself facing the pudgy man. He blocked the man's path, without raising his hands or saying a word, and tried to smile. It wasn't easy; the man had a hand inside a pocket, and if Elayne drew her knife, whatever the man had would be drawn on Mahoney.

"Nick, you bloody fool!" DeVries snapped. The pudgy man stepped back. "What the hell did you do to Keith? Is he all right?"

"Uckk," the man who'd been punched in the stomach said. With the help of a chair he pulled himself to his feet.

Mahoney decided that if he stayed he might learn something interesting but would embarrass DiVries, who was trying to defuse the whole situation. He turned and headed for Tachin's table, leaving the others talking as angrily as they could without raising their voices.

"Brian Mahoney, what are you doing here?" Tachin exclaimed.

"I might ask the same thing."

"You might then be told it isn't your affair."

"No, it's yours," Zheng said. "But if it nearly gets the rest of us into a fight with the lo—with the civilians, maybe it's our business, too. Lucco DiVries has a brother here. Can you imagine what it would have meant for him if there'd been real trouble?"

"Carlo DiVries can take care of himself," the tall man said. "As can you, Lieutenant. I respect you for that, even more than I did when I first saw you."

"Then perhaps you should also respect your friend's opinions," Tachin said. She turned to face the woman. "It seems that I misjudged the situation. For that I owe you an apology."

The woman bit her lip, then grunted, "Accepted."

Mahoney turned as the manager's daughter came up.

Kate Hennessey wore a dressing gown and a look that if translated into hard radiation would have been lethal to everyone in the atrium.

Behind her came a tall man in a weatherskin leisure suit. Mahoney had to look twice to recognize Commander Bogdanov.

"People, I think Lieutenant Tachin's apology finishes your business here this afternoon. Lieutenant DiVries and I will meet you at the north gate of Vinh Memorial Park at 1530."

"I haven't had lunch!" Zheng protested.

"You'll be lunch!" Kate Hennessey snapped. "You and your friends. Now be off with you." She shifted her grip on the riot gun.

Elayne Zheng, veteran of many a barroom confrontation, recognized an authority superior even to three stripes. She gathered up her friends and led them out, with Mahoney as rear guard.

A food stall quieted Zheng's hunger pangs and eased her temper by the time Bogdanov and DiVries appeared. Brigitte Tachin hoped devoutly that it would stay eased, no matter what Bogdanov said. If necessary, she would take even more than her share of the blame, to keep the Hermit from skinning Elayne alive with his tongue.

The trashcan by their bench was half full of discarded drink packs and sausage wrappers by the time the other two officers appeared. DiVries looked very much as if he'd rather be anywhere else, but Bogdanov was almost smiling. He let out an almost human sigh as he sat down, and Tachin's stomach began to unknot.

"Now, if I might ask what you were doing here? Lieutenant Zheng I know about from Lieutenant DiVries. But the others?"

"There weren't any orders about—" Zheng began.

Bogdanov coughed. "I was not asking you, Lieutenant."

"Elayne said that she'd checked out Kellysburg and it seemed pretty safe," Mahoney began. "Not terribly interesting, but it was a new planet."

"The woman tempted you?" Bogdanov said.

Mahoney laughed. "She did. But I didn't have to say yes."

"You're more honorable than Adam," Bogdanov said.

"He not only ate the apple but blamed it all on Eve. I've always thought that the original sin was not taking responsibility for your actions. And you, Lieutenant Tachin?"

"I'm a little like Brian," Tachin began. "I wanted to see some of the planet. This is my first time outside the Charlemagne system. I didn't think one Federation officer looking for company could arouse such hostility."

"Not until she tried to arouse something else."

Tachin remembered how conservative Russian Baptists were. Was he going to make a disciplinary issue of her little manhunt?

"That would be between you and God," Bogdanov went on. "However, I have learned that your friend was probably going to use any bedroom encounters to learn as much as possible about *Shenandoah*."

Tachin's stomach reknotted itself, more tightly than before. *"Impossible!"*

"Not that he would try."

"He would learn nothing!"

"You wouldn't say anything deliberately. But you might let something slip. Remember your intelligence course, Lieutenant, if you can't remember anything else!"

Tachin flushed and looked away. She now faced Lieutenant DiVries. He was sweating, pale, and reluctant to meet her eyes.

Several hypotheses suddenly turned into facts in Tachin's mind. "I'm sorry, Lucco. I think I hurt you more than I did that jealousy-eaten *putain*!"

"You would have, if matters had gone any further. Fortunately I'd been sent to Mount Houton and Kellysburg to coordinate with Victoria Command—arrangements—for handling just this kind of trouble. So I knew a little more about what to expect than I was letting on at the time."

Bogdanov shrugged. "All's well that end's well. We may need to improve those arrangements by discouraging liberty in the two cities. We may also still hear from Hennessey's if they find out what happened to their elevator and robot."

Tachin stared. Bogdanov grinned, suddenly looking twenty years younger. *When he is like that, one can see how much better looking he is than that string-tied clown I was chasing.*

That clown, who might have let himself be caught!

"You?" Zheng said.

"Me," Bogdanov said. "One of my boyhood vices was throwing stones. Not at living creatures, but at anything else I could hit, and I could hit almost anything."

He laughed out loud at their shocked faces. "We won't mention my other vices. I came in, saw the situation, saw a tub of gravel and exposed circuits in range, and created a diversion."

"I'll be damned," DiVries said. "Can I say 'thank you' again?"

"You can say it until breakfast on Judgment Morn," Bogdanov said cheerfully. "But gratitude wouldn't have saved you or your friends if there'd been bloodshed. That's why I'm handling this informally for now."

"For now?" Mahoney asked.

"Captain Liddell may still have something to say. Also, I can't vouch for Victoria Command. Their Intelligence people may yet be heard from. That's why I wanted to explain the possible motives of Lieutenant Tachin's sporting partner."

It seemed to Tachin that Bogdanov had left out more than he had explained. She also thought he'd done a wise and compassionate thing. If Lieutenant DiVries were only suspected of links with anti-Federation rebels, even terrorists . . .

"One suggestion, for Lieutenant DiVries," Bogdanov went on. "In case some further action is required, I would recommend that you either ask to go off active duty for a while or at least officially transfer off *Valhalla*."

"We're not going to spy on him for you!" Zheng snapped.

"I'm not asking that. Just remember that my patience is not inexhaustible. Also, remember Captain Prange's views."

Zheng gulped visibly. Prange was that rare thing among line officers of his rank, a fanatical Federation loyalist. He also set inhumanly high standards for those under his command.

Temporary duty and long leave made no difference. DiVries still hadn't been officially detached from *Valhalla*. Prange could order him court-martialed—and certainly would, if any hint of this affair got back to Riftwell.

Bogdanov stood. "Lieutenant DiVries, consider my suggestions. Consult your friends, and pray if you wish. Good afternoon."

They watched Bogdanov's tall figure recede toward the gate. DiVries looked the readiest to faint but was the first to speak.

"Can I trust him?"

"Damned if I know," Zheng said. "He's not living down to his reputation."

"We seem to have both a captain and an executive officer who are hard in some places and soft in others," Tachin began.

Zheng guffawed. "That's the way men and women are made. Just as long as the places are compatible—"

"I cannot imagine that pairing," Tachin said, trying not to laugh. "I cannot even imagine Commander Bogdanov reproducing, except by cloning."

"Mother! Fifty Bogdanovs! I'd rather have a Baernoi invasion." Zheng stood up. "But seriously, Luke. Try asking Captain Liddell. She wasn't deputy chief for Personnel for three years without picking up a few connections—"

"See the squadron! See the squadron! Only half a stellar for a look! See the squadron! Three ten-centimeter telescopes and a screen. You pay your money and you take your choice! Come see the squadron!"

The piercing voice from the south gate brought everyone to their feet. They hurried down a pruned umbrella-grass path to the music stand. It had sprouted three fat white tubes and a camouflaged shelter, and a line was already forming.

"Got any cash?" Mahoney asked.

Zheng passed around a handful of coins. "But I go first." She sprinted to the platform and wound up fifth in line for one of the telescopes.

When her turn came, she deftly adjusted the controls. Then she let out a whoop of delight and jumped off the platform.

"*Ira Hayes* and *Wu Te-Huai*. They're in orbit and they're unloading. Now I can—"

"Remember what we've just been through," DiVries said.

"Oh, I'm sure they'll find out about—what *Hayes* is unloading soon enough." She looked back at the telescopes and whispered. "Maybe that's one reason for this little show for the tourists. Shall we check out the shelter for recording equipment?"

"After attracting this much attention?" Mahoney laughed. "They'll have had a chance to hide anything they don't want us to see. Come on." He took one of her arms, DiVries took the other, and they marched her away.

Tachin brought up the rear. She knew that if Zheng did go back on attacker duty, she would be much happier. But she would also be leaving an emptiness in the bunkroom where she had been.

It can hardly be a surprise that I will miss Elayne. Not after the day I woke up and found I missed Charles Longman!

Eighteen

Captain Liddell could have held the meeting in her regular office but decided to use the small conference room. Even with the admiral's newly delivered gift of three Jersey Jems in envirocapsules, there was plenty of room for the admiral, Colonel Vesey, and herself.

"The joint exercises shouldn't take more than three days," Colonel Vesey added. "After that, we can allow at least a four-day Evaluation and Maintenance."

"I'd suggest five or six," Admiral Kuwahara said. "I plan to use the period of the dockyard's arrival in Victoria orbit for squadron maneuvers."

"How would you maintain security for Dockyard during the maneuvers?" Vesey asked.

"The squadron hasn't practiced a defensive action supported by dockyard weapons," Liddell said. "About half the weapons would be simulated this time, but we could still gain valuable experience. We would also be practically nose-to-tail around the dockyard most of the last two days of its approach. That's the only period when the Bonsai Squadron could act without giving us some warning."

Kuwahara spread his hands delicately on the tabletop and nodded. "Colonel Vesey?" he said.

"Fine," Vesey said. Sweating in spite of the climate control, she wiped her forehead with the back of her hand and pushed several loose strands of hair into different if not necessarily proper places.

"After the E & M, the squadron will deploy the attackers with full warloads for a joint operation with First Battalion.

This will attempt to penetrate and clear the Blanchard Canyon area. The planning title is Operation Raptor.

"Second Battalion will be operating on training maneuvers with Third and Fourth. They will also hold one company as a Brigade reserve, to join Operation Raptor if necessary."

"We don't expect that will be necessary. If the intelligence estimate of opposing strength is remotely accurate, we should have the military side of the crisis resolved in a few days."

A distasteful suspicion crystallized in Liddell's mind. She wouldn't call Victoria Command's optimism fatuous, but . . .

"Has a decision been reached about asking for ground reinforcements?"

Vesey spoke in carefully modulated phrases. "Informally, yes. It's negative. Not irrevocably, but the Military Council and the president definitely support us."

"What about the prime minister and the governor-general?" Kuwahara asked. In the days since the admiral's arrival aboard the converted scout cruiser *Mogilev*, Liddell had learned to recognize some of his tones. His present skepticism was one of them.

"They haven't stated either support or opposition," Vesey said. "The governor-general says he feels neutrality is appropriate."

"I will not presume to tell Victoria Command how to assess a situation," Kuwahara said. Liddell wondered if he sensed the same thing: that Vesey was passing on a decision she herself did not support.

"I concur," Kuwahara added. "Captain Liddell?"

Take a deep breath, Rosie, then dive.

"Yes, with some reservations. We can't rule out either Alliance or Baernoi influence. Both have a habit of causing minor troubles and hoping to provoke major Federation responses. A brigade would be a major response if it wasn't needed.

"Also, the reputation of the Federation armed forces for handling these little flareups is part of our strength. We may be putting our people in danger, but it's not unnecessary danger."

Vesey nodded. "What are the reservations?" She sounded like someone who knows they're not off the hook yet.

"Really just one, come to think of it. If the Alliance is involved, we may need to operate in the border areas. That's a lot of empty land for the troops we could spare. The attackers can help, but we need somebody on the ground. A Ranger team might help, and they could slip on-planet without anybody noticing."

"You can probably pry a whole corps out of Eleventh Army more easily than the Rangers," Vesey said. "But I like it. May I credit you when I pass it along?"

"Add my endorsement, too," Kuwahara said. "But whatever you do, it can wait until after lunch."

Munching biscuits spread with cheese between sips of fruit juice, Liddell leaned back in her chair and mentally reviewed the meeting.

Actually, I did have two reservations, but one of them wasn't the sort to mention. It looks as if Kornilov and Victoria Command hope to win promotion by handling this themselves.

The nonprovocation policy for divided-sovereignty planets was implemented in various ways on the thirty-odd planets in question. Some had miniscule garrisons of crack troops. Some had no garrisons and few local forces. Victoria had a brigade, normal for a planet with this many Federation citizens, but an undersized one with little support and few officers who hadn't more or less retired on duty.

Now, suddenly, Victoria Command was waking up to the fact that a crisis can be an opportunity. If Liddell had to point a finger at anyone for reminding his fellows of this fact, she would point it at General Langston.

He has never pretended not to want three or four stars. Just as well that he's the best of the lot as well as the most ambitious.

"So how's business?" Candice Shores asked.

A sepulchral voice replied from behind the bar. "Not bad, not good. People stay close to the fort because they're busy, not because they're afraid to go into town."

Something went *fzzzzz* like a bottle of inferior champagne. Foul smoke and fouler language followed. Max Jabs, the bartender at the Hunter's Rest, crawled out from under the bar. His normally cherubic pink face was dark with soot.

"When was the last time Maintenance cleaned inside the terminal? *When*?"

No one was in hearing except two serving robots and an androgynous individual with "You pay, I bounce" written large on its long face. Shores smelled an opening.

"Maintenance short-handed?"

"What isn't?"

Shores wondered if Jabs's perpetually cheerful expression was acting, chemistry, or surgery. It certainly didn't match the lugubrious voice.

"Locals not coming in on time?"

"Not coming in at all, some of them."

"I didn't know the bad feeling came this far south."

"Mostly it hasn't. It's the owner giving people vacations until things settle down."

"Makes sense. Fewer incidents, and us uniformed types don't need to watch our tongues every second we're drinking with friends."

"It makes sense, until work doesn't get done. Do you know how to fix a Goodwill Model 24?"

"I know a few people who do."

"It might be worth their while to help me."

Shores thanked the Creator that she'd found Jabs so eager. She really ought to have left this foraging mission in the south to Raoul Zimmer; it wasn't officer's work. But Zimmer was even more indispensable in the north, keeping morale up and watching out for Intelligence snooping.

"Some of them are Scouts. What's it worth to Scout Company's supplies?" She had a perfectly legal company welfare fund, but why pay when you might make a deal?

Jabs was a shrewd bargainer. They finally reached a figure of nonration food and drink that could be slipped out of the storerooms, carried north, hidden in Scout Company, and earn Max the services of a couple of Scout Company's electronics techs for some essential repairs. The bargaining was down to how many pallets each party would provide when a familiar face emerged from the mirror at Candice Shores's left shoulder.

"Good evening, Major Nieg."

"Good evening, Captain Shores. Good evening, Max. The usual."

Nieg's usual was a beer. Without being asked, Jabs also

refilled Shores's Scotch. She prayed for Max to be rewarded in this life and any future one and raised her glass.

"To peace."

"And understanding," Nieg added, then he drank. He wiped foam off his upper lip with a finger that showed signs of being a crude regen. "Captain Shores, can I talk with you outside?"

Only about ten of the fifty possible reasons for Nieg's request made him dangerous, and some of them were worth the risk.

"Lead on."

The androgyne looked disappointed as the two officers left the bar and skirted the marathon card game by the fish tank. At the door, Nieg pulled his cloak tighter around his throat.

"The wind's up, Captain. Let's sit by the windbreak."

Shores couldn't quite hide relief. Nothing immediately fatal could happen in such a public place.

They trotted the five hundred meters to the artificial dune that shielded Fort Stafford from the worst of the desert storms. To the west the Queen's Star was already below the horizon, with the Prince's Star sinking into its companion's afterglow. A flock of red devils swooped down onto the face of the windbreak, recoiled from a section of plastic mesh, and finally settled where the beervine ground cover had already taken root. The two officers sat in silence until the birds had finished squabbling over roosts.

"Captain," Nieg said, "a question I would like answered. Nothing will happen if you don't answer."

"Except you not learning something you want to know."

"Being delayed, anyway. I imagine I could at least narrow the field by going back and talking to Max Jabs."

"How long were you in the bar?"

"I didn't mean that to sound like a threat. If it was private business, it can stay private. I merely wondered if what Corporal Esteva said had something to do with you being here."

"How long were you in the bar?" Shores wanted to scream the question or even shake an answer out of the little major.

"Several hours. The card table has a regular member, an underemployed, discontented lifter mechanic. A change of clothes and a quick facial, and he vanishes. They probably think he's on the run from Intelligence!"

"Is somebody after you, Major, or are you just paranoid for the fun of it?"

Nieg stood up. "Captain Shores, you are being unnecessarily rude. I'm answering questions that I really don't have to."

Shores bowed her head. "Your Supremacy's graciousness overwhelms me."

"Do you want to learn why I talked with Corporal Esteva or do you want to stay here exchanging insults until Security asks us what we're doing?"

"The first, if I have a choice."

Nieg stood up and began to walk back and forth. In the lee of the windbreak, he could almost whisper and still be heard a good two meters away.

"Corporal Esteva is one of my best agents. He's one of my best, because he's a good actor. He can arouse any officer's curiosity or indignation, until they come to me and I have a chance to evaluate them.

"I was beginning to worry when all I had from you was sarcasm. Then I remembered your file. You have the field officer's usual dislike of covert Intelligence people, cubed and squared."

Shores nodded slowly. She was beginning to feel like a blue death, herded inexorably into killing range by ultrasonic buoys. At least she was intelligent enough to choose the moment to go over to the attack.

"Captain Shores, right now you're one of the keys to peace on this planet. Your Scouts are going to be the first on the scene of even more trouble than General Kornilov estimated. What happened at Blanchard Canyon is just the first incident."

"If I'm going to be in that deep, Major, what about my being captured? Couldn't it wait until we get a fresh brigade?"

Nieg whirled. "We're not going to get that new brigade. Not until after a few more Blanchard Canyons, if nothing worse. That's a secret, trust, along with everything else I want to tell you.

"Captain Shores, I've read your file. There aren't many officers I'd trust so completely to keep a secret. Anyone will talk under enough pressure, except the dead. You'd be very hard to take and keep alive."

Nieg's tone was almost jocular, but his words felt like a cold hand squeezing her mind. She shivered from more than the wind.

"So the desert opposition is getting militant," she said. "That means units heavily recruited on Victoria may not be reliable for suppressing it. Second Battalion's going to have some holes and we might as well write off Third and Fourth completely."

"That's what I call the realistic-pessimist scenario," Nieg said.

Shores wanted to know what the extreme-pessimist scenario might be, but she couldn't think of anything worse than open rebellion by the Third and Fourth Battalions coupled with Baernoi intervention. She also couldn't take much more of listening to Nieg spill his guts or whatever he was doing. Max Jabs, once Nieg's eye was off him, would be hustling the supplies out of the storeroom to a pickup point as fast as the robots could work.

Nieg faced her. "Our enemy is complex out of all proportion to their numbers. A couple of hundred fanatics like the ones you met. A thousand, maybe two thousand ready to take the field as a rebel army. An unknown number of sympathizers, on both sides of the border, ready to supply weapons, equipment, and intelligence."

"Both? I suppose the Alliance is feeding money and weapons to its border settlers' to pass on to ours, but does that make them—"

"The borderers in Seven Rivers are stealing supplies and weapons faster than ours. We've just learned this in the last few days. We've also learned that their Intelligence isn't telling the Bonsai Force."

Shores spat into the sand. "If you go on this way, Major, you may actually have me believing there's some difference between the two intelligence services."

"It's never too late to convert. But it is getting too late to be out here in the wind, even without Security fussing at us." Nieg started to pace again.

"So we don't know if the Alliance ties are official or not. This may simply be the result of all the desert and border people feeling neglected by both governments.

"That's why I expect the decision not to ask for reinforcements will be endorsed on Southern Cross. The Government only has a five-vote majority in Parliament. If things blow up on Victoria, the United Socialists at least will claim that this is the result of neglecting the planet. They might force a vote of censure."

"From what I've seen, they'd have a point."

"I would agree, but that's not our business. Our business is finding the best way to avoid a blowup. Troops to simply overwhelm the opposition aren't going to be available. That would need two or three brigades right off, followed by a whole corps when the crisis with the Alliance started."

"So we're going to soothe rather than slap. I'm not quarreling with that idea, Major. But what about the Baernoi?"

"So far, all the aid they've sent is either negligible or filtered through so many layers of Merishi and human that it ends up that way. The Baernoi have learned that most humans won't accept directly from them. They haven't learned how to give indirect aid and still control what its recipients do.

"When they do, we're in trouble. But sufficient unto the decade are the crises thereof. Right now, my main job is finding disloyal Victorians in Victoria Command's ranks. We want to purge them, but politely, not like Stalin or K'yung.

"We'll invite them to sit on the sidelines. Most of them should accept. By the time we're down to reliable troops and nothing else, we should know who the political leaders are. We can negotiate with them, isolating the terrorists and fanatics."

"People like that don't give up just because you're negotiating with their leaders," Shores pointed out. History, her mother had said early and often, was an infallible antidote to optimism.

"Tell me something I don't already know too well. They're more likely to repudiate their leaders and go underground. But what can they do against a whole planet? Many of the people we've purged will come off the sidelines to fight the terrorists. We could even bring in that extra brigade without offending anyone."

"Everybody except Alliance Intelligence will probably be begging us to," Shores said. "All right. You've persuaded me that we're probably not enemies. What do you want me to do?"

"I'll send you specific instructions in a couple of days. Through Corporal Esteva, if all else fails. For now, remember that we're in a race against time, more than a war against human enemies. It would still be a hard race if I had a dozen clones. As it is, I can only ask the help of the best people I find."

Shores thrust both hands forward into the major's firm, cool grip. Then he turned and seemed to fade into the darkness without taking a step.

She waited until she saw him trot out of the shadows into the lighted stretch of road by the bus station. The sense of relief was curious but real. There'd been something otherworldly about Nieg, beyond normal limits of good and evil.

Certainly he'd talked sense. Nobody but a fool thought that the best way of dealing with minor crises was major forces. Not when the Alliance and the Baernoi were only two of the parties ready to make the Federation exhaust itself chasing phantoms across two thousand light-years.

There might even be "promotion and pay" for Candice Nikolaevna Shores in the situation. Honestly come by, too. Even a single reinforcing brigade might have a whole Light Infantry Battalion, complete with armor. It would certainly have its own Scout Company, under an officer senior to Shores.

Without that brigade, Shores would be the senior Scout on Victoria. She could go on doing field-grade officer's work as an acting captain. If she did it well . . .

She started back for the Hunter's Rest. The Prince was gone and the sky star-specked. Well up toward the zenith, a spark moved swiftly across the darkness. A ship was climbing into orbit, already into the sunlight. An attacker or a shuttle, from the size.

A Security lifter hovered overhead. Shores turned until her ID would be clearly visible to the sensors, then waved. Golden lights blinked three times and the lifter moved on.

She would work with Nieg, as long as she found ways of learning more than he chose to tell her. Corporal Esteva would be a starting point. She had his good will; she would have more when he became Sergeant Esteva. And Scout Company would have another reliable sergeant.

SQUADRON ALERT

* * *

Elayne Zheng swigged half her drink and almost gagged. A misprogrammed mixer, or were the drinks going bad on her along with everything else?

She couldn't even get much satisfaction from cursing Captain Liddell and Admiral Kuwahara, because she couldn't do it at the top of her lungs. Not with half the crews of the 879th Attacker Squadron in earshot, counting those who were busy in the side rooms.

Maybe I shouldn't curse Kuwahara. After all, it was his idea to work the squadron hard. No reinforcements any time soon, so what we have has to go further. If I'd gotten into a crew by now, I could look forward to flying my tail off.

But Cozy Rosie smells empire building and slaps an "Essential Personnel" label on me. So here I am, stuck aboard Shenandoah.

Zheng pushed her drink away. Why bother to get drunk if it was no fun? Kicking off her boots, Zheng gripped both arms of her chair. Slowly she brought legs and torso up, then swiveled until her body was vertical. Finally she straightened her arms until her eyes looked over the back of the low chair.

They looked straight at the squadron commander's navel. Zheng recognized the navel; Commander Gesell had come to the party from liberty and hadn't changed out of her red, two-piece party suit.

Slowly Zheng raised her eyes to meet Gesell's, without shifting position. She met the most appraising stare she'd ever encountered.

"Are you fit for duty, Lieutenant Zheng?"

Two drinks. Strong ones, but one of them only half. Nothing else. Unless I'm losing my head before I lose my youth.

"Fit enough."

Zheng's arms flexed; she flipped to land feet-first on the table. Her abandoned drink bounced off the table, landing on Gesell's pants.

The appraising look vanished behind an armored mask for a moment. Then Gesell shrugged.

"We're on stand-down, so most of the people weren't expecting anything but partying. Then Katzanzakis went down with mite sinusitis. Don't know how he got it, but that big nose is always snuffing up things it shouldn't."

"Anyway, that leaves the duty crew short an electronic-warfare officer. Until now. You are the new EWO for Gold Three."

Zheng felt like turning another somersault. "Let me run back and get my—"

"I've sent a messenger. She may be back in time. The duty attacker is now on ten minutes' notice for long-range operations. Beg, borrow, or steal anything you can't do without, starting right now."

Zheng did turn the somersault. Two people under the table, clothed but cozy, glared at her. She bit her thumb at them.

"What's the trouble?

"Do you expect the gods to tell mere attacker swine?" Gesell said.

"Ours not to reason why, ours but to fly and fry," Zheng quoted.

"Exactly. Now stow your body aboard Gold Three before the Old Lady discovers that I'm trying to snatch it!"

Nineteen

"Time for the passenger check," Kurt Pocher said. If any of
the six passengers on their way to the Nicola Chennault
Observatory were asleep or busy, he wanted to know. In
half an hour he'd have to wake or interrupt them, as *Leon
Brautigan* prepared for rendezvous with the observatory.

Like most astronomical observatories in systems that didn't
offer a well-placed planet, the Chennault Observatory perched
on an asteroid hauled into optimum orbit by a Navy engineering crew. It had large specimens of every known kind of
astronomical instrument, a permanent staff of eighty, and
quarters for half again as many.

All the resources of Victoria couldn't have supported it
now, let alone a century ago, but they didn't need to. The
Victoria System was the only inhabited system convenient to
a number of abstruse astronomical phenomena that Kurt
Pocher had never been able to understand.

Mahmoud Sa'id, the classic amateur-astronomer spaceman, had tried to explain some of them. As pillowtalk,
astronomical curiosities were a lost cause for Pocher, and
Sa'id finally gave up.

Sa'id stretched, yawned, and began checking the passenger-
cabin monitors.

"Everybody's alive and nobody's doing anything strenu-
ous," he finally said. "Those two photo techs from the
university must have stepped out for a beer."

"Probably saw Louis on his way to fixing a snack and
decided to claim a dividend," Pocher said. "Damn! I wish
we could step up the monitoring."

"You know what the director'll say. 'Ve haff no money' and 'brivacy must be resbected.' "

Pocher laughed at his friend's imitation of Dr. Kuttelwascher's accent. "What about respecting the accident statistics? Sooner or later, we'll let a case of anoxia or cosmophobia get serious. Then she'll hear a lot more than she'd ever get from a privacy violation."

"She probably thinks her luck will put it in the next director's lap."

"Doctor Rita's going to be running the observatory when you and I are both retired to a little house outside Thorntonsburg."

"Better a little farm in the Vinh Delta."

"I thought you hated farms, Mahmoud."

"I would hate not being able to see the stars even more."

The bridge door chime tinkled. To Pocher, it always sounded like an irritable fairy. He recognized Ferraro's code and punched the opener. As the door started to open, the chime tinkled again.

Before Pocher's surprise could turn to alarm, the door slammed into its slot under the weight of bodies falling through. One body was Louis Ferraro. The second, holding a bodylock around Ferraro's torso, was one of the photo techs.

Behind the two was the other tech, holding a short-barreled, large-bore plastic scattergun.

Pocher's hands rose as his mind scrolled conclusions. *Must have broken it down into components that would pass a scan. That could mean he's short of ammo. If he's short of nerve as well—*

"Freeze!"

Everybody on the bridge obeyed, except the first tech. He rose, holding the knife he had been pressing against Ferraro's throat, and glared at everybody impartially, his partner included.

Closer to the edge, I'd guess. Problem is, he'd take one of us over the edge with him if we pushed hard. Not time for that kind of trade. Yet.

Without moving anything except his mouth, Pocher said, "All right. This looks like a hijacking. We won't be any problem, if you'll tell us what to do."

The first tech's mouth worked. The second nodded. "We

represent Action for Independence. This ship is now our property."

"I won't argue with that," Pocher said.

"You won't make jokes again, either," the knifeman said, raising his blade.

The gunman shook his head again. Sweat broke out on the other hijacker's face and his mouth worked soundlessly. *Damned good act. One tough, one nice. I wonder how long they expect it to work.*

"Disable your communications," the gunman said. "If any signal goes out, we'll know it. I'll tell you when to be ready to send and receive again."

"Do it, Mahmoud," Pocher said. Sa'id bent low over his consoles and slapped switches. A meter-square section of displays went dark.

"Good," the gunman said. "Now seal the passengers in their cabins."

Pocher saw that Mahmoud was still bending over. He decided to hesitate.

"The cabins don't have—"

"We've been in one of them for three days," the gunman said. "Seal them now."

The knifeman's hands had begun to shake. Pocher decided not to bet that he was acting. A little or even a lot of inconvenience to the passengers was better than most of the alternatives.

"Cabins sealed," Pocher said a moment later. Mahmoud finally had control of his face and was sitting upright. "Can we inform the passengers what's happening? They might panic."

"They can't do anything if they panic. They might resist if they know. None of them have any serious medical problems."

Pocher stiffened, and Sa'id's face twisted again. That knowledge implied a breach of security somewhere. Not critical in itself, but it meant that the hijackers had an informant somewhere or a tap into the observatory's ground-data files.

The knifeman seemed to be under control. At a nod from his comrade, he pulled a stun capsule from his belt and sprayed a dose into Ferraro's neck. As Ferraro slumped unconscious, the man released the bodylock and pulled it off.

"This ship has a new destination, which you will learn in

time," the gunman said. "Meanwhile, one of you will be stunned at all times. Of the two awake, one will be in the bodylock, immobile except for hands and head. Which of you will be first?"

Mahmoud shrugged. "Me, I suppose. I told you my yoga would be useful some day, Kurt."

Pocher signaled caution with his eyes but doubted that Mahmoud noticed. All Pocher could do was hope that the hijackers wouldn't notice Mahmoud's confidence and get suspicious.

Dead-man alarms on ship's communications were standard practice. What Mahmoud had done was link the dead-man sequence to the tender's radio and that radio to an external antenna almost invisible unless you knew where to look for it.

In about forty-two minutes the tender's radio would expect to receive the HOLD signal. If it didn't, the radio would automatically start broadcasting a distress signal. The tender's radio didn't have the range of *Brautigan*'s main rig, certainly not working through an improvised antenna, but it would be broadcasting in range of a radio-telescope array three kilometers in diameter.

With that array, the observatory could pick up a child's headset transmitter at ten thousand kilometers. *Brautigan*'s signal would be like a scream in a temple.

"I think we need to know when the attackers are going to embark, and how many," the first lieutenant said. "Then we'll know how much training help they'll need onboard and how much we'll need to send dirtside."

The spectacle of Commander Charbon being cooperative and polite reduced the other department heads to speechlessness. The silence gave Rose Liddell time to organize her own thoughts.

Juggling the priorities of training, maneuvers with the Victoria Brigade, Evaluation and Maintenance, bringing Victoria Dockyard into orbit, Operation Raptor, and keeping alert while doing everything else had started producing long days and short tempers. What a department-heads meeting would do about it, Liddell wasn't quite sure, but it would at least satisfy everybody that the Old Lady was on the job.

The EMERGENCY signal on her screen broke the silence. When the SECURE warning followed, she popped in the earplugs and cut off the visual. Only Fujita and Zubova had reached the point of fidgeting by the time she unplugged.

"Sorry for the interruption, everyone. The Chennault Observatory just called. They've picked up a distress signal from the observatory supply ship, *Leon Brautigan*. It was a weak signal, but they had their main radio array up for a project, so it came in loud and clear.

"They also got a visual on the ship. She missed her last maneuver for rendezvous and is now heading out of the system. They coded and packaged all their data and have it on the way."

"Communications. Priority One is decoding the data and running it through our main. I smell something.

"Engineering. I want all systems ready for a full-power run anywhere in the system in two hours."

"They'll be ready faster than that," Fujita said.

"If your people are that good, maybe I can have some of the training assets the attackers don't need," Charbon said.

"Commander, that was uncalled for. But otherwise I think you've made the critical point. The 879th needs all the help we can give them, even if we have to cut back our own training schedule. We've had ninety-odd days to work up. They've had only two-thirds of that at most.

"I can leave the details to you. Thank you all for your cooperation."

Liddell rose, returned the salutes, and headed for the door. She needed a secure line and privacy for a talk with Admiral Kuwahara.

Brautigan might have suffered a severe but routine accident. She might also have been caught up in the high-stakes games somebody was playing on Victoria. What happened in Blanchard Canyon or the bars of Kellysburg could be left to Kornilov, but what happened in space was the Navy's affair.

"Your turn for the bodylock," the gunman said. As he handed the gun to his partner, it passed in front of an active display. Pocher tried to count the rounds through the nearly transparent plastic without being too obvious.

It didn't really matter. If the hijackers had seven rounds

and the will to use them, they could turn an empty ship over to whoever was meeting them.

For eight hours *Brautigan* had been on a straight course, steadily opening the distance to the observatory. They were moving at many times escape velocity for the Victoria system, so their eventual destination would be deep space if nobody met them.

Pocher hoped that the meeting would take place within the next ten hours. Then they'd be out of range of the meteor-watch radar and scopes. The big astronomical telescopes with their fifty-meter arrays were too clumsy for tracking ships. If the hijackers' friends maintained electronic silence and painted their ship black, *Brautigan* might vanish as completely as if she'd fallen into a black hole.

With no weapon to be seized, the gunman released Sa'id's bodylock, then stepped back and retrieved his gun. Sa'id stood up, rubbing his wrists and ankles and flexing his back cautiously. The knifeman knelt, his blade at Ferraro's throat. The message was clear: Ferraro would pay with his life for any resistance from the other two.

"Oh, get on with it," Pocher grunted, holding out his own arms and legs. The gunman didn't reply, either to Pocher or to his comrade's glare. He merely fastened the bodylock's collar and belt harness into place and activated the restraints. When the last of them had clicked on, Pocher was embraced as closely as he'd ever been by a partner, but not nearly as pleasantly.

As the hijackers intended, he could use his hands on the controls and swivel in his chair. Both took an effort that brought sweat out all over him. The already sour air of the bridge grew worse.

Pocher found a position where he could see and reach most of the controls without moving enough to hurt. Since the hijackers hadn't even hinted at any maneuvers, that should be enough. The only ones he couldn't reach were the ones for the passenger cabins. Their alarm lights had been frantically blinking these past six hours, but as far as the hijackers were concerned, the passengers might have been on Monticello.

Still, another try wouldn't hurt.

"I don't know what you're planning for the passengers. But you'll be in much more serious trouble if they're hurt or killed. You might even be in trouble with your friends, if they need hostages—"

The knifeman's blade whispered through the sour air, drawing a thin line across Pocher's left hand. Blood welled up. Pocher blinked sweat out of his eyes, realizing how close he'd come to death or maiming.

That bastard with the knife is kill-crazy and his leash is fraying. I wonder if we can work it so that his friend won't trust him with the gun the next time they change the bodylock.

"Don't tell us our business," the gunman said, almost politely. "It's not yours. Don't worry about the passengers. Nothing's going to happen to them that they don't bring on themselves."

Since the passengers were in no position to even visit the head when they needed to go, what they could bring on themselves was one more mystery in a situation that already had too many. Pocher still turned the statement over and over in his mind.

Is that a hint—that the hijackers' friends will pick them up before the passengers can start hurting? Maybe. But it doesn't say a bouncing thing about who those friends are!

Every spaceman in the Victoria system had by now heard rumors of the mystery ship *Shenandoah* tracked on her way in. The ship threatened to become Victoria's answer to the ghost ships of fifty systems and a hundred planets, going all the way back to Earth's Flying Dutchman.

Pocher didn't believe in ghosts, but he did believe in outside intervention in Victoria's affairs, by somebody who could build a state-of-the-art starship and send it to play games in the Victoria System.

Which cuts the number of suspects down to seventy or eighty.

Since Pocher couldn't relax his body, he decided to relax his mind. Planning a week's menus produced nothing but a rumbling stomach. Designing the retirement cottage led to arousing thoughts of Mahmoud. Wondering where the Navy was made him sweat so much he could barely see.

Pocher finally decided that relaxing in a bodylock aboard a hijacked ship was not part of his duty as *Brautigan's* captain.

*　　*　　*

"Hey, Longman! Get your head down! A couple of hours will do you good."

Charles Longman turned from the terminal to see Rima Aschmann glowering at him from the cabin door. He rubbed his eyes until *Cooney*'s first lieutenant was fully in focus.

"Just a final check."

"That's what you said the last time. And the time before that. Take a break, before it breaks you."

Aschmann stepped into the cabin and closed the door behind her. "You don't need to prove you're not just a passenger. You've lifted your share if you drop dead right now." She frowned. "Which looks about what you're heading for."

"Nothing a bath can't fix."

Aschmann pulled a keycard out of her shirt pocket. "So be my guest."

"In a bit. I want to have the schematics of *Brautigan*'s tender bay laid out so a blind, deaf, half-witted, groundbound Merishi toddler can figure them out."

"I thought you were line, Longman. You keep talking like an engineer."

Throwing the first lieutenant out on her ear would be illegal and impossible. Longman grunted, froze the screen, and turned to face Aschmann.

But she'd slipped behind him, and strong thumbs and fingers were massaging his forehead and temples. He thought of resisting, but gradually he felt the aches being drawn out of him.

"Now," she said, sitting back on her heels. "Take the bath. That's an order. After you come back, you can have a complete massage if you want it. That's not a proposition.."

Longman took the card and tottered out the door. He was surprised that he could find his way to the first lieutenant's cabin, and how much difference the bath made.

When he returned, Aschmann was bent over the screen. He lay down in his robe and contemplated the coloring of his left great toenail. Anything more seemed to demand too much mental effort.

Aschmann swiveled in the chair and squatted on it in the easy pose. "Longman, did you ever think of a career as a teacher?"

"It's good?"

"Damned good. Did you study naval architecture?"

"Call it a hobby. I collect odd designs and components. When I heard *Brautigan* called 'thirty surplus subassemblies flying in tight formation,' I figured I might know something somebody else didn't. I didn't expect she had the same kind of bay as the transport where I did my enlisted service. That was just dumb luck."

"Good luck for us. Finish the job, get some sleep, and we'll put it on a three-ship link, with you as teacher. We really *may* be able to find our way aboard *Brautigan* blindfolded. It was a lucky hour when we had to take off so fast we couldn't unload you and your friends."

Longman had been one of a three-person team from the Dockyard crew. Their mission: to get a ship's-eye view of a landing on Dockyard by observing one from aboard *Cooney*. Their fate: to go racing off on the trail of *Leon Brautigan*, because *Cooney*'s orders allowed her no time to disembark them.

"Three-ship link?" he asked.

"*Cooney, Weilitsch,* and *Mogilev.*"

"I didn't know that overpowered piece of scrap was with us. What about *Shen*?"

"Still around Victoria, last I heard. Or overheard. The Old Lady and the exec didn't sound too happy about it, but orders are orders. Seems that the Alliance is keeping *Audacious* off Victoria, too, so our big gun has to watch theirs."

"Damn!"

Part of the chill Longman felt was wearing only his robe. Part of it was thinking of what this might mean if the ships chasing *Brautigan* ran into the same intruder that *Shenandoah* had tracked. If *Brautigan* had been hijacked, wasn't she probably heading for a rendezvous with that ship? Or at least some ship that could easily outgun everything the Federation had in-system except *Shen*?

"What about Dockyard?"

"*Pucinski, Ira Hayes,* and the attackers were scrambled to bring her in. Anyway, nothing short of *Audacious* could really hurt the dockyard, and if *Audi* moves, *Shen* will stick her nose up *Audi*'s waste-water line and keep it there."

Aschmann unfolded herself and stood up. "I'll let you get

back to work, but there's one thing I'd like to ask you: How much EVA time have you had?"

"About a hundred hours."

"Pretty good. Any EVA combat?"

"Only the basic course."

"Okay, then you can be technical support. The point is, I'll be leading *Cooney*'s boarding party. I'd like you to be in it. You'll be a real asset, one *Weilitsch* won't have."

Longman said a lot of things besides "Damn," but under his breath. Aschmann was still standing by the door when he finished.

What now, relative of too bloody many admirals? Here's your chance to mess your pants in public.

I've never done that.

There's always a first time. Hijackers shooting at you might do it.

Not going will have all the admirals shooting at you.

They haven't hit you yet.

There's always a first time. Besides, you might wind up a live hero, and if you do wind up a dead one, you won't have to listen to any more bloody admirals!

Pocher woke up and realized that going to sleep hadn't been such a good idea. The bodylock made him stiff and sore in places he hadn't known were places.

Also, both hijackers were shooting vicious looks at Sa'id. Nothing else, but the tension level was way up from what it had been a couple of hours before.

If Mahmoud has been provoking them . . .

If he has, maybe he's right? How long can we wait for the Navy?

What the Hades! The observatory might not have picked up our signal. Then the first thing they'll know about the 'jacking is when Brautigan *comes back as a Trojan horse. With a fuser aboard, she could take out the observatory, or Dockyard, or* Shenandoah . . .

"Up!" the gunman said. His voice sounded almost as harsh as his friend's. "Not you!" he snapped at Sa'id, covering him.

Mahmoud, what the Hades do you think you can do with me in a bodylock—

"I want to clean up Mr. Ferraro," Sa'id replied. "Nothing

else. In case you hadn't noticed, he's had a reaction to the stun."

Pocher couldn't be sure Sa'id was telling the truth, although the air did seem even riper than before.

"If you're concerned about his hostage value, you have to let me tend him," Sa'id said placatingly. Only Pocher knew how much such subservience must be costing his copilot. Sa'id would rather take orders from Baernoi than from these men. The Baernoi were at least open enemies. The hijackers were traitors to the Federation.

Neither hijacker said anything. Boldly assuming that silence gave consent, Sa'id stepped forward. He was kneeling beside Ferraro when the knifeman sprang.

Sa'id twisted clear of a lethal stab to the ribs but landed with the knifeman on top of him. The tip of the knife gouged Sa'id's cheek, working its way toward his eye.

The knifeman was drooling.

Pocher wished he could believe that what he saw wasn't there. The knifeman had finally gone over the edge.

"Damn it!" the gunman shouted. "Damn you! Not him!"

The knife stopped. A look passed between the two hijackers, then the gunman nodded.

Still sitting on Sa'id's chest, the knifeman turned around and cut Louis Ferraro's throat.

Pocher's throat turned to a pool of bile. He gagged and writhed. From the deck, Sa'id's voice came sharp and clear.

"If Lieutenant Pocher chokes to death, you'll only have me to run the ship. You can end up short of hostages, but what about short of crew? With Mr. Ferraro dead, the two survivors are no longer—"

The gunman looked as if he would like to shoot both Sa'id and his partner, evening up the odds. Sa'id's threat seemed to draw him back.

"Pocher. Adjust the internal gravity so that you can carry Ferraro's body. The cabins have visual locks? Do they?" The last was almost a scream.

"Yes."

"Show each passenger what happens to enemies of Action for Independence. Then put the body in the tender bay."

The knifeman didn't even wipe the blood off his hands before he released Pocher's bodylock. His eyes had an obscene look of relief, even contentment. Pocher wanted to spit in the man's face, to drive him back toward the edge.

Not while his friend's here with the gun and a bit of common sense. Not as much as he had before, though. He thinks it's important to separate Mr. Killcrazy and Mahmoud. He's right. But he's doing it at the price of having both of us out of bodylock at the same time.

Even odds, you bastard. Even odds at last. Bounce the Navy, we don't need them!

Twenty

The holographic image of Governor Hollings was so large its edges frayed against the walls of Captain Leray's cabin.

Trust His Pompous Excellency or His Excellent Pomposity to do things without style, even when he's not present in person.

At least the volume was adjustable. Leray had the volume set so that the governor's words came through loud enough to swamp any listening devices in the cabin, but not loud enough to leave listeners' ears ringing.

"It is our decision that *Audacious*'s primary mission during the hijacking situation is to monitor *Shenandoah*. It is possible that the entire hijacking is Federation disinformation, intended to provoke a response that would put the Alliance at a disadvantage.

"Even if there is a genuine effort being made to hijack *Leon Brautigan*, it is impossible that Alliance citizens can be involved. In the absence of any requirement for police action, the obligations of the Alliance under the Convention of Asok for the Safety of Life in Space is limited to refraining from interfering with the forces sent by the Federation to recover *Leon Brautigan* and apprehend the perpetrators. This obligation has already been met.

"A further obligation would exist if Alliance forces were requested under the convention to lend assistance. No such request has been recorded. Therefore this second obligation does not at the present time exist."

Nice to hear him qualify that. If the mystery ship shows up, we may hear those light cruisers screaming for help loud and

211

clear. Then the only way to keep me from taking Audacious *out would be to missile her from the ground.*

Leray decided that wasn't even good black humor. If the mystery ship were an Intelligence operation, His Mediocrity might be willing to destroy an Alliance ship to cover his friends' tracks. Destroy it, blame it on the Federation, and get credit for a valiant stand in the first battle of the next Federation-Alliance War.

Thank the Creator that was also a low-order probability. *Audacious* outgunned the rest of the Bonsai Force's ships put together, and the ground-based antiship weapons would have to be cleared through Colonel Pak.

Leray realized that his attention had wandered. He looked at Jo Marder and the navigator. This past week, they'd started letting the third-ranking officer of *Audacious* in on all but the most private sessions. Keeping too much between the two of them would begin to look suspicious, with the Victoria situation heating up. It would also make them indispensable to *Audacious*, but that didn't always stop Intelligence or the senior officers they influenced.

Life in the Alliance Navy sometimes seemed to be one long search for a way to fight Intelligence without endangering your ship.

The other two officers didn't show any signs of having heard a momentous announcement. Leray relaxed and let his mind tune in slowly.

Two minutes of routine business, described completely if ponderously (Hollings did have a knack for detail), then:

"I have decided to request reinforcements for our naval forces in the Victoria area. Our ground forces are already superior to those of the Federation for the defensive actions that are all we contemplate. Our naval forces require sufficient strength to counterbalance *Shenandoah* and the 879th Squadron.

"This request has been approved. I have no information on the strength or ETA of the reinforcements. You will be informed as soon as possible.

"Continue in your duty as you have begun, and the Alliance will prevail."

The image vanished, and Leray was master of his own quarters again. He unplugged the projector and stowed it in his desk.

"I'd better get the junior watch officers to polish up their stationkeeping," the navigator said. "I think the last time we cruised in any sort of a formation was for the New Year's party link."

"Do that," Leray said. "If you still find yourself short-handed, we'll see about requesting transfers from some of the auxiliaries. They put in more time underway than we do, in the average quarter."

"What about asking for transfers from the reinforcements?" Marder suggested.

"If they're rushed out, they may be even more short-handed than we are," the navigator said. "I can't see the regional directorate calling up a major chunk of reserves for this mite-ridden sandturd of a planet. If they're light forces, they'll be even worse off. We might get one spare watchstander out of a four-ship light-cruiser squadron."

"Anyway, we have to polish up everything aboard *Audacious* before the reinforcements arrive," Leray added. "If we're going to be the flagship, we have to set the example. If we're going to be a junior ship, we can't have some admiral grumbling about the scummy, sloppy Bonsai Force."

The ideal reinforcements would include at least one more heavy ship, plus an admiral with at least three stars. That would keep the admiral off *Audacious* and Governor Hollings in his place; the admiral would fight for the Bonsai Force simply to protect the privileges of his rank!

Common sense and a commitment to justice are nice. But in the short run, a little greed will do almost as well.

Carrying Louis Ferraro's body down to the bay hatch let Karl Pocher forget the hijacker's presence at his back. Ferraro was no lightweight, and for once the knifeman had been no fool. He'd tied the corpse onto Pocher in a position that forced *Brautigan*'s captain into a muscle-wrenching crouch. Without the reduced gravity, he would have fallen at least twice. The odds against any sort of resistance were impossibly long.

Obviously the idea that *Brautigan*'s crew were no longer expendable had managed to penetrate the hijackers' armored skull. Just as obviously, the hijackers hadn't thought it all the way through. Sa'id was even less expendable than

Pocher, and as long as he was at the controls, he might change the odds from impossibly to only improbably long.

Subtle hand signals before he left the bridge had told Pocher that Sa'id was going to do something. There'd been no way to object, and Pocher wouldn't have done so anyway. Nothing could bring back Louis, but he had to be the only one to die.

By the time they reached the passenger area, Pocher's back was a string of little balls of pain, and he was close to praying. As he passed the cabin doors, he heard furious, obscene protests from inside, but he didn't even pause. He only scanned the doors long enough to see that the external manual overrides looked intact.

The protests died for a moment as the cabin monitors came on, showing the imprisoned passengers what was passing by. The silence reeked of shock and fear.

Pocher felt another kind of shock. Unless the gunman had turned Mahmoud loose on the main computer, the copilot must have gone to the internal-systems panel to activate the monitors manually. That panel controlled more ways of changing *Brautigan's* internal environment than all the rest put together.

And if by some chance Mahmoud was on the main machine . . .

Pocher was so happy that he stumbled and nearly fell on the last ladder, to the workshop-storeroom deck. The hijacker poked him just above the belt with the knife.

"Not as big as your friend's, but a lot sharper. It'll do for you when the time comes. So don't be in such a bloody hurry to break your neck."

Not my neck, you slimeguzzler. Not mine.

They reached the inner hatch for the bay airlock. The telltales showed that both hatches were sealed and that the bay was in vacuum. Just as it should be. Pocher knelt awkwardly, measuring with his eyes the distance to half a dozen places to grip or brace. Then he pressed the switch to open the inner hatch.

Instantly Pocher knew he had underestimated his copilot. Somehow Mahmoud had slipped an automatic sequence into the computer.

The moment the hatch started opening, the artificial gravity went off.

Instantly weightless, Pocher was still able to orient himself in a single breath, begin controlled movements in the next.

The hijacker was not only disoriented, he was helpless as Pocher whirled. His hands gripped the edge of the hatch, his feet slammed into the hijacker's ribs. The man slashed wildly but cut only empty air.

Now Pocher pushed off, harder than usual. Louis' mass would slow him, not to mention cushioning his impact with the bulkheads. Grisly, but the history of zero-g combat was no reading for the weak stomached.

Speaking of stomachs . . .

Pocher kicked at the hijacker's torso as he sailed past. The kick let the hijacker grip Pocher's leg but at the cost of letting go of his knife. It also didn't keep the kick from hurting. When a two-body mass kicked a one-body mass in zero-g, the one-body mass came off worse.

Before the hijacker could recover enough to do anything with his grip, Pocher had an even firmer one on an overhead pipe. Again he whipped his legs, sending the hijacker whirling across the deck. He crashed headfirst into the bulkhead, bounced off, flailed wildly, and went on flailing as he sailed into the open hatch.

In three seconds Pocher had slammed the hatch, sorry that the hijacker's hands weren't in the way. In two more seconds he sealed it. In the second after that, he released the inner hatch into the hard vacuum of the bay.

The lock held just enough air to let Pocher hear the hijacker's first scream. He would have enjoyed watching the dying man drift away but managed to put business before pleasure.

Close the outer hatch. Never have only one barrier between you and vacuum, if you can help it. Untie Louis, but save the bodylock. Victoria Command will want the last hijacker for interrogation, if we can give him to them. Now find someplace to fasten Louis, so he won't drift around . . .

The last problem solved itself, as the gravity came on. Ferraro's body slammed to the deck, with Pocher on his hands and knees above it.

"Sorry, Louis."

Pocher staggered to his feet and scrambled up the ladder. As he reached the top, zero-g returned. He shot out of the ladder shaft and had to flip to avoid cracking his skull against the overhead.

The clamor from the passenger cabins started again.

Pocher wanted to hurl himself up to the bridge onto the last hijacker, with someone at his back. He swung himself around the passenger deck, unsealing the cabins without taking time to explain. The first two people who came out would have volunteered.

The doors swung open and three of the remaining four passengers floated out. From the last cabin floated the smell of a bad attack of space sickness.

Pocher pointed at a pair of life-support engineers, a married couple named Nyberg-Hansen. "The ship's been hijacked. I need your help taking her back." He held up the knife. "Either of you combat trained?"

Both reached for the knife. The wife—Erika, he recalled her name was—shook her head at her husband. "Hrolf, you're a paramedic, too. That means I'm expendable and you aren't."

The gravity came on again, fluctuating between one-third and one-half normal. Pocher could live with the range and so could Erika Nyberg-Hansen. She gripped the knife.

"Let's hope nobody gets expended, except the hijackers."

"There's only one left. We need a prisoner."

" 'We,' comrade?"

"The military will whine and piss if we don't try."

"Oh, we'll try."

The way she held the knife told Pocher this wasn't the bloodthirstiness of a vengeful, frightened civilian. It was the casualness of a professional who refuses to run unnecessary risks to please people who are running none at all.

I already like you, Erika Nyberg-Hansen.

It took them three minutes and four more gravity shifts to reach the bridge, with a stop for the medkit on the way. Pocher was surprised not to find the bridge barricaded— surprised and concerned.

His concern turned to fear when he smelled the blood and smoke. Hrolf Hansen smelled it too and nearly beat the others onto the bridge. They would have made a beautiful target, all three jammed in the door, if there'd been an enemy able to shoot inside.

Instead the gunman lay across the pilot's chair, his spine

bent impossibly. He was alive but unconscious. All over the bridge, the gouges and pockmarks of scattergun needles marred the consoles. From the mad pattern of the lights and the acrid smell of smoke—yes, and the wisps of it trailing from some holes and cracks—the needles had made a fine mess of the controls.

For a moment Pocher thought Sa'id had vanished completely. Then he saw feet sticking out of a locker. He bent and pulled.

Like a wounded animal, Mahmoud Sa'id had crawled into a hole to die. He wasn't dead yet, but that wasn't the fault of the gunman who'd shot him or the needles that had stitched him from ribcage to midthigh.

His teeth were buried in his lower lip. As he recognized Pocher, he smiled, and more blood trickled from his mouth.

"Didn't want to . . . shout. 'Fraid . . . you'd get . . . carried away . . . run into . . . other . . ." The scream he'd been holding back echoed around the bridge.

The paramedic knelt beside the copilot to slap a painkiller cartridge onto his neck. Pocher gripped his friend's hand.

"You put the other one away nice and neat. *Brautigan's* ours again."

"Thank God."

The smile set, then relaxed as the painkiller took hold. Pocher's eyes met the paramedic's. The man shook his head.

"Then see what you can do about our friend draped over the chair."

The gravity went off again for a moment, then on again suddenly enough to bring them all to their knees. *And I'd better see what I can do with what's left of our controls.*

Pocher shoved the hijacker unceremoniously out of his chair, sat down, strapped in, and began the standard manual tests for control malfunctions. He'd bring the main computer online when he was sure that wouldn't blow anything vital.

Meanwhile . . .

In carefully memorized Arabic, Pocher began a prayer.

"There is no God but God, and Mohammed is His Prophet. There is no God but God, and Mohammed is His Prophet. There is no God . . ."

Over and over again, keeping his tongue as busy as his hands. Mahmoud had assured him that it would not endanger an atheist's soul to recite a Moslem prayer. Even if it had, Sa'id deserved the prayers of his fathers from a friend, before anyone else had a chance to say anything.

"There is no God but God, and Mohammed is his Prophet. There is no God but God . . ."

Irritable hissing noises came from the consoles, lights swirled on the main screen, and the smoke thickened.

Five hundred meters ahead, *Leon Brautigan* twirled against the stars. Whatever had brought her to a stop had also started her rotating on her longitudinal axis and tumbling slowly end over end at the same time.

The two leaders of the boarding party put their helmets together. Twenty meters behind, Charles Longman could make a shrewd guess about the subject of their conversation: stop *Brautigan*'s motion at the risk of alerting their prey, or go in with the tumble and spin still on her, risking delays and accidents that could be just as fatal?

A moment later the decision came, announced by hand signals. They were going straight in.

Makes sense. We take the extra risks, not the people in Brautigan. *That's what we're paid for.*

Now if they'll just pay me enough not to be scared, if there's that much money in the Federation!

More hand signals divided the boarding party into two teams, assault and reserve. As technical advisor and rear lookout, Longman and his computer were with the reserve. It put him out of immediate danger but left his back feeling painfully bare.

As the assault party puffed toward the tender-bay hatch, Longman looked behind him. Two thousand meters away, *Cooney* drifted. Her bow and stern searchlights were just part of what she had trained on *Brautigan*.

Invisibly far away and keeping complete electronic silence, *Weilitsch* was providing top cover. Still farther away, keeping a listening watch, *Magiley* was doing her best to imitate an asteroid. If anything like the mystery ship did show up, *Mogilev*'s job was to record what happened, send it off, then run. Her extra cargo space came from removing her Stonemans; the rest of her scout cruiser's drive and power plant was intact, and scout cruisers were the fastest light ships in the Navy.

As the assault party landed, Longman unslung his computer to keep his hands busy. He punched up a schematic of the lock while they were laying the ring charge and was studying it when the charge went off.

A second charge was ready, but the bay had pressure. Not much, but with the spin and tumble it was enough to finish the job. The hatch peeled open until it hung by one end, and a body floated out.

It floated past the assault party before they could do more than aim their lasers at it. It floated on out into space, with its own private spin and tumble.

Longman realized that it was heading straight for him. He was the only one of the boarding party in a position to reach it without casting off and maneuvering. All he had to do was use his belt snare with its hook set and make sure that the hook sank well into the body.

Longman hadn't come so close to vomiting in a spacesuit since his training days. Fortunately, his stomach didn't control his hands; they automatically opened the hook, set the trigger, aimed . . .

He felt the quiver of the releasing spring through his arm. The hook soared forward, shoving Longman gently backward. The hairtriggered pulse charge rammed the hook's arms into the body. It pulled the line out to full length, but as the strain came on, the reserve party leader fired his own jets. The dead man joined the chain of suited figures.

The leader hand-signaled "Well done," as Longman tried to identify the body. Allowing for explosive decompression, it looked like one of the Mount Houton photo technicians, which could mean—

"All hands," came Lieutenant Aschmann. "All hands, we're in. The crew took the ship back. That body was one of the 'jackers. The other's disabled and a prisoner. Come on in."

How much that left out, Longman found out ten minutes later, when he saw the passenger lounge, the two shrouded bodies, the dying hijacker, and Karl Pocher's eyes.

"Any of you an electronics tech?" Pocher asked. The voice matched the eyes.

Longman shook his head. "Electrons and I don't get along, except in my computer. But I can juryrig your bay hatch and check out your tender. I'm not a rated pilot, but I can jack into its onboard and . . ."

He went on much longer than he usually could without boring people, long enough to start boring himself. He still kept spouting technicalities, because he sensed that Karl Pocher needed to listen to something besides the voices in his head.

"Now hear this, now hear this. The captain will address the crew. The captain will address the crew."

Rose Liddell's face appeared on the main screen in the Training Office. She looked as if she had gazed on Medusa just long enough to harden her face, without turning completely to stone.

"We have a report from *Cooney*. Their boarding party reached *Leon Brautigan* and found the ship in the hands of her surviving crew and passengers. One hijacker was killed, the other wounded and taken prisoner. No passengers were injured, but Lieutenants Mahmoud Sa'id and Louis Ferraro were killed in the line of duty. May the Creator receive them in peace.

"A memorial service will be held for Sa'id and Ferraro at 2030. All liberty is canceled until further notice. A shipboard no-duty schedule will be posted as soon as possible.

"We all want to pay back the killers, but let's not get careless. The living can enjoy vengeance a lot more than the dead.

"Thank you."

"I don't like talk of vengeance," Chief Netsch said to the blank screen. "It's unprofessional. All the people killed so far don't add up to more than one good training accident—"

"Oh, shove your religion and your sense of proportion!" Electrician Gellis snarled. "I want to go out and stamp on a few—"

"You are going nowhere except up before the captain for insubordination," Mahoney snapped.

"I'm sorry, Chief," Gellis said. "I was out of line."

Netsch made a dismissive gesture and turned back to her desk. Mahoney wanted to say something, but words weren't enough and a court-martial would be too much.

"What are we going to do with all the time we don't

spend on liberty?" Gellis grumbled. "Wire the simulators for demolition, in case we're boarded?"

"Don't laugh," Mahoney said. "The Old Lady just might. She was exec of a migrant ship once, and they train to fight riots and mutinies. So if the order comes down, keep your mind on your job and not on your grievances. I want to be killed by my enemies, not by my friends."

"Aye-aye, sir."

Twenty-one

"Victoria Command refuses to confirm or deny that there is evidence of Alliance involvement in the attempted hijacking of the observatory supply vessel *Leon Brautigan*. *Shenandoah*, flagship of the Victoria Squadron, never left Victoria orbit, leaving matters to the light cruisers *Cooney* and *Weilitsch*.

"Victoria Command does confirm that the Alliance heavy cruiser *Audacious* remains in orbit around Victoria." The announcer's cheerful face vanished, in favor of a starscape with something large and ill defined moving against it. General Kornilov sat up in bed and turned his glance from the screen to the small, well-defined woman sharing the bed.

"The son of a bitch!"

"He didn't lie," Colonel Chatterje pointed out.

"No, but he interpreted what the PIO told him rather freely. We said that the matter was under investigation, but at the present time we didn't expect to find any Alliance involvement."

"Maybe he suspected an effort to soothe people with half-truths. Media people have a Pavlovian response to that sort of thing."

"I piss in Pavlov's computer!"

"Pavlov lived before computers," the colonel replied. "Late nineteenth or early twentieth century, Russia, if I remember correctly."

Kornlilov flung his arms out in disgust and nearly poked his companion in her eyepatch. She would have been in another sort of bed, recovering from a synopt implant, if she hadn't decided to defer the operation.

222

"I can do everything but surgery with one eye, and I won't take up a bed we may need for casualties," she'd said. "When I order a freeze on nonemergency admittances and procedures, it will look better if I'm still wearing the patch."

The object on the screen had now defined itself as an asteroid with half a dozen flat areas and a random selection of metal domes. The announcer's voice returned.

"This is our staff artist's recreation of Victoria Dockyard, formerly an asteroid of the Haim Cluster. No information on its actual configuration has been released by the Navy.

"Victoria Dockyard is expected to be in geostationary orbit over Fort Stafford in less than fifteen hours. Its final maneuvers will be visible from most of the inhabited hemisphere of Victoria. Public telescopes for watching its arrival have been set up at the following places . . ."

Before the announcer was halfway through the list, Kornilov turned off the screen. He lay back with a disgusted grunt, his hands behind his head.

"I wonder how many of those telescopes are put out by the people behind the hijacking?"

"Then you really don't know who's behind it?"

"Of course not. If we did, I'd have had Major Nieg say so, instead of the PIO announcing an investigation. I find that telling the truth helps me sleep at night."

Doctor Chatterje pulled out one of Kornilov's hands and laid it on her breast. "Perhaps I can help you sleep, too."

Kornilov rolled until he could slide both hands under Chatterje and lift her on top of him.

At the latitude of Silvermouth, *Audacious* was too low to be visible behind the Pfingsten Mountains. Paul Leray had seldom felt quite so naked. His ship was invisible, Jo Marder was up there aboard her, and the governor's mansion featured hot- and cold-running Intelligence types in every *pissoir*.

Colonel Pak ignored the cough from the sentries and lit his fifth aromatic in the last half hour. Brigadier Fegeli looked carefully at the ceiling, with its vitrisand mosaic of the Battle of Kesh. The governor had commanded a regiment in the battle, well enough to lay the foundations for his promotion to general.

Leray sipped his glass of wine and spared a sympathetic thought for Fegeli. Caught between an impossible senior and two abler juniors who did most of the work, Fegeli was in a situation that would have tried a saint. He wasn't one, but he didn't do as badly as some might have, including one Paul Joachim Leray. In Fegeli's situation he wouldn't be fighting Jo's drinking problem, he'd be developing one of his own!

The guards came to attention and saluted as the Governor's military secretary emerged.

"His Excellency will see you now."

Governor Hollings's office would have made a good if unimaginative military museum. Relics of every planet he'd seen in thirty years crowded cases on the walls. A recon drone hung from the ceiling.

A robuffet crept toward the three officers and popped its lid. Fegeli piled his plate so high that Leray suspected he wanted the food as a barrier against Hollings. Leray refilled his glass; Pak merely stubbed out his last aromatic.

"We are getting the requested reinforcements faster than I had dared hope," Hollings began. "Our courier made contact with a transient fleet unit. Its commander had rank, discretionary orders, and sufficient strength to come to Victoria. I just received word that they have entered the Victoria System."

Leray sat up. An admiral who could respond to that kind of message without getting permission in advance had to outrank everybody else in the Victoria System on either side. If she commanded a force in proportion to her rank and wasn't just a passenger in a light squadron . . .

"The reinforcements consist of Battle Division Ten and the Fourteenth Cruiser Squadron, under the command of Admiral Lopatina. Their ETA in Victoria orbit is approximately sixty-two hours—"

Leray had to think of something unpleasant to keep his face from twisting into an idiotic grin. "What about attackers and supplies?"

"Embarked attackers and supplies only. Two supply ships have been requested, but the request had not been acted upon at the time of the Jump to Victoria."

If three battleships and four cruisers reached Victoria short of supplies, the Bonsai Force's spares would be a small drop in a very large bucket. Leray conjured up tactful phrases for telling Lopatina that; also methods of transporting what he had to send and hiding what he needed to keep when Lopatina overrode his protests.

Marya Lopatina looked like everybody's grandmother but was actually as benign as a starving tree tiger. Entire ships running between obscure outposts were said to be crewed by people who had taken Lopatina's appearance for the reality.

If the situation stayed political, no governor of anything the size of Seven Rivers could ignore a full admiral.

If serious shooting started, the Alliance now had about a three-to-one superiority.

Negotiating or fighting, Paul Leray's job had just become much easier.

"This is good news," Leray said, as soon as he could speak without breaking out laughing. "Damned good news." Pak nodded. Fegeli looked sullen, probably at having his already miniscule chances for getting any credit just about eliminated.

"Thank you for coming, gentlemen," Hollings said. The three officers saluted and were out in the hall before Leray could be sure his feet were still touching the ground.

Fegeli marched off to the right, still sullen; Pak and Leray turned for the door.

Outside, Leray realized how long they'd been waiting for Hollings. Twilight had swallowed the slopes of the Pfingstens; the scattered lights of housing and light industrial parks sparked yellow and silver on the purple-black slopes.

Leray let out all his delight in a full-throated whoop.

"They could have heard you in Mount Houton," Pak said. His face was no friendlier than usual.

"What's the matter?" Leray asked. He was in no mood to have his pleasure spoiled. "Afraid of losing your chance to shine?"

"Don't confuse me with the brigadier," Pak said. "Besides, you're in more danger than I am. I don't have a spaceborn's dossier with Intelligence and an XO with a dependency-risk label."

"Drop it," Leray said.

"It's true—"

"That's no excuse to be nasty. For either of us."

"Very well. Put Intelligence aside, and consider how many spare regimental commanders Baba Lopatina will be bringing and how many spare ship captains. You, my friend, have become much more dispensable. Don't let your dislike of His Excellency lead you to ignore this."

Pak was actually being polite, not mentioning the additional risk to Jo if Leray lost command of *Audacious*. Baba probably had a few spare execs along with the captains.

They walked down the stairs that wound through the gardens to the bank of the Silver River. Fifty meters farther along the bank lay the landing pad. The governor had repeatedly refused to allow a roof pad, although he'd put in enough ponds, shrubs, and miscellaneous greenery to make the walk to the pad bearably scenic.

Pak turned and lit another aromatic. "There's another reason why I'm indispensable. We may face some security trouble in the Border Counties. The regiment may have to deploy, which it won't do as well under a new CO."

"What kind of trouble? The same the Feddies are having?"

"Close enough, from what I've heard. Some of those arms caches may be leaking across the border."

"What border? As far as I'm concerned, if we fight over Victoria, the loser should get that damned desert."

"Intelligence won't love you for that, Paul. And by the way, we may have to stop dealing with our broker."

The thought of losing their independent channel of communication off Victoria took the edge off Leray's pleasure. "Is Federation Intelligence on to him?"

"He thinks it's only a matter of time. If Major Nieg is half as good as our friend says, I would agree with him. Our friend has several escape hatches, so he's not in danger. But if Nieg learns about what we are sending through the broker, he'll be in an excellent position to blackmail us. He knows what our Intelligence thinks of field officers who don't respect their communications monopoly."

"*Peste!*" Leray said. This time he could have been heard as far as the Pfingstens. He picked up a handful of gravel and threw it into the river.

Alliance Intelligence's control of military communications was proclaimed loudly but not really enforceable in fact. Every so often, however, some particularly blatant violation of that control was made into a horrible example, "to encourage the others." Add Hollings's blatant affiliation with Intelligence, and Pak and Leray would be prime candidates for the job of horrible example if their broker were compromised.

A dismal but essentially insoluble problem. Leray turned to matters where he might be able to do something.

"Shall I start running ground-support exercises with *Audacious* and the light cruisers?" he asked. "*Audacious* isn't too well configured for tactical support, but we'll extend sensor coverage."

Pak looked tempted, then shook his head. "That could make Intelligence suspect our unofficial sources. The official word from the prefects of both border counties is that the problem can be handled at a police level. Active involvement by the armed forces isn't expected to be necessary."

A searchlight beam swung across the gardens from the landing pad, settling on the two men. "That's my lifter pilot getting impatient," Pak said. He punched Leray's shoulder lightly. "Pray, at least until Baba's ships come."

The colonel ran lightly toward the pad. Leray stood until the command lifter was rising, a miniature constellation against the darkness of the mountains, then signaled for his own ground car. Returning to his own ship and Jo would at least end the naked feeling.

Coming off watch, Brigitte Tachin reached the Training Office at the same time as Brian Mahoney reached a slack period in his work. With a Weapons Department officer on hand, Mort Gellis seemed sufficiently cowed to need no supervision, even from Chief Netsch. So Mahoney and Tachin were chatting amicably when Elayne Zheng walked in.

She wore attacker-crew coveralls and boots; her hair was tangled and her face lined from too many hours in a helmet. To Brian, she looked about five years younger and twice as happy as when he'd last seen her.

She has, the saints preserve her, a sort of Antaeus relationship with those death machines. She has to get back and touch one every so often or lose her strength.

"What's this buggering off on duty?" Zheng said cheerfully. "I thought you were supposed to have the reprogrammed simulators ready for loading aboard *Mahmoud Sa'id*."

"Aboard what?"

"She used to be Gold Three in the 879th. We thought *Brautigan*'s people deserved a monument."

"I have no quarrel with that," Mahoney said. "But if you'd checked at Dock Three before you stormed up here to harass honest instructors, you would have discovered the simulators all packaged for loading. Go, thou, and load same."

Zheng tore off a mock salute. "All in good time. By the way, heard anything from Charlie?"

"He stayed aboard *Brautigan* to save time getting her fully operational," Mahoney said. "They went in to the observatory to load spares and unload passengers, then spaced back for Victoria. Their ETA is about forty hours."

"I wonder if he's chasing Pocher?"

Tachin frowned. "I doubt even Charles is so gross. Also he has machinery to fix, and he enjoys that even more than making love."

"How do you know?" Zheng said, grinning. "Has he—"

"He has not. But I am about to hang you up by your toes and tickle you under your armpits until you apologize."

Zheng said something impolite in one of her five ancestral languages and struck a look of mock horror. "Brian, have you been telling her all my secrets? How could you? Do I mean nothing—"

"Now hear this. Now hear this. The captain will address all hands."

In contrast to Zheng, Rose Liddell looked about five years older.

"It looks as if *Brautigan* was just the beginning. An Alliance squadron is in-system, ETA Victoria fifty-six hours.

"The squadron consists of three battleships, two heavy and two light cruisers, and a scout, under Admiral Marya Lopatina. We're about to get a close look at the Baba in action.

"Under the circumstances, you'll appreciate that all no-duties have to be canceled, effective immediately. There will be a department-heads' meeting at 2100. At 2200 the Victoria Squadron will go to Alert Three and remain on that status until further notice.

"Now for some good news: Victoria Dockyard will make its final insertion maneuver at 1546. *Shenandoah* will get underway to rendezvous with the dockyard at 1300. Captain Steckler has officially expressed his thanks for the quality and quantity of work done by *Shenandoah*'s people.

"Your guess about what will happen next is as good as mine. We can be sure that the Alliance is taking the situation on Victoria very seriously. But, then, so are we. The Alliance reinforcements don't mean the shooting is about to start.

"They do mean that we'll have to be even more alert than before. I know I can trust you all to do that. If the shooting does start, I know I can rely on you all to live up to the highest traditions of the Federation Navy.

"Thank you, and good luck."

Either there were no routine announcements or Mahoney tuned them out. When the screen was dark again, he saw Zheng nodding.

"That explains the in-system courier we saw heading out," she said. "A converted attacker, with a shield installed to let her work in junk space. We picked her up about an hour off-planet, heading out like there was a black hole on her tail. I guess Baba ordered a hot lunch and they wanted to deliver it before she got mad."

"Or send a confidential message," Mahoney put in. "From whom, I wonder."

He shrugged and answered himself. "God and whoever sent it know. The rest of us will just have to muddle through. For us, that means making a preliminary list of people the Training Department can second to the operational departments."

Netsch looked dubious. "Without the Head's lead? She'll scream."

"If I know Captain Rosie, she'll scream a lot louder if the list isn't ready at the department-heads meeting. And don't look so damned eager, Gellis, or I won't put you on the list for transfer back to Weapons."

"I wasn't thinking any such thing, sir."

"Tell me another. Better yet, don't tell me anything. Just go help Lieutenant Zheng load her simulators."

Twenty-two

The robot truck backed away from the lifter's rear door.

"That's the last of the organics," the pilot said. "Time to load and lift."

The pilot's use of the military term was just one of the ways he annoyed his copilot. The copilot was fair enough to realize that anyone but Wilma McKenzie would have annoyed him; he and Wilma had flown together for twenty years. Still, couldn't they have come up with somebody besides this glossy exgunship jockey with lots of military vocabulary and not much experience of outback flying?

"Have we checked the passengers?" the copilot asked.

"Have you?"

So he's going to be regulation and make that my job. Of course, Wilma and I knew by sight half the people we carried.

"Can do."

The inside of the lifter was dimmer than usual. The copilot checked the internal power displays and realized this wasn't an illusion.

Time to down the old lady for an overhaul. Or it would be if the bloody Army and the two new airfreight mobs hadn't chartered all the newer machines!

The copilot walked forward, checking off passengers as they waved their boarding passes at him. He stopped at the next-to-last row to talk to a twelve-year-old boy.

"How's the leg, Ken?"

The boy flexed it. "Good enough for kicking the Army in the arse, if they come around snooping on my da again."

More bloody Army nonsense. "What did they think he was doing, selling ortonite for bullets?"

"Da—darned if I know," Ken said. "Don't think they do either."

The copilot decided there was something to be said for a job taking a lifter from Kellysburg to Mount Houton one day and back the next. If the Army came snooping around, you could always be one stop ahead of them.

The pilot turned in his seat and glowered. "Didn't I say something about loading and lifting?"

The copilot resisted the temptation to click his heels. He wondered if he would resist the temptation to ask for a transfer.

Learning a new route's weather and terrain will be a lot easier than learning to put up with this clown.

The copilot sat down and turned on the "Fasten Harness" sign. A look behind told him that most of the fifteen passengers were old hands who'd already strapped in. A gust of wind blew sand in through the rear door. The copilot slapped the switch to raise the ramp and turned on the displays. At a nod from the pilot, he started the preflight systems check.

Outside, gusts of wind whistled and moaned louder around the grounded lifter.

"Range on that lifter," Candice Shore said.

"The one with the AD stuff deployed?" Lance Corporal Sklarinsky asked.

"That one."

Sklarinsky raised his pulser with its built-in rangefinder, while Corporal Esteva mounted guard and Shores studied the encampment. A good part of Third Battalion was there, deployed for maneuvers against First Battalion out of Camp Aounda.

The Scouts were working with First Battalion again, to keep the Third Herd on its toes. The maneuvers weren't supposed to start until the next day, but Shores and her bodyguards had decided to steal a march on the Third. If the battalion were thinking "We don't need to be alert until we're ordered to be," the sooner somebody found out, the better. Somebody like General Langston.

"Range is 2250 meters, as close as I can make it," Sklarinsky said. "The sand's beginning to blow."

"It's going to get worse before it gets better," Esteva added. "Look over there."

Shores followed the corporal's gesture. The western horizon was turning an almost twilight gray, although it was only midafternoon. A gust kicked up sand around her feet. A lull, then a second gust, long enough to reduce visibility and send pebbles clicking against her body armor.

"Filter and radio check, everybody," Shores said.

"We going to stick it out?" Sklarinsky asked.

"If they can find us in a blow like this, they're good."

"Yeah, but suppose we can't find us?" Sklarinsky asked.

"Sklarinsky, I think the captain just gave an order," Esteva said.

"Storm's building fast," the sergeant at the Air Defense console said. "We're beginning to lose signals."

"Any damage to the antennae?" the Air Defense officer asked.

"Not so far. But this is going to be a real nasty one."

"Leave everything deployed for now. If it really blows up, we'll be the camp's only defense."

"Who's going to attack us in this garbage?" the sergeant muttered.

The Air Defense officer ignored the sergeant. He had a nasty feeling that someone was out there, just waiting for him to relax. It might be only a First Battalion patrol ready to simulate an attack; it might be real enemies.

The copilot checked altitude, airspeed, position, and power on the heads-up display, then checked all windows. A lurch confirmed the deteriorating weather he'd seen in both places.

As the lifter returned to an even keel, he turned to the pilot.

"What about cutting lift a bit? With the wind getting up, we may be too light for control."

On full lift, they had effectively zero weight and the surface area of a medium-sized house. Mass was permanent, but a strong-enough wind could still generate enough windage and aerodynamic lift to make the machine hard to control. That was why they ran up the engines of the big liftliners before takeoff or else launched them from catapults.

"Not yet," the pilot said.

Nervous about the weather? Don't know how to juggle weight, lift, and wind? Or too used to the peacetime military, where there's always a shot of juice available anywhere you land? You're going to have to learn that the Victoria outback isn't an Army reservation.

"Then what about a change of course?" The copilot displayed the next two hundred kilometers of their flight path. "We drop down and ride just below the crest of Meteorite Ridge. Pop over to Stiggins' Flat, then head back to the ridge. If the wind holds, we can make it all the way to Pothole in the lee of the ridge."

"Will the wind hold?"

Sounds like you are nervous. Well, if you haven't spent years flying in these blows, you've a right to be. But get over it, man, or find a new copilot!

"It'll be a miracle if this blow doesn't last twelve, fourteen hours."

"Let's use the ridge route."

The copilot was grinning as he fed instructions into the computer.

"Low-altitude air contact, bearing 52, distance 71,000 meters, altitude 2,500 meters, speed 350 kilometers an hour," the sergeant said.

"That might be Air Victoria's Flight 6," the Air Defense officer said, but his mouth was suddenly drier than the low humidity could account for.

"Maybe," the sergeant said. "But Flight 6 is scheduled to stop at Stiggins' Flat. This one's going around to the other side of Meteorite Ridge, if it stays on course."

They watched the radar screen for two more minutes. "Definitely not the regular course for Flight 6," the sergeant concluded.

The Air Defense officer licked his lips. "Arm the missiles. All guidance modes. We don't know what this storm will do to radar. And call the CO."

"IFF interrogation, sir?"

"Of course." *This may be my first shot at a real target, but I should still have remembered that!*

"I'd recommend doing it through satellite relay," the sergeant added. Her hands were already moving without her eyes leaving the radar screen. "Between the storm and the ridge, we may not get to them any other way."

"By all means."

Out the starboard cockpit window, the copilot spotted Ankle Rock. It jutted up out of the murk, seemingly close enough to touch, even though the radar said it was two hundred meters below and five hundred meters off to the right. *Not much of a margin, in this kind of a blow.*

The pilot looked at the altimeter. "Take her up fifty meters."

"That'll put us in the wind faster."

"It'll also give us more lateral room while we're climbing up the valley. We can duck back down when we go over the top and stay low all the way to Stiggins' Flat."

Still nervous, but about a real danger. You may make a bush pilot yet.

The radio began squealing and whimpering. The copilot turned the volume down until he no longer felt his scalp peeling off his skull. Then he tried to make sense of what he could barely recognize as a signal.

"Sounds military," was all he could say after a minute.

"I heard the Army was supposed to be doing something or other about twenty, thirty kloms west of Stiggins' Flat," the pilot volunteered. "Maybe they've lost a lifter."

"Army people don't fly in this kind of crap, unless it's a war situation," the copilot said before he could think.

The pilot glared. *Maybe he's not the only one who's nervous. Or why would I have put my foot in it like that?*

The lifter climbed sixty meters higher, then headed straight up the valley, rocking and lurching as it climbed toward the crest of the ridge.

"Commander," the Communications OOW said. "One of the satellites is passing an Army IFF signal."

"Put it on my console," Bogdanov said. He put his tea down as the information came up. "That's Air Defense, from the Third Battalion. They're on maneuvers against First Battalion."

"That's a long way from the Blanchard Canyon," the lieutenant said.

"Oh, didn't you hear?" Bogdanov said. "The penetration

of Blanchard Canyon was canceled. Admiral's orders, after we heard about the Alliance reinforcements."

The lieutenant looked disgusted. "Nobody told me."

Bogdanov smiled. "Somebody always fails to get the word."

The Air Defense center now held more people than its equipment left room for, or its life support could handle properly. The Air Defense officer now smelled a lot of other people's sweat besides his own.

"Still no response to our IFF," the sergeant said. She was pale, but she was one of the few in the room without dark sweat spots at neck and armpits.

"Any communications at all?" the CO queried. She was trying to blink desert grit out of her eyes.

"Nothing intelligible."

The picture on the radar screen wavered. "Range 45,000 meters, altitude 800 meters and descending—we've lost him in ground clutter."

The Air Defense officer closed his eyes. It was a mistake. Instead of the crowded room he saw a lifter loaded with missiles skimming the ground, ready to pop up and launch.

One minute. Two minutes. Three minutes . . .

"There he is. Range 28,000, altitude 500 and climbing—no, he's peaked out."

The Air Defense officer opened his eyes, looked at the radar screen, looked at the CO, and saw her nod.

"Missile lock?"

"Confirmed."

"Prepare to fire ready missiles." His hand floated over to the firing control, seemingly without his mind commanding it.

"Fire one!"

The red plate sank into the console.

"What the hell!" Esteva shouted. The Scouts were on radio silence, but the corporal yelled loud enough to be heard over the roar of the wind.

Even the wind was drowned out by the screaming howl of missiles blazing overhead. Their boosters gilded the twilight for a moment, then light and sound faded.

Shores blinked, more confused than dazzled. She didn't have anything to say except Esteva's remark, and once was enough for that.

She waited thirty seconds, for a second salvo, then tapped Sklarinsky on the shoulder and turned on her radio. "Time to break radio silence and find out what happened. We'll use your set."

"Who first?"

"Let's try Third Battalion Air Defense."

"Commander, missile firing!"

"No need to scream, Lieutenant," Bogdanov said. "I'm right here beside you."

Also nearly as on edge. I am getting very tired of half-seen surprises lurking around the fringes.

He watched the sketchy picture of the missile's trajectory. It lost much detail in the thirty-thousand-kilometer journey to *Shenandoah*, but the outlines were clear.

Somebody in the Third Battalion area had fired at least two missiles. Maybe it was Third Battalion; maybe even if it weren't, the missiles were no danger to *Shenandoah*, but—

"Detonation!" he snapped. The radar signature was unmistakable to an old attacker pilot. "That was a live target, too."

"Call up Third Battalion, Commander?" the lieutenant asked.

"Yes. While you're waiting for them to answer, put me through to the captain and the admiral."

"Aye-aye, sir."

Both missiles had TV cameras in their noses for last-minute visual identification of targets.

In this case, the last minute was too late.

Until just before impact, the TV screen showed nothing but a rushing gray murk, lit by the missile flames.

When the Air Victoria lifter leaped at the missiles, the Air Defense officer heard screams, one of them his own. His hands were already clawing at override switches.

One missile received the override signal. Its course change would have taken it clear of the lifter, if it hadn't rammed its mate. The fratricidal explosion set off both warheads, well within their lethal radius.

On the screen, the Air Defense officer saw one large blip and a number of small ones plummet toward the ground, until their signals were lost. He sat down and held his hands between his knees until they stopped shaking.

This left him with nothing to cover his eyes, but that didn't seem to matter so much. He wasn't the only one crying.

Aboard the lifter, both pilots saw the missile flames before they saw the missiles. Both reacted, but, like the Air Defense officer, too late. The lifter was robust but unarmored, and the warheads were designed to defeat an attacker's hull.

A fragment of missile decapitated the pilot and went on to pierce the copilot's chest. He was already choking on his own blood when the lift field died. It wouldn't have made any difference if he had stayed alive to use the fans for a last desperate effort at braking. Their power and the copilot both died a moment later.

Some of the passengers also died from fragments. Others, including Ken, died from being thrown about inside the lifter as it plunged to the desert. A few survived until the final impact. They might have survived that, because what was left of the hull remained nearly in one piece, but the cargo lockdowns were not so robust. Containers of organics and other flying debris finished the missiles' work.

The lifter fell to the ground two kilometers west of the impact point, eight kilometers west of Stiggins' Flat. It was on the short-range radar of the Stiggins' Flat field, and a ground car was on its way to the crash site almost before the last piece of wreckage had landed.

The Air Defense officer looked up as a sandblown, battle-armored apparition stalked into the room. Two more stood behind her.

"What the devil happened?" the apparition demanded.

"Who the devil wants to know?" the CO snapped.

"Captain Candice Shores, CO of Scout Company."

"Were you snooping us?"

"I was close enough to see the missile launch. What was your target?"

"What business is it of yours?"

The Air Defense officer looked steadily at his CO. He was beginning to smell "cover up" or at least "no captain

237

tells *me* what to do." Both smelled worse than a mite-infected wound.

The incident was going to leak out anyway, no matter what the CO did. Then the Air Defense officer would be finished in the Victoria Brigade and probably the Army. *If I want to sleep at night, I'll have to cooperate so this won't happen again.*

"We had a bogey. Nonstandard course, no IFF, a flight profile that looked like it might be setting up a missile launch. It . . . it was Air Victoria Flight 6."

"Did you hit it?"

"Lieutenant . . ." began the CO.

For a moment it looked as if Shores would draw her sidearm on the CO.

"We had visual contact at the last moment. I tried to override, but we had a fratricidal explosion. The target went off the screen, so I assume it's down."

"Where?"

The Air Defense officer called up coordinates. Shores looked at the screen and nodded to her two guards.

"Colonel, I'd like to go with the patrol you're sending to the crash site."

The CO opened her mouth, which Shores interpreted as as agreement. "Fine," she said. "I have complete trust in the Third's integrity," she added piously. The Air Defense officer actually found himself smiling. "But I've been out in more sandstorms than your troopers.

"Besides, the locals may not trust the Army as much as I do." She paused, to let an eloquent silence fill the room.

"It's settled, then. Now, can me and my people refill our canteens while we're waiting to lift out?"

Liddell sat in the center chair, with Kuwahara to her left and Bogdanov to her right. The term "worry seat" ran through her mind; she banished it and turned back to the screen.

Before it reached *Shenandoah*, the picture had to survive the sandstorm and two scramblers. What survived was just clear enough to show Liddell what she'd expected since the radio intercepts began coming in.

In the lee of the groundcar, the bodies were being laid out. The rescue crew was bagging them as fast as it pulled them out of the wreckage, but twice a bag had blown away. Rose Liddell knew she'd seen messier corpses, but she didn't bother remembering exactly where and when.

The fringes of the wreckage itself were already blurring under windblown sand. In the murk, a laser flared briefly, someplace where the sand wouldn't block the beam or abrade the crystal. Two stooped figures backed away from the wreckage, holding another body, too small to be an adult.

Captain Shores stepped onscreen, jacked her mask radio into the screen set, and saluted.

"The local rescue crew has matters in hand," she began. "They aren't letting us touch the main wreck, but they haven't accounted for all the bodies, either."

"Are you investigating scattered wreckage?" Kuwahara asked.

Liddell saw Shores's nostrils flare and prayed for the captain's discretion. Browbeating field-grade reserves was risky enough. Trying to bite the heads off admirals led only to broken teeth, if nothing worse.

"We have only two lifters and eight people. The locals have about fifty people, more than half of them armed, and can reinforce from Stiggins' Flat by groundcar. The storm would make it difficult for us to reinforce from the camp or see anything if we went out searching."

"You realize that the storm will completely cover the wreckage in a few hours," Kuwahara said.

"Yes, sir. But the locals have warned us against any air search, and the CO of Third Battalion concurs."

"Thank you, Captain Shores. Please express my condolences to the families of the victims."

Liddell turned from the dark screen to meet Kuwahara's equally dark but much more expressive eyes.

"I would like to have the crash site searched before the locals can reach it on the ground," he said. "I want a secure circuit to General Kornilov and the chairman of the Military Council."

Liddell thought about the weather, then nodded slowly. "We need a complete investigation, but that may be more than Third Battalion can handle by itself."

She turned to her exec. "Commander, you're our attacker expert. Could an attacker with a good pilot search at low altitude in that storm maybe land salvage parties?"

"If nobody else can do it . . ."

"That seems to be the case," Kuwahara said. "I'll take the call in my quarters. Captain, Commander, thank you. This is an ugly situation. . . ."

He broke off and strode out. Liddell stared after him.

He's concerned about covering asses but not just his. Everybody who's under him has his loyalty. He also knows what to do if we have a choice between covering asses and a rebellion on Victoria.

I've known worse sets of principles. And speaking of principles—

"Pavel, we have thirty-two hours before the Alliance squadrons arrive. Do you think we have time for a sherry, if your scruples allow?"

Twenty-three

Lucco DiVries stepped into the front dustlock of his brother's house. A gust of wind followed him in, laden with grit, the smell of organics from the plant, and ozone from the dying sandstorms.

As the inner door opened, the familiar sounds of a family argument floated out. Raimondo and Teresa shared a taste for airing their differences at the top of their lungs. It sounded appalling to those who didn't know the combatants. Fortunately, those who did included Lucco and both children.

DiVries let the air blast clean his clothes. He stamped the last grit off his boots, then stepped through the inner door. His ten-year-old nephew, Carlo, popped out of the hall. The look on the boy's face made DiVries wonder if the argument were as sporting as usual.

"Sounds like your da and mum are at it again."

"Too right. Sounds like they mean it, too."

"What are they arguing about?"

"Da wants to send Mum and us away somewhere—says we'll be safer there."

"Where?"

Carlo looked suspicious. "Sure you have a need to know?"

"You've been watching too many adventure shows. I need to know, because maybe I can suggest a safe place."

"I already know where Da wants us to go."

"Where's that?"

Carlo lowered his voice to a whisper. "Promise not to tell Da I told you?"

"On my honor as a—"

241

"Carlo!" his father's voice blasted. "I told you not to talk to anybody about this!"

"It's your own brother, you *ishzir*! Maybe if he knows, he'll talk some sense into you. That's more than I can do!"

"Hello," DiVries said, as his brother and sister-in-law stamped out into the hall. Carlo had the good sense to disappear. "What seems to be the problem?"

"Your mite-witted brother wants to abandon the factory!"

"That's not what I said at all—" Raimondo began.

Teresa didn't let him finish. "It's what's going to happen, if I run off to Gar Lake and you run off—"

"Teresa, if you blab—"

"Oh, the devil stew you and your friends in their own piss! Luke knows pretty much what you're about, or he wouldn't have used your name at Hennessey's the day of the fight!"

Raimondo made a strangled noise of rage and turned on his wife. His elbow swept a vase off the side table. It shattered on the floor. DiVries took one look at Teresa's face and stepped between the couple. A second look, and he dropped into a defense stance.

"Shut up, both of you!" he snapped. "If you don't care about the kids, at least think about what the workers might be hearing."

That got their attention. DiVries looked at his brother.

"That's the Gar Lake up toward the border, isn't it?"

"What other one is there?"

"What's up there, besides an easy hop across the border into Alliance territory?" Silence. "A secret camp for rebel sympathizers, maybe?"

Teresa's grin and Raimondo's glare confirmed DiVries's guess. "So what are you planning that you need to shut down the family business for it?"

More silence, until Teresa spoke. "He says that the situation is likely to get out of hand after the Flight 6 incident. The kids and me might be taken as hostages if the Feds crack down. There's already a rumor that they're disarming the Fourth Battalion."

There'd been rumors of locals from the two militia battalions being put on indefinite leave. Garbled—probably deliberately in some cases—they were no doubt the foundation of the rumor Teresa had just quoted.

DiVries faced his brother. "I don't suppose it's occurred to you that Fed Intelligence may be on to your bloody revolutionary 'safe house.' If they decide to move against it, everybody there can be gathered up in one swell foop. If you send Teresa and the kids south—"

"What makes you think I want to go anywhere?" she said. "It won't do the kids much good to be safe with no family business to support them."

DiVries suspected that his sister-in-law was partly concerned, partly rationalizing. She'd done as much or more than Raimondo to build up the business, including being one of the lifter pilots before the kids came.

"Hear me out, and then bite my head off," DiVries said. "Now, I don't want to ask your revolting chums for help—"

"You'd bloody well not get it," Raimondo shouted. "They're not happy with you stopping the fight at Hennessey's, *or* mentioning my name there. I had to answer a lot of questions about that."

"Were any of them intelligent? Never mind, that was rhetorical. I don't have to ask those bastards for help. I can ask some of my friends—"

"Fed military!"

"More trustworthy than your dust-brained apes! If they agree, we can make our own 'safe house' for all the families at the plant. If we do that, won't the workers be likely to stay on and keep things running?"

The longest silence of all. Teresa's eyes were almost pleading with her husband to agree. Finally, Raimondo jerked his head. It might have been a nod or a mite in his ear.

"What do you want in return?"

"Nothing."

"No—information?"

"I already have enough to buy a few extra friends if we need them. I'm not going to play spy, even if I think you're a—"

"I'm no traitor!" Raimondo shouted. "None of us are. We're not in this with the Alliance."

DiVries nodded politely. Prerevolutionary illusions and postrevolutionary realities were usually a good ways apart. He didn't expect anything to be different this time. But Raimondo still had a boy's—or maybe a frontier colonist's—

innocence. Victoria might smash it; it was a waste of time for Lucco to try.

"Why don't you and Reesa talk this over for a few minutes?" DiVries said. "I'll go outside."

The wind had almost completely died, and the last of the dust was sifting to the ground. DiVries could see twenty kilometers out across the desert.

A flight of three lifters swept past, just above the windbreak to the west. DeVries couldn't read the markings, but all three had their sensor masts raised and their launcher wings deployed.

Better start with Elayne, if Reesa can talk some sense into Ray. Her squadron's got the most transport to spare for "proficiency training flights" or whatever. Don't know if she thinks she owes me anything, but on the other hand you have to start someplace, like she said the last time in bed.

Nine thousand kilometers above the DiVries family organics plant, the Alliance battleship *Fei-huang* swung by in her orbit around Victoria. At that altitude, she and her squadronmates were out of range of ground weapons but in range of the Federation's squadron in its geostationary orbit.

The Alliance ships were too high to provide tactical support for ground troops. But Baba Lopatina would worry about the ground fighting when she thought it was about to start, and meanwhile her ships were deployed so that among them they had the whole planet under continuous surveillance.

"I won't say a hopper can't leave its nest without our noticing it," Lopatina said briskly. "But anything of military importance can't go on for very long without our detecting it. What we do after we detect is one of the reasons I invited you all here."

Captain Leray looked around the conference room at his fellow guests. *Ordered* would have been a better word than *invited*, although technically a full admiral could not actually punish a territorial governor for refusing her "invitation."

That governor's chances of getting any cooperation from the admiral, however, would be negligible. In a rare attack of common sense, Governor Hollings had realized this. Watching Lopatina put Hollings in his place soothed Leray's annoyance at having to ride up in the same shuttle with the man.

"I've glanced at your reports and passed them on to Admiral Uzel," she went on, with a nod at her chief of staff. "They look quite complete. I'll expect prompt answers to any questions, and, of course, regular updates."

A ten-minute break for tea and drinks let Leray study the conference room. Samples of the Baba's famous collections of antique enamelware and leatherbound books were unobtrusively displayed in odd corners. Otherwise the room was strictly Navy issue and gave no clues about its mistress, which was notoriously the way she liked it.

The admiral set down her steaming cup and contemplated a map of Victoria.

"We're already in the most versatile formation for what we have. I'm assuming that the Federation leaders aren't paranoid or megalomaniacal, and they won't automatically assume we're a threat.

"What we need to fear is their mistaking a threat from Victoria for a threat from us. They've already made that kind of mistake once. If they make it again, we want it to be very clear that the Feds shot first, and we'll respond with only enough force to defend ourselves.

"This may mean taking casualties, but that will be our duty if there's no other way of learning Federation intentions.

"If those intentions really are hostile, of course, we can turn *Shenandoah* into an orbital-debris problem and neutralize Victoria Dockyard." Three battleship captains, a cruiser-squadron commander, a scout-ship captain, and a chief of staff all grinned.

Pak's face wasn't made to grin. Leray grinned but mostly at Hollings's look. He had clearly expected the Baba to wade into Victoria Command with all lasers firing, or at least issue an ultimatum.

"Uzel, call a staff conference for—oh, 1700. Have my steward lay on dinner. And let Victoria Command know I'd like to talk with them on a secure circuit this evening, at a mutually convenient time after our staff conference."

"Aye-aye, ma'am."

"The rest of you can return to your posts. Thank you, and good luck."

The admiral rose. "Captain Leray, I'd like a private word with you."

This polite request nearly paralyzed Leray. It accelerated

the departure of everyone else and turned the governor's sour look into a carnivorous smile.

Leray's mind wasn't paralyzed. *The enemy of my enemy is my friend, the saying goes. But what if she decides we're both enemies and she can afford to fight us at the same time?*

Lopatina remained standing until the door closed, then adjusted a wire in the brass filigree frame around one of the pieces of enamelware.

"There. That gives us about fifteen minutes, when all Intelligence will hear is a polite discussion of in-system resources for supporting my ships. We came out just five days after a full resupply, by the way, so you needn't worry about our eating your stockpiles to the bare walls." She stepped to the buffet and picked up a carafe. "More wine?"

"Thank you."

"I had an advisory opinion from the Intelligence chief on Aguinaldo before we Jumped here. He advised breaking up the Bonsai Squadron."

If the wine glass hadn't been armorplast, it would have shattered in Leray's hands. "That—"

"Let's call him a fool and leave it at that. We don't have time to work out his genealogy. I have no intention of breaking up the squadron.

"In fact, I intend to reinforce it. I'm going to transfer *Pathan* to your squadron. She's the best-configured ship I have for ground-support work."

Under other circumstances Leray would have jumped at the chance of having another heavy cruiser under his command. With this situation and this admiral, he suspected a hook inside the bait.

"Does that mean we'll do most of the ground-support work if it's needed?"

"Does sand grate in your teeth? I thought I'd better concentrate our ground-support assets under somebody who knows Pak and Victoria."

And who isn't one of your hand-picked captains, either, so if he drops the ball it's less skin off your well-padded posterior.

"*Pathan*'s captain is a little senior to you, so I'll exercise my emergency power and call you a commodore. Now, do you want to continue as CO of *Audacious* as well?"

First-class bait, I'll admit. But—Jo is what she is. Responsibility might sober her up for good. If it didn't, there's two hundred other people besides her to think of, just on Audacious.

"Unless *Pathan*'s CO is going to need a lot of my time soothing him down."

"Leave that to me." The order was good humored but still an order.

"I think I can wear both hats."

"*Can*, or *have to*?"

"Did Intelligence blather about Jo—about Commander Marder, too?"

"Her problem isn't the Bonsai Squadron's secret anymore. It will be all over the sector if she doesn't do something about it. Has she been tested to see if it's a stress reaction or heredity?"

"No."

"I can't order you to make her take the tests. But I'd hope you can persuade her before I have to order her."

On the screen, Admiral Lopatina looked younger than she did in the three-year-old picture in the file on Kuwahara's lap. The rudimentary jowls and most of the wrinkles were gone, and the muscle tone seemed better.

"I've been bombarded with situation estimates from everybody on my side, down to the bartender in the 96th Regiment's NCO club," she said. "As a personal favor, I'd like yours."

Kuwahara and Kornilov exchanged glances, and Kornilov nodded. "We thought you might ask that," Kuwahara began, "so we consulted with the Military Council. They told us to go ahead at our discretion.

"First, we can confirm that the nonprovocation policy is still in effect. We hope that a similar opinion prevails in Alliance circles."

"As far as I know, it does. I can certainly promise to inform you if I receive any nonconfidential information to the contrary."

"Thank you, Admiral. As for the situation on Victoria, we evaluate it as a medium-level security threat. We are trying to deal with it at the political level rather than at the military."

"Nice, if the other side cooperates. And if they don't?"

Kornilov took the ball. "An appropriate response, whatever that may be. We don't feel that a long-term political solution would be advanced by massive use of force.''

"Aside from the fact that you don't have massive forces to use, that's true enough.''

Kuwahara was glad his darker skin didn't flush as easily as Kornilov's. "The Federation doesn't send squadrons and brigades chasing ghosts up and down the galaxy. I'm sure the Alliance doesn't either.''

"Depends on what you mean by a ghost, but in principle, yes. The Baernoi are too, too solid flesh and need constant watching.''

"I couldn't agree more," Kornilov said. "Anyway, a pure-force solution would end up with us needing a large permanent garrison to enforce an inherently unstable political settlement.''

"You've recommended this to the Victorian and Federation authorities?''

"Well . . .''

"I'm not asking what they said. I'll learn that anyway. I'm just asking if we're both telling our superiors the same thing.''

"Yes.''

"Thank God," Lopatina said. She lifted a cup of tea in salute. "With your permission, gentlemen?''

"*Da svidanya*," Kornilov said, and the screen went dark.

Kornilov sipped his own tea, then slumped back in his chair. "I would like to believe she is telling the truth. It would make our work much easier.''

"If wishes were fishes . . .'' Kuwahara quoted.

Kornilov glared over his teacup, then subsided. "One thing we do not need to wish. We can put Intelligence to learning if she is here ahead of her authorization or not.''

"I think she's telling the truth about that," Kuwahara said. "Leray's promotion convinced me.''

"That could be a regular promotion.''

"If it was, the Baba would have brought word of a good many others as well. Besides, Leray is spaceborn. The Alliance promotes them to flag rank about once a decade, if they are very nice to the Pentarchs and the Intelligence gurus. Leray is only polite to Pentarchs and he despises Intelligence as openly as he dares.

"No, I think the Baba is here under senior-commander

initiative. Now that she's here, she's going to arrange matters to suit herself. What that will involve, we'll have to wait and see."

Kornilov set his cup down. "I confess to being happier with that course where our rebel friends are concerned. They can hardly wipe the Federation off Victoria."

The officers' shower at Camp Aounda now had running water, sometimes hot, always mineral laden. Candice Shores blew her hair dry and looked at Major Nieg trying to wipe soap from between his toes.

"We were supposed to get mineral filters on the same convoy you came on," she said. "They sent us ammunition instead."

"Tangler mines. I sat on a crate of them all the way from Fort Stafford." Nieg finished with his toes and twisted from the waist. His spine looked as flexible as a cat's. "Kornilov's got his priorities in order."

"So he has." She looked around the shower room. "You know, this visit won't do much to dampen the rumors."

"That we're lovers? Probably not." He wrapped the towel around his waist. "Are these rumors likely to cause you trouble?"

"Just tongues with nothing better to do, so far. But why are you concerned?"

"You are a loyal Federation citizen and a fellow officer. But I have no hold over you except that loyalty and your commission oath, if it turns out that I have put you in an embarrassing position. Good Intelligence officers don't use up sources like toilet paper."

"Well, you are a good Intelligence officer, if that's not a contradiction in terms."

"Some of your friends would doubtless think so."

"They say so, loud and clear. Why am I lowering myself to love an Intelligence officer?"

Nieg contemplated Shores's muscular meter-eighty. "I imagine you would have to lower yourself. Or I would have to climb up you like an ape up a tree. Our dignity would never stand it."

My dignity, maybe. It wouldn't matter to you that you're twelve centimeters shorter, but you think it might matter to me. Is your tact purely professional?

"About those Third Battalion names you gave me," Nieg went on. "I have confirmation on most of them. Good work."

Is "confirmation," spelled "Esteva," I wonder?

"I note you didn't include either the CO or the Air Defense officer."

"I haven't had enough contact with the CO to have an opinion. The Air Defense officer is openly saying he wants to help the investigation. I think letting him take leave would do worse than interfere with that investigation. It would insult somebody with a great deal of moral courage."

"I agree. He'll have his day in court. So will the rest of Third Battalion. Nobody there is going on leave if I have a voice in the matter.

"The people in Third Battalion who want out don't want it because they're loyal to Victoria. They're loyal to their own skins.

"Divided loyalties I can understand, even forgive, under some circumstances. Moral cowardice I understand the way I understand biological warfare. I can't forgive it.

"If those mewling hoppers leave the Army, it will be because we ask them. Not the other way around."

The door slid open, to reveal two second lieutenants, a man and a woman. From their elaborately blank faces, Shores knew they must have heard Nieg's last outburst.

Compared to them, I know so much. Compared to Nieg, so damned little! How many unsavory facts is each new promotion going to teach me? And how many of them will I have to act on?

The door to D-4 slid open and Charles Longman half strode, half tottered in.

Mahoney froze the text on the screen and stood to help his bunkmate. Longman didn't even have the energy to shake him off. He collapsed onto Elayne Zheng's bunk, oblivious to the amount of gear temporarily stowed there.

"Hey, Lanie gotten sloppy all of a sudden?"

"Gone back on squadron duty. She's EWO on *Mahmoud Sa'id*."

Longman pretended to goggle. "Captain Rosie stood for that?"

"Captain Liddell," Mahoney said frigidly, "considers the interests of the whole squadron."

"Meaning I don't?" Longman flared. "What the hell do you think I was doing out there, bouncing Pocher?" He put his face in his hands. "Try to meet that man sometime before he recovers and look into his eyes. You'll see Hell."

Longman's eyes were puffy and bloodshot, a good picture of Purgatory if not Hell. Was he back on the drugs?

Before Mahoney could bring himself to ask, Longman actually smiled. "Sorry, Brian. I should have stayed on the dockyard and used the no-duty time Steckler laid on. Caught up on my sleep, had a couple drinks and some real food, maybe found a bouncing partner. Then I could have come back not looking like a Hive War-surplus android."

"Why didn't you?"

"Because we've been getting the bulletins. Every few hours on the way back aboard *Brautigan*, then every hour on Dockyard. If the shooting starts, I want to be back home. Here, aboard *Shenandoah*."

Mahoney was too surprised to think of apologizing himself. Longman pulled himself to his feet with one hand and started undressing with the other.

"Where's La Tachin?"

"In the bath," floated from behind the door. "And no, I will not scrub your back. But I will rub it when you have bathed."

"What an offer," Longman said. "It might even keep me awake."

It didn't. Longman managed to finish his shower, but he collapsed on Mahoney's bunk the next minute and was asleep the minute after that.

Mahoney didn't have the heart or the energy to move him. He'd started the text again when Tachin sat down beside him, close enough to whisper.

"Brian, can I ask you to sleep in Elayne's bunk tonight?"

"Sure. It's time we secured all that junk anyway. Too many unguided missiles if we take a hit. But why put me in it?"

"*Le petit Charles* is snoring like a faulty booster. You will sleep better."

Mahoney would have compared Longman more to a ditcher with a fractured belt. "I probably will." He looked at Tachin, who met him with steady eyes and a lower lip that quivered faintly.

She's scared, but I don't dare mention it. She's too proud. Besides, if we got into a serious discussion of courage, she'd know I was the one-eyed leading the deaf. My one dangerous situation was breathing too much toxic garbage aboard Valhalla. *What I'll do if* Shen *starts coming apart around us, I don't know any better than she does.*

He activated the terminal, sat down, and started composing a letter to Candice Shores. She'd shipped out for Victoria before he got out of the hospital, and he'd never gotten around to thanking her for a couple of visits and a box of reading matter.

Twenty-four

The wind was rising and changing. It blew sand across the terrace, making Lucco DiVries put a hand over his drink. It carried the sounds of sea birds, surf, and a steady stream of lifters coming into the Port Harriet Armory across the square.

C Company of Fourth Battalion, Victoria Brigade, was assembling for its evening drill. The Fourth wasn't fully mobilized yet; its cadre had all taken leave from their jobs, but most of the enlisted were still drilling three evenings a week and one day each weekend.

DiVries hoped that would damp the rumors about their being disarmed. *Any fool knows you don't train people like that if you're just going to send them home.*

Two more lifters droned over the square, tilted their fans as they passed over the armory gate, and settled down somewhere behind the wall. That covered a good deal of territory—several square kilometers, stretching down the shore west of Port Harriet.

Both lifters had civilian markings. *Must be doing a practice TUCE run. I'll ask Elayne's friend when he shows up.*

If he shows up.

Lucco DiVries wasn't the only person on this windswept terrace for his own amusement. Elayne Zheng had sent him out here to Port Harriet, to meet someone who knew someone in Intelligence who knew a friend of Elayne's.

It wasn't much, but it was the only lead he had so far. It might be the only lead he would get without going through channels that might produce no more results and a lot more awkward questions.

Ray's probably been no worse than a damned fool, but I know a lot of officers who've forgotten or never learned that foolishness isn't a crime.

The wind was making the tablecloths flap. The host came out, watching the sky.

"We have plenty of tables inside, Lieutenant," he said. "I don't want to raise the windscreens with drills going on next door. Firing practice can crack the screens."

"Thanks, but I've been up north a while. I'd like to smell the sea." *Not to mention that this is where I'm supposed to be, so my contact can scout on the ground in advance.*

"Fine. It may get a bit noisy, though. They flew in four loads of ammunition just before you came. Doesn't sound like the Fourth is going to be disarmed, does it?"

"How many people around here believe that?"

"Quite a few. I don't know that anybody is planning to do anything . . ."

It sounded at first as if the firing practice had begun. Then DiVries realized that most of the noise was shouting, with only a few pulsers firing. One of the lifters lurched into sight. It slammed against the top of the wall as the wind caught it, then stabilized and started to climb.

From the roof of the armory, a lance of golden fire thrust at the lifter. Its belly erupted in smoke and debris. As its lift power faded, it staggered over the wall, then toppled nose-down onto the beach.

The host had already vanished back inside. DiVries ran to the edge of the terrace and flung himself over the wall. The three-meter drop ended on sand; he went to his knees, then ploughed toward the stairs to the square.

"A regular is always on duty" had been drummed into him since his second day in Basic. The drummers hadn't always defined *duty*, but this time it was easy.

Find out what the Hades is going on, then help the good guys. If you can find out who they are.

DiVries hit the square at a run. He was fifty meters from the armory gate when it flew open. Was blown open, rather, by a concussion grenade. Two people almost flew through, with a cluster of others just behind them.

One of the leaders fell and didn't get up. The other, a female lieutenant, sprinted toward DiVries.

"Stop her!" someone screamed.

The voice carried authority, and common sense added its weight. DiVries cut to the right to head off the fleeing officer. At least she might be able to explain what was going on.

Instead she drew her pistol. DiVries cut left and scooped up a handful of windblown sand. As the officer tried to keep the pistol on him, he flung the sand. She closed her eyes, which gave him all the time he needed. They went down together, she struggling and swearing under his weight.

"You fucking rebel!"

"What?"

DiVries was so startled he nearly let go. The lieutenant wriggled desperately and was almost back on her feet when the others came up. So many people piled onto her that she was reduced to screaming, kicking, and biting at hands.

One kick caught DiVries in the temple. By pure reflex he kicked back. This merely added to the confusion.

Like a bull snee, DiVries lurched to his feet, throwing off hands that clutched at him. Some of the hands' owners realized that he wasn't trying to fight back, just get loose. One set let go only when he punched their owner smartly in the jaw.

By the time he stood freely, he realized that the soldiers were trying to avoid bloodshed. The lieutenant—the name on her battledress was "Uchupi"—looked as if she'd been in a major-caliber brawl but nothing worse.

"What the Hades is going on here?" DiVries shouted. *Not original, but it'll get an answer.*

"C Company's going north—" began someone.

"C Company's mutinying!" Uchupi yelled.

"C Company is joining the fight for freedom!" someone else thundered.

"Whose freedom?" DiVries asked. A feeding-pit uproar answered him.

Looks like they know what to do next, but not why, or what comes afterward. Maybe I can talk them back to duty.

DeVries counted the number of weapons in sight and rejected that idea. It would take only one fanatic and he would be dead, along with Uchupi and her companion. Then C Company would be outlawed for mutiny and murder; they would have nothing to lose.

"I'm First Lieutenant Lucco DiVries, formerly of F.S.

Valhalla. I'm also a Victoria native, brother of Raimondo DiVries. If you'll let these two go—" he nodded at the lieutenant and her fallen companion "—I'll take their place."

"She can identify us for the executioners!" the same voice who'd invoked "freedom" chimed in.

"Idiots!" DiVries shouted, before any doubters could join the fanatic. "They've already got IDs on most of you from the Billabong." He pointed at the restaurant, hoping no one knew that the proprietor was probably a sympathizer.

"Let Uchupi go—"

"And anyone else who wants to go," the other loyalist said. He was sitting up now, breathing heavily but apparently unhurt. He wore the stripes and trefoil of a Command master sergeant.

Several heads shook. "That will take too long," a sergeant first class said. DeVries recognized her as the one who'd mentioned "going north."

"Everybody in the armory now is going north. If anybody changes their mind after that, and the Feds promise to behave themselves, we can see about letting them go. Fair enough, Lieutenant?"

Uchupi looked outraged; the fanatic started to swear. DiVries studied the man, a lance corporal with protruding ears and a snub nose, and shifted his feet. Whatever else happened, if that lance corporal raised his pulser he was dead meat.

Nothing happened, except that the silence stretched on and pulled nerves tauter. Then Uchupi nodded. The Command master glowered but rose and went to her side.

DiVries went to stand beside the first class. "Anybody else hurt in there?"

"A couple of flesh wounds and a few broken bones. Our medics are coming with us, so the casualties are, too."

DiVries decided he'd reached the limits of negotiation. Slowly he drew his sidearm and handed it over butt-first.

Ten minutes later the whole company, reluctant dragons included, was airborne and heading west along the beach. DiVries found himself strapped snugly but not uncomfortably into the copilot's seat of the Command lifter. The first class, Sophie Bergeron, sat in the turret seat, cleaning her nails.

A hundred meters below, a family was playing where dry

gray sand turned to wet brown. Two children splashed through puddles and patches of foam, while a mother held a baby up to watch the father flying a kite. The two older children waved as the lifters whined overhead.

Probably too far upwind to hear anything suspicious. The company's keeping a nice tight formation, too. Which isn't what you'd expect of a militia rifle company, twenty minutes after a mutiny.

The formation wheeled and headed out to sea. Ten kilometers across whitecapped ocean, the headlands of Cape Sanders lifted toward the sky.

"We're going around the cape and head north along the far side of the O'Neil Range," Bergeron said. "That will make visual contact harder."

"It won't matter to orbital tracking," DiVries said.

"I know. But orbital tracking can't do any harm, unless someone orders lethal force. We hope matters won't come to that, either side."

Bergeron seemed more willing to talk, with the lance corporal and self-appointed political officer riding two lifters behind. DiVries decided to listen and above all not mention that the intended course brought the company within fifty kilometers of Alliance territory at several points.

Commander Gesell was only five centimeters taller than Elayne Zheng. Zheng still felt loomed over as the squadron commander stood behind her seat, glaring at the displays. The expressionless displays only showed the rapidly closing distance between *Mahmoud Sa'id* and C Company's lifters.

"Range 65,000 meters," Zheng said. "Formation maintaining previous course, speed, and altitudes. No, the highest one is now down to about 700 meters. Looks like they're ready to hide in ground clutter."

"I can read a display as well as you can, Lieutenant," Gesell muttered. "When we close to 20,000 meters, I want an all-frequencies 'stop and ground' sent out."

"Aye-aye, ma'am."

The range closed rapidly. The lifters were at their most economical cruise speed, a sedate 250 km/h. *Sa'id* was moving three times as fast—for her, a positive crawl.

The signal went out. Some electronic fault made a horrendous squeal in Zheng's earphones. She swore and shook her head as the screen flashed for an incoming call.

"Take us up to a thousand meters above the formation and keep us there," Gesell told the pilot. "Lieutenant, let's see what these bastards have to say for themselves, if anything."

The turret seat of a command lifter came on the screen, with a middle-aged militia SFC in it. She gave the open-palmed salute used when duty required sitting down.

"Sophie Bergeron, acting CO of C Company, Fourth Battalion, Victoria Brigade."

"Sergeant Bergeron, I order you and your people to land immediately and stay in your vehicles."

"Commander, what are you going to do if we don't?"

In a less explosive situation, Zheng would have laughed at Gesell's expression. The CO looked ready to explode from sheer internal pressure.

Bergeron took advantage of Gesell's temporary speech-lessness. "Commander, you can't stop us without using lethal force. I don't think you have any orders to do that. If you do, we can't do anything except defend ourselves the best we can. But will you listen a bit anyway?"

Gesell managed to nod.

"Nobody has been killed in this . . . unauthorized leave. We didn't want to either be disarmed and immobilized, or sent out to kill other Victorians. So we decided to put ourselves out of reach.

"We left the XO and first sergeant back in Port Harriet. All the other people who resisted needed medical attention. We've got them in the medevac lifter. They'll come back as soon as the rest of us are safe, along with anyone who's changed their minds."

Gesell glowered. "Why should I take your word for this?"

"You won't have to, Commander."

"Put me through to your CO!"

"The captain's in the medevac. But—"

"Lucco!"

Zheng's screech drew another snarl from Gesell. Zheng shouted, "Lucco, what in the name of Shiva are you doing there?"

"That's my question, Lieutenant!" Gesell said. "What are you doing in the company of mutineers?"

"I went along to keep them from either kidnaping or killing Uchupi and the Top. Bergeron's telling the truth, as far as I know. I saw all the casualties loaded. They'd all been treated and they were all alive." He shrugged. "I haven't seen them since, but so far I'm pretty sure nobody's been deliberately murdered."

"This is mutiny!"

"If you say so, Commander. But if you shoot, I'll be one of the first casualties."

A "dead mutineers tell no tales" look flew across Gesell's face, then vanished as her shoulders twitched.

"Very well. You've made a valid case for avoiding lethal force. But we're going to call up reinforcements. We're also going to fly formation and maintain radar lock on you."

"Be our guest," Bergeron said. "As long as you don't mind if we keep radar lock on you."

A glance at her displays told Zheng that the lifters' air-to-air radar was precisely locked in on the attacker. What they could do with that lock depended on their weapons load, which was probably light considering all the troops on board, but so was *Sa'id*'s, because she'd rushed out in an almighty hurry.

A shooting match would most likely end in mutual destruction. Unless *Sa'id* could get under the mutineers, and they'd made that difficult by flying as low as they could and still keep formation.

"We'll be happy to keep you company until you come to your senses," Gesell said.

"Or reach our destination," Bergeron replied, and she cut the connection.

Gesell hissed at the blank screen, then grinned. "They'll find out that lethal force isn't all we've got. Check with Base to see if they've loaded those webheads yet."

"Take her up?" the pilot asked.

Gesell shook her head. "We're going to stay right on their tails. Let the terrain mess up everybody's sensors. We may not be able to get under them, but I'm damned if I'll let them get under us!"

"That's a roger."

Sa'id settled down to tail Company C, zigzagging back and forth across the rear of the formation to avoid slowing down enough to be a sitting target. Zheng put Gesell through to Base, then gripped the arms of her seat.

Damn you, Lucco! Why?

"We should have had the webheads loaded and ready," Kuwahara said.

The "we" wasn't quite enough tact for Kornilov. Either he grimaced, or the scrambler on the screen made it look as if he did.

"You will undoubtedly not be the last person to tell me that," the general said heavily. "However, the delay in bringing the webheads on the scene was less critical than a number of other factors."

Kuwahara hoped the number was small. Kornilov certainly needed to let off his rage at someone, but Kuwahara had his own list of urgent business.

Kornilov continued. "The webheads arrived aboard Crimson Two and Three. By then the mutineers were well into the mountains. They stayed low in the passes, claiming that this was out of concern for the casualties.

"They may have been telling the truth," Kornilov conceded. "However, the accuracy of the missiles was seriously impaired by the targets being low over extremely rough terrain. By the time we were making effective hits, the mutineers were out of the mountains and we were nearly out of webheads.

"With room to manuever, the mutineers were able to take the disabled vehicles in tow. The one that they claimed was carrying the casualties maneuvered so that we couldn't interfere. Then the whole formation set off again, at a lower speed but right down among the dunes and straight for the border."

That was an impressive display of discipline and cohesion for a unit that had mutinied only a few hours before. Kuwahara wondered if it might not have been wiser to bring the Fourth Battalion along ahead of the Third.

Perhaps, but then they might only have mutinied sooner and more dangerously. Kornilov will undoubtedly be cursed by enough wise-after-the-fact comments; I will not add to them.

"Did they cross the border?"

"They went within ten kilometers of it, then set a course

parallel to it. Meanwhile, they were telling everybody within listening range all about their situation."

"Including, no doubt, the Alliance border patrols?"

"Yes. They must have had some advance warning, because they brought up a whole flight of gunships from the 96th's Air Group, plus a pair of light attackers with recon pods.

"That ended any possibility of preventing the mutineers from crossing the border. Fighting for our right to violate Alliance borders in pursuit of comparatively nonviolent mutineers would be starting the war under the worst possible circumstances.

"In fact, the mutineers did not need to cross the border. Shortly afterward, the whole southern horizon was lighting up with blips. Over a hundred civilian lift vehicles appeared. They came from Mount Houton, Kellysburg, most of the small towns around and between the two cities, and individual farms.

"It was already impossible to shoot down the mutineers without a horde of hostile witnesses. When the civilians enveloped Company C's formation, it became absolutely impossible. Commander Gesell asked for permission to break off the pursuit, and I gave it."

"I concur," Kuwahara said. It was the only possible reply. It would be making a bad situation worse to comment about his not being informed about this crisis until it was over.

Kornilov had operational control of the 879th; everything he'd done had been within his right. Kuwahara's intervening would have looked as if the Navy's new admiral didn't trust the veteran CG of Victoria Command. This was not the time to have that rumor running around.

"I have seldom seen anyone as angry as Commander Gesell," Kornilov concluded. "I took the liberty of prescribing a stiff drink and a good night's sleep."

Kuwahara smiled. "I concur in that, too."

A map replaced Kornilov's face, but his voice continued. "The Victoria Brigade is on a war footing as of an hour ago. I am maintaining my HQ at Fort Stafford, with Task Force Langston in the north and Task Force Liu in the south.

"Langston controls First and Second Battalions. Liu controls the Third and the Provisional Transport Group. The Fourth remains at its depots, armed but not issued transport. That should keep everyone but the fanatics under control. With Langston between them and the rebels, the rest of the Fourth won't get away so easily.

"Will you have any problems supporting that deployment?"

"No."

That was assuming the First and Second were going to clean out the Blanchard Canyon area or at least hold it against any rebel offensive southward. There should be plenty of warning if anything else turned out to be needed, such as an offensive into rebel territory.

"One problem, Sho. I need a Navy representative at my HQ, so we can do full real-time consultation. The Military Council's either going to move to Fort Stafford or send Karras and probably Brothertongue. Who can you send?"

A problem as old as radio: do you send complete information and risk the enemy hearing or do you keep the enemy ignorant at the risk of doing the same to your own people? Every advance in communications had made things worse, and the Federation doctrine of HQ representatives was one rearguard action against chaos.

The light cruiser and transport captains were too junior for the job. The dockyard needed Wolfgang Steckler. Kuwahara had no chief of staff.

This left himself and Rose Liddell. Which one?

If he sent Liddell, he would command in any action in space and the Navy would be well represented at HQ. It would also look as if he wanted to deprive Liddell of her chance to command in combat. The squadron would do just a little better under Liddell than under him, in a situation where any small advantage could be decisive.

Not to mention that Liddell knew Kornilov's mind well enough to work with him from orbit. Kuwahara would be more likely to overload communications circuits and/or guess wrong.

"I'll come down myself. I'll also pull as many people as the squadron and Dockyard can spare for HQ security and an improvised staff. That way we'll have a few extra trigger fingers if our opponents' next move is a kamikaze assault on the fort."

From Kornilov's expression as he signed off, it was hard to tell whether he'd been given good news or bad news.

That makes two of us, Kuwahara realized as he contemplated the blank screen.

He wouldn't be bringing very many people, not from a squadron so shorthanded he was using as a chief of staff a captain who had a capital ship to run and not even a secretary to call her own. He would, however, give preference to anyone with Intelligence experience.

It was time the Navy had its own Intelligence network on the ground, at least enough to bypass the Military Council. It was also time that Kuwahara sat down quietly with Major Nieg.

There'd been too many security leaks. At first Kuwahara had been ready to suspect sloppiness or General Liu. But Kornilov had tightened up on loose tongues, Liu was no longer chief of staff, and the leaks went on.

This had to be changed, immediately, without offending either Kornilov or their common civilian superiors.

This is also impossible, but I would be letting my people down if I didn't at least try.

"Commander, *Audacious* has launched a shuttle. It's losing altitude rapidly, but staying well inside Alliance territory."

Bogdanov didn't sit upright. He wanted to appear calm and not crack his head again. For someone of Bogdanov's height, Fujita's private cubicle in Engineering Control had barely sitting headroom.

"Have you told the captain?"

If a voice could glare insubordinately, this one did so. "All done and logged, Commander."

Bogdanov wondered when Captain Liddell would finish her briefing with the admiral. Instead, he thanked the sensor officer and cut the circuit. Turning back to Fujita, he found a cup of tea in front of him. The two officers had managed to compromise on a strength that pleased both of them, even if Bogdanov wanted it stronger and Fujita wanted it weaker.

Bogdanov sipped politely. "I came around to find out if there are any problems in your department that the captain and I could solve before the Alliance and the rebels start taking up all our time."

"Nothing we can't handle ourselves with the seconded people. They're settling in better than I expected. Personnel and Training really checked the shape of the holes before they started shipping out pegs."

"I suspect a collaboration between Lieutenant Mahoney and Warrant Officer Hobson," Bogdanov said. "Only don't depend on him staying in Training much longer. Charbon and I want to polish him up for JOOW as fast as we can."

"Mahoney? Isn't he on limited duty, from the *Valhalla* accident?"

"Yes, which is probably why Prange let him go. That's one advantage of Kuwahara going dirtside. He won't be around to quote regulations if we start a limited-duty officer training for watchstander."

Bogdanov took another polite sip of tea and looked out the clear wall of the cubicle. One control usually looked much like another, unless you got close enough to read the displays, but Engineering had subtle differences. The emergency gear was ready to hand, even on Alert Two, and the watchstanders were mostly older people.

Engineering watchstanders normally took no more radiation than anyone else aboard a starship. When they had to keep their machinery going in the middle of a battle, though, part of their job was to risk massive doses.

Modern medicine could repair radiation damage that would have been fatal as late as the Starworld Rebellion. It still helped to have fewer years to lose and no need to hope that your stored germ cells were in good shape.

Bogdanov finished the tea just in time for another call from the Combat Center.

"Commander, we have an altitude and course for that shuttle from *Audacious*. She's down to 9500 meters, on a course roughly parallel to the border but sixty kilometers clear of it."

"Speed?"

"Slow but variable. Minimum 700 kilometers per hour, maximum 1100."

"Electronic signature?"

"Nothing distinctive."

"Can you put them through to me?"

"On the way, Commander."

The electronic signature of the shuttle came up on Fujita's displays. Bogdanov frowned.

"Everything's nominal, except . . . Show me the position of the Alliance border patrols!"

Fujita jumped at the whipcrack in Bogdanov's voice.

"The last reported positions," the sensor officer said.

"Thank you," Bogdanov said. Now he was grinning. "If those patrols are still on station, we know what the shuttle's doing. With lasers, the patrols can transmit on line-of-sight to her. Very reliable in clear weather and no way we can intercept.

"Lieutenant, start scanning for another lifter-borne unit. It'll be far enough from the border to be under the horizon from the patrol areas but close enough to be a quick-reaction force."

"Reacting to what, sir?"

"I don't think they know themselves. Start looking, tell the captain, and expect me in Combat Center in five minutes."

Twenty-five

Behind the command lifter, darkness was swallowing the hills. Ahead, the peaks of the O'Neils were still in sunlight.

Candice Shores stared alternately at all four quarters around Scout Company's formation, until her eyes began to ache. It seemed unreasonable that by sheer will power she couldn't draw some sign of the enemy out of this dismal landscape.

Beside her, Jacob Koritz grinned. "Relax, Captain. You gave good advice back before we lifted out. Just remember to take it yourself."

Shores stared sideways at Koritz. She was satisfied that the captain's insignia he wore now weren't a hallucination. She still wondered what he was doing here.

With Scout Company operating semi-independently, it needed a liaison with Langston's HQ. Was Koritz also around in case Shores tackled another field-grade job and this time mucked it? Koritz had an LI badge, but how recent were his qualifications?

Simplest solution is not to muck it. And was that a flash off to the southeast? No, it was several flashes.

The radio crackled, then turned to gibberish and finally to speech as the scrambler codes matched.

"Baker Four to Zulu One, Baker Four to Zulu One. We have a hot LZ. Repeat, we have a hot LZ. Request suppressive fire."

Baker Four was Company B, First Battalion; Zulu One was Langston. The flashes went on, and high overhead a copper-glowing dart changed course, then plunged into the darkness. One of the standing-patrol attackers was on her way to help Baker Four.

"Sure the advice applies anymore?" Shores asked. "This is two missile-snipings and a hot LZ before we're even touched down."

"Maybe the rebels take the job of getting those caches out more seriously than we thought," Koritz admitted. "The advice still applies."

Shores remembered standing on the bow of the Command lifter, facing Scout Company. "Break ranks and gather round," she began.

"We're going out as Scouts, one platoon in rotation with each battalion of the task force. We're also going out as part of the task force reserve, three of our platoons and a company from each battalion.

"First Battalion cleans out Blanchard Canyon. Second Battalion hits anybody who tries to interfere."

"What about anybody who tries to run?" somebody asked.

Shores hadn't called for questions, but this one had to be answered.

"If they're just running, not firing, we let them go. I mean that. Heavy trigger fingers are going to be exhibited for the media after this is over, whether or not they're still attached to their owners!"

Shores wasn't ecstatic about that policy, and she knew she had company. But it was the only way to go if the rest of what she'd said was true.

"Our job is to prevent a war, not start one. We're to do this by disarming the rebels and limiting their territorial gains. The less firepower they have, the less they'll be tempted to fight it out or make trouble on the Alliance side of the border."

"Why the hell don't we let the Alliance have those damned bushrangers?" somebody shouted.

"When you get to be a general, you can decide to throw people to the Alliance," Shores said. "Meanwhile, we play it straight."

"Any questions?" The silence lasted until Shores nodded to Top Zimmer.

"Scout Company, load and lift!'

That was three hours before. Now, in not much more time than that, Scout Company might be in a full-scale battle. Shores's comment about not starting a war had left one thing out.

The decision had to be mutual. If the rebels or the Alliance didn't cooperate . . .

Fainter flashes, off to the north, in the shadows below the sunlit peaks. Then a harsh flaring of blue-white light, unmistakably a heavy power plant exploding.

A gabble of voices on the radio, straining the limits of the scramblers. Koritz and the radio operator listened, until Shores ordered the whole formation into nuclear-alert formation.

In two minutes Scout Company had opened out to three-kilometer intervals. The station-keeping lights of the flanking lifters were no brighter than fourth-magnitude stars.

"Don't think that was a fuser," Koritz said.

"Hard to tell, isn't it?"

"Radiation signature's different."

"Got a recording?"

"Recorder's down," the pilot said. Koritz said something impolite.

"Try to get me through to Zulu One," he told the radio operator.

Shores decided to ignore Koritz's acting without her permission. He was within the limits of his liaison job, and anyway, intelligence about who was doing what to whom ahead was more important as Scout Company flew straight toward it.

Joanna Marder's left buttock was going to sleep. She shifted as much as the seat would let her.

It wasn't really the seat's fault. It was the fault of having to be strapped in, and of having three extra people aboard the shuttle to handle the plug-in modules.

The main map display flickered, and the red line across Federation territory shifted. Marder whistled at the new action code.

"Somebody popped a fuser?

The sensor chief shook her head. "Attacker power plant. Could have been hit by a fuser, maybe. Maybe a laser, a slughead, or an accident, too."

Modern sensors and communications, Marder decided, merely increased the range over which you could be confused. At least the actual fighting so far was on the Federation side of the border.

"Show the positions of our patrols," she said. She could call them up on her own screen, but its smaller scale would distort the density of the patrols' coverage. No more than sixty lift vehicles and five hundred men were spread across four thousand kilometers of border.

That was slightly more than token coverage; large and conspicuous enemy formations could be detected, even engaged with some hope of success. Marder doubted that the Federation would be stupid enough to use anything of the kind, and against low-altitude or ground infiltration the patrols were—call it "porous"—at best.

Oh well, they'll register on Fed sensors as much as they do on mine. The Feds won't think they can get triggerhappy and not have us notice.

The deck tilted as the shuttle changed course, to hold her distance from the border. At seventy kilometers, she was out of range of any Federation energy weapons unless they'd grossly violated the border. Any legally placed Feds were also out of her range. Marder hoped they knew it.

"Thanks." The patrols vanished from the screen. Four suspicious sightings—no, five now—remained.

"What's that new badger?" At least it looked like a ground contact, instead of an airborne bogey.

"Radiation pulse," the sensor chief said. "Matches the signature and location of an old mine plant. Somebody probably decided the chamber was too radioactive to bother removing when the area was way outside any possible—"

A giant kicked the shuttle up and sideways. Every light aboard went out. Somebody shouted incoherently. Marder added orders.

"Emergency power! Evasive action!"

The deck tilted again, then gyrated madly. With no power spared for internal gravity, the g-loads slammed everybody aboard into their chairs, which automatically swung back and down into acceleration couches. Marder was still sure she was going to end up as a thin second layer of upholstery on her chair.

Emergency lighting flickered twice, then steadied. The intercom stayed dead. So did most of the displays. The copilot opened the emergency panel and took course, airspeed, and altitude.

Marder thanked the dim lighting for hiding her bemused

expression. She knew what had happened: a particle-beam strike with a missile or two riding the beam to very close to lethal radius.

She also knew that was *don't say impossible, say possible only under extreme circumstances.* The beam and the missile would have had to be launched from Alliance territory. But then who'd launched them? Missiles that could guide on a particle beam specifically designed to fry electronics were sophisticated equipment. Nobody on Victoria would have them except the Federation.

"Report to Crystal, we've been attacked by a Federation infiltration team," Marder said. She was glad the intercom was out; it gave her an excuse for raising her voice. "They used a beam-and-missile attack with a—slug or fuser?"

"Slug, I think," the pilot said. "I guess, anyway."

That guess was good enough for Marder. She didn't want to think about the Federation not only infiltrating Alliance territory but arming the infiltrators with fusion-warhead shipkillers.

The tension this relieved came right back when the pilot said, "We've lost all communications. Well, maybe not the emergency radio. But it's got no scrambler or coder."

"Can you reprogram it?"

"Not with the main machine 85 percent down. We'll be in visual signaling range of Patrol Onyx in twenty minutes, assuming the gauges aren't as big a mess as everything else."

"Can't we cut that time?"

"Not at low altitude. Power plant's almost nominal, but I think we've got some hull damage. I wouldn't want to push her too hard. Besides, fast and low on the gauges is a good way to make your heirs rich if your death bonus is up to date."

Which reminds me: who is going to get the money if this shuttle does fall apart? Maybe I should make a new assignment, to Paul?

"We can always climb."

"Is that an order, Commander?"

Marder heard the hostility of light-craft pilots for big-ship spacers and something more. She clawed her wits together.

"Think our friends may have a few more shots in their locker?"

"Nobody sets up a heavy beamer to guide just one missile. Maybe our patrols can keep them busy, but I don't want to be a fat, dumb, happy target if they can't."

"I want to live to spend my retirement bonus, too. Use your judgment."

"Thanks, Commander. Leo, get back and make an eyeball check. I want you to stick your own finger into every hole, instead of keeping it where you usually do."

Brigitte Tachin ducked as a crate of high-velocity decoys rumbled past on the conveyor. She was getting good at ducking fast-moving equipment, so good that eighteen hours of continuous duty hadn't destroyed the reflex.

May this continue. Being squashed like a grape by a load I didn't see is a fate too ignominious to contemplate.

Morton Gellis lifted his head from the plug-in screen on his knees. "That's the last one we're supposed to load. Shut down the conveyor?"

"How long to launching the attackers?" *I should remember that, but* mon Dieu, *I am so tired!*

"They launch at 0430, it says here."

"Forty minutes . . . That's time enough for orders to be changed. Does it need any maintenance?"

"No."

"Then leave—"

"Now hear this, now hear this. All attacker crews report to the docking area immediately. All attacker crews report to the docking area immediately."

Few of the sixteen crew of the four attackers reloading weapons and consumables had left the docking area. One who had was Elayne Zheng. A minute later she sprinted out of the elevator, a considerable feat even under reduced gravity with the load she was carrying.

"Brigitte! I didn't see you on the way in. How goes it?"

"I live. And you?"

Zheng dropped her two bags to the deck and flexed her shoulders. "Just picking up some cabin stores. Brian had them all laid out, or I'd have never made it. How's he, by the way?"

"Frustrated."

"You really ought to—"

"Elayne, do you want me to break every jar in those

bags?" Tachin swayed and gripped a stanchion to steady herself. "Not that kind of frustration. Training's virtually shut down, but nobody's going to let him on the bridge or anywhere else he'd be useful. He may stage his own mutiny if this goes on."

"Take care of him. Oh, and yourself, too."

"I'll do my best. He's even put the fear of God into Gellis. If God is worth fearing, compared with what we face."

Zheng frowned. "Brigitte, you're getting cynical."

Tachin saw the other woman was genuinely concerned. "Only tired."

"Get used to it. Things are going to get worse before they get better. We have to make a courier run to the two light cruisers with somebody's mail. A shuttle or a tender could do it, but oh no, they won't let any unarmed outside Dockyard's defense perimeter."

A dark bearded face thrust around the rim of the nearest dock hatch. "Elayne, get your tail in here right now. If you don't, there's a chunk of antimatter just dying to nibble on it!"

"On the way, Skipper."

Zheng threw an arm around Tachin's shoulders, kissed her lightly on the nose, and picked up her bags.

Tachin watched her practically dive through the hatch. *Question: do I want this to happen often enough to get used to it?*

The explosion registered on all the CP's sensors; displays promptly told everyone about its force, location, and altitude. Probably fragment pattern, chemical residue, and casualties, too, but Candice Shores wasn't looking at the displays once they told her the location.

She was looking at the wall, as if her eyes could not only pierce it but the hundred kilometers of darkness to Zion Four. A platoon of D Company, First Battalion, and 4th Platoon, Scout Company, ideally positioned to command a main route into the Blanchard Canyon area.

Ideally positioned, it also turned out, to be surrounded by the rebels. Nobody thought the rebels could surround a salt well, but nobody had thought they would mass that hundred-lifter formation for an offensive, either.

A hundred lifters, all blatantly civilian, none obviously armed, using only civilian electronics to hold formation and track their Fed visitors. No sign of the missile used on the attacker—and the rebel radio had actually apologized for the attacker's destruction.

"We only wanted to keep it from tracking us," the rebel spokesman said. Someone recognized the voice as a retired lifter-maintenance tech, who'd dropped around both First and Second Battalions as late as the previous month, visiting old friends.

"Probably pumping them for intelligence, too," Major Kufir had growled.

With no positive identification of a military target and no authority to stop traffic outside the prohibited area, Task Force Langston found its hands tied. So it pushed its outposts farther forward than planned, to where they could monitor ground traffic in the Blanchard Canyon area.

"They can't send that mob into the prohibited area, so they'll be bringing the stuff out on the ground," Langston said. "We'll hit as much as we can before they load and lift. Then we'll have legitimate military targets and won't have to pussyfoot around with webheads."

That got nods and mutters of approval all around the CP. Nobody thought the apology over the attacker was worth a cup of manure. Task Force Langston was operating on the basis that the other guys had started a war, and now it was time to make them understand they'd made a big mistake.

The outposts went forward, and the enemy's lifters thickened up. Now there were *two* hundred.

"Where in God's name do they all come from?" Kufir blazed.

"They've got a real high ratio of lift to population," Shores said. "Most of the machinery is one generation short of museum pieces, but it lifts and flies. That's all the bushrangers can afford, but that's all they need."

"They'll be using up power cells like beer barrels," Langston said. "If we can find and hit their charging bases, they'll be up the creek without a paddle."

"Even better if we could knock out their whole power grid," Kufir said. "But I suppose they won't do anything stupid like mounting a missile launcher on top of either generating plant."

"They won't," Langston said. "They also have a lot of solar cells, all nicely plastered over civilian dwellings."

The outposts grounded and set up their sensor nets. Not many sensors remained from a few weeks before, and Shores suspected the outage rate had very little to do with Victoria's rancid weather.

The rebels must have been monitoring the sensor emmissions—passively, but reliably. Minutes before the sensor nets would have become operational, all four outposts came under attack. With three of the four Zions it was nothing but heavy sniping and an occasional HE warhead, lobbed by rockets so crude they were probably homemade and certainly easy targets for the attacker section.

Until the attacker sections started running out of ammunition. Even then, the cover might have held if there'd been more attackers available. With twelve of the 879th's seventeen machines reverted to Navy command for some unspecified reason, the remaining section was trying to fix a banquet with one microwave and a campfire.

"I'm going to yell and scream at Kornilov and Kuwahara after this is over," Langston said. "We had a firm promise of the 879th's being available for tactical support before we moved. What the hell happened?"

One of the things that happened was trouble across the border; word of that came about the same time as the air cover over the Zion line evaporated. This mollified the people in the CP, but it didn't save the four outposts from a salvo of airbursts that mangled vehicles, sensors, communications, and even a few soldiers.

Only Zion Four faced a ground assault, and there was another nasty surprise. Some of those civilian lifters must have dropped rebel troops close enough to let them close the distance on foot. The rebels were determined and well-organized enough to make use of their edge in numbers, and they packed a surprising amount of firepower.

None of this did them much good against two platoons of regulars. They were beaten off, but by the time they were, Zion Four was nearly out of ammunition. Major Kufir took off with a resupply; a platoon of heavy launchers took off to set up a firebase covering the whole Zion line.

"The rebels should make one more push before they figure out where the firebase is," Langston said. "If we slap that one down hard enough, they'll have to pause and regroup. Then we can resupply the whole Zion line and use that as our base. They can't use a mob of 'civilian targets' against it after that. They'll be off balance, and we can start getting them reacting to us for a change."

Now Kufir was probably dead, his mission a failure, Zion Four as dry of ammo as before, the enemy alert and ready to attack again. Shores listened to the fragments of radio messages from the outpost confirming all this.

Now she wanted to hurl more than her senses across the darkness. She wanted to fly to Zion Four herself, be with her people, do what could be done for them even if it was only to make sure Scout Company's KIA list would include the CO.

"If we're sending another mission to Zion Four, I volunteer to lead it," Shores said.

Her answer was silence, broken only by the hiss and crackle of a radio carrying static and an occasional distant pulser burst.

Lucco DiVries sat on an empty water barrel, legs dangling. Three robot pallets loaded with ammunition crates rumbled by. The rider on the third glared at him, but DiVries was immune to glares by now and didn't expect anything worse.

He still didn't know what he was, here in the rebel base outside Kellysburg. It would have been a joke learning that the rebels didn't know either, except for the few fanatics wandering around.

Those fanatics were DiVries's only big worry. Everybody else seemed to know that randomly shooting Federation prisoners was injudicious.

The hotheads probably know, too, but think that if they kill me the Federation will retaliate and their comrades will be desperate enough to follow them wherever they lead. Including into the arms of the Alliance.

A lifter took off in a cloud of dust. Three more pallets emerged from the cloud, the last one carrying two passengers. As the pallets went by, the second passenger dropped off.

It was Sergeant Bergeron, wearing a tan civilian windbreaker over fatigues. What looked like captain's bars were stenciled on either shoulder of the windbreaker.

"Congratulations on your promotion," DiVries said.

"I didn't ask for it," Bergeron snapped. "But they thought that where I was going, it would help."

"I meant it," Di Vries said. "Where are you going?"

"I can't tell you," she said, then smiled. "I mean that, too."

"Well, if you want my advice—"

"Could I stop you if I didn't?"

"If you were someone like that wild-eyed corporal, yes. Otherwise, you'll have to pay the price of being an officer and a lady."

"I have time for quite a few things but not flattery."

"Sorry," DiVries said. "Just this: how much of your arsenal is Baernoi?"

In the near-blackout DiVries couldn't see a blush but he could hear strain in a voice. "Anything off-planet came through Merishi traders."

"Who are perfectly willing to trade in Baernoi weapons if the price is right."

"Are you sure you aren't seeing things?"

"I'm seeing what I taught a course on at Alcuin Arsenal. The Baernoi usually do a better job of matching human designs, or even I wouldn't have spotted it. Either the Baernoi, the Merishi traders, or your leaders don't care if the Baernoi connection is traceable."

"And suppose it is? Who will blame desperate people?"

DiVries had never heard a worse imitation of defiance. "You sound like the corporal. Although you must be pretty desperate if you're planning trouble for the Alliance."

Even the darkness couldn't hide another glare. The sound of a lifter heading north also didn't drown out Bergeron unsnapping her holster. She didn't quite draw, but DiVries was suddenly careful to keep his hands in view.

"You shouldn't have been allowed to wander around loose. You've seen too much. The minute somebody realizes just how much, you're in trouble."

"If you think that, then take me in yourself. But remember that what I've seen I can't unsee. If I survive, maybe I can be useful to both sides."

"You won't survive 'til morning, wandering around where anybody can take a shot at you."

"Wandering around, I'll be hard to shoot without witnesses.

Locked up, all it takes is a bribe to one or two guards or even a little poison slipped in the porridge."

Bergeron closed her holster and threw up her hands in disgust. "You're impossible."

"You're about the hundredth person to tell me that, starting with my brother."

"Not your parents?"

"My mother died when I was four and my father took to space. Raimondo pretty much raised me."

"Is that why you're here?"

"Part of the reason. Look, I suspect you've got work to do and it'll look suspicious if you stay here much longer. I don't want to get you into trouble."

"You think my new rebel friends will do that for you?" But she had a smile in her voice.

They shook hands, and Bergeron faded into the darkness and the dust. DiVries climbed back on the drum and beat out an old song with his heels.

I thought I was coming home. Instead I found I'd come to cloud-cuckoo land.

"They want you to *what*?" General Langston exploded.

The sergeant now commanding Zion Four sounded apologetic.

"Well, maybe not exactly surrender. They've simply shown us how completely we're surrounded. They even illuminated a couple of their positions to show us their people and weapons."

"Didn't you fire?" Langston sounded ready to climb through the radio and shake information out of the sergeant.

"Sir, we've got about five minutes worth of ammo. That's with what we took from the wounded and a little we salvaged. They totaled Kufir, but the other lifter jettisoned a couple of crates before it hit."

"What do they have?"

"At least two full companies and lots of direct-fire heavy stuff. Maybe the firebase can help with the weapons, but if the infantry comes again they'll be too close too soon."

"That bad?"

"Sir, we can put maybe thirty-three, thirty-four people on the line. That's counting the walking wounded and leaving all the bad cases to take their chances. We got five, six people who aren't going to make it if they don't see a medic pretty soon."

"What makes you think the rebels have any medics, at least for you?"

"They've promised us legal treatment as prisoners of war and exchange as soon as possible. I've seen them picking up their own wounded, at least."

"Thank you, Sergeant," Langston said. "How long did they say they'd wait?"

"Another ten minutes is about all I'd expect," the sergeant said.

"We'll be back to you faster than that," Langston said. "Meanwhile, you've all done well—if a general's opinion counts for anything at a time like this."

"Well, sir, some generals count for more than others," the sergeant concluded.

Langston stood up and stretched until his fingertips touched the overhead. "Well, people?"

Shores had seen this moment approaching since the sergeant came on the radio. Military protocol required that Langston consult her and the CO of First Batallion about surrendering a unit of their commands.

Her hesitation let Captain Koritz speak first. His only claim to a voice was long association with Langston, but Shores knew that claim was worth more than a whole stack of TOs.

"I'd say this is a pretty straightforward case of their trying to get us out of the way without a fight. Give them a fight, and maybe we'll have time to bring the firebase on line and push everyone up to Zion."

"That your recommendation, Captain?"

"Yes, sir."

"Captain Shores?"

"We can assume the sergeant's telling the truth. We can't be so sure about the enemy, except that they've showed their hand. It's a winner."

"Then, surrender?" Koritz made it sound obscene. His lips were tight.

"They could fight to the last trooper and the last bullet without lasting more than about five minutes. We get that many people killed on both sides, it's war to the death. Do we want that, with maybe two and a half battalions with no air support and the Alliance ready to do Creator knows what?"

"It's going to come to a death fight sooner or later," Koritz said. "Or is sleeping with Intelligence making you think we can be so nice the rebels will feel guilty about fighting us?"

"Koritz, how many of my people do you want to see killed to prove how tough you are? Is that the only way you can get it—"

Langston stepped between the two captains. "Shut up, both of you. Or step outside. I don't care which."

He sat down again and rested a hand on the radio controls. "As soon as I've consulted with First Battalion, I'm going to allow Zion Four to surrender.

"I'm also going to order reinforcements up to the Zion line. Captain Shores, that includes your reserve Scouts.

"Captain Koritz, you'd be in the right if we needed to fight at Zion Four in order to keep the enemy concentrated. As it is, they've already concentrated too much to disperse on foot before we can reinforce.

"They could send in some of those two hundred junkyard rejects. But every one they send in is one less for hauling ammunition. Every one we see loading troops is also a legitimate target. I think by sunrise we can do quite a bit by way of both disarming and grounding our rebel friends."

Rose Liddell looked across her desk at her executive officer. Either the draft plan she'd handed him was no surprise, or he was doing a better than usual job of keeping his handsome face blank.

Liddell pulled out her emergency grooming kit and went to work on her fingernails. If a significant number of things went wrong, she would be vaporized or at least explosively decompressed. If they went right, she would be spending more hours on-screen in the next two days than she'd done since *Shen* Jumped to Victoria.

She was so absorbed in a piece of recalcitrant cuticle that Bogdanov had to hand the draft back to her to get her attention.

"Everything seems to be in place, Captain. Except for the Alliance attack."

"I won't be disappointed if it doesn't come. But I'll be

surprised. Alliance policy is fairly rigid, and besides, Lopatina may smell an easy victory."

"Which you and the admiral intend to deny her." Bogdanov sat back in his chair and steepled his long pale fingers. "Has General Kornilov been consulted?"

"Afraid of the court-martial? Sorry. That was nerves talking."

"Captain, if you weren't nervous over this, I would be tempted to supercede you in command. As it is, I'm only concerned about lack of coordination between the naval and military units. We've already asked a lot from our Army colleagues by keeping back air support without telling them why."

Because Kuwahara suspects that not everyone on the staff of the Military Council is what they seem. I'd better put that in my 'Exec's Eyes Only' memorandum, in case Pavel inherits my job without a chance to consult with the admiral.

"Victoria Command and the Military Council agree that Alliance action requires a different response from us than the rebels do."

"The rebels aren't a strategic threat. They may not even be capable of presenting one. Even before the reinforcements, the Alliance was one. Now . . ."

She shrugged. "Everything's in place, except one element: you handling *Shenandoah*."

Bogdanov laughed. "You'd have to place me under arrest to keep me from volunteering."

"Don't insult your commanding officer. I know you're the best shiphandler aboard."

"The first lieutenant and the navigator could do as well with *Shenandoah*."

"Maybe they could, but *Shenandoah*'s only part of the squadron. You've commanded attackers and light cruisers. You'll know what they can do and even maybe what their crews are thinking.

"Close coordination's going to be critical. It will be a lot closer with you at the helm."

Twenty-six

Admiral Lopatina frowned. "I'm not proposing that we start a war. That's not my plan or my orders."

Leray thought it would help to know what the Baba's orders were, or if they existed at all outside her own mind. The Alliance doctrine of Senior Commanders' Initiative so far hadn't produced many would-be Bonapartes. It had produced a good many confused subordinates.

Leray hoped he would be unconfused fairly soon. He was sure to be the Navy's point man for whatever Lopatina was planning.

"What I am proposing," Lopatina went on, as her large hands danced over computer controls, "is something like this."

The display showed a rectangular strip of territory with the border zone wiggling down the middle of it. The Alliance side of the zone was pockmarked with red, showing where hostile weapons had been detected, sometimes through their firing on Alliance patrols.

The families of eight of Pak's soldiers were already due for condolence messages. If the hostiles hadn't apparently been more interested in discouraging curiosity than in shooting to kill, the figure would have been much higher.

Another dance of the large hands. Two blue arrows darted across the border, while a grid of blue lines formed on the Alliance side.

"My staff's estimate is that the 'rebels' are being used by the Federation as a screen for infiltrating into the disputed territory."

"The rebellion seems to be fairly authentic," a battleship CO put in.

Admiral Uzel grunted. In his invidious position, he seemed to find grunting a useful method of communication. Leray knew that if he had been chief of staff to a legendary admiral who was clearly running wide open and hellbent, he would have done more than grunt.

Seeing that the grunt wasn't considered a complete report, Uzel shook his head. "I'm not denying its authenticity. But can we rule out collusion between the rebels and the Federation authorities? Considering the signatures of the electronics we've recorded—"

"Half of them are ambiguous," a second battleship captain pointed out.

"My Intelligence staff and I are more concerned about the other half, unmistakably Federation military issue."

The two battleship captains looked at each other, then subsided. Leray wondered if they really doubted the Baba's conclusions or were just simulating doubt for the record— and for Intelligence. Field Intelligence was going to be very rude to everyone who participated in this affair if it went badly wrong, unless they'd throw out a wind anchor beforehand.

"The Federal deployments are even more suspicious than the Federal equipment," Uzel continued. "They're very much on the defensive, against an opponent who seems to be launching an offensive in the opposite direction. Those deployments also mean they're doing damned little to stop the flow of weapons and equipment north."

"Exactly," Lopatina said, neatly taking the ball as Uzel passed it to her. "I'd be prepared to consider this a tactical mistake if it wasn't for our files on Kornilov. He wouldn't make a mistake of this order without somebody tying his hands."

"That somebody could be—" began one of the battleship captains, but glares from both the admiral and his colleague converged on him and shriveled the rest of his speech. Lopatina waved at the map again.

"If we send two battle groups to the high ground at either end of the disputed area, we'll have both observation and reserves on hand. Meanwhile, we can gridwork the infiltration area. Anybody who shoots at one of our patrols is going to have two others on his tail before he can evaluate his shot.

"Brigadier Fegeli, we're asking for a pretty heavy commitment of ground troops. Can you plan on the basis of not holding anything back for internal security?"

"Yes," Fegeli said. Only Leray seemed to recognize his reluctance. Not having a battalion ready to peer under beds would make Hollings fretful, and when he grew fretful Fegeli suffered first.

Then the brigadier's reluctance evaporated, as either training or ambition carried him away. "This is the kind of situation where we have to move fast and with maximum force. If we're facing Federation regulars, we'll need the force to fight them. If we're not, we may impress the enemy into surrendering.

"So I left my staff with Colonel Pak. He and they should be planning along roughly the following lines.

"The 96th has five rifle battalions, plus its Weapons and Air groups. The battalions are already largely committed to patrols in the infiltration area. We commit a third battalion with supporting weapons, and there's the grid. The other two battalions can provide the flanking battlegroups and a small reserve."

"You sound optimistic about the internal security aspects," Lopatina said.

"Realistic, rather. The main threat to Alliance citizens is in an area the 96th is about to saturate. Low-level terrorism in the rear is something for the police. Any strategic terrorism—do you want me to doubt that the Navy can deter or avenge that?"

Even the glared-at captain smiled at that one.

"Any suggestions?" Lopatina asked.

"The Low Squadron's going to be spread fairly thin covering both the deployed 96th and our rear areas. I'd like permission to use as many of our auxiliaries as we can get off the ground as extra sensor posts. *Audacious* isn't the best ship around for tactical support, but if we thicken up the sensor grid and link it to her computer, we can manage a lot better."

"No problem," Lopatina said. She looked at the clock. "Anything you can lift in three hours is yours."

"Three hours!" somebody exclaimed.

Roland J. Green

The admiral's face lost its benignity. "We'd better move fast if we want to settle this without a big fight. Our Federation colleagues damned well aren't going to sit around playing with themselves in the middle of a border incident."

Liddell pulled the security hood up from her display and stuck her head inside. The blackness inside seemed almost dazzling, and the silence roared in her ears. It made "the isolation of command" an almost brutally physical fact.

The blackness gave way to the screen, and the silence to Kuwahara's voice, low and clear, the words coming only a trifle faster than usual. The screen displayed the positions of the Alliance ships and battalions, then flashed "INTENTIONS PROJECTION" and moved two of the battalions across the border.

Never mind that they moved into what was now, effectively, rebel territory. By law it was Federation territory, and the Federation armed forces had the duty of defending it.

"The movements we've detected don't have any other logical objective," Kuwahara said. "We don't know whether the Alliance suspects us or has a rebellion on their side of the border, too.

"We also don't care. Certain members of the Military Council probably do. I don't wish to discuss that, even in a Command Secret message, but I can say that my suspicions have been largely confirmed, with the exception we all hoped we would find."

That meant General Kornilov's loyalty wasn't in doubt. Liddell let out a sigh that was half a prayer of thanks. Federation Security investigators weren't as quick on the trigger as Alliance Field Intelligence, but they could do quite as thorough a job of butchering the careers of the innocent and the guilty alike.

"One virtue of our plan is that both the loyal and the disloyal to the Federation will benefit from our success. The Alliance won't, which doesn't bother me at all and I doubt it will bother the rebels."

Liddell was glad the communication was one-way now. She'd probably have twitted Kuwahara about his new tolerance for anti-Federation people who weren't pro-Alliance.

Kuwahara's voice slowed. Liddell could imagine him sitting straight and breathing from deep in his belly, to say what must be said without seeming uneasy.

"If the Alliance forces a confrontation, you are authorized to consider the Victoria Squadron expendable, if you can destroy the 96th Regiment and the Low Squadron.

"Substantial naval reinforcements are on the way. If you can destroy one or more capital ships of the Alliance squadron, we will have naval superiority when the reinforcements arrive."

That close, are they? Eleventh Zone Command must have decided that one good initiative deserves another—which is just what I would have expected of Schatz and Berkson.

So far, so good.

"Believe me, I'd be far happier up there with the squadron than down here with the politicians. But up or down, I have complete confidence in you and your people.

"Captain Liddell, execute Operation Walkabout."

The change of tone almost made Liddell salute. She sat in the silence and the darkness for a moment, hearing each heartbeat and breath.

Then she folded the hood and pulled on her battle helmet. The intercom circuit was already live.

"Pavel?"

From the Auxiliary Combat Center, the executive officer answered.

"Ready and waiting."

Liddell took a deep breath. "Commander Bogdanov, you have the con. Execute the first maneuver for Operation Walkabout."

Three words in Russian that sounded like a prayer, then: "Aye-aye, ma'am."

At *Mahmud Sa'id*'s last Maintenance Availability, Elayne Zheng had gone from having the oldest of the crew seats to the newest. The padding still squeaked under her as she shifted to relieve an itch under her left armpit. She would have given a month's pay to unstrap and scratch.

"Coming up on regular course change," the pilot said. "Watch your distance."

"I'm watching it," the copilot replied. "But I'm not sweating it, either. The Hermit's got too many attacker hours to give us grief."

"I don't care if the Hermit really is God, instead of just thinking he is. When he's conning something the size of *Shen*, he needs elbow room."

Zheng shifted her display to visual, with the electronic data overlaid. Sixty kilometers ahead and fifty kilometers below, *Shenandoah* was sliding down through the sky of Victoria. She'd already passed the forty-kilometer altitude; now she was coming down on thirty-five. Not fast, but steadily.

How low was she going to go? And were the light cruisers going to remain a third layer, above the attackers, climb, or come down and join the party?

The pilot cocked his head to listen, then tapped the copilot. "Maintain present altitude."

Shenandoah was still descending. On high magnification, she seemed to be wavering. Atmospheric buffeting? Hardly, with a ship that size at that altitude. *Shenandoah* could develop some aerodynamic lift but not enough to seriously affect the maneuvering of her mass.

Zheng hoped it wasn't rogue field interaction with Victoria's gravity field. The Stoneman equations covered only most of the things that could go wrong. Over the years, the Navy had lost enough ships to fight a small war to the things the equations didn't cover.

One of them was either lift or drive field becoming radically unstable as it fought a planet's gravity at low altitude. When this happened slow (like *Shenandoah*'s present Mach Four) as well as low, only a miracle could keep the ship from spattering herself and her crew all over the landscape—assuming the generators didn't blow up or the warring fields rip her apart before she hit.

Don't rockhop with that ship, Captain Rosie. I've got too many friends aboard.

"Still on course, still descending," the copilot said. She sounded as if she had something stuck in her throat.

To hide the fact that she felt the same way, Zheng shut off the visuals and scrolled all her data. Internal electronics nominal, navaids and targeting sensors ditto, jammers ditto, enemy bouncing quite a lot of radar off *Shen* but nothing the jammers couldn't handle . . .

I've heard of this tactic. It's designed for bloody light cruisers! How low is Cozy Rosie going to go with a battlecruiser!

In five more minutes, they had their answer.

"God help us," the pilot said. "*Shen's* leveled out at 6,000 meters."

"That's 2,000 above the highest terrain in our area," the copilot said. Zheng wondered who was supposed to be reassured by that. What was the turning circle of a battlecruiser at Mach Two on the deck? And how far outside the area were the Lizardspine Mountains with their summits climbing to 7,000 meters and their rocks just waiting to gut *Shenandoah* if she missed her turn?

I hope this is impressing the Alliance. I know it's impressing me.

Twenty-seven

Rose Liddell suppressed the urge to switch her display from sensor repeat to visual. Four consoles in the Combat Center and two more on the bridge were eyeballing friends, foes, and the passing landscape. She didn't need to join them, and if she did she'd only start the rumor that the Old Lady was nervous.

Which would be true. She couldn't recall if anyone had ever used this tactic with a ship the size of *Shenandoah* before. Certainly she'd never expected to do it.

But Kuwahara was right. With this tactic, any major Alliance border violations simply gave hostages to fortune. In this case, fortune was spelled *Shenandoah*.

To be sure, the tactic depended on a precise combination of *Shenandoah*, the attackers, and the light cruisers. *Shenandoah* provided an enormous ammunition supply wrapped in a hull invulnerable to most ground-based weapons. She also carried energy weapons that could fry any target, ground or air, that came too close.

The attackers provided a sensor net, deployed on the high ground, able to detect enemies and engage them with either their own weapons or missiles launched by *Shenandoah* and controlled by the attackers. At any given time, the attackers' coverage included more than two-thirds of the border area in question and three of the four identified enemy battalions.

The light cruisers had the least to do until the shooting started and probably the shortest life expectancy once it did. Down at hilltop height, even a ship the size of *Shenandoah* would be a hard target for ships' heavy weapons. But if *Audacious* or *Fei-huang* came down and flew formation on her, they could engage her with some chance of success.

The light cruisers' job was to keep that from happening until *Shenandoah* could ascend enough to maneuver freely. They probably wouldn't survive carrying out their job, but by the time they were gone, so would the Alliance's Low Squadron.

Then it would be *Shenandoah*'s turn. Liddell hardly expected her ship to survive such a fight, but she expected that any Alliance victory would by Pyrrhic. If enough of the attackers had finished their tactical mission and joined *Shen* in space, the battle might even be a draw.

"Coming up on Jenkins' Jaws now," Bogdanov said.

"Steady as she goes," Liddell replied.

The twin peaks barely touched 3,500 meters, and the valley between them was twenty kilometers wide, enough for a battlecruiser squadron to fly through in line abreast. Or at least wide enough if each one had a Pavel Bogdanov at the con. There were good and sufficient reasons why low-altitude maneuvering was a very occasional part of Navy SOP, and one of these reasons was the shortage of Bogdanovs.

Liddell realized that the gnawing in her stomach was not an incipient, ill-timed case of diarrhea. She was hungry. Come to think of it, she couldn't remember having eaten in the last fourteen hours.

She hand-signaled the Combat Center orderly.

"Scherbakova, get me a cup of tea and dial up a sandwich. Whatever they can get the fastest, with lettuce in it. Then have the steward send me up a book. One of my bound volumes. *Alice in Wonderland*, I think."

"Yes, ma'am."

It would be a mild distraction to read about someone also thrust into a situation not of her making that generated surprises, apparently at random.

Bogdanov studied the display tank with minute attention. Jenkins' Jaws was no sort of navigational hazard, but it might be a tactical asset.

Another look at the display gave him two attacker numbers. He made sure that the formation would need no course changes, then called the captain.

"I'd like to send Gold Four and Purple Two to make a tactical sensor scan of this pass from outside. It might be a good hiding place for either side."

Captain Liddell might have some vices, but resenting others suggesting what she should have thought of would hardly be one of them. He heard her swallow a mouthful, then reply.

"Go ahead. Maximum communications security, though."

"Aye-aye, ma'am."

He shifted to Communications. "Immediate tight-beam signal to Gold Four and Purple Two. Maneuver on course —285 and 140 respectively, with sensors on maximum scan. Record and report, at visual range."

"On the way, Commander."

Bogdanov heard acknowledgments, watched the two miniature attacker shapes break out of formation, and flexed his shoulders to relieve a knot of tension that seemed to creep up his back at times like this. Taking the two attackers out of formation even for twenty minutes was a risk. Being without any data you could possibly obtain was a greater one.

Fujita had heard of engineers who stationed themselves by the bulkhead of the main field generators at tense moments. Some claimed that they could actually feel any unusual pulsing or vibration before it registered on the instruments. Most admitted that it was simply a good way of not being bothered when they had a lot on their minds.

Fujita couldn't have said which of about twelve bulkheads would tell him the most. After many weeks of clambering about *Shenandoah*'s powerplant and studying drawings when he wasn't clambering, he was still not quite sure where everything was. He could tell whether it worked or not, but if it didn't work he might have to look up where it was before he could start fixing it.

This, Fujita knew, wasn't living up to the legend of chief engineers. His memory simply wasn't quite good enough to hold a complete picture of a capital ship's vital systems in ready reference. Diagnosis, repair, and administration were his fields, preferably with plenty of help on hand.

Another problem was *Shenandoah*'s layout. Warship powerplants were supposed to be fairly well standardized for mass production if some crisis outstripped the supply of old ships to be recommissioned. But every dockyard and private builder always added their own minor variations.

Add the fact that *Shenandoah* had been built to the standard of fifty years before Fujita was born, further modified on her first recommissioning, and still further worked over this time; it was a minor miracle that her layout wasn't completely idiosyncratic. With good people and not too many obsolete components cannibalized from long-scrapped ships, he'd kept the problem in manageable bounds.

Fujita scanned the basic displays again, then scrolled full readouts. A minor anomaly made him call the Combat Center.

"Captain, how much notice are we likely to have before full-power manuevers?"

"How much notice do you need?"

"Do you want a hundred-percent fail-safe figure?"

"Have you noticed our altitude lately?"

Ask a stupid question, get a sharp answer. "For that, two minutes."

"We can live with that. If it changes, let me know five minutes in advance."

"Aye-aye, ma'am."

Sounds nervous. Well, if I were threading mountains down where I could see them coming, I'd probably be even worse.

A cup of tea sounded like a good idea, but the need for a visit to the heads after that didn't. Fujita pulled a throat lozenge out of his desk, sucked on it, and split his screen to display basic readings and scroll the rest simultaneously.

If the captain thinks I can read these engines' minds, I'll try not to disappoint her too much.

Brian Mahoney was in full damage-control gear, like the others in the Training Office. He also had his eyes fixed on the screen of one of the simulators, like everybody else.

Chief Netsch might appear regulation. In fact, there was enough "give" in her attitude to let her use her electronics skills in a variety of unorthodox ways. One of them was tapping a simulator into the communications between the two combat centers. To the limits of the simulator's graphics, the Training Office gang could see whatever *Shenandoah*'s sensors were feeding to her decisionmakers.

It was strictly illegal, and Netsch intended to cut the circuit as soon as the present crisis was past. Meanwhile, it helped take some of the edge off Mahoney's tension. He didn't like being barely more than a passenger aboard his ship, a ship he'd been trained and commissioned to help fight as well as just run.

The two attackers ordered out of formation were now drifting back toward *Shenandoah*. Mahoney saw people stiffening as they seemed to be following a collision course. He hoped it was just the distortion of distance caused by the simulator's small screen.

When the attackers finally stopped, they seemed to be right on top of the flagship. They squirted in messages that were transmitted to the Auxiliary Combat Center still scrambled and therefore unintelligible to the simulator. Then they resumed their place in the formation, just before it began a slow, wide, 180-degree turn.

"We must be down to something under Mach One," Netsch muttered. "If we have an appointment anyplace, I'm going to get out and walk."

The alarms on the consoles in the Weapons Center were muted. That didn't keep Brigitte Tachin from starting when one chimed softly. If she hadn't been strapped into her seat, she'd have jumped up and banged her helmeted head against the ventilation duct that overshadowed her bank.

A moment's study of displays ended fear and began annoyance. "Who hooked the weapons-status panel to the alarm system?"

Chief Nakamura gave her a look full of the innocence that proves guilt. It also warned her against raising the question again.

Tachin looked around the Weapons Center. Zhubova was in the Combat Center. The two officers senior to her looked preoccupied. If she could go one-on-one with Nakamura . . .

"I won't ask who, if it doesn't happen again," she said sharply. "A cracked circuit or a loose booster attachment isn't worth overloading the alarm system. We can't trust our people to notice defects using SOP."

Nakamura's look now told of a challenge noted and accepted. The looks from the other people showed relief, either at the modest size of the crisis or somebody else prepared to take on Nakamura.

Tachin isolated the missile, ran the standard diagnostics and a few she'd learned at Alcuin Arsenal, and sat back with a sigh of relief.

"Looks like our old friend 085D is playing reluctant dragon again. I'm going to pull him and recommend that he be downed for a special overhaul. This is the third time his self-diagnosis hasn't been worth a stone stellar."

At a nod from Tachin, the people on two other consoles began the procedures for pulling a missile out of the loading sequence and storing it in an accessible maintenance bay. It took ninety seconds before the "LOADING SEQUENCE RESUMED" signals lit up.

Which is twenty seconds under the allowed time. Put that in your cup and drink it, Nakamura. Drink it and digest it, before the next time you think these people need false alarms to test their reactions.

Tachin surreptitiously loosened her seatbelt and ran a hand inside her trousers to rub where the waistband chafed. Three hours into the crisis and already she was afraid to stand upwind of anyone she cared about.

She cinched the belt again and turned back to her console. The steady march of missiles from the magazines into the launchers continued.

In another twenty minutes, *Shenandoah* would be able to salvo half her missile load in four launches. Half of *Shenandoah*'s missile load, delivered on target, could obliterate civilization on Victoria. Concentrated on a narrower selection of targets, it could overwhelm most defenses and kill those targets several times over—or force them to flee, if they were mobile.

From the warhead and guidance-mode selections Zhubova had ordered, Tachin suspected that flight would serve *Shenandoah*'s goals as well as destruction. She hoped she was right. The day of shooting to kill and kill only might come, but every year it didn't was one less year she would have to live with the memories.

With *Shenandoah* on Alert One and cruising at hilltop height, Charles Longman was actually bored. When he'd identified the sensation an hour before, it had surprised and encouraged him.

Now it did neither. The surprise vanished when he realized that, after all, he'd already done most of his share of the day's work. The launchers were in nominal condition, even Problem Child Two. He'd sweated and slaved and loaded himself up with more surreptitious doses of Vessegol 14, but the job had been done.

Now all he needed to do was watch the loads assembling in the launchers, check to see that they fit properly, and be manual backup to the automatic launch sequence when Combat Center gave the order. Everything was nominal for that sequence, too; he probably wouldn't have to lift a finger.

Even if he had to launch manually, he wouldn't be responsible for anyone's life. That was up to the people who targeted and released the missiles.

If he'd been responsible for actually feeding instructions to a missile to fly down a particular valley and spray an Alliance outpost with fragmentation clusters, that would have been a different matter. This meant that his long-standing qualms about Weapons qualification were still there, and the confrontation with his family just as inevitable.

"This is a sweater, Charlie," Lieutenant Uhlig said from his console. "Hope the Weapons types have all the boosters checked out. I saw a low-altitude launch like this once, when they had a bunch of boosters that had been reloaded once too often. Half of them MFed and we put half a dozen duds into the side of a mountain. The sonic booms and the impacts triggered a couple of avalanches, and some very high-ranking officers had their ski lodge and love nest wiped out. I was too junior for them to notice, thank God."

"Well, I hope we're not too junior for the Old Lady to let us know what's going on," Longman grunted. "I'd like to whistle up a crate of spares for quick repairs after the launch. But how can I do that if I don't know that I can take my eyes off the displays for two seconds?"

"Any problems you haven't told me about?" Uhlig asked with a frown.

Longman shook his head. "You know me. I'm just a High Church Murphyite, trying to get all my worrying done in advance."

* * *

Rose Liddell unstrapped, stood, stretched as much as the limited space in Combat Center allowed, and did thirty seconds worth of breathing exercises. Then she signaled to the intercom console.

The camera swiveled, red lights turned green, and her face and voice were all over *Shenandoah*.

"Good afternoon. I'm sorry I haven't been able to speak to you before now.

"Briefly, our situation is that Alliance ground forces with tactical air support have crossed the border. At least two task forces are more than a hundred kilometers inside Federation territory.

"They haven't made any hostile move, but they have no business in Federation territory. It's territory currently controlled by the rebels, but as long as it's not controlled by a hostile government we have the duty to defend it.

"Besides, we're not going to throw anybody to the Alliance without more reasons than the rebels have given us.

"So *Shenandoah* is patrolling the border at low altitude, supported by the rest of the Victoria Squadron. At the moment, we aren't doing more than patrolling. But if the border-crossers start shooting or the other Alliance forces join them, we shoot back.

"Where we are, we can take out most of the Alliance ground forces on Victoria within an hour. Either that, or force them back across the border with their tails between their legs. I'd prefer the second, but I'll take the first if there's no other choice.

"If we fight, our first job will be the ground forces. Then we take out the Alliance's Low Squadron, starting with our old friend *Audacious*, and as much of Lopatina's reinforcements as possible.

"If that means expending ourselves, then we have to do that, too.

"With their ground forces wiped out and their naval support crippled, the Alliance will be in a nice mess on Victoria. They can't retaliate against our civilians without blowing this up into a major confrontation. They can shoot up the Victoria Brigade, but what then?

"A good part of the rebels currently seem to come from the Alliance side of the border. If nobody has any ground forces to fight them, the bushrangers will own Victoria. Can the Alliance swallow that prospect?

"A good question, and I hope to have the answer in about an hour. That's when we warn Baba Lopatina and Governor Hollings that we're going to have to start shooting if they don't start withdrawing their troops.

"If we get the wrong answer, we'll all be too busy for any more farewells. So I'll turn over the intercom for private calls now. For myself, I'll just say it's been a pleasure and a privilege to be your commanding officer, and I trust every one of you to live up to the traditions of the Federation Navy—including the victory party when we've sent the Alliance packing!

"God bless all of you until we meet again."

Twenty-eight

The missile alarm screamed and the lifter tilted wildly. The maneuver dumped Candice Shores nearly into Captain Koritz's lap. He growled something impolite and fended her off into her own seat.

By then the lifter was diving rapidly while pilot and copilot called off range, altitude, and missile lock. Shores had just decided their babble meant safety when a thundering explosion told her she'd misunderstood.

If Koritz hadn't pushed Shores back they'd both have been exposed to a sleet of fragments. As it was, Koritz and the others on the left side of the lifter absorbed most of the fragments. Shores felt something gouge her cheek and something else slam her helmet against her head, heard the copilot announce they were losing power, and just managed to brace herself before the lifter crashed.

It hit on its belly armor, tore off a skid, and slid another twenty meters, bucking and twisting wildly, throwing the dead and living around with ruthless impartiality. The final jerk that stopped it nearly threw Shores on top of the copilot, who'd abandoned useless controls to try stopping the pilot's bleeding.

The pilot's bleeding finally stopped because he was dead. Shores peered out through a starred and bloody windshield, then swore in relief. If the lifter had been ten meters higher, it would have sailed over the crest of the ridge and been fifty meters above the far slope when the power died. Nobody would have survived that crash.

At the foot of the ridge, something was moving. Several

somethings. Shores started counting before she bothered identifying, and she only recognized what she was counting when she'd reached twenty.

The copilot recognized the moving objects at the same time. "Good lord, we've found a rebel lifter park!"

"So much for our skyspies," Shores snapped. A lingering sense of proportion reminded her that the rebels and the troops fighting them were no longer the most important part of the Victoria crisis. The dead and wounded around her and her own discomfort kept her from going any further.

She slapped the copilot on the shoulder. "Report what we've found and our position. Then get the wounded clear and set up a strongpoint with the ablebodied."

"What—"

"The turret's intact, isn't it?"

"Yeah, but—"

"I'm going to stay and do one of the Scouts' jobs—knocking out enemy transport."

"You'll need me on the radio, Captain."

"That's—oh, what the Hades! I'm sure Graves Registration has enough bags and markers for both of us. Now get on the horn!"

Shores's adrenal high evaporated when the copilot wasn't able to raise anybody on the radio. Meanwhile, she made a head count, and the rest of her determination to wade into the rebels faded. Five ablebodied people would have to take care of six wounded, only two of them able to walk. If Shores had waited with the turret until the casualties were clear, the rebels would have been long gone. If she'd opened up soon enough to be effective, she'd have signed a death sentence for the wounded.

She still sat in the turret, hands resting lightly on the controls, counting the rebel lifters scrambling away in twos and threes. She counted thirty-four before the park was empty.

As the last pair vanished, a metallic glint above the northwestern horizon drew Shores's eye. Magnification on the optical sight showed a pair of Federation attackers, in open formation, low and slow.

"If they were just close enough for visual signals . . ." Shores muttered. Then she poked the copilot in the shoulder again, this time with a toe.

"Can you rig the sighting laser for signaling?"

The copilot gave a cautious nod.

"Good. We're just close enough to the squadron's course to maybe reach them with the laser after it gets dark. We'll keep trying to raise somebody on the radio, but if we can't, we'll try the laser at intervals until the power's gone."

The copilot looked at what was left of the displays. "That may not wait until dark."

"Then we'll slip down and see if we can scavenge something," Shores said. "The way those bushrangers took off, I don't imagine they policed up too well."

"What if the shooting starts and the attackers all move north to hit the 96th?" the copilot pointed out. "They'll be way out of our range."

"All the more reason for our staying here. We've got good observation on a chunk of rebel territory. If serious shooting starts, I'll bet a case of beer that we'll have rebels coming back through here, lots of them and fast."

"If that's a serious bet, you're on," the copilot said. "I guess playing OP until somebody finds us isn't the worst thing we could do."

"You have any better ideas?" Shores snapped.

Either nobody did or nobody was ready to argue with a large captain in a bad temper. Shores stamped off, not wanting to dump any more frustration on the people around her.

She also wanted to find a reasonably private patch of sand. She hadn't quite managed to mess her pants on the way down, but she had a nasty feeling that something was going to let go before long.

"You are through to *Fei-huang*," the Communications officer said.

Rose Liddell, conscious of all the eyes on her, took a deep breath and stared at the screen, as if by sheer willpower she could conjure Admiral Lopatina's face onto it.

Conjured or not, a face appeared: a nondescript, middle-aged male face, surmounting powder blue Alliance coveralls with a rear admiral's stripes.

"Admiral Uzel. Good afternoon. May I speak to Admiral Lopatina?"

"You may, if I decide it's worth her time."

"I think you're stretching a chief of staff's powers a little far. What I have to say is something she'll want to discuss with you, so you don't need to worry about being cut out. But it's definitely something she'll want to hear herself, directly from me, and as soon as possible."

Uzel's face was coloring before he blanked the screen.

Two minutes later, Uzel reappeared. He jerked his head once, then vanished. Admiral Lopatina took his place.

The Baba's legendary benignity hadn't vanished, but it was so blatantly a disguise that Liddell almost laughed. She didn't quite catch herself in time, either.

"Captain Liddell, I'm curious what you find amusing in this situation. The Federation has committed an act of war against the Alliance, crossing our borders and arming rebels. We are making a limited, appropriate response to this act. From the way your squadron is maneuvering, you seem to object to this."

"Admiral, the only true part of that speech is the last sentence." Liddell raised both hands, open palmed. "That's not saying that the rest is a lie. Let's say that you are speaking from inadequate data."

She summarized the Federation's intelligence estimate in as much detail as she could without revealing sources. "I won't say that we know the rebels' capabilities, let alone their intentions, and about their strength we are mostly guessing," she concluded. "But we do know where our own people are, and none of them are on the Alliance side of the border.

"You, on the other hand, can't say the same about your troops. Units of the 96th Independent Regiment, acting under orders, have crossed the border into Federation territory. We would prefer that they be removed, within two hours from the end of this discussion or by 1900, whichever comes later."

"You seem to think we have a great deal to say to each other," Lopatina said. "Has it occurred to you that I might not have so much to say to a captain who could be exceeding her authority?"

"I've been given full authority by the Military Council of the Dominion of Victoria, General Kornilov, and Admiral Kuwahara," Liddell replied. She decided to assume a tone of indignation. "None of us thought that the Alliance Navy was so obsessed with rank that they'd refuse to hear sense unless it came dressed up in stars."

The mask of benignity slipped briefly. "We aren't, but I haven't heard any sense yet. Suppose you begin by explaining why you're talking to me."

"I'm talking to you because I command the squadron that is going to remove your forces from Federation territory if they don't leave voluntarily. I know where every ship is and I can order them all into action in two minutes. I can do a very efficient job of wiping the 96th Independent Regiment off the face of Victoria, along with any of your ships that get in the way."

Talk about having somebody's undivided attention.

Lopatina quickly recovered her voice, if not even a simulated benignity.

"I think the next point is persuading me that you can do this."

Liddell shook her head. "There really isn't a next point. I would be insulting the Alliance Navy and you personally if I thought you didn't know the capabilities of my ships in their present formation."

"Formations can be changed."

"I won't change them, and I beg to doubt that you can change them without more violations of Federation territory and probably opening fire. That would add firing the first shot to making the first border violation. You'd be taking a lot on yourself.

"Actually, Admiral, there is a second point. But it's not what we can do to the Alliance forces on Victoria. It's whether we're ready to sacrifice ourselves to do it. You know that if we're prepared to do that, any victory you'll win would be Pyrrhic at best. Your initiative would be repudiated, and any survivors who'd followed you into this would have pretty grim prospects for the future.

Give the Devil her due. If somebody has been loyal to her, she'll do her best to keep their tails out of cracks if she has any choice. Will she recognize that she has one now?

"You don't know whether or not I'm bluffing," Liddell went on. "I can only beg you, in the name of whatever highest power you honor, to believe that I'm not.

"Federation territory can only be violated with impunity

when there is not one Federation fighter left alive to defend it."

Which doesn't quite square with our policy toward the rebels, but they aren't the Alliance, and I hope Lopatina has the wits to know the difference.

Lopatina remained on-screen long enough to put her benign mask back on. The smile didn't quite reach her eyes, and a muscle was jumping just below the left eye.

"You've given me an interesting decision to make. I certainly can't guarantee that I'll decide in the way you want me to. Will you be content with my word of honor that I will render the decision on the schedule you require?"

"That will be quite satisfactory, thank you. Shall I call you back at 1900, or will you call me?"

"I'll be at home to any call from you, Captain Liddell."

Lopatina's face remained on the screen until Liddell realized that she was being allowed to sign off. She waved farewell, cut off her screen, and signaled Scherbakova for water. Even herb tea would be too much for her stomach now.

It seemed to Candice Shores that she'd spent a lot of time since she came to Victoria peering out from behind rocks. Tonight she was lying behind the jagged crest of the little ridge where the lifter had crashed, studying the abandoned rebel vehicle park. She had a full charge and magazine in her pulser and a grenade in the launcher, but a slingshot would probably be enough for any target that showed up.

Fortunately they were too high for the worst of the mites, but she suspected frustration would nibble her away as thoroughly before the night was over. They'd seen neither rebel lifters nor friendly attackers nor any visual signals since they'd settled into their improvised OP. Two of the wounded weren't going to make it if they didn't get help soon, while an improvised combination of survival radio and main powerpack was still fighting to get through the static.

In another half hour, Shores decided, they were going to unlimber the salvaged targeting laser and start signaling to the wide wild sky, no matter who might answer. Rebels with a lifter would at least be able to medevac them to a doctor.

Shores shifted position, to expose a different set of aches to the rising wind. No fragments had penetrated her battledress, but a good many had tried hard enough to leave bruises.

"Hey, Captain," the copilot whispered behind her. "We can receive at least. I'm going to try to figure out what's going on, then transmit a Mayday."

"Well done, Sergeant . . . Butler, isn't it?"

"Budler."

"Sorry. Budler."

"No problem, Captain. It's been kind of a busy day. I'll—what in Mother's name is that?"

"That" was an ordinary civilian lifter ambling at low altitude into the abandoned rebel vehicle park. It was larger than the average civilian machine on Victoria, but the stains and patches could have been on any one of a hundred Shores had seen since she landed.

Shores watched as the lifter entered the park area, slowed, and began to circle just above the sand. Finally it grounded, so hastily that it rocked back and forth several times before settling down on its skids.

The rear door opened, and two people in civilian clothes climbed out. As Shores and the copilot dashed for the wrecked lifter, the rebels began walking around their machine. Shores let the copilot man the turret while she lowered her binoculars and watched the rebels.

"Can we join the party, Captain?" one of the walking wounded called.

"That's a negative, until we know what they've—well, I'll be damned."

"Captain?"

"Never mind. I think we've got a bunch of civilian evacuees here. Most of them look like kids."

The lifter was unloading a steady stream of passengers now, and no more than a quarter of them were anywhere near adult size. Some of them were being carried in the bigger ones' arms, and a couple were on stretchers.

Shores jacked her helmet radio into the lifter's system and ordered the copilot to cut in the loudspeaker. The battered system came on in a shriek of feedback that made Shores want to rip off her helmet and left her ears ringing, but it stayed on.

"Attention, civilian lifter! Attention, civilian lifter! Remain where you are. You are covered by two lifter guns and a rifle squad. Attempt no hostile action, please. This is Captain Candice Shores, Scout Company, Victoria Brigade, Federation Ground Forces. I am coming down to meet you."

As she climbed down from the lifter, the ablebodied troopers hurried into position. Shores surveyed them, nodded, and said, "Anybody got a flag of truce on them?"

The cleanest light-colored neckscarf wound up tied to a strip of insulation from the lifter. With that in hand, Shores scrambled down the ridge, more concerned about falling than about rebel treachery.

"Good evening, Captain," the man who came to meet her said. "I am Dr. Nosavan. My assistant, Dr. Carlisle, and Superintendent Eddings of the Duikkersberg Children's Home have been evacuating the children. We were supposed to have an armed escort, but the last we heard, the park had to be evacuated in haste. We came here anyway, hoping that somebody would have stayed behind to round up strays."

Shores had a distinct suspicion that it was her dropping in that had spooked the lifters into fleeing. She felt disgusted, as well as frustrated. All she'd accomplished in return for three dead troopers was inconveniencing a bunch of orphans!

"Do you know if general war has broken out?" the doctor went on. "We have no way to unscramble military signals."

Shores shook her head. A close look at the doctor and his charges suggested that they were both ethically and physically incapable of treachery. So why not make common cause with them, as long as they were all going to be stuck out here overnight?

"We've been out of radio contact with our own forces since one of your missiles shot us down. I doubt if general war has broken out, because we'd have seen the fighting in space. However, I don't know if the Alliance has responded to our—to the Federation ultimatum yet.

"Doctor, could I propose a truce? I have some wounded who badly need a doctor. We have some extra hands to help you with the children. Shall we trade?"

"Do you have any food to spare? We're nearly out."

"I'm afraid not. But if we can use your radio, we may be able to punch through the interference and reach friendlies."

"What will happen to us?" Eddings asked. A tall woman,

she looked maternal but in the steel-souled way Shores knew far too well.

"If friendlies answer, you'll be interned until an exchange is worked out. If rebels answer, we'll be POWs for the same—"

"Captain Shores!" came a faint yell from up the hill. "Captain Shores! The Alliance gave in! They're evacuating Federation territory right now."

Superintendent Eddings proved she was more human than she looked by fainting on the spot. By the time Nosovan had her awake, Shores was seated at the lifter's radio, using the Mayday frequency to talk to Sergeant Budler.

"The Baba got on the horn to Rosie Liddell about an hour ago," he said. "Circumstances made the course of action proposed by the Federation prudent at the present time, or some such fancy wrapping up the fact that we scared the Hades out of her.

"Anyway, the northern task force of the 96th's back across the border already. The southern one's lifted out and is on course for doing the same. The troopers in the grid across the border are still working, but they're keeping fifty kloms clear of the border.

"First Battalion's sending a company to each of the two evacuated positions. The squadron's going to stay on station until they arrive, then keep a light cruiser and a flight of attackers down low until whenever."

"How long will that be?"

"Nobody knows. Nobody's popping the seals and lighting up the pipes, either."

"Sensible," Dr. Nosavan said behind her.

"Who—" Budler said.

"Doctor, eavesdropping on military communications opens you to a charge of espionage," Shores said.

Nosavan smiled. "Sorry, Captain. I just couldn't help agreeing with the idea of not celebrating too soon."

"I'll drop the charge of espionage if you'll explain."

"The Alliance's intervention might have done us—the rebels—more harm than good. Once they discovered that the hostiles in their own territory weren't Federation agents, the 96th would have been all over us. As it is, we have only the Federation's rather weak and wobbly brigade to fight on the ground. Nothing personal intended against you and your company, Captain, you understand."

"Maybe I do. Go on."

"The withdrawal of Alliance troops doesn't mean the end of the Alliance's ability to influence events. They'll just try something else. It will be quite a while before they admit defeat."

"If they do," Shores added. She stood up, banging her head against the soundproofing of the lifter's cockpit.

"I think the designer of this lifter must have been about a meter seventy," Eddings said. "I'm always doing that too."

Paul Leray knew that he was only imagining that Baba Lopatina's cheeks were pale and sunken. It would take more time and worse defeats to do that.

Across the table, Jo Marder met his eyes. She looked sober in all senses of the word. He suspected he looked much the same. They had, after all, both supported an intervention that might have been based on inaccurate intelligence and had certainly led to a major confrontation with the Federation.

"Local knowledge" deserved its reputation only as long as it led to more effective action. If it just led to equally big mistakes . . .

Not to mention that the confrontation had been avoided by Admiral Lopatina backing away from it. Backing away from inferior rank, inferior forces, and an inferior tactical situation—unless the inferior forces in the inferior tactical situation were prepared to sacrifice themselves.

Captain Liddell, it seemed, had done her best to persuade Lopatina that the Federation forces were prepared to do exactly that. Her best had been good enough.

Lopatina cleared her throat. Maybe intentionally, it sounded very much like the signal for missile lock-on. It got everyone's undivided attention.

"I don't want or need any help with excuses or explanations. We all acted on the best estimate of the situation we could make. We weren't the first, and we won't be the last, to find out that wasn't good enough.

"I do ask that everyone consider seriously what I am about to propose. If anybody does not concur, I ask that they go through channels in registering their opposition."

Leray studied the faces around the table as intently as he could without being obvious. Did sweat prove secret ties to Intelligence or just faulty ventilation in the flag suite?

The only officer who was openly uneasy, Brigadier Fegeli, raised a hand.

"Admiral, does this cover communications with Governor Hollings?"

"Only for the duration of this meeting. We'll go over the proposal, and I want you all to evaluate it and comment on it. After that, it's both my duty and my intention to communicate with His Excellency and seek his concurrence."

Leray noted that the brigadier looked no happier, and with good reason. The Baba had left unsaid what she would do if the concurrence wasn't forthcoming. Had she yielded to the Federation to clear her flanks for a fight with Hollings?

Leray would have been delighted to witness that battle, if he'd been certain that he'd only have to witness it. He suspected, however, that casualties among bystanders would be high.

Two Marines rolled in a massive three-decker tray of *zakuski*. Leray looked meaningfully at the ceiling when Jo poured herself a double-sized slug of vodka.

The Baba let everyone stuff and guzzle for twenty minutes before waving a hand at the display tank behind the table. It lit up with a detailed map of the Alliance's border area and the Federation territory currently held by the rebels.

"We have withdrawn our forces from Federation territory and from the first fifty kilometers of our own. I propose that we withdraw our forces from all the rest of the territory beyond this line."

A red zigzag darted across the map. The Baba contemplated it with what seemed to Leray satisfaction bordering on smugness.

"I further propose that we recognize the rebel government and negotiate an armistice with it. A formal peace treaty and an embassy can follow in due course.

"Whether we'll need an alliance with them against the Federation depends on the Federation's reaction."

Fewer officers kept their masks on this time. Leray frowned at Jo, who was choking on a combination of laughter and vodka, but wanted to laugh himself at Fegeli. The brigadier was also choking, but laughter had to be light-years from his mind.

"I trust that Governor Hollings will evaluate this proposal on its merits, Brigadier Fegeli." It was phrased as a question but uttered like an order.

"He may be slow to see the merits of giving up Alliance territory," Fegeli said. "I'd be happier with an explanation, myself."

"I can give you a very quick one," Lopatina said. She munched a forkful of golden prawns in grape leaves, washed it down with red wine, and made a steeple of her hands. Those hands were large and powerful but quite elegant, so unlike the rest of the admiral that Leray sometimes wondered which was a projection, the solid body or the fine hands?

"We're not giving up Alliance territory. We're giving up part of Victoria held by about 200,000 people who don't seem to want to be part of the Alliance anymore. That's too many people for us to fight with our available ground troops. Far too many, if they draw on support from their fellow rebels across the old border.

"It's not enough people to cripple the remaining Alliance territory. We'll still have well over a million loyal citizens. The 200,000 will be a large minority of the population of a new nation. Once their political grievances are settled, we can find nonpolitical ways of reaching that minority.

"Or, who knows? The Federation has been very shrewd this time around, but show me the government that never makes a mistake. If we avoid a confrontation over some two-thirds of a million people who don't want to be under either government, we have a better chance of winning the next round."

That was a classic understatement. If the Federation continued to fight the rebels while the Alliance made peace with them, the 96th would suddenly be all the ground forces needed. Facing it would be only the battered, bruised, and lame Victoria Brigade; fighting on its side would be the rebels, if necessary, armed and trained by the Alliance. . . .

Federation naval reinforcements were supposed to be on the way. Ground troops, too, probably—but to handle the situation Lopatina was proposing to create, the Federation would have to send a corps, not just one or two brigades.

It was unlikely, to make another understatement, that the Feds had a corps to spare for fighting over a few hundred thousand dust-grubbing Victorians.

So then maybe he and Jo were off the spot for their recommendations. They and Colonel Pak could even be clear as far as Intelligence was concerned. The Bonsai Force was no longer the only tree around, but at least it wasn't going to be uprooted or used as a toilet box by somebody's cat.

Leray felt a glow that had very little to do with the wine and almost shouted his toast to the Bushranger Republic.

Twenty-nine

Brian Mahoney looked up from his cluttered desk to the cluttered view through the dirty window of his cubicle. Was it just his imagination, or had half his view of the desert disappeared in the three days since he moved in here for his assignment with the Armistice Commission?

Good scenery was one of many chronic shortages on Victoria. The desert around Camp Aounda was even less scenic than average. To Mahoney, the sprouting field buildings, domes, and shelters were no improvement. Not to mention the defenses for the critical installations, the defenses for the defenses, and the continuous cloud of dust kicked up by all the comings and goings.

And everything with a flag. The eight-pointed star of the Federation, the yin-yang of the Alliance, and the new flag of the Bushranger Republic (a silver field hat on a fatuously optimistic green field) seemed to be everywhere.

At least the lifters have scared away most of the birds. The flags should maintain a little dignity for a few more weeks.

The door slid open behind him. He swiveled his chair. "Didn't they teach you to—Candy!"

Captain Shores shrugged. "Your buzzer's lost its buzz."

"Never had any to begin with, I think. What can I do for you?"

"You're billeting officer?"

"For my sins, yes. All the legitimate supply and support people were too busy preparing for reinforcements to be spared for handling what we already had. So I got yanked out of my refresher course for JOOW and plugged in here."

"You sound a little sour."

"Well, if I'm not going to stay in Training, I don't want to be jerked around from one crap detail to another."

"You could look at it another way," Shores said. "They think you're a jack of all trades, at a time when we need those more than we do specialists."

"You're an optimist, Candy."

"Only on an off-day. Anyway, I'm in here basically to kill time while Sergeant Esteva and Corporal Sklarinsky scout. The rest of my company is coming in this evening to do its turn as Fed security for the Armistice Commission."

"I'd have thought you'd be the first company sent out."

"I think we're supposed to use our local knowledge to see if the Alliance or the Republic is up to any tricks. Sending us out three weeks ago would have been a bit obvious, but now . . ."

Mahoney looked meaningfully at the walls and tapped his ears. Shores shrugged again.

"If the Alliance can't guess that, they're a lot dumber than they've given us any reason to believe. Got a drink?"

Mahoney rummaged in his desk and came up with an empty flask, souvenir of the previous owner of the desk. "If you can wait until they deliver today's shelter shipment and I log it in, I'll take you to lunch. Or we can order in."

"Shelter shipment? Eight 12-3-3s, by any chance?"

"That's what I've been told to expect."

Shores laughed. "Brian, you may have a long wait. I think Kornilov's diverted that one for the new battalion."

"What new battalion?"

"Hey, the Army hasn't evaporated. We're getting a new rifle battalion with its own scout company, a tactical transport battalion, and a whole bunch of new officers and NCOs. Enough to provide deputies and assistants and XOs for everybody who doesn't have one."

"When do they show up?"

"That transport, the *Showalter*, who came in Sunday—she had most of the officer draft. Most of them Hentschmen, too."

"What?"

"Frieda Hentsch's picked people, from I Corps. I don't know if they're planning on bringing her out personally. But she'll have the ground spied out beforehand if they do."

Mahoney decided not to ask any more questions about Ground Forces politics. He didn't want to strain Candy's loyalties, and they made him feel dirty anyway.

Of course, it's partly luck that the Navy isn't in the same muck up to its drive generators. Nobody expected us to fight on the ground, and what we did win, we won without fighting at all. But that was damned good leadership, too. Show me the Army's answer to Kuwahara and Captain Rosie—who would use a little extra help, too, come to think of it. . . .

"Nobody told me anything about the shipment going adrift," Mahoney said, changing the subject. "I'll check. Meanwhile, the lunch offer still stands. The Mess doesn't deliver, but I can call Hennessey's or Khasim's."

"Khasim the Cook?"

"The same one who broke up that riot. He's got a permanent shelter over by Refugee Property Storage. That old lifter of his runs supplies out every couple of days. From the prices he charges, he's either stealing his stuff or getting subsidized by somebody, but it's good if you don't mind grease. His liquor runs mostly to raki and vodka, but—"

"Good for Khasim, whatever he's serving. We owe him one. And Hennessey's? The one in Kellysburg where you and Brigitte Tachin—"

"They've got a branch here, too. Over in the Bushranger Zone, but they take orders from all parties."

"Let's try Khasim. And how are the rest of the D-4s, by the way? The next time you're in a ship right overhead and I get one letter in two months, I'm going to break something."

"Brigitte may join us for lunch," Mahoney said. "Charlie Longman's probably taking somebody's launcher apart. Elayne's either on duty or pouting over Lucco DiVries."

"Was she seriously—"

"She's seriously wounded in her pride. You know Lanie. She thinks she's the best EWO and the best judge of men in the fleet. Lucco defecting or whatever you want to call it, that shook her confidence."

"Maybe you should grab her while she's down."

"Candy, none of your ancestors used matchmakers, so don't you start. Besides, she's got me firmly classified as 'friend,' not 'intimate partner.' "

"Maybe I should start a new tradition. Or trip you myself." Mahoney wasn't aware that he'd stiffened, but it didn't escape Shores.

"Sorry. If that would strain things with La Tachin . . ."

"We're not that far."

"I hear the word *yet*, Brian."

"Hear what you damned well please," Mahoney snapped.

Shores glared, then smiled one of those disarming smiles that made you forget her height, strength, and lethal skills. "Sorry, Brian. What are friends for, except to make asses of themselves about what's none of their business?"

"Right now, it's to help me get through a double order of Khazim's falafel and stew."

"If you'll hold off while I make a call, I think I may get a fourth for lunch."

"Anybody I know?"

"Have you heard of a Major Nieg?"

"Intelligence, by any chance?"

"That one."

"Candy, you're keeping strange company these days."

"You're a fine one to talk, Brian. Remember that axe-thrower?"

"I remember quite agreeably, Candy. I also remember that Yvette taught you to throw axes, and you've been using it to fluster people ever since."

"A Scout has to keep up her image."

"Go make that call, Candy, and let me see if I can steal back our shelters from General Kornilov!"

Rose Liddell hopped off the treadmill and joined Admiral Kuwahara at the display tank in the corner of the exercise room. Sweat trickled off her, some of it falling on the lid of the tank; she toweled herself off and dabbed at the lid as the display came up. The blue-gray globe of Victoria and the sparks of ships and squadrons turned before their eyes.

The balance of forces was holding. The Federation had *Shenandoah* and her attackers, Dockyard bristling with weapons and a second attacker squadron, three squadrons of light cruisers, and four armed transports.

The Alliance had Lopatina's three battleships and four cruisers, the Bonsai Squadron with *Audacious* and two light cruisers, and the newly arrived light carrier *Brilliant*, with her two attacker squadrons and escorting heavy cruiser.

With such a balance, the two navies were doing little more than keeping each other out of mischief. Significant changes would have to come from the ground forces or the politicians.

Liddell was not particularly happy about such a standoff; it left Federation interests at the mercy of people who hadn't shown anything like the competence of the Navy. But it was preferable to the kind of bowel-churning, throat-drying confrontation she and Kuwahara had forced. Too many of those, and the situation would destabilize simply because somebody's nerves had snapped!

When the tank went dark, Kuwahara sat down in the perfect pose and draped his towel over his head. "Would you like to go a few falls with me, Captain?"

"I'm afraid I'm nowhere in your class, Admiral."

"Most of the people who are, are too junior to be willing to go all-out. Rank hath its limitations. . . ."

"Thank you, sir, but I've got to go clean up. I'm guest of the Wardroom tonight. Partly it's celebrating our fifth month in commission, partly it's an excuse to let the stewards into my quarters to scour them out. I have a nasty feeling I'm going to be doing even more entertaining than before."

Kuwahara started drying himself off. "Would your Wardroom be able to accommodate me?"

"We'd be honored, sir." *Which is true, but why . . .*

"I have to be dirtside by 0800 tomorrow, to prepare for the meeting with the Senate Military Committee. Until then, I'd rather be out of Kornilov's reach."

Liddell thanked God that Kuwahara seemed in a mood to answer questions she wasn't supposed to ask. If Army-Navy relations were about to reach terminal delicacy . . .

"I just learned that I've been promoted to acting vice-admiral."

"Congratulations, sir!"

"I hope that's the appropriate response. Unfortunately, Kornilov hasn't received a similar promotion. Meanwhile, he's surrounded by new officers loyal to Frieda Hentsch, who may be setting her cap for a combat command. Victoria's the only place in the Eleventh Zone where she can find that."

"I hope somebody will tell Eleventh Zone that it's not

worth upsetting the ground balance just to give Hentsch her fourth star."

"I'm sure somebody will. I just hope they listen. Schatz wouldn't originate the idea, but he might go along with it to maintain good relations with Eleventh Army."

Being an adult, Liddell did not pound on the bulkheads, much as she felt like it. "I hope they've at least accepted Kornilov's recommendations for awards and promotions. Even if they think he didn't come up to requirements, why penalize his people?"

"Exactly," Kuwahara said. "I've also heard that my recommended list has gone before the Board of Awards, while Kornilov's has been tabled. This isn't official, by the way. It's a rumor that came out on *Showalter*.

"I am going to learn the truth. If Kornilov's list has been tabled, then I am going to file a protest with the Board that will fry their terminals. Would you be prepared to join it?"

"Is space a vacuum?"

Kuwahara's smile was much less austere than usual. "Thank you, Captain. The more feet we use to kick the Board, the more justice we may kick out of them."

More softly he added, "There's never enough justice for the people who do most of the dying."

He tossed his sodden towel into a corner and turned toward the head.

The handiest officer to inform (or warn) the Wardroom about Kuwahara's visit turned out to be Lieutenant Longman. Even in dress uniform, he didn't look quite at ease, but maybe that was just fatigue. Or being more at home in working kit.

He had a right to either, certainly. Liddell decided that if Longman continued to shine in engineering assignments, she would sit down with Fujita and Uhlig and see about an in-ship transfer. Longman would still have to fight his own battles with his rank-laden, battle-starred family, but she could at least give him a year or two of congenial work.

This wouldn't be charity, either. *Shenandoah* and the Victoria Squadron would have an officer working—indeed overworking—where he was an expert. With everyone certain to have two jobs and likely to have three before matters were settled, they could use a few more like Longman.

Which tells me we need another department-heads' meeting. I think the announcement can wait until Officers' Call tomorrow, though.

Liddell gave Longman ten minutes to reach the Wardroom and find Bogdanov. She gave Bogdanov another ten minutes, as president of the Mess, to rearrange or hide anything that might not be fit for an admiral's eye.

Then on Kuwahara's arm she marched down the passageway to the Wardroom. As they passed the mirror and display outside the door, she caught a glimpse of herself, every hair in place.

But were quite so many of them gray the last time I looked?

The display showed the surface of Victoria below *Shenandoah*. They were passing three thousand kilometers above Jenkins' Jaws, where forty days before, she, her crew, and their ship might have found an improvised grave if a few decisions had gone some other way.

They hadn't, so everyone was alive to celebrate. Was this a reprieve or a pardon?

A reprieve, Liddell decided.

In the first crisis, no one who had a voice in its outcome had wanted war to the last drop of blood. There were others not so scrupulous on Victoria, watching the planet, or on the way.

They would be heard from.

ABOUT THE AUTHOR

Roland J. Green is an active SFWA member, and the author of the PEACE COMPANY series, as well as co-author (with Jerry Pournelle) of two military SF novels in the JANISSARIES series. SQUADRON ALERT is the first book in his STARCRUISER *SHENANDOAH* trilogy. He lives in Chicago.

⊘ SIGNET SCIENCE FICTION   (0451)

WORLDS OF IMAGINATION

☐ **THE DARKLING HILLS by Lori Martin.** When the beautiful Princess Dalleena and the handsome nobleman Rendall fall in love, defying an ancient law, they invoke a searing prophecy of doom. Betrayed and exiled by their homeland, the couple must struggle to remain together through a brutal siege from a rival empire. "An exciting, charming, and irresistable story."—Tom Monteleone, author of LYRICA   (152840—$3.50)

☐ **JADE DARCY AND THE AFFAIR OF HONOR by Stephen Goldwin and Mary Mason.** Book one in *The Rehumanization of Jade Darcy.* Darcy was rough, tough, computer-enhanced—and the only human mercenary among myriad alien races on the brink of battle. She sought to escape from her human past on a suicide assignment against the most violent alien conquerors space had ever known.   (156137—$3.50)

☐ **DREAMS OF FLESH AND SAND by W.T. Quick.** When corporate computers rule the world, who can separate the moguls from their machines? Within the largest corporation in the world, the two founders launch a private war against each other. Their weapons are the best computer whizzes in the business! A brilliant cyberpunk adventure!   (152980—$3.50)

☐ **DREAMS OF GODS AND MEN by W.T. Quick.** "A lively hi-tech thriller" —*Publishers Weekly.* When a human-generated Artificial Intelligence becomes humanity's god, whose reality will survive—ours or the computer's? "Fast-paced, technologically glib"—*Locus*   (159349—$3.95)

Prices slightly higher in Canada

Buy them at your local bookstore or use this convenient coupon for ordering.

NEW AMERICAN LIBRARY
P.O. Box 999, Bergenfield, New Jersey 07621

Please send me the books I have checked above. I am enclosing $_____
(please add $1.00 to this order to cover postage and handling). Send check or money order—no cash or C.O.D.'s. Prices and numbers are subject to change without notice.

Name_____

Address_____

City _____ State _____ Zip Code _____
Allow 4-6 weeks for delivery.
This offer, prices and numbers are subject to change without notice.

Ⓞ SIGNET

(0451)

ROBERT ADAMS' CASTAWAYS IN TIME

☐ **CASTAWAYS IN TIME by Robert Adams.** It was a storm to end all storms, but when the clouds finally cleared, Bass Foster and his five unexpected house guests find they are no longer in twentieth-century America. Instead, they are thrust into a bloody English past never written about in any history books.... (140990—$2.95)

☐ **CASTAWAYS IN TIME #2. THE SEVEN MAGICAL JEWELS OF IRELAND by Robert Adams.** Drawn through a hole in time, twentieth-century American Bass Foster finds himself hailed as a noble warrior and chosen to command King Arthur's army. Now Bass must face the menace of an unknown enemy that seeks, not only to overthrow Arthur's kingdom, but to conquer and enslave the whole world. (133404—$2.95)

☐ **CASTAWAYS IN TIME #5. OF MYTHS AND MONSTERS by Robert Adams.** As Bass Foster's fellow castaways in time struggled to save Indian tribes from Spanish invaders, it was only natural that they use the advance technology that had been left by travelers from a future beyond their own, but what awaited them was a horror even modern weapons of war might not be able to defeat.... (157222—$3.95)

☐ **CASTAWAYS IN TIME #6: OF BEGINNINGS AND ENDINGS by Robert Adams.** This time Bass Foster and his fellow castaways have attracted the attention of mysterious, awesomely powerful beings who might bring the world tremendous benefit—or destroy it with terrifying force. Hidden enemies are tracking their every move, scheming unspeakable dangers to lay in their path.... (159721—$3.95)

Buy them at your local

bookstore or use coupon

on next page for ordering.

· Ⓞ SIGNET SCIENCE FICTION   (0451)

THE HORSECLANS RIDE ON

☐ **FRIENDS OF THE HORSECLANS edited by Robert Adams and Pamela Crippen Adams.** For over ten years, Robert Adams has been weaving his magnificent tales of the *Horseclans*. Now he has opened his world to such top authors as Joel Rosenberg, Andre Norton, John Steakley and others who join him in chronicling twelve unforgettable new tales of Milo Morai and his band of followers.   (147898—$3.50)

☐ **FRIENDS OF THE HORSECLANS II edited by Robert Adams and Pamela Crippen Adams.** So popular have Robert Adams' tales of the Horseclans proved that many other authors have longed to send their own characters roaming the plains and valleys, swinging swords and aiming bows against the Horseclans' foes ... And now Robert Adams once again welcomes some of these top writers into this world of excitement and adventure, of courage and honor....   (158466—$3.95)

☐ **MADMAN'S ARMY (Horseclans #17) by Robert Adams.** When the Horseclans defeated the army of the tyrannical King Zastros, High Lord Milo Morai offered them a full membership in the new Confederation of Eastern peoples. But Milo didn't bargain for the evil hidden in the heart of the land's new government—an evil that could threaten the Confederation itself....   (149688—$3.50)

☐ **CLAN OF THE CATS (Horseclans #18) by Robert Adams.** When undying Milo Morai found the tower ruins, they seemed the perfect citadel to hold off the ravenous wolves that howled for his warriors' blood. but in its depths lay The Hunter, the product of genetic experimentation gone wild, who would challenge the High Lord himself to a battle to the death....
                                                         (152298—$3.50)

Buy them at your local bookstore or use this convenient coupon for ordering.

NEW AMERICAN LIBRARY
P.O. Box 999, Bergenfield, New Jersey 07621

Please send me the books I have checked above. I am enclosing $_____
(please add $1.00 to this order to cover postage and handling). Send check or money order—no cash or C.O.D.'s. Prices and numbers are subject to change without notice.

Name_____

Address_____

City _____ State _____ Zip Code _____
                    Allow 4-6 weeks for delivery.
            This offer is subject to withdrawal without notice.